Now I was angry . . .

I scrambled to my feet. Without a word, I headed for my horse. I stopped when he grabbed my arm and spun me about.

"What the devil is the matter with you, Heather?" His ebony eyes flashed with impatience.

"I am not a child! I don't like you thinking of me as a child. I will soon be twenty!"

"How should I think of you, Heather?" His voice and eyes softened.

"As . . . as a woman. How would you like it if I thought of you as a boy?"

Before I knew what was happening, his arms were about me, his head lowering. His mouth covered mine in a passionate kiss of exploration. The worldly kiss was so sensual and lusty that my hands went to the heavy sinews of his back. I could feel muscle move against muscle as he deepened the kiss. I was lost in a new world, a world of sheer physical pleasure. I never wanted to move from his arms.

GOTHICS A LA MOOR—FROM ZEBRA

ISLAND OF LOST RUBIES
by Patricia Werner   (2603, $3.95)
Heartbroken by her father's death and the loss of her great love, Eileen returns to her island home to claim her inheritance. But eerie things begin happening the minute she steps off the boat, and it isn't long before Eileen realizes that there's no escape from *THE ISLAND OF LOST RUBIES*.

DARK CRIES OF GRAY OAKS
by Lee Karr   (2736, $3.95)
When orphaned Brianna Anderson was offered a job as companion to the mentally ill seventeen-year-old girl, Cassie, she was grateful for the non-troublesome employment. Soon she began to wonder why the girl's family insisted that Cassie be given hydro-electrical therapy and increased doses of laudanum. What was the shocking secret that Cassie held in her dark tormented mind? And was she herself in danger?

CRYSTAL SHADOWS
by Michele Y. Thomas   (2819, $3.95)
When Teresa Hawthorne accepted a post as tutor to the wealthy Curtis family, she didn't believe the scandal surrounding them would be any concern of hers. However, it soon began to seem as if someone was trying to ruin the Curtises and Theresa was becoming the unwitting target of a deadly conspiracy . . .

CASTLE OF CRUSHED SHAMROCKS
by Lee Karr   (2843, $3.95)
Penniless and alone, eighteen-year-old Aileen O'Conner traveled to the coast of Ireland to be recognized as daughter and heir to Lord Edwin Lynhurst. Upon her arrival, she was horrified to find her long lost father had been murdered. And slowly, the extent of the danger dawned upon her: her father's killer was still at large. And her name was next on the list.

BRIDE OF HATFIELD CASTLE
by Beverly G. Warren   (2517, $3.95)
Left a widow on her wedding night and the sole inheritor of Hatfield's fortune, Eden Lane was convinced that someone wanted her out of the castle, preferably dead. Her failing health, the whispering voices of death, and the phantoms who roamed the keep were driving her mad. And although she came to the castle as a bride, she needed to discover who was trying to kill her, or leave as a corpse!

Available wherever paperbacks are sold, or order direct from the Publisher. Send cover price plus 50¢ per copy for mailing and handling to Zebra Books, Dept. 3217, 475 Park Avenue South, New York, N.Y. 10016. Residents of New York, New Jersey and Pennsylvania must include sales tax. DO NOT SEND CASH.

THE MIDNGHT HEATHER OF BRIDEE CASTLE

BEVERLY C. WARREN

ZEBRA BOOKS
KENSINGTON PUBLISHING CORP.

Chapter One

My sister was beautiful. I was not. Perhaps that is why I am still alive today and she is dead.

A long time ago I learned not to compete with Diana. She was a petite, blue-eyed blonde with a figure that turned men's heads. Her oval face and tiny bow lips gave her an aura of great delicacy. She was twenty-one, two years older than I, and Father's pride and joy.

When my mother died shortly before my tenth birthday, I was left to my own devices after our tutor's lessons. I preferred the rough and tumble games the boys played: horseback riding with my legs astride the animal. At five foot six, I was not petite. My copper hair was unruly which made me constantly appear disheveled. My green eyes were too large and my full lips too wide. Generous freckles splashed across my small nose and cheeks.

Looking back, I would have to say it all started in May of the year 1857 when we lived in India. Father had been stationed there since I was one and Diana three. I remember the day well for it was the day after my nineteenth birthday.

The heat was oppressive, the dust choking. I almost looked forward to the coming monsoon. Diana and I sat in the stand along with other families to watch the entire garrison parade before the divisional commander. I enjoyed the precision of these parades while Diana found them tedious. The only thing that engendered enthusiasm in her was the parties and balls to be held in honor of the divisional commander.

I craned my neck as our father's infantry and cavalry regiments began to pass the review stand. Swords, buttons, and braid scintillated when caught by the blazing sun. Tufts of dirt spewed into the heated air as the horses pranced in their best parade manner.

Brigadier James Angus MacBride, our father, was handsome and resplendent as he sat on his horse leading the cavalry regiment. His back was rigid as his head snapped to the right and he whipped his sword in front of his face in salute.

My eyes shifted to the man behind him, young Lt. Patrick Danton. He was twenty-seven, handsome, with sandy hair, green eyes, and a pencil-thin mustache trimmed to precision. He was serious and grave of nature, but, for some unknown reason, he took a fancy to me. Then he met my sister Diana. I was soon relegated to the position of an annoying child. I sensed he would soon ask Father for Diana's hand in marriage. I knew Diana would not be marrying him and it gave me a modicum of pleasure. Diana was not ready to settle down with any one man. She enjoyed the company of many admirers. Flirtation was as dear to her as horseback riding was to me.

"Such handsome men, don't you think, Heather?" Diana's smile was dazzling as we rode in the carriage back to our home.

"I suppose so," I replied indifferently. I was anxious to get back to our spacious bungalow which was situated on a hill in the northeast corner of India. If there was a cool breeze to be had, it usually found its way to our house. On a clear day I could see the Himalayas in the distance. The sight of their snowy, jagged peaks stretching to poke at the sky never failed to excite my imagination. How I longed to stand at the foot of them and feel the power of their majesty.

"What are you wearing to the ball tonight, Heather? I certainly hope you wear something other than that old white gown of yours. And do try to do something with that hair of yours. You are such an embarrassment to Father and me. Your deportment at these functions is a disgrace too. If you don't think you can act like a lady, I do wish you would stay home."

I had planned to wear my more fashionable blue gown, but now I would definitely wear my old white one. Nobody looked at me anyway when Diana was around. As far as my behavior went, I was always polite, but did have a tendency to speak my mind. I remained silent, knowing Diana didn't expect a reply.

When the carriage came to a halt before our bungalow, I hopped out. Diana sat there until the driver came to assist her.

"Samrú," I cried as I dashed into the house, "is tea ready?"

Samrú Singh was our ayah, or nanny as they would say in England. She was a thin woman but taller than me. Her black hair was webbed with gray and she bore the tilak on her forehead, a spot of colored paste which had religious significance among Hindu men and women. Even though she was our surrogate mother, I never felt close to her. She was reserved and distant as though wrapped in a mysterious cocoon. Her English was precise and clipped.

"Tea will be ready by the time your father arrives, Miss Heather," she replied.

"Samrú, have a bath drawn for me," my sister demanded as she entered.

"Yes, Miss Diana."

"And be quick about it. I don't have much time to get ready for the ball tonight." As Diana turned to me, Samrú scurried from the foyer. "Aren't you going to bathe, Heather?"

"After tea."

7

"How can you think of food when the ball is only a few hours away?"

"I am hungry. Besides, it won't take me long to get ready."

"Perhaps you should take more time. Remember what I said about looking decent." She flounced down the hall.

I shook my head and smiled at her imperious departure. Her personality would take on a whole new aspect at the ball. Sweetness, charm, and coquetry would be summoned forth to mask her domineering, self-centered, priggish nature.

When I came into the foyer in my white gown, Diana gasped, "Oh, no," gave me disdainful glare, then marched out of the house on Father's arm. She wore a lovely peacock blue taffeta gown with numerous flounces, puffy off-the-shoulder sleeves, and a tight bodice which revealed her creamy shoulders and a good deal of cleavage. My white gown also had a tight bodice, but it came up to my neck, circling it with a lace mandarin collar. My balloon-like sleeves came down to my elbows. I didn't care how old or unfashionable it was. The cotton gown was cool and comfortable.

On either side of Father, we entered the splendid home of Major General Hewitt. The house sparkled with oil lamps and candles. As we entered the ballroom, the colorful uniforms of the men vied with the brilliant gowns and glittering jewelry of the women.

Musicians took their places and the room became flooded with music. Lt. Patrick Danton strode across the room, tall and handsome in his uniform. After giving me a terse greeting, he swept Diana onto the dance floor. Father had gone to join a group of his cronies.

I watched the dancers for a while then glanced around the room at various clusters of people. Though there was an outward appearance of gaiety, I felt an undercurrent of insidious discontent. I glanced at Father. His expression was serious with a trace of anger. The high-ranking officers around him also had grim expressions. I soon noticed that a number of the faces in the ballroom had masked fear and worry with smiles of forced gaiety.

I scanned the room for Edith Mason, the daughter of a captain in my father's regiment. She was my closest friend in India and adept at gleaning the latest gossip. When I didn't see her in the ballroom, I sauntered into the spacious dining room where a large buffet held an array of delectable foods and drinks.

I spied her sitting in a corner eating. I put some of the spicier foods on a plate and joined her.

"What has happened? A lot of people in the ballroom look positively glum," I said.

"I don't know. I have asked around, but everyone is mum. Why aren't you dancing?" Edith was a rather plump young woman. Her bright red gown did not have a slimming affect.

"Why aren't you?" I countered.

"I would rather eat."

"Want to go riding with me in the morning? We could go watch them work the elephants," I suggested.

"I can't leave the house," Edith replied between bites.

"Why?" Edith was a placid young woman. I couldn't imagine her parents punishing her for anything. She submitted to their every wish.

"I have a feeling it has to do with everyone acting so strangely. The other day I started to come over to visit you. I never saw my mother get so excited. She screamed for me to come back into the house. Even my father is edgy. Has your father said anything?" Edith asked.

"No. I will question him tomorrow and insist on answers." I finished the food on my plate and washed it down with a glass of punch. "Let us go into the ballroom and watch them dance."

"You go ahead. I will join you later. Right now I want

to try some of those desserts," Edith said.

I went back to the ballroom to find Patrick Danton standing alone, his eyes burning with jealousy as he watched Diana being swirled about the floor by a dashing captain.

"Has Diana deserted you, Patrick?" I asked with glee.

His head snapped to look at me with irritation. His long, delicate forefinger flipped over his mustache. "Would you care to dance, Miss Heather?"

"Why, I would love to, Patrick." I enjoyed dancing and was quite good at it.

He whirled me around the floor with the precision of a drill master. His curly sandy hair was thick with pomade and never moved an inch as we twirled about the floor in a vigorous waltz. His green eyes were emotionless. Father said Lieutenant Danton was an officer's officer and perfectly attuned to the rigors of service in India. To me, his reserve was maddening. I was glad his attentions turned to Diana. He exuded a frigidity even a well-stoked furnace couldn't melt. And his dancing was mechanical, not at all induced by the music.

When the dance was over, Patrick walked me to a chair against the wall. I didn't sit. He was about to depart when I said, "Let us walk outside for a spell. It is stifling in here. I suppose I should be used to the heat, but I am not."

"I really shouldn't leave, Miss Heather."

"I know for a fact that Diana is taken for the next four dances."

He stiffened. "I shouldn't go outside with you unchaperoned. Gossip would develop."

"Let it. Perhaps some gossip would cheer everyone up. Why are they so glum, Patrick? Father looks like a grumpy old owl that has lost its prey."

"Hasn't he told you?"

"Told me what?"

He took a deep breath. "Perhaps you should ask him."

10

"I want to know now. If you don't tell me, I will tell Diana you flirted with me."

"You know that is not true. Really, Heather, you can be exasperating at times. I think it is shabby of you to resort to blackmail." His shoulders heaved with a sigh. "I suppose I may as well tell you. You will hear it soon enough. The Sepoys have mutinied. We have just learned that four days ago Indian regiments released certain imprisoned and condemned Indian men. This past Sunday, while British officers and their families were at evensong, our Indian troops burned buildings and slaughtered anyone in their path. Then they marched to Delhi. We dread to think what has happened there. Our Delhi barrack is not responding to our urgent telegrams. We fear there has been a general uprising."

"What are they doing about it?" The news didn't upset me as Delhi was some distance away and the fracas didn't sound too serious: an isolated incident that wouldn't affect this part of India.

"Excuse me, Miss Heather. I see some fellow officers I wish to speak to concerning the uprising."

He was gone before I could utter another word. The smoke from the candles, pipes, and cigars hung heavy in the hot, motionless air of the ballroom. I went outside alone and took great gulps of the cooler, but still humid, air. I looked toward the Himalayas, but the moonless sky merged with the land, forming one black shadow. I yearned for the sight of those mountains and vowed to travel there someday. The Sepoy mutiny faded from my mind as I dreamed of travel and great adventures.

At breakfast several days later, Diana was still gaily chattering about the ball at Major General Hewitt's. She was enumerating the new male conquests she had made.

"What about Lieutenant Danton?" I asked, carefully cracking the shell of my egg.

"I suppose he is all right, but he has the nasty habit of wanting to kiss me all the time," Diana replied as she daintily munched on a piece of toast.

"I should think you would like that."

"I hate it. That silly mustache of his pricks my tender lips. I don't like to be kissed in general."

"It is all a game to you, isn't it, Diana?"

Diana looked thoughtful for a minute, then smiled. "I suppose it is. It is like a hunt. Once the prey is caught, I lose interest. What a pity you don't have the attributes to join me."

"I am glad I don't. I don't consider love a game."

"Love? Who is talking about love? Love is an illusion. When I marry it will be for wealth and position."

"I will wait for love and my knight in shining armor," I said.

"The trouble with you, Heather, is you buried your nose in fairy tales as a child. Someday you will have to face the world as it really is."

"I do now," I protested as Father took his place at the breakfast table.

"You are late this morning, Father. Didn't you sleep well last night?" Diana asked him in a honey-smooth voice.

"Well enough, child, well enough." Dark circles under his eyes belied his words. He began to crack his egg in his ritualistic manner then looked at Diana. "Is that all you are having for breakfast? A piece of toast and tea?"

"I must keep my figure, Father. You wouldn't want me to look like Edith Mason, would you?"

He smiled indulgently at her then went back to his egg. I was about to come to Edith's defense when Father suddenly looked up with an expression that signaled he had come to a decision.

"I am seriously thinking of sending you girls home for a while," he announced.

"But we are home," I ventured.

"I mean to Bridee Castle in Scotland." He completed his

12

attack on the egg, severed the top, and began to spoon the contents into his mouth.

"You can't do that, Father. I am committed to a number of social engagements here," Diana said.

"Any special reason, Father?" I was intrigued by the idea.

"This devilish Sepoy business. The news from Delhi is not good. More slaughter of British and Europeans. Buildings burned to the ground. Rumors are rampant that more native regiments will join the uprising. Stupid wogs. They are making things messy in India. I would like to know the two of you are safe in Scotland before I leave."

"Leave?" Diana's fine eyebrows arched.

"I suspect my regiments will be called out to alleviate the siege at Delhi. I am waiting for orders now. They might come any day, any minute."

"Oh, Father, I am sure the army will put down the rebellion in no time. It would be foolish to send us all the way to Scotland. By the time we got there, this tempest will be over," I said.

"Heather is right, Father. Please don't make us leave."

"If the situation worsens, I am determined to have you girls well out of it. You are always talking of adventure and travel, Heather. I should think you would welcome the opportunity."

"She may, but I don't." Diana's small mouth puckered in a pout.

"Bridee Castle sits on a vast estate. The castle itself is a remarkable piece of architecture and houses many valuable antiques. Your neighbors are barons and earls. The two of you will inherit the entire estate one day and you should show some interest in it."

"Barons and earls?" Diana mused. Her entire expression changed, her eyes sparkling with sudden interest.

"I thought your sister Clarissa owned Bridee Castle," I said.

"Nay, lass. When she married Pickering and moved to

13

London, she lost all claim to our ancestral home. Your grandfather gave her a meager dowry, then declared she had relinquished any and all claim to our Scottish lands and Bridee Castle. Your grandfather didn't like Pickering and was greatly riled by her choice of a husband. The entire estate came to me on his death and shall go to the two of you upon my death."

"I thought Aunt Clarissa's name was Ross, not Pickering," I said.

"Pickering died. He left Clarissa with a small annuity. Unfortunately it was not enough for her to maintain their residence in London. I gave her my permission to live at Bridee Castle for as long as I served abroad. Seven years ago she remarried a widower with three children. Being childless, she welcomed them. I haven't heard from her since. We have never been close."

"Perhaps we wouldn't be welcomed there," Diana offered.

"Nonsense. My daughters have more right to live in Bridee Castle than my sister. Always remember that," James MacBride declared.

"Couldn't we stay here, Father? Already I don't like Aunt Clarissa," Diana said.

"No. My mind is set."

"Perhaps we could come to a compromise," I suggested.

"What kind of compromise, Heather?" Father asked.

"If the situation isn't resolved by the end of June, we will leave without argument."

"Speak for yourself, Heather," Diana said.

"I am not finished. If the rebellion is under control, we stay. I call that a fair bargain."

"What do you think, Diana?" Father asked.

"If you agree to it, Father, then I shall comply," Diana said with her usual pout.

"All right then. But if things worsen before the end of June, you will leave immediately." He pushed his chair back and stood. "I have to get down to the garrison. Orders might have arrived. I will speak to Samrú tonight and

14

give her instructions regarding your departure if I am suddenly called to duty."

"What about Samrú? Will she go with us?" I asked.

"I haven't thought about it yet. In the meantime, I want both of you to stay close to home."

"Yes, Father," Diana said. She rose, slipped her arm through his, and walked outside with him.

I poured another cup of tea, sipped at it, and thought about Scotland. On those few occasions Father talked about his sister, he characterized her as a very silly woman. Though I liked children, I wondered if I could tolerate living with three little ones. I knew Diana was not at all fond of children. Anyone's children. I decided a good hard ride would clear whatever doubts about Scotland I might have.

"Where are you going?" Diana asked. She came back into the house as I was leaving.

"Riding."

"You heard Father. He told us to stay close to home. Why are you defying his wishes?"

"I am not going far."

"I am going to tell him."

"I thought you would and I don't care." I pushed past her and went to the stable.

Father did not come home for lunch or supper which concerned me. I lay in bed wide awake. It wasn't until the wee hours of the morning that I heard Father's voice coming from the parlor. Curious about his long absence from home, I got out of bed and padded down the hall toward the parlor. I stopped short of the room when I realized Father was not alone. Samrú was with him. I should have left discreetly, but the tone of their voices stopped me and I stooped to eavesdropping.

"I will not leave you, James," Samrú said.

"You will do as you are told, Samrú. You are a servant, not my wife," James MacBride said with rising irritation.

"I have been more than a servant to you over the years.

15

You cannot treat me in this manner, James. I will not go to Scotland. I will stay here with you."

"You will go to Scotland or go to the devil. Once my daughters are gone, I have no further use for you."

"Who will warm your bed when you have need of a woman?"

"I have already taken care of that. A younger woman. Much younger. You are getting old, Samrú. Your skin is starting to dry up and sag."

"A younger woman is inexperienced. She will not be able to arouse you the way I can. I know your desires, the little movements that bring you ecstasy. To send me away will be a great mistake, James. You will miss me in your bed."

"Not for long."

"And if the mutiny is subdued and the girls stay, what are your plans then?" Samrú asked.

"From what I learned today, this rebellion will take longer to quell than anyone expected."

"I will not go to Scotland."

"Then you will be in the street when the girls leave. I do not wish to speak of it again."

"You will regret this, James."

"Don't threaten me, Samrú, or I will put you in the street this minute. Now leave me."

I slipped into the library, stunned by what I overheard. My mind was in a muddle as I stood in the dark. The house was so silent I could hear the faint footsteps of Samrú going down the carpeted hall. After several minutes, I peered into the empty hall, then tiptoed to my bedchamber. I took off my robe and slipped back into bed.

I was shocked to learn that Samrú was Father's mistress. I wondered if Diana knew about it. I would question her in the morning. The way Father spoke to Samrú astonished me. Father never had high praise for me, but he was never as cruel or insulting as he was to Samrú. This was a side of him I never knew existed. For the most part he was

16

pleasant around the house. He was fairly strict, but gave us wide latitude in thinking for ourselves and doing as we wished. I struggled against sleep for I had so much to think about. Sleep won.

"Where is Father?" I asked, taking my place at the breakfast table.

"He left early," Samrú replied in a subdued voice.

"Is my sister up yet?"

"Yes. She will be down soon."

"After I have had breakfast, will you please have one of the lads saddle up my horse?"

"I am sorry, Miss Heather. Your father has instructed me to make sure both of you stay in the house today. People are being killed on the roads and in the fields."

"Murdered?"

"Yes. Roaming rebels have drifted into our area and they are murdering anyone they come across. You must excuse me, Miss Heather. I have some work to do."

As Samrú left the dining room, Diana entered.

"Have you heard we are confined to the house? Rebels are murdering people around here," I blurted out when Diana took her place at the table.

"Where did you hear such a tale?"

"Samrú told me."

"Surely you don't believe everything *she* tells you," Diana said.

"You sound like you don't like Samrú."

"I detest her. She is under the illusion she is a grand duchess around here when she is nothing more than a servant."

"You sound like Father." I went on to tell her what I had overheard last night.

"Didn't you know Samrú was Father's mistress?"

"No."

"You are a naive dunce. It is time he got rid of her. He

17

is still a handsome, youthful man. Speaking of men, did you see the lovely bouquet that Patrick sent me this morning?"

"No."

She commenced to talk on her two favorite topics—men and herself.

The end of June was fast approaching. Father's absences from home became longer and more frequent. Scotland was not mentioned on those few occasions he was home.

Being confined to the house and a small area outside was beginning to take its toll on the household. Samrú was acerbic. Diana was whiny and ill-tempered. I retreated into my books and dreams of far-off lands. Occasionally I would sit on the veranda and stare at the vistas our hilltop bungalow presented.

The monsoons were late and there wasn't a cloud in the sky. The heat increased and parched the land brown. In most places wells were dangerously low, if not completely dry. Each footstep on the ground caused puffs of dust to swirl in the air. If the rains didn't come soon, famine would cause people to die and the earth would soon follow suit, I thought.

Samrú had become a shadowy figure around the house. Her absence was obvious when Father was present. Though Diana seemed pleased at the new arrangement, I was uncomfortable.

"I am so glad you made it home for supper, Father," Diana cooed. "June is almost over so I guess we won't be going to Scotland after all." Triumph gleamed in her blue eyes.

"The month is not over, lass. Unfortunately the rebellion is widening. You and your sister are isolated here and are not aware of the serious and deteriorating situation. Most of Oudh and a wide strip of India are now in rebel hands. This troubled state of affairs will not be cleared up before

18

the end of June. You have only a few days left, lass."

"If this rebellion is as widespread as you say, Father, why hasn't your regiment been called to duty?" I asked.

"I would like the answer to that question myself, Heather. I have written furious letters to Calcutta about it. They don't seem to have any definite course of action at headquarters. The march on Delhi has been delayed again and again by the untimely deaths of army commanders. It is devilishly exasperating."

At first I thought Father was exaggerating the circumstances, but the look in his eyes told me the truth. I didn't know what to say. As I groped for words, a highly distraught Patrick Danton came dashing into the dining room. Diana smiled and opened her mouth to speak, but Patrick was quicker.

"Excuse me for barging in like this, sir, but . . ."

"What is it, Patrick?" Father asked, his brow furrowing.

"Cawnpore," Patrick managed to blurt out, obviously agitated.

"Sit down, lad." James MacBride motioned toward a seat at the table, then called, "Samrú, more tea and a cup for Lieutenant Danton." He turned to Patrick. "Calm yourself, lad. Have a sip of tea and the telling of your tale will be easier."

When Samrú had complied with Father's order and left, Patrick sugared and milked his tea, took a sip, then began his tale in a controlled voice.

"About a thousand men, women, and children were besieged for weeks at Cawnpore by Nana Sahib and his mutineers. Nana Sahib heard there was a British relief column on its way there so he sent a message to the besieged stating they would be allowed to go to Allahabad in safety. He would supply the boats. Lack of food and water made the people march out of their entrenched refuge at Cawnpore.

"The minute the boats were loaded with the people, the native Indians jumped overboard. Nana Sahib's men on

19

the shore opened fire, killings hundred of them in the boats."

"Did any of them escape?" Father asked.

"One man made it down the river." Patrick took another sip of tea. "Many others survived and that is the tragic part. They were herded ashore. The surviving men were immediately shot. The rest, women and children, were herded together in one of the main houses. They think three of the women were taken away by the rebels, including General Wheeler's daughter." Patrick hesitated. He flicked a finger over his mustache, then pinched the bridge of his nose with his thumb and forefinger.

"Get on with it, lad," Father urged.

"There are ladies present, sir."

"My girls are army bred and born. I neither pamper them nor shield them from the realities of life."

Patrick took a deep breath and gazed from me to Diana then back to Father. "From what I was told, about two hundred women and children were crowded into the house and courtyard. When the Sepoys lost heart to kill them, butchers were summoned from the bazaar. They worked their knives over the hapless victims, butchering until not a body moved. Some of the bodies were dragged down to the Ganges and thrown in while others were stuffed down wells.

"Havelock's column reached Cawnpore the day after the massacre. Evidence of the heinous deed was fresh. Rooms and floors of the house were smeared and spattered with blood. Outside, blood was caked everywhere. I have left out the more horrible details in deference to the ladies," Patrick concluded.

"What is being done?" Father's face was red with raw anger. His eyes glinted like a racehorse straining at the gate, anxious to join the race.

"Havelock has moved on to Lucknow, leaving Neill in charge at Cawnpore. You are to join Havelock with your regiments. As you will have to pass through Cawnpore, you will see the atrocities for yourself, sir."

"At last! I have been wondering when those bloody dolts in Calcutta were going to give me marching orders." His eyes gleamed with excitement. "Well, lassies, you will leave for Scotland in the morning. Best you see to your packing immediately."

I knew the events at Cawnpore sealed our fate. Scotland it was for us. I tried to think of it as an adventure, but didn't really want to leave India anymore than Diana. Her face was contorted in disbelief and outrage at being sent away.

"Early tomorrow morning I want you to bring ten of your best men here to escort my daughters and Samrú down the trunk road to the railhead, Patrick. See that they get onto the train to Calcutta safely. You can catch up to me later."

"Yes, sir." Patrick stood when Father did. "I must get back to the garrison."

"Tell them I will be there shortly."

"Yes, sir." Patrick smiled. Blatant eagerness for battle shone in his eyes.

"Well, Diana. Come give your father a kiss and a hug. It might be a long time before we see each other again."

A dry-eyed Diana did as she was told. I could tell her mind was preoccupied.

My eyes misted as I went to him for my hug and kiss. I tried not to cry. I wanted him to see I was as brave as Diana. Tears trickled over my cheeks as he marched out of the house.

Diana and I stood on the veranda and watched him ride off into the night. A shiver tickled my spine. I had the eerie sensation I would never see him again, even though he promised to send for us when the revolt was over.

Stoically standing in the foyer when we came into the house, Samrú said, "Would either of you care for my help in packing?"

"I can pack myself," Diana said imperiously and brushed

21

past Samrú.

"I would like your help, Samrú." I wiped the tears from my eyes with the back of my hand. "Will you be coming with us?" Even though I knew the answer, I asked the question rather than have her suspect I might have overheard her argument with Father.

"Yes, Miss Heather. I have already packed my belongings. A trunk of your father's will be going with us," she informed me as we walked down the hall to my room.

"Why is he sending a trunk of his to Scotland?"

"He said there are papers which you and your sister might need, along with his memoirs and some of your mother's personal things. He expressed a desire for you to recopy his memoirs and perhaps get them to a publisher," Samrú replied.

I nodded. We began the tedious task of packing.

Trunks, valises, and hatboxes were piled on the veranda waiting to be loaded onto the wagon. Patrick and his men arrived as our carriage drew up to the porch. I could see Patrick was not thrilled with this assignment. I suspected he would have preferred to ride at Father's side.

While Samrú oversaw the loading of the wagon, Diana chatted with Patrick, but her eyes were on the ten uniformed men on horseback. Occasionally she would flash them an irresistible smile and tip her parasol coquettishly. Patrick seemed not to notice her little flirtations.

The platform at the railhead was a mass of colorful saris while men and children were more plainly dressed. When the train puffed and hissed to a halt, it disgorged a multitude of troops.

Patrick took Diana's hand, raised it to his lips and kissed it. He repeated the gesture with me, only his lips never touched my hand.

Finally we boarded. I went to our compartment while Diana posed and waved good-bye to the soldiers.

After a long and uncomfortable journey, we chugged into the station at Calcutta, the engine whistle screaming our arrival. Calcutta was an undulating sea of people. The babble of voices created a din that pricked the ears unmercifully. The stench of the city was so strong Diana pressed a lace-edged lavender-scented handkerchief over her nose. My handkerchiefs were packed in my trunk.

Our ship was waiting as our carriage delivered us to the port. As we began to board, the wind picked up and I felt a drop of rain on my face. I looked up at the chaotic sky. The monsoon had begun.

Chapter Two

The ship belonged to the East India Company. The majority of the people aboard worked for or were attached to that company, including a great number of bachelors. Diana was in her glory throughout the long voyage to Plymouth, England. My enjoyment came from watching Diana manipulate her admirers. I would sit and commiserate with whichever young man was out of favor with Diana at the time. All in all, the voyage was more pleasant than I thought it would be.

We docked in Plymouth then took the train to Victoria Station in London. We stayed at the posh Clarendon on New Bond Street. The plan was to stay in London for a week to rest before embarking on the long trek to Inverness and Bridee Castle in the Scottish Highlands.

While Diana concentrated on the fashionable shops of Regent and Bond Streets, I dashed around seeing the sights. Hearing Big Ben's chimes enchanted me. Madame Tussaud's Wax Museum sent chills up my spine. I stood outside Buckingham Palace hoping to get a glimpse of the Queen, but all I saw was the changing of the guard. The Zoo, the galleries, the museums, the parks, and notable buildings filled my rapidly diminishing days in London.

As we ate dinner in a quiet restaurant, Diana chastised me. "You must stop running all over the city, Heather. You have to get yourself some decent clothes. Do you want to shame Father before his sister? I have asked all the seamstresses about suitable apparel for the Highlands. They said it gets bitter cold there in the winter. The clothes we wore in India are not at all suitable for the Scottish Highlands. I insist you come shopping with me tomorrow. I refuse to have my sister disgrace me," she declared.

She did have a point. My clothes were not suitable for a cold climate. "What about Samrú? I don't think she has warm clothing."

"I am not her keeper. Let her fend for herself. Now promise me you won't leave before I get up in the morning."

"I promise." Though I was not close to Samrú, I did have compassion for her. I would get her size and make sure she had what she needed for Scotland.

By the time we had finished shopping, three more trunks had been added to our retinue.

Diana and I agreed on one thing: we would have liked to have stayed in London longer, but our train and coach connections had been made and we were expected at Bridee Castle on a certain day.

The train sped northward. Little gray towns amid lush greenery flew by my window. I had purchased several magazines to read on the long train ride, but I was so mesmerized by the alien scenery that I barely opened them. Diana, on the other hand, was captivated by the numerous ladies' periodicals she had bought.

Samrú slept. Garbed in English dress, Samrú didn't look like the Samrú I had known for most of my life. She didn't look ludicrous, nor did she look like an Englishwoman. She just looked different.

At the end of the rail line, everything was transferred to a coach, including ourselves. The fat black cattle of the Lowlands gave way to the shaggy brown Highland cattle. Sheep dotted the landscape like cotton balls strewn over green velvet. Heather-covered hills rose in the distance, and stone mountains soared like giant sentinels guarding the glens and lochs. Though it was summer, the air maintained a crisp coolness, a far cry from the stifling heat of India. I silently thanked my sister for insisting that I purchase a warmer wardrobe.

As the coach rattled onto higher and more desolate country, dark gray clouds did battle with lighter ones. A soft mist began to coat the land causing the scenery to waver dimly.

The coach deposited us in front of a tea garden on the south side of the River Ness. While we waited for the carriage which would take us to Bridee Castle, I strolled the railed walk that hugged the riverbank. Diana and Samrú went into the tea garden for refreshments. I preferred the river. My nostrils flared at the exotic aroma. The sweet greenery and chill of snow-kissed mountains mingled with the sweet water of the amber river. As a capricious breeze came in from the east, the smell of salt water dashed over Moray Firth from the North Sea. Across the river various shaped houses were pinched together as though in a vise. Down from me, on my side of the river, church spires were thrust into the air proclaiming their dominance of Inverness.

Diana and Samrú came out of the tea shop as though on cue, for the carriage from Bridee Castle pulled up at the same time. Once again we were on the road traveling. Diana's mood had become quite sour by now. Her sighs of impatience and disgust became frequent.

The light mist thickened. My heart beat faster when a dark edifice loomed before us like some primeval monster waiting to claim unsuspecting victims. That vague impression of Bridee Castle was enhanced as the carriage rolled up the crescent driveway.

The mansion was built on a vast block with cross wings. The wings reached out as though to clutch its visitors in an all-embracing, almost smothering, welcome. The skyline of the imposing structure was accented with tall chimneys in the form of clustered columns while onion domes crowned a multitude of turrets. Obelisks rose behind an arched parapet. Orieled windows dotted the main section of the house.

An old keep hovered in the background like a giant rounded monolith. As we drew closer to the melancholy castle, I could detect the intricate moldings and expansive arches upon which leered grotesque gargoyles. The castle exuded all the gloom of fallen grandeur. Bridee Castle allured and repelled me simultaneously.

I swallowed hard when the carriage halted before the portico and wide marble steps. Apprehension filled me as I gazed at the huge oaken doors. The footmen were attentive and we were soon approaching the entrance.

"At last," Diana muttered. "I don't think I could have gone another inch. Do hurry, Heather, and stop your gawking. You can do that tomorrow."

As usual, I paid little heed to her. Only when the oaken doors opened did I increase my pace. A well-liveried butler stood before the portal, while footmen dashed to unload the numerous trunks and baggage.

"Ladies," the butler said with a slight bow of his head.

He was a tall, lean man with unremarkable features. I judged him to be in his mid-fifties. A short, stout woman stood behind him, her hands clasped in front and lost in the folds of her voluminous skirt.

"I would like to be shown to my room and have a bath arranged at once," Diana said, pushing past him. She was in one of those overbearing moods I detested.

"The Ross family is waiting for you in the drawing room," he announced in a tone that would brook no argument. "Mrs. Burns, our housekeeper, will see to your luggage, then she will escort you to your rooms after you have met with the family. This way, ladies."

Diana speared the butler with a hateful look. She removed her bonnet and cape then thrust them at Samrú. I gave mine to the stout, unsmiling woman behind the but-

27

ler. I smiled, but it was not returned.

The foyer was a minor masterpiece of pink and white marble with niches holding Oriental vases or reproductions of Greek statues. The ceiling was festooned with plaster cherubs intertwined with floral swags. My head swiveled as I took in the wonder of it.

The butler slid open the sliding doors and announced us. "Miss Diana and Miss Heather MacBride."

Two of our sizable Indian bungalows would have easily fit into that vast drawing room. I looked at the scene before me and was reminded of Madame Tussaud's Wax Museum. The five people in the room were as stiff as a diorama.

A woman in her mid-forties stood and came toward us with outstretched hands. Her russet-colored hair was touched with gray and fashionably coiffed. Her figure was youthful, but I suspected corsets masked a tendency to plumpness. Even though her smile was warm, her gray eyes held a sadness. In her youth she must have been a fetching woman, I thought. She hugged both of us then stood back, her gaze shifting from me to Diana then back to me.

"Oh, dear me." Her eyelashes fluttered rapidly as she blinked in confusion. "I am afraid I don't know which of you is Heather and which is Diana."

"I am Heather, Aunt Clarissa," I ventured, then nodded to Diana who was staring at the young man seated in an overstuffed chair. "She is Diana, my older sister."

"My, you are a pretty little thing. And red hair just like your father when he was young. How is he, Heather?" Aunt Clarissa asked.

"Fine when we left. His regiment was called out to assist in putting down a rebellion."

"So this is Diana. What a beauty you are, my dear," Aunt Clarissa gushed, ignoring my words.

"Aunt Clarissa, why don't you introduce us to the others?" Diana asked as her eyes surveyed the three men in

28

the room.

"How silly of me. Come along." Aunt Clarissa snaked her hand through Diana's arm then mine. The two seated men stood as she pulled us across the room. Her smile was tremulous and her eyelashes fluttered with adoration and anxiety as she looked up at the tall man. "This is my husband, John Ross."

He was a handsome man in his mid-fifties. His lean body was showing signs of an indolent life. His formal attire was stretched taut over an incipient paunch. His gray-streaked dark hair was carefully groomed. He took our hands in turn and kissed the air over them. I noticed he held Diana's hand for several seconds longer than necessary and smiled languidly at her. I had the feeling his smile was forced and insincere. I was developing the impression he was against our presence at Bridee Castle; still, he showed a definite interest in Diana.

We were then drawn to a woman seated in a red velvet Queen Anne chair. "This is my stepdaughter, Jane Ross." Aunt Clarissa smiled benevolently. The younger woman's smile was shy and tentative.

Jane Ross looked to be in her mid-thirties. Neither beautiful nor ugly, she fell somewhere in between. Her warm brown hair was pulled back tightly, making her ears protrude. She had hazel eyes and her white skin was translucent to the point of pallor. Her lavender frock of taffeta emphasized that wanness. Though she seemed cool and distant, I liked her. Diana and Jane's eyes reflected instant antagonism. I flashed Jane Ross a smile before Aunt Clarissa dragged me away. I don't know if she returned it. Diana turned on her full charm at the next introduction. I couldn't blame her. He was a pleasant-looking young man in his early to mid-twenties. If I had charm and knew how to project it, I would have done so myself.

"This is my stepson, Bruce Ross," Aunt Clarissa said.

Ritual hand kissing ensued. When he looked up, his grin indicated he would retain a perennial boyish aura.

His light brown eyes were warm, friendly, and mischievous. Thick brown hair curled over his head. He was a few inches taller than me with a stocky body. He was appealing instead of handsome.

"I do hope you young ladies plan to stay with us for a while," Bruce Ross said.

"We have been looking forward to this visit for some time." Diana smiled and tilted her blond head.

"We shall be returning to India once the rebellion there has been quelled," I added.

"You must tell us about India and the rebellion," Bruce urged.

"It will be a pleasure," I said.

"Oh, you don't want to hear about India. Quite boring, I assure you. I do hope you will have time to show me Scotland," Diana cooed. Her voice always resorted to cooing when she wanted to make a favorable impression. I noticed she didn't include me in that proposed tour of Scotland.

We then met the last member of the family. I caught my breath and wilted inside. He stood by the ornate fireplace, his feet apart, his hands behind his back under his coat tails.

"This is my other stepson, Adrian Ross," Aunt Clarissa said.

I thought his father was tall, but this handsome, thirty-ish man towered over me. His black eyes glittered like new coals. When they caught my eyes, I knew what it was like to be hypnotized by a cobra. His black hair curled down to rest on his collar while wide shoulders and a broad chest tapered down to slim hips. He exuded a potent, virile masculinity. My feelings toward him were ambivalent. I wanted to warm to him, but a deeper emotion warned me to be wary of him. He appeared to be a dangerous man.

"Welcome to Bridee Castle, ladies." His smile was arrogant, his voice deep as he bowed over our hands. He did not pretend to offer the ritualistic kiss.

30

I forced myself to look away from him and glance at Diana. She was transfixed. I knew that look in her eyes and sighed. She wanted him and what Diana wanted she usually got.

"Really, Clarissa," began John Ross. "You should have more consideration for our guests. These young ladies have traveled a great distance. I am sure they would like to retire to their rooms and freshen up. You are being quite remiss."

"Oh . . . why yes." Aunt Clarissa's hands began to flutter nervously. Her eyes darted about the room as though she was searching for help.

Jane Ross stood. "Why don't you show Miss Diana Mac-Bride to her room, Clarissa? I will take care of Miss Heather."

"Oh, yes. Yes, my dear. We shall do that. Where is Mrs. Burns? She should be here."

"I suspect she is still busy with the baggage and that Indian woman. Mrs. Burns will have to find a suitable room for her," John Ross suggested.

When we reached the sliding doors, Diana turned, smiled, and gave her dainty wave to the three men in the drawing room. With Jane leading the way, we went across the foyer to the main staircase, whose mahogany newel posts were intricately carved.

"I do hope you girls will like your rooms," Aunt Clarissa said as we climbed the staircase. "I had the maids working on them for days, didn't I, Jane?"

"Yes, Clarissa." Boredom coated Jane's voice.

Reaching the landing, Aunt Clarissa led Diana in one direction while Jane led me in the other. I could hear Aunt Clarissa's chattering even though we were headed in separate directions. Halfway down the dark corridor, Jane opened a door and ushered me in.

The room was done in pale green and cream highlighted with gilt. A fourposter dominated the room. I trailed my hand over the quilted satin cover. A dressing table, a chest

31

on chest bureau, and a night table were made of highly polished cherrywood. A chaise longue with a small table by its side rested by the travertine marble fireplace. Dresden figurines, along with an ormolu clock, graced the mantel. Two large wardrobes flanked the passageway to the water closet. Beyond that was a small sitting parlor which contained an escritoire, and a round table near the window whose two chairs had embroidered seats. Bookcases lined a small portion of the wall while miscellaneous bits of furniture gave the room a finished appearance.

After the brief survey, I went to the window in my bedchamber to see tall green hills sweep down to a glen where a long, fingerlike loch ribboned its way through the mist. The imposing and ancient keep dominated the view.

"It is béautiful," I exclaimed as I turned to face Jane.

Her arms were folded across her chest, her expression stoic. "I am thirty-five, the oldest Ross child, and a spinster by choice," she said without preamble.

The statement startled me. I shrugged and said "So?"

"I saw the look on your sister's face when she learned my name was still Ross. I thought it best to clear the air immediately."

"I wasn't aware the air needed clearing. As long as you brought it up, I am nineteen. My sister is twenty-one. How old are your brothers?"

"Adrian is thirty and Bruce is twenty-four. As you must have noticed, my brothers got the good looks in our family."

I laughed. "I believe it is obvious who has the beauty in our family."

"Don't underestimate yourself." She was serious. I had a feeling she was always serious. "A maid will be up to fill your tub and put your things away."

"Where is Samrú?"

"Who?"

"The Indian woman who came with us."

"I suspect she is in the servant's quarters. If there is

anything you need, the bellpull is by the bed. Dinner is at eight sharp." She turned to leave. When her hand fell on the doorknob, she stopped. "By the way, do try to be tolerant of Clarissa. She is a bit flighty and her mind has a tendency to wander." With that, Jane departed.

As promised, a maid soon arrived and began to lug hot water from the dumbwaiter to the tub in my water closet.

"What is your name?" I asked of the maid.

"Jean, miss. Mrs. Ross said I am to be your personal maid."

"Samrú usually sees to my needs."

"Is that the Indian lady, miss?"

"Yes."

"She was called to tend to the other young lady," Jean informed me.

"I see. Would you please help me wash my hair, Jean? I can manage everything else."

"Yes, miss."

I undressed and slipped into the hot tub. The water had been scented with lemon verbena. I closed my eyes and soaked while Jean began the tedious task of unpacking my trunks. I tried to erase all thoughts from my mind and enjoy the bath, but the dark eyes of Adrian Ross began to haunt me, disturbing me in an unfamiliar way.

After Jean washed and dried my hair, I browsed through the wardrobe where she had neatly hung my frocks and gowns. Wanting to make a good impression on the Ross family and Aunt Clarissa, I settled on a dress I had purchased in London. It was a shimmering green silk gown, off the shoulder with a voluminous skirt. The only ornament was a green silk rose which nestled between my breasts.

Dressed, I sat down at the dressing table and struggled to do something with my long, unruly hair. Seeing my difficulty, Jean offered her assistance which I gratefully accepted. To my surprise she worked wonders. With the aid of combs and hairpins, she had secured my hair in a crown atop my head with curly reddish gold tendrils framing my face.

"You have done a marvelous job, Jean. My hair actually looks neat for a change." She smiled with pleasure. "Now if only I could do something about these freckles."

Her eyebrows raised as she studied me. "There is some rice powder on your table." She nodded toward a Limoges box. I pressed the puff into the powder, then dabbed it across the bridge of my nose and upper cheeks. I peered into the mirror and decided that I didn't look like myself without freckles. I quickly brushed the powder away.

"I will unpack the last trunk while you are at dinner, miss," Jean said.

"The one in the sitting parlor?"

"Yes, miss."

"Don't bother. It is my father's trunk. I will tend to it myself when I have the time."

"As you wish, miss."

I was early. No one was in the drawing room. I wandered about the spacious room studying its contents. I observed that many of the objects must have come from foreign lands where my father had served. None of them helped to make me feel at home though. The entire room was alien. In India a certain lightness of decor helped to form my tastes. Here the furniture was heavy, dark, and ornate, making the room appear ponderous. The only spark of color was in the Oriental rugs scattered over the parquet floor.

A grand piano squatted in a far corner. On the closed lid were numerous photographs. The newer ones were of the Ross family done in the new wet-plate process invented by Scott Archer in 1851. I was surprised to see an old daguerreotype of Father, Diana, and me. He was in full uniform. Diana must have been twelve at the time. She was smiling sweetly while I was giving my best ten-year-old pout. I picked it up to study it more closely.

"Why weren't you smiling when that was taken?"

His deep, mellifluous voice sent tremors along my spine. Still holding the picture in its silver frame, I spun around to face Adrian Ross. I drew my eyes from his and looked down at the picture, fearing my eyes would betray my bizarre anxiety.

"If I remember correctly, I wanted to go riding that day and abhorred the fact that I had to get dressed up for the sitting." I put the picture back on the piano.

"I take it you like to ride," he said.

"Very much."

"We have a fine stable here." He paused to light a long, thin cheroot. "Do you always pout when you don't get your way?"

I smiled. "Only when I was ten."

"Do you play?" He nodded toward the piano.

"Yes. After a fashion." Learning to play the piano was the one concession I made to feminine accomplishments. Diana never had the patience to learn.

"Play for me. It is early and the rest won't be down for a while."

"Why are you down so early?" I smoothed my skirts as I sat down on the piano bench.

His smile was enigmatic, yet there was a trace of the sardonic in it. "Play," he urged softly.

My fingers executed a simple Chopin étude. I could feel his dark eyes studying my face as he leaned on the piano. I wondered if he were counting my freckles and wished I had left the rice powder on.

"That was pleasant," he said when I finished. "I am surprised you are so accomplished."

"Why?"

"I always thought of India as remote and primitive."

"We are not uncivilized, Mr. Ross. We *can* read and write," I countered sarcastically.

He smiled down at me. "I suspect your temper can be

35

quite as fiery as your red hair."

"Did I hear music?" Bruce Ross asked as he entered the drawing room.

"Miss MacBride was giving me a sample of her musical talents," Adrian answered.

"I knew it couldn't be you, Adrian. You never play the piano. You attack it."

"You play?" I asked, my attention going back to Adrian Ross.

"A little."

"A little is a gross understatement, Miss MacBride. He plays like a man gone mad. Fingers pounding all over the keys. I am surprised the piano doesn't crumble under his onslaught," Bruce said.

"Do play for me." I started to rise but Adrian Ross held up a staying hand and sat next to me. He was so close I could feel the heat of his body against mine.

"You will see for yourself, Miss MacBride, what a warped devil he is," Bruce said.

Adrian glared at his brother for a moment. Suddenly the air was filled with tension. A dark scowl crept over Adrian's face. His fingers came down on the keys with a fury as he pounded out a work of Beethoven with skill and emotion.

"Oh, dear me. Must you play, Adrian? You know how it shatters my nerves," Aunt Clarissa chirped as she sailed into the room, John and Jane Ross behind her. The music ceased instantly. Adrian's expression darkened further with incipient rage. "Oh, that is so much better. I am sure you were shattering our dear Heather's ears with that dreadful noise." Her fan fluttered like a wild metronome as she collapsed into a chair.

"I think he plays well and I was enjoying it. Don't you care for music, Aunt Clarissa?" I asked.

"Not his. Much too loud and furious."

"Our dear stepmother has delicate sensibilities," Bruce Ross offered.

"You know Clarissa has a weak heart, Bruce. Adrian should play softer, more gentle music in this house," Jane said.

"It is not in Adrian's nature to be soft and gentle," Bruce said.

"I think the lassies in the village would argue with you on that point, Bruce," John Ross laughed.

"John, dear, please don't speak of such things. Whatever will our Heather think of us?" Aunt Clarissa's admonishment was delivered with a smile.

"I will say what I wish in my own house," John Ross declared.

"Whose house?" Diana swept into the room with a regal air. "I was under the impression this is my father's house. You live here by his generosity."

"Oh, dear me." The speed of Aunt Clarissa's fan increased.

Evidently Diana had touched a raw nerve. Everyone fell into a gloomy silence. My sister then spied me sitting next to Adrian with Bruce leaning on the piano. Her demeanor altered dramatically as she came toward us: the sweet smile; the fluttering eyelashes; the fan covering her daring décolletage then subtly moving away.

"Are you teaching the gentlemen to play, sister dear?" she asked, her eyes devouring Adrian.

"On the contrary, Diana. I believe Mr. Ross could teach me much about music," I answered.

"Perhaps Mr. Ross should teach me."

"Anytime, Miss MacBride." Adrian rose to his feet.

"All this *Mister* and *Miss* is far too formal. As we will be living together for a spell, I do believe it would be proper to use our Christian names, don't you?" Diana pursed her lips and tilted her head.

"That is a capital idea, Diana," Bruce agreed.

John Ross approached Diana saying, "Forgive me, my dear, for being so presumptuous." He took her hand and raised it to his lips.

Diana adored the gallantry. "Your apology is accepted, John. I may call you that, may I not?"

"Of course, Diana. What a beautiful name — Diana. Goddess of the hunt."

I laughed, causing everyone to stare. Diana glared at me. I muted my laughter to a low twitter.

"I don't hunt," Diana said.

"Ah! but you are certainly a goddess," John said.

Adrian suppressed a smile. Bruce and Jane expressed indifference. Aunt Clarissa had a beatific smile as she snapped her fan shut.

I was grateful when dinner was announced. I was hungry and Diana's flirtations always embarrassed me. She wormed compliments from men the way a flute sways a cobra.

John offered Clarissa his arm while Adrian escorted his sister. Bruce crooked his arm for Diana. I felt like an extra thumb no one wanted. I found consolation in Diana's annoyed expression. She would have preferred Adrian's arm.

The barley soup was followed by poached salmon. The saddle of lamb had been carved in the kitchen and was offered on a silver salver as were the boiled potatoes, creamed cauliflower, and brussels sprouts. Dessert was rice pudding. I enjoyed the meal even though my palate found it a trifle bland after the spicy Indian food.

Conversation was desultory at the table with Aunt Clarissa and Diana doing most of the talking. Though I concentrated on the food, I could almost feel an undercurrent of discontent among the Rosses. Perhaps my imagination was overwrought from the day's long travels and coming into a house of strangers.

After dinner we retired to the drawing room where the ladies were offered tea or sherry while the men had their whisky.

"Tell us about India, Diana," Bruce urged, once we were seated.

"Hot and dry," was Diana's terse reply.

"What about this Sepoy rebellion?" John queried as he leaned forward in his chair.

"You will have to ask Heather about that. I deplore speaking about the natives. They are so crude and dirty." Diana crinkled her delicate nose as if an Indian beggar had stumbled into the drawing room.

When eyes turned to me, I related what I knew of the situation, going into detail about Cawnpore.

"Oh, dear me," Aunt Clarissa gasped when I had finished. "Why didn't our people put those Indian rebels in their place? They should have stopped them immediately. Don't those natives realize we are superior to them?"

John shook his head in exasperation. He tried to explain to Aunt Clarissa the plight of the captives at Cawnpore, but gave up when her gray eyes stared at him vacantly.

"It must have been grisly for you," Bruce said.

"I only heard about it. Perhaps actually seeing it might have produced a different reaction in me," I replied.

"What do you do around here, Adrian?" Diana asked, then added, "You don't mind if I call you Adrian, do you?"

"Not at all, Miss MacBride."

"Oh, do call me Diana." She snapped her fan open.

"I am a breeder," Adrian replied to her first question.

"You look like an excellent breeder," Diana said tossing him a flirtatious smile.

One corner of his mouth lifted as though he wanted to laugh aloud, but was restraining himself. "I breed sheep, cattle, and horses."

"Adrian's animals are renowned throughout the British Isles. He always wins first prize at county fairs. His stud services command high prices," Bruce said with a certain amount of pride.

"I can see where they would," Diana said, her eyes never leaving Adrian.

I glared at her sharply. Her remarks were not only

pointed, but obvious and risqué.

"Do you think it would be possible for me to see your prize animals, Adrian?" Diana asked.

"I think it could be arranged."

I didn't let the smile rising in me reach my face. I knew what Diana had in mind and it wasn't four-footed beasts. Her interest was in the two-footed animal called Adrian. Diana detested all creatures. We could never have any pets in the house because she claimed to be allergic to them. She was about as allergic as I was. She plain hated them.

"You must see our beautiful glens and lochs before winter's mantle hides their beauty," Bruce said to both of us.

"I have heard of your Scottish 'sleety dribble,' 'cruel blasts,' and 'howling tempests' of winter," I said.

"I take it you have read the works of our great bard Robert Burns," Bruce said.

"He is a favorite of mine. But before I go galloping around the countryside, I would like to see the house," I said.

"Whatever for?" Aunt Clarissa's back went rigid, her fan stopping in midair as she leaned forward.

"Curiosity," I answered. "Father talked a lot about his ancestral home in the Highlands. He described every room in the castle. I am curious to see if his descriptions were accurate."

"I am not up to taking you through this enormous place. My heart wouldn't take all the clambering about. I suppose you would like to see the house too, Diana," Aunt Clarissa said in a thin, tired voice.

"Not really. I am far more interested in Adrian's animals."

"I would be happy to show you around the castle, Heather," Jane said. "I probably know the castle better than Clarissa."

"Thank you, Jane," I said, giving her my best smile.

Adrian took out his pocket watch and stood. "You will have to excuse me, ladies. I have some business to attend

40

to in the village." His long legs took him from the room in seconds.

Bruce grinned.

"Keep your thoughts to yourself, Bruce," his father admonished. "We have company."

"As you wish, Father." Bruce turned to face us. "After you have seen the house, Heather, and you have seen Adrian's animals, Diana, you must let me take you to the great glen and our famous Loch Ness."

"I don't ride. Those beasts terrify me. I prefer the comfort of a carriage," Diana said, her interest in conversation waning after Adrian left.

"Then I shall take you in our trap," John Ross said.

"Oh, dear me. You men shouldn't have our guests running about so. I am sure they would prefer to rest in the afternoon, wouldn't you, my dears? After all you have just completed a long, tiring journey," Aunt Clarissa said.

"I, for one, am most anxious for some activity. We did nothing but rest on the journey," I said.

"Speak for yourself, Heather," Diana said.

"I am."

"Actually, I was rather busy on the ship. So many fine gentlemen. We danced and took many walks around the deck. All that sea air can be exhausting," Diana claimed.

"Oh, I know what you mean, Diana. Getting everything ready for your arrival was positively fatiguing. The ordeals I had to go through with the servants were quite enervating." She paused for a moment. "I am ready to retire now. Are you coming, John?" Aunt Clarissa snapped her fan shut and stood.

"Not right now, Clarissa. I have some work to do in the library."

"Good night, my dears." Aunt Clarissa kissed Diana and me on the cheek then flowed out of the room.

"I, too, shall say good-night," John said then left on the heels of Aunt Clarissa.

"How far is the village?" Diana asked.

"Not foo far," Bruce answered. "Perhaps a half-hour by trap."

"What possible business could Adrian have in the village at this time of night?" When Diana was interested in a man, she was persistent.

"Wine, women, and song," Bruce said gleefully. "But I am here. That should assuage the absence of our enigmatic Adrian."

"Bruce is jealous of Adrian," Jane declared.

"Don't listen to old Jane. She is jealous of my youth."

"Nonsense. I am nothing of the sort. Don't try to deny your jealousy of him. He makes a good living for himself while you have no prospects of doing anything worth while."

"I do wish you would find someone to marry you, Jane. You can be quite tiresome at times."

"You always find the truth tiresome."

Diana yawned. "I think I shall follow Aunt Clarissa, and retire."

"I will go up with you," Jane said, casting a look of disdain at Bruce, then departing with Diana.

"There. Now I have you all to myself. I knew mentioning marriage would get to her." Bruce smiled triumphantly.

"Why?" I asked.

"She hates the thought of marriage. When she was twenty, she was betrothed to one Edward Carter. The day before the wedding, he disappeared. They searched for him with no success. Naturally, Jane was beside herself with what everyone thought was grief. Frankly, I think she was thoroughly humiliated. She went into seclusion for years waiting for Edward Carter to appear. I suspect during that seclusion she whipped up a hatred for men. She never again showed interest in any man. She is resigned to being a spinster now."

"If you know it bothers her, why do you torture her about marriage?"

"She can be frightfully bossy at times. She forgets I am

twenty-four and tries to direct my life as though I am four years old. I wish that Carter chap hadn't disappeared. By now Jane would be married and have children of her own to boss about. Make sure she doesn't start on you and Diana," Bruce said.

"I have been managing my own life for some time now. Not even my father could tell me what to do if I had my mind set on it. As for Diana, she can give the impression she is doing what you want, but, she too, has a mind of her own."

"Still, beware. Both Jane and Clarissa can be subtle."

"I shall," I said smiling at his warning. "After hearing Jane's story, I feel sorry for her."

"Don't feel sorry for Jane. I don't think she was really in love with Carter. Carter had scads of money. Father's finances weren't in the best of shape at the time. I learned later he promoted the match as the marriage would have eased his financial situation."

"What does your father do for a living?"

"He speculates. Land, stock, inventions. That sort of stuff. Unfortunately his plans didn't always prove profitable. When our mother died, her small trust was left entirely to Father. The money was enough to maintain us, but not in the style Father wished." Bruce chuckled. "He even started bringing young heiresses home for tea when Adrian was present. Few women can resist Adrian, as your sister proved. Though the young ladies were more than willing to marry him, Adrian was having none of it. When he threatened to leave, Father decided to find a wife of his own. He found your aunt and married her," Bruce explained.

"Why? Aunt Clarissa isn't rich. My grandfather disinherited her some time ago, leaving everything to my father," I told Bruce.

He shrugged. "She always seems to have plenty of money. When Father saw this place, her wealth was confirmed in his mind. Are you telling me she is actually

43

poor?"

Feeling I had said too much already, I decided to drop the subject until I found out more about Aunt Clarissa.

"Today was the first time I met our Aunt Clarissa. I have no knowledge of her finances. She might have made some wise investments." I paused, thinking it was time for me to retire before I said something I shouldn't. "Well, I should go to bed like everyone else. I want to be fresh for tomorrow."

"In case no one told you, breakfast is served in the dining room from six to eight, unless you prefer to have a tray in your room. Clarissa usually does," Bruce said.

"I will be down. I don't care for breakfast in bed. See you tomorrow, Bruce."

"Good night, Heather."

When I entered my bedchamber, I was startled to see Samrú standing at my window. She turned when I closed the door.

"What is it, Samrú?" Her dark eyes were wide as though she were terrified.

"There is a great evil here, Miss Heather," she declared in all seriousness.

"Don't be ridiculous, Samrú. Whatever put a notion like that in your head?" Though my expression was serious, I couldn't keep the laughter out of my eyes.

"Death is nothing to laugh at, Miss Heather. I have knowledge of these things. My senses are tuned to the spirits. The walls, the very air in this place reeks of death. We must leave here and never return."

"Be sensible, Samrú. We have only been here a few hours. A new place always feels strange at first. Give it some time. Once you get used to Bridee Castle, I am sure those feelings will disappear. Besides, where else would we go?"

Her face became a mask, her eyes without emotion. "I have warned you as I have warned Miss Diana. That is all I can do." She took a deep breath. "Miss Diana has requested I attend to her personally. She doesn't care for any of the maids. Do you mind, Miss Heather?"

"No."

"If you need me, I shall come. Good night, Miss Heather."

"Good night, Samrú."

Though Samrú's notions were far-fetched, I didn't ignore her predictions entirely. I decided to think about them later. At the moment I had more pressing things on my mind.

A mental picture of the dining room table and its occupants formed in my mind. The men were impeccably dressed in finely tailored and expensive clothes. I switched the mental image to Aunt Clarissa and studied it. I hadn't paid much attention to her dress at dinner, but, having time to reflect, she became sharper in my mind.

Around Aunt Clarissa's neck was a necklace of diamonds and blood red rubies. Matching earrings dangled from her lobes. Two rings on one hand, another ring on her other hand sparkled like giant lighthouse beacons.

Where did Aunt Clarissa obtain these fabulous jewels? From what Father told us, her first husband was not a rich man. Father paid for the upkeep and staff at Bridee Castle. Was he also giving Aunt Clarissa huge sums of money? Or did John Ross make some shrewd investments? I went to bed without any answers to the questions.

Chapter Three

Having slept soundly, I rose early and went downstairs. I helped myself to the lavish array of ham; kippers; sausages; rashers of thick-sliced bacon; shirred, scrambled, or coddled eggs; and oatmeal. I put some ham and scrambled eggs on my plate, then ladled oatmeal into a bowl. I took a place at the table whose only other occupant was Adrian. I felt a tug of joy at his presence.

"Where is everyone? Am I too early or too late?" I flashed him my best smile.

"You are early. Clarissa has a tray in her room. Father and Jane come down around seven. One never knows when Bruce will put in an appearance. He has a tendency to be erratic. Where is your sister?" He leaned back in his chair and stared at me with those magical black eyes of his.

"Probably having a tray in her room. She usually did back home."

"Do you miss India, Heather?"

"I haven't had time yet. Where is the sugar?"

"Right in front of you."

"That brown stuff?"

"Brown sugar is all we use here."

"Diana won't approve of that." I spooned the brown

46

granules over my oatmeal and tasted it. "Rather good. Do you use it for everything?"

He nodded.

"Including tea?"

"Either the brown sugar or honey. How long do you and your sister intend to stay at Bridee Castle?"

"Until the troubles in India are over and Father sends for us."

"For you and your sister's sake, I hope that is soon."

"Why do you say that?" I thought about Samrú's warning last night.

He poured himself another cup of tea. "What are your plans for today?"

"You were there when we discussed them last night."

"I had my mind on others things and wasn't listening."

"Jane is taking me on a tour of the house this morning and Bruce has offered to take me riding to see Loch Ness this afternoon."

"Ah, yes. Try not to take my brother too seriously. He is young, impressionable, and highly impulsive. He may say something then just as quickly change his mind."

"He appeared to be sincere and sober last night."

Adrian smiled and I felt like I would melt like the butter on my toast. "We were on our best behavior last night. The longer you stay here, the more personality changes you will notice."

"Will your personality change?"

"Probably more than the others. As you will find out sooner or later, I have been called Rogue Ross."

"Why?"

"I never did find out."

"Is it because you carouse and seek the company of wanton women?"

He laughed, his deep baritone voice reverberating around the room. His eyes sparkled like black pearls. "You are a blunt little vixen. I shall have to watch my step with you."

47

"I didn't know anyone could make you laugh so early in the morning, Adrian," Bruce said as he entered the dining room.

"Heather has the incredible knack of saying exactly what is on her mind," Adrian said.

"You probably goaded her. You are not the epitome of subtleness yourself, Adrian." Bruce scrutinized the breakfast fare on the sideboard.

"At least I know what I think and can articulate it," Adrian said.

"I suspect you mean I don't. No matter. At least I don't go around insulting people to their faces." Bruce took a seat at the table with a well-laden plate.

"I understand you are going to take Heather on a gallop to Loch Ness this afternoon. I hope you don't fill her head with Scottish tales of terror, Bruce."

"Only if she wishes to hear them. Do you like scary stories, Heather?"

"I adore them."

"Do you believe in ghosts and the like?" Bruce asked.

"No. But I think the tales are great fun."

"Did you ever think that superstitions and legends might have some basis in fact?" Adrian asked with a sardonic smile.

"They might," I answered. "I believe they are distorted and exaggerated as each narrator tells his or her own version over the years. Perhaps simple, believable stories are twisted into tales of horror, each narrator adding his own ideas to stimulate the listener."

"Well, if you don't believe in ghosts and the like, Bridee Castle should hold no terror for you," said Bruce.

"Don't start that, Bruce," Adrian admonished.

"Why not? I am sure Heather would like to know about her ancestors."

"My ancestors?"

"Yes. Back in the sixteenth century—"

"If you are going to dredge up that old tale, I have

48

better things to do," Adrian said.

"Aren't you going to wait for my sister, Adrian? You told her you would show her your animals."

"I told her I would arrange it. This morning is not convenient."

"She will be upset. I believe she is under the impression you meant this morning."

"Her assumption was incorrect. I have work to do this morning."

"Work? I think your animals do all the work. You just watch. I wouldn't call that an enterprising pursuit." Bruce's expression and voice carried a jeer, a taunt.

"At least I have a pursuit, my dear brother." Adrian departed with a sly look at Bruce.

"Exactly what does Adrian hope to produce with his breeding schemes?" I asked.

"With the cattle he claims he is trying to produce a breed of animal with a wide, deep chest, short legs, and a higher, finer grade of meat. In sheep he wants well-developed legs and loins, along with a wool whose fibers will maintain their brilliance when mixed with other wools. He fancies he will revolutionize the meat and wool industry," Bruce explained.

"What about the horses? I think it was mentioned last night he also breeds horses."

"Speed, beauty, and stamina are the features he is striving for with horses."

"Do you think he will succeed?"

"He already has to a degree. Adrian always gets what he wants in the end."

"Tell me about my ancestors. Are there any ghosts here?"

"All Scottish castles have ghosts," he said grinning. "Didn't you know that, Heather?"

"Be serious, Bruce. It is Bridee Castle I want to hear about."

"All right. Bridee Castle has been expanded over the

49

centuries. Originally, in the sixteenth century, it was only a keep which housed Laird MacBride, his wife, Lady Anne, and their son. The laird died in battle and the keep became the sole domain of Lady Anne, a domineering and ambitious woman who loved to display her authority over others, especially her son.

"When the young laird was seventeen, distant neighbors came for a visit. Among them was a lovely sixteen-year-old lass. She and the young laird enjoyed each other's company and spent long hours riding together over the hills and moors. When her parents were called to Edinburgh, the young laird pleaded with the parents to leave their daughter at Bridee Keep. The parents, seeing the fondness between the two young people, agreed.

"Lady Anne, on the other hand, was not at all pleased watching the two young people grow closer. She had other plans for her son, namely marriage to a high-born noblewoman. One day, when the young man returned from the field, he found his young beloved dead, poisoned by Lady Anne and laid out on the dais high in the keep. He left Bridee Castle to build his own keep.

"One night, at midnight, Lady Anne sat in her chair in the main room. A sudden, icy wind blew through the chamber, wafting the tapestries. Thinking it was the young lass seeking revenge, Lady Anne screamed and fell dead on the floor. What do you think of your ancestors now, Heather?"

"Sounds like a plausible story. But where does the ghost come into it?"

"There are times when drapes move for no apparent reason. Moans have been heard whistling down from the keep. After you have been here a while you will notice strange events going on here."

"Who is the ghost supposed to be?"

"There are two theories: Lady Anne forever earthbound in Bridee Castle as punishment for her crime, or the young lass stalking through the castle seeking the young laird. Which one do you like, Heather?"

"Searching for a lost love is too sad. I hope it is Lady Anne being punished."

"But Lady Anne would be an evil ghost. The young lass would be a sweet ghost."

"I still prefer Lady Anne."

"Lady Anne?" echoed Jane as she and John Ross came in for breakfast. "Has Bruce been telling you the tale of Bridee Keep, Heather?"

"Yes. Will we see the keep during our tour this morning, Jane?" I asked.

"Do you *want* to see it?"

"Of course. I would love to be able to tell my father about it when we go back to India," I said as John and Jane took their seats at the table.

"I will have to get the key from Mrs. Burns," Jane said.

"Is it locked?" I asked. Jane nodded. "Why?"

"By order of Clarissa," John said. "The mere mention of a ghost, especially Lady Anne, gives her the vapors. I do believe her heart would give way if she knew you were going to open that door. She has forbidden it, fearing the ghost will be let loose on the castle."

"Then perhaps we shouldn't," I said with reluctance even though Bruce had whetted my curiosity.

"Nonsense. Who will know?" Bruce said.

I looked at John.

"If you have your heart set on it, Heather, by all means have a look at the keep. No one here will tell Clarissa. I know Bruce and I will remained silent. What about you, Jane?"

"I have no reason to tell Clarissa."

"No reason to tell Aunt Clarissa what?" Diana asked as she stood in the doorway.

I swiftly glanced around the room with a warning look in my eyes. Diana always did like to tattle about my little escapades. "No reason to tell Aunt Clarissa that Fa-

51

ther might be in danger in the Indian rebellion," I offered as an answer.

"Aunt Clarissa probably already knows that a career in the army is a dangerous profession. I am looking for Adrian. Where is he?"

"He left some time ago," Bruce answered.

"What! He was supposed to show me his animals this morning. How dare he leave without me. I arose earlier than usual just to meet him. Now what am I to do?" Her hands flew to her hips as a pout settled on her tiny bow lips.

John rose, went to her side, and took her hand in his. "There, there, Diana. I don't like to see a creature as lovely as you become so upset."

"Would you care to join Heather and me in a tour of the castle?" Jane asked.

"No. I had my heart set on Adrian showing me his animals."

"Do let me try to amuse you this morning," urged John.

Diana tilted her head and looked up at him, her blond curls bouncing. "How?"

"A tour of Inverness, lunch at a charming restaurant, then a leisurely drive home," John suggested.

"You won't get to see Loch Ness with Heather and me this afternoon," Bruce said, his brow furrowing.

"Who cares about some silly old lake? John's excursion sounds like more fun." She looked up again at the older, but still handsome man and smiled.

Pride flushed John's face. He stood up straight and pulled in his slight paunch. "Have a cup of tea, Diana, while I finish my breakfast, then we will leave."

"I will not be drinking tea until the housekeeper gets in a supply of white sugar." Diana sat down. "Are there any shops in Inverness?"

"Several," Bruce replied with blatant disappointment on his face.

Diana chatted about the luxurious shops in London. I patiently waited for them to leave and hoped my eagerness to explore the castle wasn't evident to Diana. If she sensed my eagerness, she would become suspicious.

"I will see you at lunch, Heather. We can take that ride after we have eaten." Bruce stood and took his leave.

"Are you ready for your tour, Heather?" Jane dabbed at the corners of her mouth with her napkin.

"Yes." I pushed myself away from the table and stood. "Please excuse us," I said to John and Diana. They were deep in conversation and paid no attention to me.

As I had already seen the living quarters of the castle, I followed Jane down the long, dim gallery where portraits of various MacBrides hung on the walls.

"Is there a portrait of Lady Anne, Jane?" I asked.

"The portraits date from the Elizabethan period forward. The legend of Lady Anne goes back to the Middle Ages," Jane said as we entered that portion of the castle which was seldom inhabited.

"Bruce said something about the sixteenth century."

"Bruce is not a historian. He never could keep his centuries straight."

Worn, faded tapestries graced the walls of the armory room. A musty odor did nothing to enhance the tarnished suits of armor. Ancient weapons, covered with dust and cobwebs, hung wearily on the walls between the tapestries.

"Why has this room been so neglected?" I asked.

"You will find all the rooms in this wing are in a state of neglect. No one uses them. A much larger staff would be required if the entire castle was to be maintained. Clarissa thought it a waste of money to hire servants to maintain rooms no one used."

"Quite frugal of her," was my only remark.

Jane arched her eyebrow and gave me a look I couldn't fathom. We moved through several rooms where the only bright spots were provided by the great number of dust sheets. Even they had a gray look about them.

Dark blue velvet drapes, a dark blue Aubusson carpet, and dark maroon leather furniture conspired to make the library depressing. I had the feeling if I took one of the books from the stacks of shelves, I would create a minor dust storm.

"I am surprised the library is unused. I should think your father or Adrian would find it a convenient place to do their paperwork."

"Father abhors paperwork of any kind. Adrian uses the library in the living quarters."

"Surely the books here must have some use."

"Outdated," was her terse reply. As we stepped into the next room she announced, "This is the morning room."

"Gloomy old place," I remarked. For a morning room it presented all the obscurity of an onrushing moonless night.

"Upstairs are bedchambers, sitting parlors, and game rooms. They have been uninhabited since I have been here. On the floor above that are old servants' quarters. I haven't been up there in years. There really isn't much to see up there. Do you want to look at them?" Jane asked.

"I don't think so."

"How long has it been since your father was here?"

"Shortly after my grandfather died, my father was sent to China. He closed the castle, leaving it in the hands of caretakers. He came back to marry my mother, then was posted to South Africa. After a year there, he received orders to take command of certain regiments in India. Was the castle in a terrible state when you arrived?" I asked as we leisurely walked through more rooms and galleries.

"Clarissa was living here when Father met her. The section we now inhabit was clean and quite habitable."

"Where is the keep? I can see it from my bedchamber, but with the maze of corridors and galleries, I have lost my sense of direction."

"We are heading toward it. It is at the very rear of the castle."

She led me through a labyrinth of corridors, each one more dismal than the next. Bright sunlight greeted us when we came to an enclosed courtyard. On the opposite end of the yard stood a large rectangular building made of rough-hewn gray stones, yellow lichen creeping over the blocks like a marching army. Windows consisted of mere slits and were fitted with thick, hand-blown glass. The towering keep behind appeared to be attached to the stone edifice. Jane pushed open the heavy oaken door of the building.

We entered an immense open hall. Carved posts rested on stone corbels and supported a vaulted ceiling of wooden tie beams. The high ceiling soared into the air in a manner reminiscent of a Gothic cathedral. The light was poor, but the dank, foul smell of the air betrayed the mildew covering everything.

I walked across the mossy stone floor to stand before a mammoth fireplace in which a host of people could gather. "Imagine the logs this fireplace would take," I said, gingerly stepping inside.

"You will get covered with soot and dust in there," Jane warned.

I stepped out, examined my skirt, and brushed a spot of soot off. It was a fruitless gesture for I was covered with dust and the gossamer threads of industrious spiders. As I peered around the vast room, I spied crates, boxes, and trunks nested off to one side.

"What are in those?" I asked, nodding to the odd assortment.

"I have no idea. No one has ever bothered with them. I suppose the place should be cleaned out. Clarissa gave orders for nothing to be touched until her brother came home."

"Shall we open them?"

"I thought you wanted to see the keep. I don't think

either of us want to get filthy mucking about with them. It is servant's work. Besides it would take weeks, if not months, to go through all of them. I suspect they contain old clothes and old furniture which do not interest me," Jane declared with an air of dismissal. "Shall we go on to the keep?"

I nodded. I was surprised by Jane's lack of interest. Curiosity bubbled over in me. I would satisfy my inquisitiveness on my own at a later date.

I followed Jane to the keep's door. As she fumbled the key into the lock, I felt like a naughty child disobeying an adult. I looked around to see if we were being watched. I felt utterly wicked and delighted in the sensation; then told myself this was my father's ancestral home and I had every right to see whatever I wanted, regardless of Aunt Clarissa's orders.

"Stand back," Jane said as she pulled the heavy door open.

A musty, acrid odor assailed our nostrils as a chilling blast of icy air swept through the door. A spiral stone staircase dominated the empty circular room. Jane started up the steps. Not wanting to be left behind, I quickly trailed after her. The succeeding tiers were empty so we proceeded until we reached the top.

"There it is." Jane pointed to a stone dais on which rested a marble slab.

"What?"

"The young laird is supposed to have found the dead body of his beloved lying on that marble slab."

"Do you believe the legend, Jane?"

She shrugged. "Someone might have been up here ages ago, saw the slab, and made up the tale." She walked to one of the slotted windows. "Come here, Heather. The view is excellent."

As she moved aside, I took her place. The panorama was breathtaking. I looked down to see what must have been a moat at one time. The great depression in the earth made an arc around the rear of the keep. Instead of water, the moat was covered with green grass with white dots of sheep nibbling away. The rest of the moat seemed to have been filled in with dirt ages ago. The manicured lawn, stretching out from the rear of the castle, was studded with topiary sculptures. Swans, peacocks, running foxes, deer, and lions rose from the green grass in living shrubbery. Two were formed like people. A ten-foot privet hedge enclosed the green menagerie.

"You can see the Great Glen and Loch Ness," Jane informed me. "Can you see them?"

"Yes. I also see the beautiful topiary below. How does one get to it?"

"The French doors at the rear of the drawing room lead to the rear terrace. The topiary garden is off the terrace. You can't see it from this angle," Jane explained. "We occasionally have lunch on the terrace in the summer. Have you seen enough?"

"Let me take a quick look around, then I will be ready to leave." While Jane went back to the narrow window, I wandered about the circular room where a wooden chest caught my eye. Something was amiss, but I couldn't discern what it was. I lifted the lid to find the chest empty, then closed it. Besides the dais and marble slab, it was the only other object in the room. "I am ready to leave, Jane."

By the time I washed and changed, lunch was ready. With the exception of John Ross and Diana, the rest of the family was present.

"What did you think of the castle, Heather?" Bruce asked me.

"Huge. It is a pity that so many rooms have been left unattended."

"I thought I would leave all that to your father, Heather. I do not want to put a lot of money into making them usable if your father is perpetually stationed abroad. He can do as he wishes with them when he re-

57

tires," Aunt Clarissa said.

Aunt Clarissa wore a fashionable rose satin day frock trimmed with black velvet ribbon. Besides the expensive frock, three strands of pearls looped about her neck. Their luster shined the word "costly" at me.

"Did you find any skeletons?" Bruce grinned and winked at me.

"Nothing but dust and cobwebs."

"What did you show her, Jane? You didn't take her to the old part of the castle, did you?" Apprehension formed on Aunt Clarissa's face.

"We had a brief tour of it," Jane answered.

"You didn't go into the keep, did you?" Aunt Clarissa appeared on the verge of panic.

Jane looked at me. Not only did I feel I had a right to see the keep, but I couldn't lie. "Yes. We did have a brief tour of the keep. In fact, we went up to the very top."

Aunt Clarissa turned white, put a splayed hand on her breast, and leaned back in her chair, eyes closed.

Bruce took a deep breath and shook his head in exasperation. "Are you all right, Clarissa?"

"Oh, dear me, dear me," she moaned. "You have let *her* out. We shall be trembling in our beds now that the creature is on the loose. I can't eat another bite. I feel faint. I must go to my room."

"Really, Aunt Clarissa. I assure you there was nothing there. The keep was completely empty." I thought it best not to mention the icy breeze swirling past us when we opened the keep's door. Even though I thought it of no consequence, Aunt Clarissa would become frantic.

"Jane, please take me to my rooms. I can't make it on my own knowing *she* now has access to the entire castle." Aunt Clarissa rose unsteadily to her feet. A dutiful Jane rushed to assist her.

When they left, Bruce looked at me with a silly grin. "I suppose she will have the vapors for a week now. She

58

firmly believes the ghost of Lady Anne has targeted her as a victim."

"Why?" I asked with laughter in my eyes. Father was right. His sister was a silly woman.

"Oh, something about her disobeying her father's wishes and marrying a man not favored by old Mac-Bride," Bruce answered.

"This is very good. What is it?" I asked, spooning the flavorful stew into my mouth.

"Mutton and barley with root vegetables. Have another biscuit." Bruce passed the biscuit tray. "Did you see the marble slab?"

"Yes. I wasn't impressed."

"Good for you, Heather," Adrian said.

"Don't tell me you finally decided to become sociable, Adrian," Bruce said, raising an eyebrow at his brother.

"I had nothing to say until now," Adrian replied.

I loved the sound of Adrian's voice.

"Have you ever been in the keep, Adrian?" I asked.

"On several occasions. The view is excellent."

"And you, Bruce?"

"Once. The place is too filthy for me."

"Do either of you have any idea what is in all those crates and trunks?" I gazed from one man to the other. Perhaps a little longer at Adrian.

"Clarissa said they have been there for as long as she can remember. When I questioned her about their contents, she informed me they were old clothes and furniture," Adrian answered.

"I think our father opened a trunk one time and found nothing but old clothes in a deteriorated state," Bruce added. "Nothing worth going to the trouble of opening."

"If you wish, we could have them opened, Heather," Adrian offered.

"No. I don't think we will be here more than a month or two. I don't want to spend that time going through old trunks and the like. I want to see as much of Scot-

59

land as I can."

"Then we had better get started on our ride to Loch Ness. I will wait while you get into your riding habit," Bruce said.

"I have already changed." I stood up and showed them the division in my full skirt. "Almost like pants, but they look like a skirt. Father calls them my flouncy riding pants."

While Adrian toyed with a smile, Bruce's raised eyebrows indicated astonishment.

"Don't tell me you are going to sit astride a horse, Heather." I nodded. "And where is your hat?"

"I don't use one." Seeing the incredulous expression on Bruce's face, I added, "If the occasion warrants it, I do wear proper riding apparel, hat and all. I thought our ride was an informal exploration."

"It is. But I thought . . . well . . ." Bruce shrugged.

"I'm going to the stables. I will have them change the saddle," Adrian said and promptly left.

"I rode a lot in India and found it easier to control the horse if I sat astride. For the amount of riding I did and the way I rode, sidesaddle was impractical," I offered as an explanation.

"I often thought I would like to go to India. See other parts of the world besides these gaunt, wretched moors and mountains," Bruce said.

"Then why don't you? Do you have a sweetheart holding you here?"

"I have no sweetheart in my life. But now that you and Diana are here, that may change." His boyish smile was endearing. "Lack of money keeps me from becoming a world traveler. I suspect even if I did have the money, the ambition would be lacking. The thought of all those tedious preparations fatigues me."

"You must have some money. What do you do for a living?"

"As little as possible. With the exception of Adrian, we

60

live off your aunt's generosity, which, I may add, can be substantial at times. I do have some luck with the ponies on occasion. I daresay Jane is the only one who works for her stipend. She caters to Clarissa's every whim."

I had the urge to question him further regarding Aunt Clarissa's wealth. I decided against it. I had only been at Bridee Castle for little more than a day. I needed time to ferret out everyone's personality and their true relationships to one another. I might learn more by keeping my eyes and ears open. Direct questioning might put everyone on their guard and I wouldn't learn a thing.

"Shall we go?" Bruce asked.

I nodded. "Why has Adrian remained a bachelor?" I asked as we left the castle and headed for the stables.

"Same reason as Jane—left standing at the church. He was young then, but never truly got over it. He believes women can't be trusted. Unlike Jane's betrothed, Adrian's future wife left him for an older man with scads of money. Though Adrian claims he doesn't trust women, he certainly doesn't avoid them, if you know what I mean. Perhaps being left at the altar runs in the family, or it might be our curse. I have never been tempted to find out."

We mounted our horses and were soon off at a brisk trot. The August day was bright and sunny. I was happy to be riding again, to feel the clean, crisp air caress my face. My long hair was pulled back and tied at the nape of my neck with a ribbon.

I looked around, then up at the keep. "When I was up in the keep, Loch Ness seemed in the other direction."

"It is. Culloden is not far from here. I thought I would show you that first. It won't take long," Bruce said.

Bridee Castle faded into the distance as we urged our horses to a gallop. Soon Culloden Moor was before us, a bleak, treeless plain high above sea level. Slowing our horses to a walk, we reined them to a halt upon reaching the center of the mournful spot.

To the northeast lay Moray Firth emptying into the North Sea. To the southwest, a saucer rim of purple-hazed mountains rose in the distance. Stretching before us in primordial splendor was the barren moor. I felt suspended in a lost world, a world consisting of pure space and time.

"What a beautiful, yet frightening place this is," I commented.

"A bloody place. Didn't your father teach you Scottish history?" Bruce asked.

"We had a tutor who was intent on teaching us world history."

"Every good Scotsman knows of Culloden and the bloody battle of 1746. Bonnie Prince Charlie's Scottish Royalist Army was defeated by the English here. Hungry, with their leaders fighting among themselves, the Highlanders were easy targets for the British artillery. The Highlanders are still very sensitive about the topic. It was a humiliating, costly, and decisive defeat. It was the last attempt to make a Stuart king of England and Scotland." He stared at the moor for several seconds before saying, "Well, shall we head for Loch Ness now."

I nodded. We spun our horses around to gallop toward the Great Glen below and the loch. We slowed down when the terrain became uneven. Our horses gingerly picked their way down to the flat fields and meadows.

"Loch Ness." Bruce swept his hand over the scenery of the Great Glen which lay as far as the eye could see. Nestled between the high stone hills was a vast freshwater lake. From a distance the lake appeared to be blue, but as we drew closer it darkened to a russet-violet color.

"What is so special about Loch Ness? I will admit it is beautiful, but why were you so anxious for me to see it?"

"Don't tell me you have never heard of our Nessie, the great monster that dwells in the loch."

"I am afraid not."

"I see your education has been sorely lacking. The

monster has a very long neck and a tiny head. Some claim that it has a large body with humps on its back. Saint Columba first sighted it back in the sixth century. One has to believe a saint, doesn't one? Besides, others have seen it on a number of occasions," Bruce claimed.

"Have you seen it?"

"No, but I know some people who have."

"After a visit to the local pub, no doubt." I smiled.

"Don't mock the monster, Heather. He might be a vengeful creature. Let us get down and watch for a while. He might make an appearance seeing you are a disbelieving visitor to Scotland. I will pray he appears for your sake. I would like to make you believe our legends and that ghosts do exist."

Bruce dismounted. Though I didn't need it, he helped me down, then tethered our horses to a larch tree. We sat down on a grassy meadow and watched the loch. I hoped the monster would show itself and make Bruce's story credible, but deep down I knew it wouldn't. I leaned back, bracing my hands on the ground.

Almost an hour had past when the ground trembled beneath me. I turned to see a horse and rider speeding toward us. As he came closer, I recognized Adrian astride a muscular, finely bred black stallion. Adrian's black hair raged about his head like dark storm clouds. Black boots covered his tight black breeches to the knee. A white shirt with large loose sleeves billowed behind him. His potent masculinity enthralled me. No man had ever had this effect on me. I had to smother my growing feelings for him or I would end with a broken heart. Every time my interest in a man became more than platonic, Diana sensed it and she would go out of her way to lure him away from me. Unfortunately for the man, as soon as Diana was sure he was infatuated with her, she would turn her attentions elsewhere.

Reaching us, Adrian drew his stallion to an abrupt halt, causing the animal to rear and paw the air fruitlessly. He dismounted before the stallion assumed a restful pose.

"What brings you here, Adrian?" Bruce asked and scrambled to his feet.

"One-eyed Angus is looking for you, Bruce. He is waiting back at the castle and refuses to leave until he sees you. I would advise you to come immediately before he thinks you are avoiding him. He is angry enough," Adrian said.

Bruce turned white. "I can't leave Heather here to fend for herself."

"I will take care of Heather," Adrian assured him.

"I can take care of myself." I never did like people talking about me as if I weren't there.

"Make sure she gets back safely," Bruce called as he untethered his horse. He galloped off without a good-bye.

Adrian sat down beside me after securing his horse to a branch. "I suppose Bruce told you of the Loch Ness monster."

"He did. He called the creature 'Nessie.' Have you ever seen the monster?"

"No." He stretched out and used his elbows to prop his torso up. "I never really looked for it."

"Do you believe there is a monster in the loch?"

"I will believe it when I see it with my own eyes."

"Who is One-eyed Angus?"

"A tout."

"Tout?"

"A bookmaker. Bruce has a fondness for horse racing and a weakness for gambling. He probably owes One-eyed Angus a sizable amount of money."

"Bruce told me he doesn't work. Where does he get the money to gamble?" Here I was asking questions again even though I had vowed to listen and watch.

"He cajoles Jane into giving it to him. Lately he has been on a winning streak. If I know Bruce, he probably thought his luck would hold and bet heavily on some

64

horse. One-eyed Angus's appearance here and the look on Bruce's face leads me to believe he lost this time."

"Does Jane have a lot of money?"

"She never has large amounts of cash. If it is a huge sum, Bruce will have to ask Father. My money is tied up in breeding stock and land. I never have large amounts of cash. Bruce can be quite charming when he wants, as can my father."

"Is charm a trait among the Ross men?"

"Do you think I am charming?" His smile held a trace of mockery.

"Along with your father and Bruce."

"You are frank, I will say that. Not many young women would tell a man he is charming to his face."

"I have never been able to stop myself from saying exactly what I think. Father says I am unladylike. He claims I am an incurable hoyden, especially when I ride a horse in a mannish style. He doesn't care for the way I dress nor my lack of interest in keeping my hair stylishly coiffed. I am a disappointment to him."

Adrian reached out with one hand, his finger trailing over a loose tendril of my stray hair. "I think your hair is beautiful as it is. If I were your father, I would not be disappointed in the least."

I reddened and pulled back. "If you had a daughter like Diana, then me, even you would be disappointed."

He smiled.

I looked away.

As though sensing my embarrassment, Adrian changed the subject. "Have you enjoyed your day, Heather?"

"Very much. Bruce took me to Culloden Moor early this afternoon. There is a fearsome beauty to that place."

"There is a fearsome beauty to all of Scotland, especially here in the Highlands with its gaunt mountains and haunting glens."

"At least the lochs are serene," I added. "Look at Loch Ness. Hardly a ripple. Are all the lochs that peaceful?"

"Usually. They are protected by the hills and mountains. I suspect our Highlands are much different from your India."

"Quite different. Does your father have a profession?"

His smile was rakish. "Not one that can be categorized."

"What do you mean?"

"Nothing important. Only I would understand the humor of it."

"Does he keep the estate books and collect the rents?"

"No, lawyers in Edinburgh do that. They have an agent in Inverness who collects the rents then forwards them to the office in Edinburgh."

"Where do you pasture your animals?"

"The cattle and horses use the fields belonging to Bridee Castle. It was a shame to see them lying fallow. As for the sheep, I purchased a large tract of land abutting the estate and pasture them there."

"You own land near here?"

"Sizable acreage. I bought it far below market price. I couldn't pass up the deal. I am looking for more. The tract isn't quite large enough to pasture all my animals. I need the fields of Bridee Castle for them."

"If there is room for them here, why do you want more land?"

"I like owning land on principle. There is the chance when your father returns that he will want to use the land for his own purposes. I hope I can find more acreage before he does return," Adrian said with a concerned stare at the loch.

"What will you do if you can't find more land?"

He turned to me and smile. "I will worry about that when the time comes." He stood and offered me both his hands. When I placed my hands in his, they were dwarfed. He pulled me up with such force that my body slammed into his. As I pressed against him for a moment, my pulse sped up and sensations became heightened. He looked down at me. His smiled faded and his expression darkened.

"I think I had better get you back to the castle." He held me at arms length then dropped his hands.

He brought our horses and helped me mount. We galloped back in silence. I tried to cope with the fact that my body had been so close to his. Lt. Patrick Danton had given me a chaste kiss or two before he was smitten by Diana. We had never embraced.

Chapter Four

When we entered the stableyard, a groom was unhitching the horses from a carriage and I assumed John Ross and my sister had returned from their jaunt to Inverness. Adrian stayed at the stables while I entered the foyer to hear Aunt Clarissa's voice emanating from the drawing room.

"Oh, dear me. Oh, dear me," came the pitiable moan.

I went into the drawing room to see Aunt Clarissa prostrate on the settee with Jane standing over her swooshing a fan back and forth over my aunt's face.

"What happened?" I asked.

"Father and Bruce had an argument. Their shouting upset Clarissa," Jane informed me.

"So much noise. And the language!" Aunt Clarissa declared putting the back of her hand to her forehead. "All that shouting is not good for my heart, Heather. And poor John. Bruce does aggravate his father so. My husband will be in a sour mood for the rest of the evening."

"I hear that fathers and sons always argue. You must not let it bother you, Aunt Clarissa," I said, hoping to soothe her. I looked at Jane. Her face was impassive, as though she had gone through this many times. I turned back to Aunt Clarissa. "Perhaps a spot of sherry will ease your distress."

"An excellent idea, my dear. Jane, do get me a glass of sherry."

Jane went to the sideboard to comply with Aunt Clarissa's wishes. I followed her.

"What was the argument about?" I asked in a whisper.

"Money," was her clipped answer.

One-eyed Angus, I thought. "Where is Bruce now?"

"I presume he got the money. He took off several minutes ago. A big ugly-looking man was here for him." She took the sherry to Aunt Clarissa and helped her sit up.

"Where is my sister?"

"She went upstairs the minute they returned. She wanted to wash and change before dinner," Jane said.

I glanced at the clock on the mantel. The dinner hour was fast approaching. "I had better do the same. Will you be all right, Aunt Clarissa?"

"I don't know, Heather. So many annoyances in one day. You never should have opened the door to the keep. The ghost of Lady Anne is free to bedevil me now."

"I am sorry." I wasn't all that sorry. I sensed Aunt Clarissa was delighted she could use the ghost of Lady Anne as an excuse for her weaknesses and imaginary troubles. I went upstairs without another word.

Jean was preparing my bath when I reached my bedchamber. She had laid out my royal blue gown which had a tight bodice ending in a vee at the first tier of a three tiered full skirt. At the edge of each tier, bright green embroidered leaves and vines circled around in a loose pattern. Short sleeves flared from off the shoulder.

When I was bathed, dressed, and my hair nicely done, it was time to go down to dinner. I met Diana on the landing.

"Wait until you see what John bought me," Diana exclaimed with a touch of breathlessness.

"What?" I asked.

"I am not going to tell you."

"Then why did you bring it up?" I hated her little games. She only did it to annoy me.

"You are in a foul mood."

"I was in a perfectly good mood until you started with your guessing games." I began to descend the stairs.

"Don't you want to know what he bought me?" She hurried to follow me.

"Only if you want to tell me. It is up to you."

"It was very expensive."

I said nothing as I continued down the stairs.

"A beautiful ermine muff. He said he didn't want my pretty hands getting cold when winter comes. Isn't that sweet of him?"

"Very thoughtful." Why would John Ross give my sister such a costly gift? I wondered.

"Don't tell anyone. John said it was to be our secret," Diana said.

"I won't."

Everyone was in the drawing room when we entered. Bruce stood and came to greet us.

"I see Adrian brought you home safely, Heather," Bruce said, causing Diana's head to snap in my direction before she turned back to Bruce.

"I thought *you* were taking my sister on a riding tour," Diana said.

"I had to come back to the castle on business. Adrian brought the message and I made him responsible for Heather," Bruce explained.

"I see." Diana had that hard glint in her eyes which always appeared when she was annoyed. She said no more.

* * *

I was tired that night and crawled into bed ready to welcome sleep. Whether it was the change in temperature and climate, or because my body touched Adrian's, sleep eluded me. I was wide awake. Sitting up, I leaned over and lighted the oil lamp. I swung my legs over the edge of the bed and dangled them while I decided which course to take. If I were in India, what would I do? Read a book, I answered myself. I rose, put on my robe, then put the matches, still in my hand, into my pocket. I opened the door a crack and peered out. The dim light from the scant oil lamps showed the corridor to be empty. I slipped out and went down to the foyer where more oil lamps flickered shadows on the walls.

As I moved down the hall to the library on the inhabited side of the castle, the foyer's light began to fade and I became part of the shadows. I went into the darkened library and groped for an oil lamp. As I passed one of the large windows that looked out on the terrace and topiary beyond, my peripheral vision caught a movement outside.

I blinked several times, thinking I had seen the sculptured plants move. I tiptoed to the window and peered out into the murky night. The topiary was stationary. The shadowy movement was on the terrace. My eyes began to adjust to the dim light. What I saw caused me to shudder.

No one could mistake Diana's golden curls. She was in the arms of a tall man and deep in a passionate kiss. I felt as though my life fluids were draining out my toes. My insides became hollow. For a moment I thought my heart had stopped. Diana was working her wiles on Adrian. I should have known he was being gallant this afternoon. His real interest was Diana. I couldn't blame him. Why should he have affection for

71

me when the beautiful Diana was available? I stood and stared, transfixed by the sight of them locked in an embrace. I didn't mind too much when Patrick Danton left me to pursue Diana. But this hurt. I felt betrayed. Though I had warned myself on more than one occasion since seeing Adrian Ross, I knew I was falling in love with him. I was about to turn away and fight the tears forming in my eyes, when the clouds scudded off the moon to chase a new breeze. Moonlight flooded the terrace.

My eyes popped with astonishment and my mouth fell silently agape. Adrian wasn't kissing my sister. It was John Ross, Aunt Clarissa's husband. My astonishment gave way to a mixture of embarrassment and relief. I knew my sister was flirtatious, but she had never used her wiles on a married man. Why was she playing this dangerous game with John Ross?

Not wanting to light a lamp and give my presence away, I forgot about a book and fumbled my way back to my bedchamber.

The dining room was empty when I came down for breakfast. My mind was still whirling with last night's incident. As her sister, I felt I should have a talk with Diana, not that she would listen to me. I felt it necessary to point out the perilous path she was embarking on. As I mulled over my tea, I was trying to formulate a speech to give her when Adrian walked in.

"You are up rather early, Heather. Any particular reason?" he asked as he filled his plate at the sideboard.

"I found it hard to sleep."

"Didn't you sleep at all?"

"On and off."

"I suppose you are too tired to look at the horses and cattle."

"No, but I do have to talk to my sister first. I don't know how long it will take."

"Perhaps some other time then."

"I hope so. I like horses."

"What about cattle?"

"I never thought much about them. They are sacred in India. No one there would dream of eating them."

"I will be here for a while if your talk with Diana is brief."

I smiled, nodded, and went upstairs.

I knocked then entered my sister's bedchamber. Pillows propped her up and a tray lay across her lap.

"Really, Samrú, you should know by now I don't like my breakfast cold. Take this back to the kitchen and bring me a *hot* breakfast," Diana demanded.

"Yes, Miss Diana." Samrú took the tray. Her head was lowered as she walked past me. Her stance was one of defeat.

"Why do you treat Samrú so shabbily, Diana?" I asked.

"If she had brought me a hot breakfast, I wouldn't have had to chastise her. At least someone has purchased white sugar."

"This isn't our bungalow in India, Diana. The kitchen here is three floors down and some distance away. If you would eat breakfast in the dining room like the rest of us, you would have a hot meal."

"Us?"

"With the exception of Aunt Clarissa, everyone takes breakfast in the dining room," I said, my temper rising.

"Adrian too?"

"He is down there now waiting for me. I would like to have a talk with you first."

"Why is he waiting for you?"

"To show me his animals."

"He was suppose to take me." Her voice was strident

73

and her familiar pout surfaced. She was out of bed in an instant. "Help me dress, Heather."

"I said I wanted to talk to you, Diana."

"Then talk while you help me dress. I want to get downstairs before Adrian leaves."

Why did I open my big mouth? "Samrú will be bringing your breakfast up soon."

"Let her eat it," Diana snapped. "Fetch my yellow day frock with the white lace."

"Get it yourself." I turned and started to leave.

"Don't get all riled up, Heather. I need your help. I can't lace this corset alone."

I sighed with resignation. I knew she would throw a tantrum and wake the whole castle if I didn't help her. I took the yellow frock from the wardrobe and tossed it on the bed, then went to do her corset laces.

"I don't know why you bother with a corset. I don't use one."

"And look at you," she snipped.

I jerked the laces tight, hoping they would pinch her.

"Tighter. I want to have the smallest waist Adrian has ever seen."

I pulled with all my strength as anger boiled within me. "I don't see why you care what Adrian thinks when you have his father wrapped around your little finger."

"What are you talking about, Heather?"

"I saw you last night on the terrace kissing John Ross." There, I had said it. It wasn't the lecture I had been practicing, but at least it was out in the open.

"So you have taken to snooping on me. Really, Heather, I never thought you would sink so low."

"I wasn't snooping. I saw you by accident."

"Hmph!"

"Toying with a married man is risky, Diana. Besides he is old enough to be your father."

"What difference does that make? He has been sweet

74

to me. I felt I should repay him for the lovely muff he bought me. Do hurry, Heather. I want to get downstairs before Adrian gets impatient and leaves."

"I suppose you are going to set your cap for him too."

"Why not? He *is* the handsomest of the lot. And so very masculine. I rather think he fancies me. Have you noticed the way he looks at me?"

"You are liable to cause friction between father and son. That isn't right, Diana."

"Oh, pooh! You make too much of things, Heather." She scooped her yellow frock off the bed and tossed it over her head. "Do the buttons for me."

I saw the futility in trying to talk some sense into her. I buttoned her frock quickly. She went to the dressing table and coiffed her hair. I had to admit she had a flair for arranging her tresses in a most becoming manner. After she tied her bonnet on, we went downstairs. Adrian was coming out of the dining room as we stepped into the foyer.

"Heather tells me you are taking her on a tour of your animals." She flounced up to him and preemptively snaked her arm through his, her smile dazzling.

Adrian raised a querulous eyebrow when he looked at me. I shrugged in return.

"Have you had your breakfast?" Adrian asked.

"Yes," Diana answered.

"Where is everyone going?" John asked as he and Jane came down the stairs.

"We are going to see Adrian's animals," Diana said gaily.

"I thought you wanted to go into the village this morning," John said, a frown creasing his brow.

"Perhaps this afternoon, John." Diana gazed adoringly at Adrian.

She is looking for trouble, I thought when I saw the scowl on John's face. I was about to grab my bonnet

75

from a table in the foyer, then thought, why bother? I trailed after Adrian and Diana as they went outside.

The horses were beautiful as they frolicked and grazed in the green fields. A number of them were yearlings. I was enchanted and said little. Besides, Diana dominated the conversation with inane questions. As we started to walk to the pasture where the cattle were grazing, Diana twisted her ankle and would have fallen to the ground if Adrian hadn't caught her.

"Are you all right, Diana?" Adrian asked.

"I am afraid not. I can't seem to put any weight on my foot. Could you help me back to the castle, Adrian?"

He scooped her into his arms. He started back toward the castle, but stopped short. "Aren't you coming, Heather?"

"No. I think I will wander around for a while."

When they had disappeared from view, I went back to the horses. I sat on the ground, my arms wrapped around my knees, and watched the placid creatures. I tried to concentrate on their beauty, but the image of Diana in Adrian's arms kept haunting me.

Mists alternated with rain for the next several days. I searched through the newspapers for information about the Indian rebellion and found only general news, nothing specific.

Diana intensified her dalliances with Adrian and John. The air was thick with tension during evening meals. Poor Bruce looked like a lost puppy who wanted to join in Diana's games, but was constantly pushed aside. Aunt Clarissa babbled away during meals with all the innocence of someone who has no idea what is happening beneath her nose. Jane was no fool; she knew what was going on. Adrian looked uncomfortable while

76

John made no attempt to hide his displeasure with Adrian. Diana was enjoying every minute of it. I wished Father would summon us back to India. Diana's amorous antics became more embarrassing every day.

During the inclement weather, I thought about opening Father's trunk and starting on those memoirs he wanted me to write. I didn't open the trunk. I decided he might like to write them himself when he retired. Beside, I didn't want to get embroiled in the project then be summoned back to India.

When the weather broke and a clear, sunny day dawned, I went down to breakfast with a lightness in my heart. I was surprised to see Bruce there at so early an hour.

"Don't look so startled, Heather. I am capable of rising early too," Bruce said, his eyes twinkling merrily.

"Usually only Adrian is up this early," I said.

"He has eaten and left. Don't tell me that along with Diana, you also have a fancy for my brother."

"We have nice chats at breakfast. That is all."

"Then we will have a nice chat."

I filled my plate and sat down. "Are you up this early for a reason, Bruce?"

"I am off to the races today. Would you like to come?"

"I don't think so. I plan to visit my mother's grave, then have a good ride while the weather is fine."

"I forgot your mother is buried on the premises. Your father sent the coffin back here, didn't he?"

"Yes. He wanted her to be buried at Bridee Castle."

"Do you know where the private cemetery is?"

"Yes. I asked Aunt Clarissa. Why don't you ask Diana to go to the races with you? She likes excitement."

"I did last night. She said it was too early for her to rise and too far away. Besides, she said she had promised my father she would go to Inverness with him. I don't think she likes me, Heather."

"Of course she likes you."

"She refuses to go anywhere with me." He leaned forward and in a conspiratorial tone said, "I will tell you something if you promise not to tell anyone else. Promise?"

"I promise."

"I saw her kissing Adrian when he carried her from the fields the day you went to see his animals. I thought what was fair for one brother was fair for the other. When I was alone with her in the drawing room one day, I impulsively kissed her. Do you know what she did?"

"Slapped your face?"

"I wish she had. No, Heather, she laughed at me. Called me a silly little boy. It was not only a blow to my pride, but it crushed my sense of manhood. After all, I am twenty-four. I don't mean to offend you, but your sister isn't a very nice person. I felt thoroughly insulted."

I didn't know what to say. Propriety told me I should defend my sister, yet I didn't know how.

"I probably shouldn't have said anything," Bruce continued. "She is your sister. I had to tell someone and I felt you might be sympathetic."

"I am, Bruce. I know my sister is a terrible flirt. I don't think she means any harm though. She is just thoughtless when it comes to anyone else's feelings."

"You won't tell anyone, will you?"

"Of course not. I respect your confidence, Bruce. I am pleased that you trusted me enough to tell me."

"Thank you, Heather. Well, I must be off. Pray that I win."

"I will."

The sun felt good on my face as I rode to the small private cemetery about a mile from the castle. I tethered the horse to one of the iron railings that formed a fence about the graveyard. Before entering the sacred ground, I picked a bunch of wildflowers from the surrounding field. I swung the gate open and perused the ancient headstones. The cemetery had been sadly neglected. Thistles and a profusion of weeds smothered the ground, in some cases hiding the headstones. White and yellow lichen obscured the names on some of the marble, and in some cases, erosion had all but made the ancient stones impossible to read. I had to keep pulling my riding skirt from the numerous thistles whose obstinate thorns delighted in impeding my way. When I found my mother's grave, I gently placed the flowers on it, after clearing the weeds away. I said a prayer, lingered a moment, then left.

I guided the horse in a canter down the lane, trying to memorize the route so I wouldn't become lost. I traveled for some time, each glimpse of the Highlands more wondrous than the next. Suddenly I was faced with a thick stand of white pine, larch and various evergreens. Though a narrow dirt lane led into it, I decided against entering and began to turn my horse around. I stopped as a faint musical sound emanated from the woods.

Concentrating, I strained to listen. Song birds trilled, masking the previous sound. I waited for the stillness to resume. When it did, I heard the sound again. I couldn't resist the lure of that strange music. I was sure it was produced by a human. I paced the horse cautiously toward the woods and entered the path. The full force of the sun disappeared to leave scintillating and sporadic shafts of light in its wake.

The deeper I went, the clearer the sound. Definitely the music of man. I was astonished when I recognized the chords of a piano. A piano in the middle of the woods? The thought was absurd until the dense woods began to give way to a clearing ahead of me. As my horse pranced into the clearing, a charming two-story house nestled on a spacious lawn.

The second story jutted over the first and oak timbers striped the white plastered facade. A cluster of chimneys rose in the center, while one chimney soared from each wing. Occasionally a window would bounce a sunbeam back at me. I felt like Gretel approaching the ginger-bread house of the witch.

I knew no witch could produce the music with such emotional élan. I had heard music like that once before, if only briefly. Adrian.

After sliding off my horse, I tethered the animal to a shrub. I boldly walked up to the door and rapped quite loudly with the brass knocker. The music continued un-abated. Realizing my efforts were probably not heard over the din of the music, I tried the doorknob, which moved under my hand. Soundlessly, I went in and headed toward the source of the loud and soulful music.

Adrian's back was toward me as I entered what I thought to be the front sitting parlor. He wore a loose white Byronesque shirt and black breeches. His thick black hair quivered as his fingers pounded out a pas-sionate piece by Beethoven. I quietly stood and watched and listened.

As the tempo changed, he stopped suddenly and turned.

"What are you doing here, Heather?" His dark eye-brows clashed together over the bridge of his nose in a frown. Anger glittered in his black eyes.

"I heard the music." My voice was hoarse and whis-pery. At that moment his eyes frightened me.

"How did you find your way here?"

"I was out riding, saw the path, and followed it when I heard the music."

"Does anyone know you are here?"

I shook my head and wondered why my presence angered him.

"You shouldn't sneak up on a person like that." His anger began to dissipate.

"I knocked. When no one answered and I found the door open, I thought it wouldn't do any harm if I came in. Please don't stop playing because of me."

"I have lost the mood."

"I had better go."

He left the piano and came to stand before me with a softer expression. "Now that you are here, do give me the opportunity to display a small amount of hospitality."

"Are you sure? I feel as though I have unwittingly intruded on your privacy. I don't want you to think me a nuisance."

"I will let you know when your company is undesirable. This way." He cupped my elbow as he steered me into the back parlor. "Wait here. I will bring tea."

"Can I help?"

"You are a guest. Make yourself comfortable."

I did just that and lowered myself onto a thickly padded sofa. The room was pleasant, geared more toward comfort than style. I particularly liked the paucity of heavy furniture. The room was light, airy, and certainly not overfurnished. The smell of lavender hovered in the air, a refreshing change from the dank and musty smell of Bridee Castle. Noticing a large orieled window behind the sofa, I rose and went to it.

A small garden stretched in a circle at the back of the house. In the center of the flowering curve was another garden consisting of various herbs which were planted and trimmed to form a hexagonal pattern. A brick path led through it. The entire rear area was well maintained. I wondered if Adrian tended to it himself. My musings were cut short by the appearance of my host carrying a tea tray.

"Admiring the gardens?" he asked, putting the tray down on the low table before the sofa.

"Yes. They are lovely."

"Past their prime now. In spring and the early part of summer they are at their best."

"Do you have a gardener?" I walked back to the sofa and sat down.

"On occasion. I like to do some of the work."

"Where do you find the time?"

"Will you do the honors and pour?" I complied with his wishes. "For the most part, the gardens consists of perennials and require very little maintenance," he informed me.

"Is this your house?"

"You seem to have a penchant for asking questions. Are you always so inquisitive?" he asked, smiling.

"Only when I am interested." I returned the smile.

"The house and other buildings came with the land I purchased."

"Then I must have been trespassing on your property while I was riding. I am sorry."

"Don't be. I won't draw and quarter you. Not this time anyway."

"Does your family know you own this house?"

"Probably, but I don't encourage visits from them. I consider this my place of refuge. A place of peace and quiet."

I smiled. "A place where you can play the piano without Aunt Clarissa scolding you?"

"Exactly."

"I am surprised you aren't swamped with their company. It is such a lovely place. Quite the opposite of Bridee Castle."

"My family isn't the adventurous type. Bruce gravitates toward race courses and pubs. Jane seldom ventures farther than the village. Cities hold more fascination for Clarissa and Father. Although lately, my father seems to prefer the company of your sister to that of his wife."

"Aunt Clarissa doesn't seem to mind."

"I sometimes think she isn't aware of it. Her mind has a tendency to flutter from one event to another like a butterfly seeking another flower."

"You don't think much of my aunt, do you?"

He shrugged his broad shoulders. "I don't think about her one way or another. As far as I am concerned she has no function in my life."

"She does house and feed you," I said on her behalf.

"I didn't mean to put you on the defensive. You asked for my opinion and I gave you an honest one. Before you and your sister came, I spent most of my time here. I have a well-stocked larder and can cook the basics. Usually I have a cook that comes and does breakfast and dinner for me."

"Why has our arrival altered your habits?"

"Let us call it a show of friendliness."

"My sister is quite beautiful. Is it because of her you have chosen to stay at Bridee Castle?"

"You are a blunt little minx, aren't you?" His smile was wide and generous.

"You didn't answer my question." I poured myself another cup of tea.

"In a way perhaps."

"Then you are interested in her."

"Not the way you think. Are you jealous of Diana?"

I sipped my tea slowly while I thought about an answer. "No. I don't think so. I like being me. Diana is a slave to fashion and her looks."

"I take it you are not."

"As long as I am neat and clean, I am satisfied. I will admit she makes me angry at times. She also embarrasses me with her outrageous flirting. Are you jeal-

83

ous of Bruce?"

He laughed easily. "Hardly. If you were me would you be jealous of Bruce?"

"I guess not." My gaze drifted around the room. "The house seems quite large from the outside. How many rooms do you have?"

"You have seen the two downstairs parlors. Also downstairs are a dining room, a morning room, a game room, a butler's pantry, a library, and a kitchen. Upstairs are bedchambers, some with their own sitting parlors. The stable and carriage houses are outside along with a solarium. The carriage house has servants' quarters above it."

"Quite an estate. You must be a proud owner," I commented.

"I am."

"I better go back now. I wouldn't want to overstay my welcome." I put my empty cup on the tray and stood.

"If you can wait a few minutes, I will ride back with you."

"You don't have to do that."

"I know." He took the tea tray and left the room.

I walked back to the front parlor and the piano. Almost unconsciously my fingers trailed over the keys. A hollow feeling settled in the pit of my stomach as I recalled Adrian claiming an interest in Diana. I should be used to standing in her shadow. It never bothered me before. Somehow, with Adrian, it did. At least he accepted me as a friend, even though my feelings went far beyond friendship.

"Are you ready to go?" he asked.

I quivered when his hands came down on my shoulders. I turned around and mumbled, "Yes." His hands remained on my shoulders.

"Have you always had that many freckles?" he asked, his hand lifting, one finger tracing over my cheekbone.

84

"Ever since I can remember. They aren't very lady-like, are they?"

"They are adorable, especially on you."

His head tilted to one side and lowered. For a fleeting second I thought he was going to kiss me. Instead his fingers plucked a leaf from my hair. My pulsing blood warned me not to stand too close to him. I headed for the hallway and front door.

We threaded our way in single file through the closely grown trees. Once we reached the fields and I was sure of the way back to the castle, I turned to Adrian and said, "I'll race you back to the castle."

"I will win," Adrian said.

"Perhaps."

I pressed my feet into the horse's flanks, loosened the reins, and we were off. Adrian gallantly gave me a good start before thundering behind me. He soon passed me, but I managed to keep the distance between us short. I arrived at the stableyard in less than three minutes after Adrian. My face was flushed with excitement. Adrian was grinning rakishly at me.

"I told you I would win," he said swinging off his horse.

"It was a good race. I enjoyed it." When I dismounted, he came over and put his arm around my shoulders.

"You are a good sport, Heather. You knew I had the better horse," he said as we headed for the castle.

We were discussing the ride as we entered the foyer. Diana sashayed out of the drawing room.

"Where have you two been?" she asked, hands on hips.

"I thought you went into Inverness with John," I said.

"We came back early. Where have *you* been?"

Adrian glanced at me, one eyebrow arched.

"I went to see Mother's grave. I met Adrian and we

85

raced back here. How was Inverness?" I didn't want her to know Adrian had a house of his own, or she would haunt it.

Diana peered down her nose at me, then gave her attention to Adrian, flashing a toothy smile at him before snaking her hand through his arm. "I have been waiting for you to show me the gardens here, Adrian. The topiary looks fascinating, but I don't recognize all the shapes. I was hoping you would explain them to me."

He patted her hand then removed it. "I am sorry, Diana. I must get washed and changed if I am to be presentable at dinner tonight."

Diana pouted, her bow mouth forming a perfect O. "You are not being very hospitable, Adrian. I am beginning to think you are avoiding me."

"Now why would anyone try to avoid a beautiful creature such as yourself?" His smile was most charming.

Diana appeared mollified for the moment. "Tomorrow?"

"Perhaps." Adrian headed for the staircase, his long legs allowing him to vault the steps two at a time.

"Chasing after an older man doesn't become you, Heather. You are much too young for Adrian. Father would not approve," Diana said.

"I suppose John Ross is your age. For your information, I am not chasing after any man. I leave that occupation to you," I declared.

"Well, I never! You are becoming brattier every day." She spun on her heel and stalked back to the drawing room.

With anger in my heart, I followed her. I was surprised to find Aunt Clarissa and Jane there. I had expected John Ross dancing his attentions on Diana.

"How was your ride, my dear Heather?" Aunt Clarissa asked.

"Fine." I flopped into a chair. "I was dismayed to see my mother's grave left unattended. In fact, the entire MacBride cemetery is neglected."

Aunt Clarissa began twisting her lace-edged handkerchief in her hands as though wringing out the family laundry. "I didn't know. This whole place is much too large for me to see to everything," she whined. "Besides, my small pittance doesn't stretch nearly far enough."

Small pittance? Money didn't seem to be in short supply where Aunt Clarissa was concerned. The jewels . . .

"I will ask the gardener for some shears and tend to it myself."

Jane sat prim and quiet. Every now and then her eyes would furtively slip to Diana. The envy was evident. Diana made no secret of the fact that she thought Jane Ross too prosaic and homely to bother cultivating anything resembling friendship.

Aunt Clarissa was soon bemoaning her difficulties with the staff. In a twinkling her conversation rotated to the harshness of the approaching winter. Diana left the room in the middle of one of Aunt Clarissa's sentences. I patiently heard her out until the time came to prepare for dinner.

After the meal, Diana managed to get Adrian to take her onto the rear terrace. Raw anger flared in John Ross's eyes. Aunt Clarissa babbled about the rice in the pudding being not quite cooked enough to her liking. Jane worked at her needlepoint. Bruce hadn't returned from the races. I sat at the piano playing soft, quiet music.

I was ready for bed, but not really sleepy. I went to the window in my bedchamber and stared out into the dark night. I couldn't stop thinking about Adrian and

87

the lovely time I had at his house.

While engaged in wishful thinking, a faint light caught my eye, then disappeared. I focused on the area near the keep. Like a lighthouse beacon, the light flickered on and off as it moved higher and higher up the keep. When it reached the top, the tenuous glow became steady, though weak. After some time, the mysterious light began descending, then vanished completely.

Was there really a ghost? "No," I whispered aloud. But if there wasn't a ghost, who was in the keep at this hour of night, and what were they doing?

Chapter Five

It was midmorning when I decided to go to the keep. Despite the dark clouds and misty rain, I was determined to look for a clue there that might indicate a human visitor. After securing the key from Mrs. Burns, I started the trek through the old part of the main castle. This time the pace was leisurely. When I went through it with Jane, it was like a timed march.

I looked at things more closely, even though the light coming through the windows was like tarnished silver. I slowly began to realize that the majority of objects in the various rooms belonged in a museum.

In the old library I perused the titles of the books which lay sleeping under the dust of eons. I started to pull a volume of Shakespeare's Tragedies from the shelf only to envelop myself in a swirl of dust. When the sneezing began, I decided against examining any more of the volumes. I moved on to the room housing the weaponry.

Though dust was just as prevalent there, cobwebs were more dominant. Suddenly a menacing laugh echoed around the room. I froze. The fine hairs on the nape of my neck snapped to attention and my skin rippled with fear. The low, groaning laugh came again. It seemed to come from one of the suits of armor. I cautiously moved closer to one suit whose metal fingers clutched a long spear. My hand trembled as I reached out to lift up the visor. The spear snapped down. I gasped and jumped aside. As I turned to speed away, a normal, robust laugh emanated from the armor suit.

The spear fell to the floor, the metal hands creaking their way to the helmet. With the helmet off, the face of Bruce Ross grinned at me.

"Did I scare you, Heather?" he asked.

"You most certainly did and it is not funny." My breathing still was shallow and quick.

"It was only a little prank."

"I don't call scaring people out of their wits a 'little prank.'" I started to walk away.

"Heather . . . please come back," Bruce called.

"Why should I?" I turned my head to look at him.

"Once I got into the suit the catches clamped down and I can't open them with my fingers like this." He raised an armored hand.

It was my turn to laugh.

"Heather, please."

"I really shouldn't help you, Bruce. I should leave you right where you are for a couple of hours. It might teach you not to play wicked pranks on people." Despite my threats, I went over to him and opened the catches on the top and sides of the metal suit. After some maneuvering, the suit came unhinged and Bruce stepped out of the armor.

"Thanks, Heather."

"How did you know I was coming here?"

"I watched you. I heard you ask Mrs. Burns for the key to the keep so I knew you would be coming this way."

"What if I had changed my mind and decided not to come."

90

"I guess I would do a lot of screaming," Bruce said, scratching the top of his head.

"How did you get into that suit so fast?" I asked curiously.

"Years ago it was soldered together on one side and hinged so it could be displayed upright. All I had to do was swing it open, step in, and shut it. I guess I shut it too hard and the catches sprung. He paused momentarily. "Why are you going to the keep again? I thought Jane gave you a thorough tour already."

"She did."

"Then why would you want to go up to that gloomy old place again? Nothing is up there," Bruce declared.

"I saw a light going up to the top of the keep last night. I thought I would investigate."

He laughed. "You probably saw the ghostly glow of Lady Anne."

"What I saw was no ghost." I turned on my heel and marched toward the ancient hall.

"Want some company?" he called after me.

I shrugged and kept on walking. He was beside me in minutes.

"Did Mrs. Burns hesitate when she gave you the key?" Bruce asked.

"No. She looked as though she was glad to be rid of it. I think I will keep it. Did Mrs. Burns have the only key to the keep?" I asked.

"I don't know. If there are more, I don't know about them."

"I thought you were still at the races."

"I came home late last night. Everyone was in bed."

"Did you win or lose?"

"I should have won, but the track was wet and muddy. It turned out my horses weren't mudders." He tilted his head and smiled.

We came to the open courtyard then entered the decaying and ancient hall. I soon had the key in the locked door of the keep. That same chilling draft swirled about us the minute I had the door open.

"Whew, it's cold in here," Bruce commented.

"Have you been here before, Bruce?" I noticed his lack of interest in the place. His eyes fixed on the spiral staircase without glancing about the rounded room we entered.

"Once, a long time ago. After I heard the tale of Lady Anne, I cajoled Mrs. Burns into giving me the key. It wasn't the exciting place I thought it would be. In fact, I found it dirty and boring. All those stairs to climb. Not worth the effort, I thought."

"Do you want to stay here while I go to the top?"

"No. I wouldn't want it on my conscience if Lady Anne got you." He ventured a tight-lipped smile.

With me leading the way, we quickly began our ascent. I braced my hand on the curving stone wall only to find it cold and clammy.

"Take it easy, Heather. Not so fast. Let us take a rest on the next floor," Bruce said with gaps and gasps between words.

We left the staircase at the next landing. With the exception of unseen spiders and their visible gossamer webs, the circular room was empty. Panting, Bruce leaned against a wall.

"You should get more exercise, Bruce," I said, then went to stare out one of the slotted windows. A faint mist covered the landscape, turning everything gray and bleak.

"Climbing those stairs is enough exercise for the rest of the year."

I patiently waited for Bruce to regain his wind. When he nodded his head and pulled himself from the wall, I eagerly rushed to the spiral staircase to resume the ascent.

As I reached the top and final room, a scene of indescribable horror lay before me. My hand clamped over my mouth. I took an involuntary step backward, my body crashing into Bruce.

"What is the matter, Heather?"

I raised my arm and pointed a finger toward the dais with the marble slab.

"Good Lord," Bruce cried.

Samrú lay stretched out on the stone, her arms rigid at her sides. Rats were gnawing at the flesh of her torso, which was covered with blood. Dried blood stained the side of the dais. I turned and buried my head in Bruce's shoulder.

"Let's get out of here," he said, drawing me away.

By the time we reached the drawing room, I was shaking. Bruce went to the sideboard and poured two snifters of brandy.

"Drink this," he ordered, and handed me one of the glasses.

I took a swallow and almost choked as the fiery liquid burned its way down my throat. I noticed Bruce's hands were shaking and he needed both of them to raise the glass to his lips. He took a hefty swallow.

"I thought I heard someone in here," Adrian said, coming into the drawing room. "Drinking before lunch, Bruce?"

Bruce stared at him then took another swallow. Adrian turned to me.

"You too, Heather? This is a shocking surprise."

"Tell him, Bruce. I—I can't right now." This time I sipped the brandy. I was too numb to talk.

Bruce drained his snifter, poured himself another, sat down, and proceeded to tell Adrian what we had found in the keep.

"You had better send one of the lads to Inverness and have the constabulary come here posthaste."

"What about Heather? She shouldn't be left alone after seeing that," Bruce said.

"Don't worry about Heather. I will stay with her. Now hurry," Adrian said with authority.

Bruce drained his glass and left.

The brandy relaxed me. I stopped trembling and sat down on the settee. Adrian joined me. My calmness was momentary. Tears began to roll down my cheeks. When the racking sobs came, Adrian put his arms around me and held my head to his chest.

"What is going on here?" asked an angry Diana as she stalked into the room. "Has she been playing on your sympathy about missing Father and India? Don't let her fool you, Adrian. She couldn't care less about either of them." Venom coated her words. She knew she lied, but I was in no mood to argue with her.

"Diana, will you please go and find my father, Jane, and Clarissa? Have them come here quickly," Adrian said.

"Of course, Adrian. Anything you wish." Diana flashed a winning smile then swooshed out of the room, her taffeta day frock sounding like bacon frying.

Adrian stoked my hair saying, "There, there." His voice was mellifluous and soothing. My tears finally spent, I pulled away and tried to collect myself by taking several deep breaths.

"Are you going to be all right?" Adrian asked.

I nodded. I didn't dare speak. He handed me his handkerchief and I gave my nose a good blow. I was returning to normal when Bruce came back.

"I have sent for everyone," Adrian informed him. "They better know what happened before the authorities get here. Did you tell the lad what to tell the police?"

"I told him to tell the police there has been a suspicious death here." Bruce sat down in a chair opposite the settee. "How are you feeling, Heather?"

"I will be all right. The shock is starting to wear off. I was fond of Samrú."

"I understand she raised the two of you when your mother died," Adrian said, taking my hand in his.

"I guess she tried to be a mother to us in her way, but I never could get close to her, her religion and way of life were a mystery to me. Though she held herself aloof, she was good to us."

When the others came into the drawing room and took seats, Bruce began his narration. I thought he went into more detail than necessary. Aunt Clarissa swooned causing her to slump in her chair. John Ross covered his mouth and chin with his hand. Jane paled. Diana frowned.

"I can't imagine why Samrú would go up in the keep, lie down on a slab, and die," Diana said. "Why would she want to kill herself?"

"I don't think she was happy here, Diana," I said.

"I don't think she killed herself. I think someone else did," was Bruce's suggestion.

Jane was waving fan over Aunt Clarissa face. When it didn't seem to help, Jane laid the fan aside and began to rub Aunt Clarissa's wrists.

"Murder? Don't be ridiculous, Bruce," Diana said with a slight sneer. "Who in the Highlands would want to kill Samrú?"

"And why?" I added.

"I think we should leave all speculation to the police," Adrian suggested. He was still holding my hand. From the direction of Diana's gaze and the look on her face, she seemed more concerned about the hand holding than she did about Samrú's death.

"Nasty business this," John Ross declared. "How is Clarissa doing, Jane?"

"I think she is coming around, Father," Jane said as Aunt Clarissa's eyes began to flutter open.

"Oh, dear me, dear me. Is that Indian woman really dead?"

"Yes, Clarissa," John answered as he stared at the floor.

"Luncheon is served," the butler Jeffrey announced.

"I won't be able to eat a thing with a dead body in the castle," whined Aunt Clarissa as she pushed herself out of the chair.

"Do you want something to eat, Heather?" Adrian asked me.

"I suppose I should eat something. The brandy is making me a bit dizzy."

He helped me up from the settee and was about to offer me his arm when Diana glided over.

"Adrian, dear, this business about Samrú has left me weak. I don't think my legs are strong enough to take me to the dining room. Do you mind giving me your arm?" Diana asked.

Adrian glanced at me. I gave him a faint smile which told him to go ahead, and pulled my hand away.

The silence at the dining table was ominous. For one who claimed to have no appetite, Aunt Clarissa managed to consume a sizable amount of food. Jane was exceptionally quiet and kept glancing at Diana furtively. I couldn't tell whether it was with envy or anger.

"I suppose I shall have to post an advertisement in the newspaper for a personal maid," Diana declared with a touch of ennui.

"Don't you think you should wait until after the funeral, Diana?" I was seething with anger. How could she be so callous? Poor Samrú wasn't even buried and Diana was already thinking of her personal needs.

"Maybe you can go for days on end without someone to do your hair and see to your needs, Heather. I can't," Diana answered.

"I don't think you have to bother with an advertisement, Diana. I am sure you can find someone in Inverness. The town is always full of young women looking for work. I will take you there tomorrow, if you wish," John offered.

"Thank you, John. I can always depend on you," Diana cooed.

"Would you care to come with us, Clarissa?" John asked.

"Oh, dear me, no. I suspect I shall be thoroughly weary by the time the police have beleaguered us with their questions."

"Jane? Heather?"

"I have a lot to do tomorrow. I must write Father and let him know what happened. And I shall have to see to Samrú's possessions," I answered.

"What about you, Jane?" John asked without much enthusiasm.

"I think the trip to Inverness would be a pleasant diversion. The weather will soon prevent frequent excursions," Jane said.

"While you are in Inverness, could you see an undertaker, Diana?" I asked. "We will need a coffin."

"What a horrid thought! I couldn't bring myself to speak with an undertaker."

"Would you like me to handle it, Heather?" John asked.

"I would appreciate it."

"It is settled then. I will make the necessary arrangements."

"Must we talk about funerals at the table?" Aunt Clarissa grimaced.

We had finished eating and a maid was clearing the table when Jeffrey informed us that the police were waiting in the drawing room. Three men were standing there as we filed in.

"I am Inspector Walter Andrews." The thick-set man came forward to shake John's hand. Compared to the

Ross men, he was short. He had a florid face and tired eyes. With a directional wave of his hand, he introduced the others. "This is Detective Thomas Gordon, my assistant, and Dr. Robert Drummond. I thought it best to have a medical man on hand."

John made the necessary introductions.

"Who discovered the body?" the inspector asked.

"We did," Bruce informed him.

"We?"

"Heather MacBride and me."

"Mr. Ross, would you care to direct us to the corpse. I don't want to put Miss MacBride through it again."

"I am afraid I don't have the stomach for it, Inspector. My brother knows the way to the keep. He can show you. Do you mind, Adrian?"

"Not at all. Where is the key?"

"I forgot to lock it." I plucked the key from my skirt pocket and handed it to Adrian.

"Come along, gentlemen," Adrian said.

"I will come with you," John said.

"I would appreciate it if the rest of you would stay here until we return," said Inspector Andrews.

We remained silent as the men left the room. I debated whether or not to tell the inspector about the light I had seen in the keep last night. One light didn't make sense to me. If I had seen two lights glimmering their way up to the keep, it might have had some significance. Perhaps there was a second light. It might have gone up to the keep before I looked out the window. I decided not to mention it until I could sort it out in my own mind. The shock of seeing Samrú made me forget what it was I thought odd about the top floor of the keep. Another visit to the building would have to wait. I was not of a mind to go up there soon.

Suddenly Diana jumped out of her seat and went to the window. "Doesn't the sun ever shine in this godforsaken place?" she asked of no one in particular.

Bruce rose, walked over to her, and put his arm around her. "You are under a strain, Diana. The weather will change."

She shrugged his arm off. "Don't tell me how I feel, Bruce. You know nothing about me. You are barely out of puberty and could never understand the complexities of a woman."

Bruce's face flushed. A fire of anger glinted in his light brown eyes. "I am sorry, Diana. I was only trying to comfort you."

"Well, you are not comforting me, only annoying me."

Bruce turned on his heel and went to the sideboard where he poured himself a drink. As usual, Diana's behavior embarrassed me. Even Jane had a rosy glow on her normally pallid cheeks. The silence in the drawing room made the time pass slowly. Aunt Clarissa was becoming fidgety, twisting her handkerchief beyond recognition. I was relieved when the inspector, doctor, and John returned.

"Where is Adrian?" Diana asked.

"He is helping Detective Gordon with the body," Inspector Andrews answered.

"Beastly mess up there," John commented, then proceeded to the sideboard where he poured himself a whisky. "Would you care for a drink, Inspector? Doctor?"

Both men declined. "What happened to Samrú, Doctor?" I asked.

"Difficult to say. The rats have made absolute chaos of the body. I shall have to have it in my surgery to do a proper examination," Dr. Drummond said.

"Can someone give me the background on this woman and her name?" the inspector asked, retrieving a small notebook and pen from his dark vest.

"Her name was Samrú Singh." I went on to tell him as much as I could about her.

"Can you add anything, Mr. Ross?" Inspector Andrews asked when he finished his notes.

"We hardly knew the woman. She kept to herself. Took her meals in her room. I don't think she mingled with the staff," John answered.

"Did she have any enemies?"

"We haven't been here long enough to make an enemy of anyone, Inspector," I said. "She hadn't left the castle since we arrived."

Inspector Andrews continued to question us. He received very little useful information. His tired eyes seemed to grow wearier. Adrian came back with a pale Detective Gordon. I didn't envy the task they had to perform. When Adrian offered the detective a glass of whisky, the detective took it.

"Where is the body, Gordon?" the inspector asked.

"In an old storage room at the base of the keep. We wrapped her in an old rug."

Inspector Andrews turned to John Ross. "I am afraid we will have to leave the body here for the moment, Mr. Ross. Being in a hurry, we came by horseback. I will stop at the village and have someone with a wagon fetch her. I don't think anyone here wants to prepare the body for burial." He started to follow Detective Gordon and the doctor to the foyer. At the entrance to the drawing room, he turned. "I expect all of you to stay in the vicinity. Good day."

Jane took a trembling Aunt Clarissa upstairs. I followed them, leaving Diana in her glory surrounded by men. I went directly to my escritoire, and, with a sad heart, began a letter to my father.

Thinking the letter was important enough, I decided to post it immediately. I changed into my brown riding skirt, white shirtwaist, and brown velvet jacket. I grabbed my brown merino hooded cape and left the bedchamber. As I crossed the foyer, ripples of laughter came from the drawing room, Diana's fluttering trill dominant.

I kept the horse at an even gait, neither fast nor slow. On the road ahead of me, a wagon rumbled along. As I came alongside, I knew what the wagon contained— Samrú's body. I rode up to the driver and greeted him. He politely doffed his cap.

"Are you going to the village?" I asked, keeping my horse abreast of him.

"Nay, Inverness is where I be heading. More gruesome business at Bridee Castle." He was a small, wiry man, bent with age, his hands gnarled with years of labor.

"More? Has there been trouble there before?"

"Aye. Old Charlie MacBride was found with his throat cut from ear to ear many a year ago."

Charles MacBride was my grandfather. Why hadn't Father told us about the murder of our grandfather? The news stunned me into silence.

"Always some mischief going on in that old castle." He nodded his head back toward the contents of his wagon. "If you be asking me, I would be saying the old castle is cursed, it is. It stands there like an edifice of evil. A mist-shrouded hell it is, miss. The MacBrides have been cursed since the days of Lady Anne."

"I am a MacBride. Miss Heather MacBride," I informed him, trying to appear proud even though a shiver was nibbling at my spine.

"Sorry, miss. I should have been knowing 'tis better to be quiet than sing a bad song."

"That's all right. I don't believe in superstition."

"These hills and mountains will soon be learning you to heed the warnings of legends. When you hear the skirl of phantom pipers roaming the moors, you'll believe as I do."

"You have heard them?" A small amount of amusement crept into my tone.

"Aye, especially when the mists are heavy. You'd best

stay off the moors when the mists come, miss. As surely as I'm talking to you, that is the time when all sorts of beasties and kelpies stalk the moors. When they become bored or irritated, they sometimes decide to play havoc in a person's home. If you see a mist coming acreeping under the window sills or under the doors, beware. It might be a beastie or a kelpie who will change from mist to human form to do you mischief."

I smiled. Though I gave some credence to the tale of Lady Anne, I couldn't believe in kelpies, beasties, or ghosts. "Did they ever learn who killed my grandfather Charles MacBride?"

"Nay. The constabulary put it down to thieves. There are those of us who think otherwise."

"Who do you think did it?"

"Black Donald."

"Who is Black Donald?" I asked him.

"Auld Clootie, the master of witches and warlocks."

"Do you mean the Devil?"

He put his index finger over his lips and furtively looked around. "Don't be saying that, miss. In these parts we call him Black Donald. Don't be tempting his wrath, lass."

His belief in the supernatural amused me. Black Donald, indeed! We rode in silence for a spell. I had the feeling the old man wanted me to go away lest he be tainted by my reference to the Devil. He reined his horse to a halt. I followed suit as we reached a fork in the road.

"The village lies that way, miss." He pointed to the right. I'll be leaving you now."

"Good-bye," I said congenially.

"Good day to you, miss." He doffed his cap, snapped the reins, and the wagon rolled along much faster than before.

With a shake of my head and a smile on my lips, I

urged my horse along the road to the village.

The village wasn't the cheeriest place I had ever seen. All the buildings were of gray stone. Even the cobbled street was gray. It was as though my vision had lost its ability to discern color. Everything was gray, even the slats on the roofs. Gray smoke from gray chimneys rose to a gray sky. A colorless world. What troubled me even more was the lack of people.

As I rode along the street, a greengrocer, a butcher shop, a chemist, and a bakery were sandwiched together on one side of the cobbled road. A sundry shop, a bootery, a draper's, and a pub huddled together on the other side. Passing all the shops, I came to a gray church that stood apart in quiet contemplation. To the left of the church was a cemetery which boasted some green grass. Color, at last, I thought, in of all places a cemetery. I hadn't seen a sign in any of the shops which claimed to be a station for posting and receiving mail.

I stopped before the church, slid off my horse, and tethered her to the iron fence around the church and cemetery. I pulled the church door open and entered. The interior was as dull and colorless as the exterior. Realizing no one was there, I left.

As I walked the stone path to the gate, a man came around from the back of the church. His attire clearly marked him as the minister. He was tall and thin with bright red hair which was slowly receding, elongating his brow. His blue eyes were merry and full of mischief.

"Can I help you, lass?" he asked.

"I hope so."

"I am Rev. Douglas Campbell," he said, offering me his hand.

I shook it. "My name is Heather MacBride."

"Well, well. I presume you are one of James Mac-Bride's daughters. Is your sister here too?"

"Yes. She is at Bridee Castle."

103

"I read about the trouble in India. It is good to have you in the Highlands. Will your father be following you here?"

"No. As soon as the situation in India has resolved itself, my sister and I will return there."

"A long time has passed since I have seen your father. It was long before he went to India. It would be nice if he came to the Highlands to escort you back. We had some good philosophical discussions." Reverend Campbell's eyes softened in remembrance.

"I don't think he will, Reverend."

"I officiated at your mother's funeral. Your father had her sent back to the Highlands in a very beautiful casket. The domed lid was intricately carved with gilt traceries. A true work of art. Those Indians are excellent craftsmen." He sighed. "I always thought it a shame to put that lovely casket in the ground. But here I am going on about the past when it is evident you are seeking help of some sort. What can I do for you, Miss MacBride?"

"I am looking for some place to post a letter," I explained.

"That is a simple problem. I will take care of it for you. The sundry shop has a small post office. Unfortunately it is closed today."

"Thank you." I handed him the letter. "Where is everyone? The town looked deserted when I came through."

"My dear child, today is Sunday. All the shops are closed. I imagine the people are staying inside due to the impending storm," Reverend Campbell said with a sympathetic smile.

"I am sorry, Reverend. I have lost all track of the days since coming to the Highlands."

"No need to be sorry, lass. Not many from Bridee Castle come to Sunday services. Once in a while Jane Ross comes."

"We will need your services soon. There has been an

unexpected death at the castle."

He frowned with concern. "Who?"

"Our ayah from India. We shall want a proper burial for her in the MacBride cemetery. Would that be a problem, Reverend?"

He shook his head then looked up at the darkening sky. "I think you had better ride back to the castle. I fear we are in for a heavy storm."

I looked at the sky. Dark clouds boiled into lighter ones and the smell of rain permeated the chilly air. The hills and the moors were tarnished black by the rapidly threatening sky.

"You won't forget my letter, will you, Reverend Campbell?"

"I won't."

"I will be back another time to make arrangements for funeral services."

He nodded and smiled as I untied my horse and mounted. His eyebrows shot up in astonishment when he saw me sit astride the animal, but he said nothing. He waved then went back the way he came.

I urged the horse to a gallop as the air thickened with moisture. I raced through the village wishing I was sitting in a villager's home with a good peat fire to warm me. Cutting winds began to pierce my merino cloak. Stray, fallen leaves swirled about in a mad dance. Solitary trees and the more abundant brush bent in reverence to spurting gusts of wind.

As the strong breeze sailed over the loch and soared up the hills and mountains, a sound akin to the mournful wailing of souls in hell lingered in the air. I was halfway back to the castle when the clouds opened. In slicing, solid sheets, the chilled rain teemed down. Lightning flashed in the distance. A second or two later, thunder shuddered through the air. My cloak was soon saturated, the dampness starting to penetrate to my skin.

My vision was curtailed by the thickness of the rain. I veered back and forth between the road and the surrounding moor. The time between the bolts of lightning and the thunder was getting shorter. Soon, they were simultaneous. A swift, jagged crack of lightning whipped down directly in front of me. My horse whinnied and reared with such force I that was thrown to the ground. The horse raced off as though demons had conspired to chase him.

I sat there, angry with the horse, the weather, and myself. I had been on rearing horses before and had never fallen off. Why was I so careless this time? I shook my head in disgust and scrambled to my feet. I would have to walk. At least I wasn't more than a mile from the castle.

At first I ran as if I could avoid the rain by running through it. When I realized I was already soaked through, I slowed to a comfortable walk, my feet making sucking noises as I sloshed along the muddy road.

I didn't see the rider until he was almost upon me. There was no mistaking Adrian's black stallion. He stopped and lowered his arm.

"Come on. Hop up here," he ordered.

My hands clamped over the thick sinews of his arms. I felt the power of the man as he effortlessly pulled me up behind him on his horse.

"Hold on," he said.

I wrapped my arms about his waist and laid my head against his back. I no longer felt the rain nor heard the thunder. My heart was making thunder of its own. Though there was water all around me, my throat was too dry for me to speak.

Once we stood dripping in the comparative comfort of the castle's foyer, I asked, "What made you come looking for me, Adrian?"

"Two reasons. One, your horse came back to the stable

without you. Secondly, your sister has taken ill. I didn't want you dawdling in the village."

"Diana ill?" I wasn't too concerned. Ever since she was little, she found feigning illness was a successful ploy to get what she wanted.

"Yes."

"Did she ask for me?"

"Not really. I thought you might want to be with her. I suggest you have a hot bath and get into some dry clothes first. It wouldn't do to have both of you down ill. Clarissa is beside herself as it is trying to nurse Diana."

"What is wrong with her?" I asked, involuntarily shivering.

"Right now you had better think about yourself." He undid the string of my cloak and flung it off my shoulders. "I will have Mrs. Burns get the hot water up to you. Go along, Heather. We will talk later."

I dashed up the stairs wondering what illness Diana had concocted. What did she want so desperately to fake an illness?

Chapter Six

Jean had brought lots of towels. I rubbed my damp skin with one of them until it glowed. She took my wet clothes away and returned in time to fetch the hot water that was coming up in the dumb waiter.

The hot water took the chill from my bones as I sat in the tub. Jean scrubbed my hair, then rinsed it with clear, tepid water.

As dinner was only a few hours away, I donned my peacock blue gown with white lace trim. Though the sleeves came down to my wrists, the gown was still slightly off the shoulders.

"Shall I do your hair, Miss Heather?" Jean asked after brushing it dry.

"Not tonight, Jean. Just tie it in back."

"Such beautiful red-gold hair, Miss Heather. It won't be long before it reaches your waist. It's almost there now."

"Unfortunately it has a tendency to get too curly. You seem to be the only one who can do anything with it."

"Thank you, miss."

"Mr. Adrian Ross told me my sister is ill. Do you have any idea what is wrong with her, Jean?"

"No, Miss Heather. I heard Mrs. Burns say something about an upset stomach, but I don't know if she was talking about Miss Diana or not."

"I will see if there is anything I can do for her."

I had only gone several feet down the corridor when a flustered Aunt Clarissa approached me.

"Oh, my dear Heather. Your poor sister is so sick. I don't know what to do for her."

"What is wrong with her?" I asked.

"Evidently she has eaten something that doesn't agree with her," Aunt Clarissa explained.

"Have you sent for the doctor?"

"She won't have one. She looks so pale and it fair worries me." She put her hand on my arm. "Heather, do try to talk some sense into her. Make her see a doctor. I would hate to think she got bad food in my house."

"I will see what I can do, Aunt Clarissa. I don't think it was the food. We all eat the same food and none of us has become ill. Has she been eating anything we haven't?" I asked.

"Only the box of chocolates John bought her in Inverness."

"There you are. She probably ate too many chocolates after a heavy meal."

"Perhaps you are right. Jane is with her now. I can't tend to her needs and run the house too. Oh, dear me. I can't seem to get all the work done," Aunt Clarissa whined.

"Is there anything I can do to help?"

"I can't think right now with this crisis in the house. I am sure I will think of something. None of this would have happened if you hadn't opened the door to the keep, Heather."

"Nonsense, Aunt Clarissa," I said sharply.

"It isn't nonsense. The ghost of Lady Anne is taking

109

her revenge on all of us. First that Indian woman. Now our dear Diana is ill." The back of Aunt Clarissa's hand went to her forehead and her eyelids fluttered. "I left Diana to get something. Now I don't remember what it was. Perhaps it will come to me once I am downstairs. Do see your sister, Heather."

I nodded as she glided away. I continued down the corridor to Diana's bedchamber. The door was ajar. I was about to knock and enter when my sister's voice stopped me.

"Really, Jane. You should try to do something with yourself. You look like a walking cadaver. Of course you never will be beautiful, but you could do something with your hair. It looks in need of a good wash. And your clothes are horrid—dowdy and out-of-date. If I looked like you, I would keep myself hidden."

"I will have you know I wash my hair frequently," Jane retorted indignantly.

"It doesn't look it. I guess I can't change the habits of a spinster. If you want to be slovenly, there is nothing I can do about it." Diana sighed. "Do go and fetch me some hot tea and scones with marmalade, Jane. You may as well be of some use around here."

I raised my hand as if to knock when Jane opened the door.

"Oh, Heather. You startled me." Anger was hidden deep in her hazel eyes.

"I am sorry, Jane. I thought I had better see how my sister is doing."

"I would say she is back to normal. Excuse me." She stepped past me and went down the corridor.

I slipped into my sister's room.

"It's about time you showed up, Heather. Don't you care what happens to me?"

"Of course I do, Diana. How are you feeling?" I sat

110

down on the edge of the bed.

"Much better. At least the horrible cramps and pains in my stomach have stopped. Where were you?"

"In the village."

"What in heaven's name were you doing there?"

"I went to post a letter to Father telling him of Samrú's death."

"Why did you bother? Father isn't interested in her anymore. He probably feels well rid of her."

"That's a horrible thing to say, Diana. She did help raise us."

"She didn't work very hard at it. She was more interested in pleasing Father. Do fluff my pillows, Heather."

I complied. Diana always did like being pampered.

"Where is Adrian?" Diana asked smoothing the coverlet over her.

"I imagine he is getting into some dry clothes. Why?"

"He hasn't been to see me. John was in here in a flash. Very worried, he was." She looked thoughtful for a moment. "Why would Adrian be getting into dry clothes? Did he leave the house?"

I told her of my misadventure and how Adrian came to my rescue. Her face darkened, her blue eyes flaring with rage. "Why did he go? Why didn't he send one of the lackeys from the stable?"

I shrugged.

"Don't you know anything, Heather?"

"I don't know Adrian well enough to read his mind."

"Hmph! I wonder where that Jane Ross is with my tea. She is such a drone. Good for nothing except to wait on people. Look how she caters to Aunt Clarissa's every whim," Diana declared.

"She only left a minute ago. Why didn't you use your bellpull? The maids are meant to fetch, not Jane."

"I was sick of looking at that homely face of hers.

111

Besides, the maids in this place aren't very swift. If we stay here much longer, *I* shall take over the running of this household."

"Aunt Clarissa does her best," I offered as a weak defense.

"Aunt Clarissa? Pooh! She doesn't know her hand from her foot. And I am tired of her referring to Bridee Castle as hers. I told her in no uncertain terms that Bridee Castle belongs to Father and we shall inherit it when he passes away."

"Why did you do that? She is flustered enough. A statement like that will only confuse her further."

"I wanted the old goat to know she is here because of Father's generosity and that she had better be good to us or we will kick her out."

"Really, Diana. Why do you want to make trouble? Aunt Clarissa doesn't harm anyone. The castle is large enough to hold several families."

"Will you go and see what is keeping Jane? I am parched and hungry."

"Gladly." Any excuse to leave her company was welcomed. "Will you be down for dinner?"

"If I am up to it."

As I came down the main staircase, a distraught maid was rushing up with what I presumed was Diana's tray. She nodded and bobbed a curtsy. I smiled. With a few hours to wait before dinner, I decided to pass the time playing the piano. Reaching the foyer, I turned and headed for the drawing room. Jane was sitting in a far corner softly crying. When she noticed my presence, she quickly whipped a handkerchief from her sleeve, dried the tears on her cheeks, and smiled weakly.

"What is wrong, Jane?" I asked as I went to take a seat beside her.

"Nothing. Nothing at all."

"I don't make a habit of listening to other people's conversations, but I did overhear what my sister said to you. The door was ajar. Try to forgive her, Jane. She was always the darling of the family. Father doted on her and, I am afraid, greatly spoiled her."

"I am sorry you heard, Heather."

"Don't shed any tears over her words. It isn't worth it. She has a habit of taking it out on others whenever she is upset."

"Her words hurt all the more because what she said is true. Your sister has a wicked tongue. I hate her. I have tried not to, but she makes it so easy."

All I could do was sigh in sympathy. I had no words to defend Diana. I knew from long experience how cruel her words could be.

"Why don't I play something gay on the piano? It might cheer you up," I offered.

Jane nodded and I went to the piano. I launched into a sprightly tune I had heard the regimental band play so often. Jane took a seat nearer the piano. After an hour the rest of the family drifted into the drawing room. My heart melted when Adrian strolled in, handsomer than ever. When Jeffrey announced dinner, we began to cross the foyer. All heads turned to watch Diana, looking radiant, make her grand entrance from the stairs.

Aunt Clarissa rushed over to Diana as her foot touched the floor of the foyer. "Are you sure you are up to it, my dear?"

"Of course. I wouldn't have come down if I weren't." Diana brushed by Aunt Clarissa and sidled up to Adrian. "You are a naughty boy, Adrian. You didn't come to see me once while I was so ill." She slid her hand through his arm.

"Too much company when one is ill might prolong

the illness," Adrian graciously replied.

"Clarissa," John called gruffly, extending his arm to his wife. He was like a boiling kettle whose lid was tightly held down. His eyes threw darts of anger at Diana and Adrian.

"May I escort you ladies in?" asked Bruce, offering Jane and me his arms respectively.

The icy chill of the oncoming winter began to caress the air. The moors and the fading gardens were as familiar to me now as our home and environs in India. I had managed to talk Jane into attending Sunday services regularly with me in the village. No one else ever expressed an interest.

As we rode home one Sunday, we met Inspector Andrews on the road.

"Good day, ladies." He tipped his tall hat.

"Good day, Inspector," I said. Jane nodded to him. "Are you on your way to Bridee Castle?"

"Indeed I am, Miss MacBride. I hope everyone is there."

"As far as we know. What news do you have of Samrú Singh?" I asked.

"I shall relate all the information when I have everyone present," he answered.

"When will we be able to have the funeral? Almost two weeks have passed," I declared.

"A wagon will bring the casket to the castle tomorrow. I suggest you keep it closed. Dr. Drummond had to do quite a bit of work on the body."

I nodded. "I intend to have her buried in our cemetery. Would that present a problem?"

"Certainly not."

I turned the trap into the driveway, Inspector Andrews on his horse abreast of us.

With everyone, except Adrian, gathered in the drawing room, a seated Inspector Andrews cleared his throat and began.

"First off, I must inform you that Miss Singh did not die of natural causes. According to Dr. Drummond's findings she died of multiple stab wounds to the abdomen. Miss MacBride, you said before that Miss Singh had no enemies here in the Highlands. Can you think of anyone who would want her dead?"

"No. No one here really knew her," I replied.

"Was she despondent?"

"She hated to leave India and didn't want to come to Scotland. She brooded about it a great deal," Diana said.

"Do you think she might have taken her own life?" the inspector asked.

"Nothing she did would surprise me," Diana said. "She had strange, mystic beliefs. She might have been despondent enough to take her own life to my way of thinking."

The inspector scratched his head. "I think I heard somewhere that Indian women take their lives when they lose someone dear to them."

"That was a long time ago, Inspector," I began. "It was called suttee. Wives would throw themselves on their husband's burning funeral pyre. Some not willingly. It was made illegal in 1829."

"Do you think Miss Singh might have taken her own life?"

"I don't see how someone could commit suicide by stabbing herself several times," I said.

"Frankly, Miss MacBride, I came to the same conclusion." The inspector braced his hands on his knees and pushed himself out of the chair. "Well, that is about it for now. As I said before, the casket will be at the church tomorrow. I appreciate everyone's cooperation. If anyone of you can think of something you haven't told me — no matter how trivial — that might shed some light on Miss Singh's demise, I would like to be informed as soon as possible. Thank you."

With hat in hand, Inspector Andrews was escorted out by Jeffrey who had been standing in the foyer.

"You really don't believe Samrú committed suicide, do you, Diana?" I asked.

Diana shrugged. "Who knows? And who cares? She was acting strange before she died."

"Oh, dear me. So much commotion lately. It is quite unbearable. I shall have to have a rest after lunch," Aunt Clarissa declared.

While everyone seemed inclined to have a rest after lunch, I went to the stable and had my horse saddled. I needed time alone to think. I rode to Loch Ness. After tethering my horse, I strolled to a grassy knoll where I sat, my arms pulled around my legs. I rested my chin on my cloak-covered knees and stared across the loch at the heather-covered hills. Shadows from the clouds raced over them creating an undulating sea of varying shades of green.

I wiped a tear from my eye as I thought of Samrú. I had never thought of suicide until Inspector Andrews mentioned it. Was her despair so great that leaving my father made her feel as though she had nothing to live for? Had the humiliation of my father's rejection pushed her beyond endurance? But what was she doing in the keep? There was no way I could convince myself that she could have stabbed herself several times. The whole thing put my head in a muddle. I decided to leave it in the hands of Inspector Andrews. The more I thought about it, the more it frustrated me.

I lowered my gaze to the loch where a foggy mist crawled over the water like a harbinger of evil. Though there was no breeze, I shivered.

"Looking for Nessie?" came the deep baritone voice.

I spun my head around to gaze up into the handsome face of Adrian Ross.

"Not really. I was thinking about Samrú." My gaze went back to the loch.

"Would I be intruding if I sat next to you?" he asked.

"No." I waited until he was seated on the grass. "Why weren't you at the house today when Inspector Andrews was there?"

"I didn't think my presence was required. I had no light to shed on the woman's death. What did the inspector have to say?"

I related all that was said in the drawing room, including the mention of suicide. "I don't think anyone would take her life by stabbing herself several times, do you?"

"I doubt if the ordinary person could manage such a feat. I hear the Japanese commit suicide by the knife, but they use only one blow. I should think after the first blow, one would be too stunned and in too much pain to continue. I don't want to frighten you, Heather, but I believe someone murdered your nanny."

I nodded. "Still, I have been whirling it around and around in my head and I can't think of a single soul who would have had a reason to kill her."

"Did Diana have any special grudge against the woman?"

"Don't even think such a thing, Adrian. Diana may be a bit difficult at times, but she would never use physical violence against anyone. It is preposterous to even mention it."

"Sorry. It was a passing thought. You and your sister

117

are the only ones who knew the woman well. Diana made it clear several times she didn't like the woman much." He placed his elbows on the ground and leaned back.

"I suppose you will be accusing me next." Anger was building in me. He had no right to point a finger at me or my sister. "If either Diana or I wanted Samrú dead, why did we wait until we came to Bridee Castle?"

"I said I was sorry, Heather," he replied calmly.

"In our own way, both Diana and I had affection for Samrú."

"From what I observed, Diana had a strange way of showing it."

"What do you mean?"

"She treated the woman like the lowliest of servants. I heard her heap abuse on Samrú on more than one occasion."

"That doesn't mean anything. Diana always thought of her as a servant. If she were abusive toward her at times, it might have been because she resented Samrú's association with our father. No matter how she treated Samrú, she never would have physically harmed her. Can we drop the topic? I am tired of talking and thinking about it." Even though my cloak was heavy, I could feel his hand rubbing gently over my back in a soothing manner.

"You haven't had a very good introduction to the Highlands, have you, Heather? I imagine the castle was a big disappointment to you. Besides a change in weather and landscape, you now have to deal with the death of your nanny. The burden must be heavy for one so young. A child shouldn't have to bear the ills an adult sometimes finds hard to bear."

Now I was angry. The feelings I had for Adrian were not those of a child. His thinking of me as a child

118

crushed my ego. I scrambled to my feet. Without a word I headed for my horse. I stopped when he grabbed my arm and spun me about.

"What the devil is the matter with you, Heather?" His ebony eyes flashed with impatience.

"I am not a child!"

"Right now you are acting like one. You are too quick to take offense."

"I don't like you thinking of me as a child. I will soon be twenty."

"How should I think of you, Heather?" His voice and eyes softened.

"As a woman. How would you like it if I thought of you as a little boy?"

Before I knew what was happening, his arms were about me, his head lowering. His mouth covered mine in a passionate kiss of exploration. The worldly kiss was so sensual and lusty, my hands went to the heavy sinews of his back. I could feel muscle move against muscle as he deepened the kiss. I was lost in a new world, a world of sheer physical pleasure. I never wanted to move from his embrace. When he finally held me at arm's length, I knew I had a silly look of wonder on my face, but could do nothing to alter it.

"Was that the kiss of a boy?" Adrian asked, his eyes slightly glazed.

"No. Did I respond as a child?"

He laughed, tossing his head back. "You are a brazen lass. No, it wasn't the response of a child. When I called you a child, I meant in the ways of the world. I assume you led a sheltered life in India. You never had to deal with the realities and horrors of life. You were locked into a closed British society where only polite Englishmen, women, and Europeans circulated. I don't imagine you ever mingled with the natives. Am I wrong?"

"No. We *were* sheltered from Indian life. We lived in compounds where the only Indians we saw were servants. Galas and socials were with people of our own stock."

"I take it you were never exposed to the sinister passions of man," Adrian said.

"That doesn't mean I am a child."

He released me, put his arm around my shoulders, and said, "When you are my age, nineteen seems like part of childhood. I didn't mean to offend you."

"You are not that old, Adrian. Why, I don't think of my father as being old."

He looked up at the sky. "I think we should go back. The fog in the hollows is starting to creep up the hills which means the weather is about to turn for the worse, I fear."

We quickly mounted our horses and returned to the forbidding castle.

The gloom of the small funeral, which was held in Bridee Castle's private plot, reflected the day. The gray sky was mottled with inky clouds which scudded before an ever-increasing wind. Leaves left the trees in scattered groups then danced in the air before succumbing to the beckoning earth. A fine mist was the precursor of heavier rains to come.

I stood between Adrian and Bruce while Jane stood on the other side of Adrian. John and Aunt Clarissa didn't attend. Diana claimed another unsettled stomach.

Reverend Campbell gave a brief eulogy. Even though I knew Samrú was a Hindu, I thought a Christian service was better than no service at all. Diana told me she thought a funeral with a service was foolish and a waste of time.

Reverend Campbell handed me a small silver scoop. I duly shoved it in the loose dirt beside the hole and tossed it onto the lowered coffin. Adrian, Bruce, and Jane followed suit more out of deference to me than any sense of duty.

When we returned to the house, I went directly upstairs to wash and change into a plain bodice and skirt. I unpinned my hair and brushed it. Rather than fuss with it, I tied it back with a ribbon at the nape of my neck. By the time I had finished, lunch was ready.

I descended the stairs, entered the dining room, and was surprised to find many empty chairs.

"Where is everyone?" I asked as I took my seat.

"John needed some supplies in Inverness. Diana decided to go with him. She thought the trip might take her mind off her digestive problems. Poor child," Aunt Clarissa mused. "I am afraid she misses the excitement of military life in India. It must be gloomy and lonely for her here. Perhaps you and she should take a trip to Edinburgh, Heather. Have a little holiday for yourselves before the weather makes traveling difficult."

"You are thoughtful, Aunt Clarissa. I am expecting a message or letter from Father. I don't want to be away when it comes. Jane, perhaps you could take Diana down to Edinburgh," I suggested, knowing that Jane would decline.

"I wouldn't be much of a companion for Diana. She doesn't care for my company," Jane said.

I didn't pursue it. "Where are Adrian and Bruce?" I inquired.

"Adrian left the minute we returned from the cemetery. Bruce went to the village pub. He considers himself an expert at darts," Jane informed me.

"I suspect he enjoys waging on them more than the

playing," Aunt Clarissa added. "That boy has no sense when it comes to money."

"Perhaps if he took a position and earned his own money, he might come to appreciate thrift," I suggested.

"I don't think the boy knows the meaning of the word *work*." Aunt Clarissa sighed.

"Heather has a good idea there, Clarissa," Jane said.

"Oh, dear me. I really don't want to think about it today. There are too many other things to worry about. Does this hotch-potch taste too salty to either of you?"

"No," I answered while Jane shook her head.

"Well, the barley is definitely undercooked while the peas have been overcooked. I hate mushy peas. I will have to talk to Cook," Aunt Clarissa said.

The promised rain pelted down sounding like tiny pebbles being rhythmically tossed against the window panes. Aunt Clarissa went for her usual after lunch nap while Jane retired to her room to read. I thought of playing the piano but dismissed it in favor of going to the ancient hall and rummaging through some of the boxes and crates there.

I wore my heavy merino cloak and brought the oil lamp. I knew the lack of heat in that part of the castle would render it icy and damp. With the pervasive rain, the ancient hall would be dim, dank, and musty.

When I reached the open courtyard, I tossed my hood over my head and made a dash for the large door. It was heavier than I thought. I had to put the light down and use both hands to swing the door open. I picked up the lamp and went in.

After lighting the wick, I went to the storage area and set the lamp down on one of the boxes while I struggled to open the trunk next to it. The hasps had rusted, making it near to impossible to open. I looked around for a tool, and quickly spied an old iron poker in the oversized fireplace. I retrieved it, then used it as a lever to pry open the hasps. I pushed the lid up only to find the trunk filled with old clothes, most of which had begun to rot.

Disappointment washed over me. I had hoped Bruce was wrong about the contents. Ever the romantic, I had expected treasures of great worth. I slammed the top down and decided to ignore the trunks and try one of the crates.

I select a large oblong crate, once again using the poker as a lever to pull away the pieces of wood. The object was loosely wrapped in canvas. Dust swirled in the air causing me to cough and sneeze as I tore away the old canvas. Revealed was a painting in an ornate gilt frame. I stood it against a trunk, got the lamp, and brought it close to the painting.

Though I knew the painting was a portrait of my grandfather, he was unrecognizable. He didn't look like the man Father had described so many times. Evil glinted in his eyes. There was a hard, cruel set to his mouth. He was not the benign old man my father had described to us.

I couldn't take my eyes off the portrait. His eyes were so real and seemed to be trying to tell me something. Or were they warning me?

With that demonic expression on his face, I could understand why someone might cut his throat. Aside from a description and a few remarks, Father seldom talked about Charles MacBride. I would make it a point to question Father about him when we returned to India.

In the meantime, I wondered if Reverend Campbell knew anything about Grandfather. Knowing he had disinherited Aunt Clarissa, I didn't think she would be the one to question. Not only might she be biased, but it might upset her fragile sensibilities.

Reluctantly, I forced my eyes from the portrait and continued my explorations of the boxes, trunks, and crates with the unquenchable hope that there was treasure to be found.

I suppose some of the items I uncovered could be called minor treasures. Tarnished silver candleholders, salvers, tea sets, porcelain figurines, delicate dishes, and various *objets d'art*. Some of the crates had their contents marked on the outside. I didn't bother with them as they were, for the most part, odd pieces of furniture. I went back to the trunks.

Bruce was right. The trunks held nothing but clothes. I pulled a few of the gowns out to find they were very old. Diaphanous white material, now turned gray, of a lady's gown had the high waist and small puffed sleeves indicative of feminine fashion during the Napoleonic era.

To my surprise, a couple of the trunks held clothes of the sixteenth century. Tight bodices narrowed down to a vee in the front before erupting into a profusion of skirt material. Long sleeves ended in elongated lace cuffs, a style Queen Elizabeth adopted to hide the fact she was missing a finger. Perhaps a museum would be interested in owning them, I thought.

Throughout my explorations, I felt my grandfather's eyes following me about. My gaze went to the portrait again. What power in those eyes! Was it the amber glow of the oil lamp that made his eyes glint with a bizarre, satanic flame? The fine hairs at the nape of my neck bristled. I took the canvas and rewrapped the portrait.

With my curiosity sated, I prepared to return to the inhabited part of the castle. I blew out the lamp and began to walk toward the massive door, the fading twilight barely guiding my way.

Suddenly a chilling gust of wind blew into the already

cold room. I turned toward the direction of the icy gust. I dropped the oil lamp as my blood careened through my veins like a river gone mad. My mouth fell agape and I began trembling uncontrollably. The door to the keep had been flung open. Gliding toward me was a luminescent figure without a head. As it swept across the floor, a pitiable wail issued from it. My head spun with fear as the specter's arm flowed upward to reveal a glittering knife in its hand.

As the glowing figure came closer, my legs weakened, a dizziness consuming me. I crumpled to the stone floor in oblivion.

Chapter Seven

When the coldness of the dank stone floor penetrated through my cloak to my flesh, I knew I was alive. I opened my eyes warily lest the glowing apparition was hovering over me. A black void yawned around me. I could see nothing. I assumed the door to the keep was closed as the icy breeze had stopped. I put my hands on the floor to push myself up. A small scream of pain issued from my throat. I had pressed my hands into the broken glass of the oil lamp. In the dark I couldn't tell if the unctuous fluid on the palms of my hands was lamp oil or blood.

I cautiously got to my feet. The blackness disoriented me. I knew I was near the door, but I did not know which way I had fallen. Was I facing the door or the vast room?

Remembering I had turned to view the specter, I took the chance I was facing the room. I pivoted ninety degrees, put my hands out before me, and slowly started to walk.

My guess was correct. My hands touched the stone wall. Groping along the wall, the tips of my fingers touched wood. The door! Lowering my hands, I found the latch, lifted it, then, putting my shoulder to it, I forced the heavy door open and stepped out into the courtyard.

Damp air filled my lungs as a heavy rain pelted down. I was beyond caring if I got wet. I raced across the open yard, anxious to be in the secure comfort of my bedchamber.

I wended my way through the darkened rooms of the closed part of the castle. The dim, deserted rooms took on a different aspect after my experience in the ancient hall. They appeared eerie and menacing. I walked as quickly as the obscure light would permit. When I reached the weaponry room, the standing suits of armor looked threatening. I remembered Bruce's prank and breathed easier as I considered he might have been playing the specter. But how did he make himself glow like that? No matter how hard I tried to rationalize the spooky event, I couldn't shake the belief it might have truly been a ghost.

A weak smile tried to form on my lips as I reached the well-lighted foyer. The smile never materialized.

Luck stayed with me. I reached my bedchamber without being seen. I closed the door behind me, leaned on it, and let out a long low sigh. I remained there for a few seconds before pushing myself away. I went to the dressing table and peered into the mirror. The sight appalled me.

A mass of cobwebs and dust coated my hair, face, and clothes. I looked like a mussalachi from a city's bustee in India. In short, a scullion girl from the slums. I raised my hand to brush a cobweb from my forehead. The gesture left a red smear on my forehead. I quickly turned my hands over and stared at the bloody gashes. My nerves were taut and a loud gasp behind me caused me to jump and turn around.

"Oh, Jean. You frightened me," I said in relief, my splayed hand coming to rest on my breast.

127

"What happened, Miss Heather?" She had the look of a startled sparrow about to take flight. Her eyes darted over me and my wet, oil-stained cloak.

"I had a mishap."

"Your hands are bleeding."

"I fell down and broke an oil lamp. When I got up, my hands got cut on the lamp glass. Do you think a bath is possible, Jean? Or is it too late?" I glanced at the ormolu clock on the mantel relieved to learn I had two hours before dinner.

"Yes, miss. I will go down to the kitchen and start the water up. While I am there I will see if Mrs. Burns has anything for your cuts along with some bandages."

"Thank you, Jean."

I divested myself of my clothes despite the growing pain in my hands. After the bath I slipped into my robe. Jean, with great gentleness, put the salve on my hands then bandaged them. The salve began to draw out some of the pain. With Jean's much needed assistance, I got dressed.

Downstairs, I went into the drawing room fully expecting to see everyone waiting, but the room was empty. I sat down for a few minutes, then went into the dining room. Only one place was set for dinner. Jeffrey was standing by the sideboard. He swiftly moved to hold my chair.

"Where is everyone, Jeffrey?" I sat down.

"Mr. Ross and Miss MacBride have not returned from Inverness. Mr. Adrian and Mr. Bruce are still out. I expect the storm will keep them from returning soon, Miss MacBride," he answered.

"And Mrs. Ross and Miss Ross?"

"Miss Ross has a headache and Mrs. Ross is not feeling well. They preferred to have trays in their respective rooms."

"I see."

My meal was served with the same impeccable correctness as if it were a dinner party for thirty people. I wished there had been thirty people at the table. I felt terribly alone. I ate without tasting the food. Finished, I wandered into the drawing room, sat at the piano, and softly played. I soon gave it up as my hands pricked with pain. Besides, my mind wasn't on music. My grandfather's portrait hovered before my eyes, alternating with the glowing apparition. I knew the portrait wasn't my imagination. But was the specter? Did my mind want an explanation for Samrú's death and conjured up a malignant ghost to account for that death? I sighed and wished Adrian or Bruce was here. I wanted to talk with someone. Too much introspection would have me thinking in circles.

I was about to resign myself to eating breakfast alone the next day, when Adrian came striding in.

"Good morning, Heather," he said, going directly to the sideboard. "That was a terrible storm we had last night."

"Yes, it was."

He turned and was about to take his place at the table when he noticed my freshly bandaged hands. "Good Lord! What happened to you?"

I explained my little adventure, but purposely omitted seeing a glowing specter. Such an improbable tale would only make me seem more of a child in his eyes. The story satisfied him and he sat down to eat.

"Did you find any great treasures in that ancient hall?" he asked after a few minutes.

"Some nice pieces of silver and china. Otherwise most of the items belong in a museum. Do you know if my sister returned from Inverness last night?"

"I just got here myself."

"Oh. Where were you?"

"That is really none of your business. But seeing you already know about my house, I will answer you. I spent the day and the night there."

"I don't blame you. This castle is gloomy, especially when there is a storm. You said you stay here out of hospitality. I would understand it if you would prefer to return to your house and normal mode of living."

He leaned back in his chair, his fingers still curled about the handle of his teacup. He wore a heavy black sweater, black breeches, and black boots. He could have passed for the Devil incarnate with his black eyes and hair. To me, he was elegant, majestic, and manly. I forgot about ghosts and specters.

"You are a sweet child, Heather," he said.

"I am not a child. When will you realize and acknowledge that fact?" I sputtered a little too loudly.

"I will try," he said with a bemused smile. "Clarissa requested that Bruce and I should help entertain you and Diana during your visit here. She wants the two of you to return to India with a good impression of Bridee Castle and its inhabitants. She wants her brother—your father—to know his daughters were well treated and entertained."

"Then you see us as a duty you must perform." I smiled but there was no mirth in my heart. I wanted Adrian to think of me as someone special. That he didn't cast a pall on my soul.

"For the time being. Did you have anything planned for today, Heather?"

"No."

"Would you like to ride over the moors with me? I can have Cook pack a picnic lunch. We can ride over Culloden Moor to where Moray Firth flows into the North Sea."

"You don't have to entertain me, Adrian. You can

130

assure Aunt Clarissa that I will give a glowing account of my stay here. I don't like being patronized. You can save that talent for Diana."

He laughed and shook his head. "My dear Heather, haven't you realized by now I don't do anything I don't want to do. There is a new bull I want to look at over at Farmer Brodie's place. Lord MacFarlane has a ram I want to see. I am going with or without you. Knowing you like to ride, I thought it would be nicer to have company than ride alone. I am not devising the trip to amuse you."

"In that case, I would be pleased to accompany you. I have to change my clothes."

"Take your time. We will have to wait for Cook to pack a lunch. I will tell Mrs. Burns right now."

We left the dining room together. In the foyer we went our separate ways.

On the staircase landing, I met Jane. "How is your headache?" I asked her.

"It seems to have played itself out," she answered. She looked down at my bandaged hands. "I heard about your accident. Are the cuts very painful, Heather?"

"Not very now. The salve Jean put on them has helped greatly. How is Aunt Clarissa?"

"She has developed a slight cold. Aside from a little sneezing and coughing, she is fine. I just left her."

"Do you think I should stop in and see her?"

"I wouldn't bother her if I were you. She practically tossed me out of her bedchamber. She is having her breakfast and doesn't like to be disturbed."

"Have you seen my sister?"

"No. I haven't seen my father either. I suspect that the vicious storm last night prevented them from leaving Inverness. The roads can be treacherous during a torrential rain storm. Bruce probably stayed in the village rather than ride his horse in a storm like that. Have

131

you had your breakfast yet, Heather?"

"I just finished. I am on my way to change clothes and go riding with Adrian."

"Have a good ride," Jane said before descending the stairs.

The day with Adrian was soothing, and for a time I forgot about the haunting apparition. Our time together, though, passed all too quickly, and dusk was about to make its appearance when we returned. Our noisy chatter in the foyer brought Bruce out of the drawing room.

"Adrian. Come have a drink with me. I'm celebrating. You come in too, Heather," Bruce said, looking as thought he had a head start on the celebrating.

"What are we celebrating?" Adrian asked, obviously in a good mood as he ushered me into the drawing room.

"I won at darts," Bruce crowed. "A sizable sum, I may add. What would you like, Heather? Sherry?"

"A small glass would be fine," I replied.

When we were seated, drinks in hand, Bruce raised his glass in salute. "To me. For having defeated David Stewart in a deadly game of darts." He tossed his entire drink down his throat.

"Bravo!" Adrian cried, then took a sip of his whisky.

"I don't think Heather appreciates the enormity of the feat," Bruce said turning to me. "I have been trying to beat this Stewart fellow in darts for two years. And the real coup de grace was the large wager I had on the game. I feel like a bloody king." Bruce rose and helped himself to another drink.

"Aren't you going a little heavy, Bruce?" Adrian asked, one dark eyebrow raised.

"Don't be so bloody self-righteous, Adrian." Bruce's

words were starting to slur.

"Watch your language, Bruce. There is a lady present," Adrian admonished.

"Indeed there is," John Ross said from the doorway, a radiant Diana by his side.

Adrian glanced at Diana before glaring at his father. Was it jealousy or anger in his eyes? I couldn't tell, but I did know turmoil stirred within him.

"Ah, the fair Diana," Bruce exclaimed, raising his glass to her. "I trust Father kept you amused during your night's stopover in Inverness."

"What are you insinuating, young man?" John boomed.

Bruce's smiled was wicked. "Really, Father. We are all adults here. You and the she-devil have been gone for the better part of two days. I'm not naive."

"Do make him stop, John," Diana whined.

" 'Do make him stop,' " Bruce mimicked in a falsetto voice. "You are building quite a reputation for yourself in the Highlands, Diana. In the village they are beginning to call you the Hussy from India. Parading yourself around like a peacock looking for a mate. Why—"

"That is enough, Bruce," John declared, his voice reverberating through the room, red blood vessels mottling his face. "Don't pay any attention to him, Diana. He is obviously drunk."

"I wouldn't dream of paying him the courtesy of any attention. Spoiled brats do not deserve attention. You should pull his breeches down, John, and give him a thorough spanking," Diana said.

Raw hatred spewed from Bruce's eyes as he stared at Diana. His hands began to twitch as though he would like to put them around her throat and squeeze.

"I think you are the one who needs a spanking, Diana. I should say it is long overdue," Bruce said, a snide, taunting smile curving his lips.

"I am getting quite irritated with you, Bruce. If you don't change your attitude and improve your manners, I shall have you thrown out of here. I urge you to remember this is *my* house, not Aunt Clarissa's," Diana exclaimed, her hands on her hips. With her skirts swishing, she stalked out of the room.

John Ross walked to the sideboard where he poured himself a drink and swallowed the contents in one toss. "Bruce, I think you had better take yourself to the pub immediately. Do not make an appearance at dinner tonight. Give Diana a chance to forget this incident. In the future, I would think it best if you avoided her."

Bruce glared at his father, slammed his glass down on the table, then marched out of the room without a word.

"Crass young devil," John muttered as he strode toward the foyer.

"That was quite a little scene. I suspect it took the edge off Bruce's accomplishment at darts," Adrian said with a wry smile.

"I don't think Bruce cares very much for my sister."

"I believe you are underestimating the depth of his feeling. Bruce has a temperament that swings from high to low. He never settles in the moderate middle. Your sister shouldn't taunt him. He can be abnormally vindictive if the mood strikes him."

"Are you the same way, Adrian?" I asked.

"More so. I never forget an injustice done to me or an attack on my character. It may take a while, but I always exact my revenge in the end." Adrian's mouth was a grim line. The stern, set expression on his face revealed a determined man.

"I had better keep on your good side then," I said with a flickering smile.

"It might be advisable." A smile slashed across his face and a twinkle danced in his dark eyes.

134

"Is my sister in your good graces?"

His countenance hardened. "Let us say she has not incurred my wrath so far."

I finished my sherry. "I want to thank you for the lovely and interesting day, Adrian. I have never seen such stocky and huge bulls. One can see the ribs and hip bones of the cattle in India. The sheep were so fat! I really enjoyed looking at all the animals. Are the people around here always so hospitable?"

"Quite. Cottages and demesnes are so far apart and isolated, people relish visitors and new faces. Gives them a chance to chat and hear the news of surrounding estates. I am glad you enjoyed the outing. Traveling to distant holdings can be tedious without a companion. Bruce and Father have no interest in animal husbandry," Adrian said.

"The picnic was wonderful, too. Again, I thank you." I stood and so did Adrian.

"We must do it again before the winter's blasts set in."

I nodded and went upstairs to change for dinner. When I reached the landing, I decided to see how Aunt Clarissa was faring. I padded down the corridor, tapped lightly on her door, and was told to enter.

I found my aunt propped up in bed by a plethora of lacy pillows. There was color in her cheeks and she looked cheerful.

"How are you feeling, Aunt Clarissa?" I asked, going to the side of her bed.

"Much better, my dear Heather, much better. I heard you went on a picnic with Adrian. Did he show you a good time?"

"Yes. The moors can be beautiful. We had a glimpse of the North Sea."

"I don't see how you can possibly think the moors are beautiful. They are bleak and treacherous. Hidden bogs everywhere."

135

"Regardless, we had a nice time."

"Have John and Diana returned from Inverness?" Aunt Clarissa asked.

"Yes, about a half-hour ago."

"Poor dears. I am glad they decided to stay in the city instead of attempting to return during that horrid storm. They might have been killed by lightning. Do hand me that other magazine, Heather. Well, my goodness! What happened to your hands, child?" she said shocked, as I gave her periodical.

"I cut them on some broken glass."

"Did you call the doctor and have him look at them?"

"No, Jean took care of them quite nicely. They are much better, I assure you. Is there anything I can do for you, Aunt Clarissa?"

"No, Jane will see to my needs."

We talked for a while before I dismissed myself to get ready for dinner.

On the arm of her husband, Aunt Clarissa unsteadily walked into the drawing room where, with the exception of Bruce, all were present. After the usual small talk, dinner was announced.

I hadn't forgotten the sinister portrait of Charles MacBride. The next day I set out for the village, intending to have a talk with Reverend Campbell about my grandfather. He was not in the kirk. I rode the short distance to his manse, tethered my horse, then went up to the door. I was about to knock when the reverend himself opened the door.

"Miss MacBride. What a pleasant surprise." He opened the door wide and, with a sweeping gesture, bade me enter. With an outstretched hand, he indicated I should go into his small sitting parlor. "Would you care for some tea, Miss MacBride? Mrs. Lamont, my housekeeper, makes excellent scones."

"If it isn't too much trouble."

"No trouble at all. I shall be right back." He scurried out of the room.

I looked around. The small parlor was cluttered in a neat way. The heavy, overstuffed sofa and chairs were old and slightly threadbare. On the mantel stood several daguerreotypes: the reverend when he was young, a woman, and a small child. I assumed it was the reverend's family, but there wasn't a family in evidence at the manse.

I was still gazing at the photographs when Reverend Campbell came back into the parlor carrying a tea tray laden with tea items, a plate of scones, and a jar of marmalade.

"Have a seat, Miss MacBride." He nodded to one of the padded chairs by the fireplace where a slow peat fire glowed. Placing the tray on the table between the chairs, he then poured the tea, and took a chair opposite me. "Now, to what do I owe the pleasure of your visit?"

"Did you know my grandfather, Reverend Campbell?"

"Charles MacBride? Only slightly. He was a solitary man. I heard more about him than I actually knew. You do know he was murdered."

"Yes. Who were his enemies?"

"I fear just about everyone around these parts."

"Was he hated that much?" I was astonished.

"He wasn't a popular figure," the reverend said, shaking his head.

"Do you know why?"

"Well, it was said he used a heavy hand with the tenants, sometimes unjustly. There was a young tenant farmer with an ailing wife. He had four very young children and was two days late paying the rent. You see, he had to nurse his sick wife and couldn't leave his cottage. His children were much too young to be sent such a distance on foot with money in their pocket. Your grandfather evicted them. When the young farmer pleaded his case and offered to pay the full rent immediately, Charles MacBride turned a deaf ear. When the farmer became angry and demanded he be paid for all the improvements he made on the land—which was his due—Charles MacBride trounced the fellow soundly with his walking stick."

"How awful! I never knew my grandfather. I was under the impression he was a benign old gentleman. This comes as a great shock to me," I said agitatedly. "Can you tell me more, Reverend?"

"I understand he was especially cruel to his servants— physically cruel. A young maid broke a not very valuable vase. Old MacBride was furious. He severely beat the lass, in the course of which he broke her back, rendering her paralyzed from the waist down. The lass's father was livid and repeatedly threatened to kill Mac-Bride," the reverend informed me.

"Do you think he did?"

"At the time, the constabulary thought he did. But there was no proof. Many of the man's friends swore he was with them during the time of the murder. Everyone thought they were covering for the man. No one said anything and the case was listed as unsolved."

"Is the young woman still alive?"

"Sorry to say, no. She died about a year after the incident," the reverend answered.

I shook my head slowly. Absorption of this unexpected news was difficult. I wondered if Diana knew about our grandfather.

"How did he treat my father and Aunt Clarissa?"

"I never knew too much about Charles MacBride's relationship with his children. For fear of his wrath, the servants never talked about events in the castle. I did hear he was a very strict parent. Of course everyone knew he hated the English. When his daughter announced her plans to marry an Englishman, he disavowed her. Other than what I have told you, that is about all I know about Charles MacBride. He was not a churchgoer. The only time I spoke to him at any length was when I officiated at his wife's funeral."

"What was she like? I mean my grandmother."

"She died shortly after the birth of Clarissa MacBride. I never knew her. She seldom, if ever, left the castle. I think she died about four years after their marriage. Pretty young woman. Blond and petite. Almost fragile. I heard she was shy and retiring. My guess would be that she was intimidated by her domineering husband. He was a forceful man. May the good Lord help anyone who went against him."

His characterization of our grandfather reminded me of Diana, although I didn't think Diana would ever abuse anyone physically.

"I hope I have been of some help to you, Miss MacBride," said Reverend Campbell after finishing a scone laden with marmalade.

"You have been most helpful, Reverend. And do call me Heather."

"Heather. What a pretty name."

"Thank you."

"I believe your sister's name is Diana?"

"Yes." I finished my scone and tea then nodded toward the daguerreotypes on the mantel. "Is that your family, Reverend Campbell?"

"Yes." There was a note of pride in his voice. "My wife died a few years ago. My son is a solicitor in Nova Scotia, Canada. We correspond fairly frequently. I have two grandchildren and a lovely daughter-in-law."

"You sound quite proud of them."

"I am."

139

"Thank you so much for the information and the delicious tea, Reverend. I must get back to the castle now," I said, rising from the chair.

"It was a delight to have you, Heather. I do hope you won't be a stranger. You are welcome here anytime," the reverend said as he escorted me to the door.

Having so much to think about, I paced the horse slowly back to Bridee Castle. I tried to recall if my father ever exhibited any of the cruel traits of his father. The only thing that came to mind was his treatment of Samrú shortly before we left India. Other than that, he was a man of moderate temper—at least in our presence. How he behaved toward his regiments or in battle, I had no idea.

I left the horse in the hands of the stablemaster and went into the castle. I was anxious to talk to Diana. I searched for my sister and when I couldn't find her, I went into Jane's sitting parlor.

She put her petit point aside when I asked, "Have you seen Diana?"

"I believe Adrian took her in the carriage to see Loch Ness," Jane replied with a wan smile.

"Oh." Disappointment registered in my voice. I wasn't sure if it were the thwarting of my urgent desire to speak to Diana or if it were the frustration I felt learning she was with Adrian.

Jane lifted the small watch pinned to her bodice. "I see it is almost lunchtime. I seem to lose track of time when I am working on my embroidery. What do you think of it, Heather?" She held up the work for my inspection.

"Lovely. You have a way with the needle, Jane."

"It keeps me busy when Clarissa doesn't need me."

"You should let Aunt Clarissa take care of herself and live your own life, Jane."

She smiled indulgently. "You are young, Heather.

140

You have so much to look forward to in life. You still have the exuberance and zeal of youth. As for me, I am satisfied with the life I lead."

I wasn't about to argue with Jane. "Did Diana say when she would be back?" I asked, changing the subject.

"Probably this afternoon. They took a picnic lunch."

"I see." The words were hard to speak as my emotions were in turmoil. I thought his taking me on a picnic was a special adventure meant only for me. Realizing I had not been singled out tore my heart asunder. I had to leave Jane's parlor before I burst into tears. "I think I will examine the topiary more closely."

"I will see you at lunch," Jane said with a nod of her head.

I left the parlor and the castle.

To my surprise, the tears didn't flow once I was outside. My thoughts dwelled on the sensible. Either Adrian had a strong sense of fair play or Diana had found out about my picnic with him and cajoled him into taking her on one.

I turned my attention to the well-trimmed topiary. I had to admit the gardener was a special sort of artist. The animals and figures he created were life sized and cleverly depicted. Suddenly I saw a flash of red vanish behind the spread tail of a large topiary peacock.

Lifting my skirts, I ran to the spot to find out if I had seen a leaf or a piece of material. When I reached the peacock and peered around the extended tail, I was startled to learn my objective was human. A figure was running to the cover of the woods beyond the topiary.

A flaming red skirt and bright yellow blouse disappeared into the trees, the jangle of bracelets and earrings echoing on the breeze. I smiled. I had heard about gypsies, but had never actually seen one. I thought of pursuing her, but decided against it. Obviously I had terrified her. Gypsies near Bridee Castle! The thought amused and aroused my interest. I went back into the castle with the notion that I would search them out in a day or so.

The tension at the dinner table that night was palpable. Fury glinted in John's eyes while hatred reigned in Bruce's. Jane appeared to have endured another one of Diana's vociferous harangues. Adrian was grim, black thoughts seemed to be haunting his dark eyes. Diana was her usual smug and haughty self. Aunt Clarissa kept sighing as though the world had issued her too much with which to cope.

"I saw a gypsy in the topiary today," I said hoping to dispel the gloomy atmosphere.

"Oh, dear me," Aunt Clarissa gasped. "Don't tell me we are going to be plagued with those creatures again. They will rob us blind. John, you must do something."

"Yes, Clarissa."

"I don't want them on my property," Aunt Clarissa added.

"When will you stop talking about this demesne as *your* property, Aunt Clarissa? You live here by the grace of my father," Diana declared.

"I am sorry, my dear. I have so much on my mind, I tend to get carried away. I try so hard to do a good job of my brother's estate, I have a tendency to think of it as my own." Remorse lingered on Aunt Clarissa's face.

"Did you talk to the gypsy, Heather?" Jane asked.

"She ran away before I could say anything."

"Devilish creatures," John muttered. "We had trouble with them some years ago."

"What kind of trouble?" I asked.

"Stealing sheep and cattle. But they never came close to the castle before. I wonder why she strayed so near?" John mused aloud.

"Perhaps she needed help," I offered.

142

"They neither need nor seek help from outsiders," Adrian said.

"Where do they live?" I asked of Adrian.

"Out and around Culloden Moor. Usually they head south long before this. I am curious as to why they are still here."

"Who cares about some silly old gypsies. If they steal anything, have them arrested," Diana said. "I would much rather talk about Loch Ness and the lovely day we had sitting beside it."

Before anyone could comment further, Jeffrey appeared in the doorway and, addressing himself to John Ross, said, "There is a strange gentleman at the door who insists on entering, sir."

"Who is the fellow?" John asked gruffly.

"I have never seen him before. He is most untidy and has the look of a mendicant, sir."

"I will not have our dinner disrupted by a beggar, Jeffrey. You should know better. Tell him to go to the servant's entrance."

"Yes, sir."

As Jeffrey turned to obey John's order, the stranger crashed into the dining room. Diana gasped. My mouth fell open and my hand went to my bosom.

Chapter Eight

A bedraggled Patrick Danton stood with one hand braced on the door frame. He was breathing hard. Once he caught his breath, he said, "Sorry for the intrusion and my appearance. I have been on the road for sometime and riding hard. Urgency compelled my arrival."

"What are you doing here, Patrick?" Diana asked. For some reason, she seemed indignant at his presence.

"You know this man?" John asked, his face expressing total astonishment.

"He is in my father's regiment," I explained.

"You still haven't explained your presence here, Patrick," Diana said, her bow mouth pursed in irritation.

"Why don't we let the poor man refresh himself before deluging him with questions," Aunt Clarissa said with compassion.

"Good idea, Clarissa," John concurred. "Jeffrey, show this gentleman to a guest room and see he gets what he needs."

"Yes, sir."

"Have you eaten, Mr. Danton?" Aunt Clarissa asked.

"Not since breakfast."

"Jeffrey, have Mrs. Burns send a tray up to the gentleman's room." Aunt Clarissa turned her attention back to Patrick. "When you have eaten and refreshed yourself, we shall be in the drawing room awaiting your presence, Mr. Danton."

"Thank you. You are most kind, madam." Patrick left on the heels of Jeffrey.

"I wonder what he is doing here." Diana's porcelain brow creased in a frown. She made no attempt to hide her displeasure.

"I hope Father is all right," I said anxiously.

"If something was wrong with Father we would have heard," Diana said. "I hope he doesn't plan to stay here."

"I thought Patrick was your dearest beau, Diana." My comment clearly annoyed her and caused the men at the table to glance her way. In some small measure, I felt a sense of triumph. She lured Patrick away from me and now I wanted her to be stuck with him.

"Patrick was never my beau," she said airily. "He hung around me like a parasite. He is such a bore. You know very well, Heather, I couldn't get rid of him. And don't try to deny it." She cast me one of her "I dare you" looks.

Tension resumed its hold in the dining room. With dessert over, we filed into the drawing room. Aunt Clarissa was agitated for no apparent reason as we took our seats. Sherry was served to the ladies while the men had port, whisky, or brandy. After a couple of sips of sherry, Aunt Clarissa calmed down to her usual fluttering self.

"Exactly who is Patrick Danton?" Adrian asked.

I explained.

"I hope he goes right back to India," Diana said.

"Perhaps the troubles in India are over and Patrick has come to escort us back," I suggested with a mixture

145

of happiness and despair. I did not want to leave Adrian. I was beginning to realize he meant more to me than all of India.

"Wouldn't that be nice for you girls," gushed Aunt Clarissa. "I know you must miss your home and the balmy weather there, especially when we soon will be faced with the bitter winter cold of the Highlands."

"At least there are parties and socials in India," Diana said.

"Heather, why don't you play something soothing for us while we are waiting for Mr. Danton?" Aunt Clarissa suggested, a beatified smile on her face.

"That would be pleasant," John agreed.

I took my place at the piano and played a soft, slow sonata. As I finished, I looked up to see Patrick politely standing in the doorway. Except for his trim mustache, his face was freshly shaven; his clothes had been brushed and pressed. His military bearing gave him a distinguished air. He certainly looked nothing like the man who disrupted dinner. John Ross noticed Patrick's presence before the others.

"Ah, Mr. Danton! I would hardly recognize you. I hope your meal was satisfactory. May I offer you a drink?" John asked, rising to his feet.

"The meal was excellent, Mr. Ross. My compliments to your cook. A glass of whisky would be most welcome," said Patrick as he strode across the room to seat himself in the vacant space next to Diana on the settee. When John handed him the glass, Patrick took a large swallow.

"What is the purpose of your visit, Patrick?" Diana asked, a spark of rekindled interest in her eyes as she gazed at him.

"I am afraid I am the bearer of sad tidings," he began.

146

"Father?" I interrupted, anxiety on my face and in my voice.

"I am afraid so, Heather."

"Has he been injured?" My fear was mounting.

Patrick's face flashed pain. "No, Heather. Your father is dead. I am sorry. He died in my arms, if that is any consolation." He paused a moment to let the dreadful news sink in. He then continued, saying, "His last wish was to be brought to Bridee Castle to be buried. The wagon with his casket and my trunks should be here in a day or so. I rode posthaste to get here and apprise everyone of the terrible news. I didn't want the wagon to arrive before I did."

Tears streamed down my cheeks. I covered my face with my hands when the sobbing started. Adrian came and sat beside me on the piano bench. His arms went around me in a comforting gesture. Aunt Clarissa's gasp was hollow, then nothing. She had fainted. John poured two brandies. He brought me one then delivered the other to Diana. Adrian gave me his handkerchief as my sobs subsided. I wiped my eyes and blew my nose before taking a hefty sip of the brandy.

Some time passed before I got myself under control and Jane roused Aunt Clarissa. No one spoke during those moments of grief. When the blurriness left my eyes, I glanced at Diana, expecting to see her weeping. Instead she was staring into space, her face a blend of sorrow and fear.

"What happened, Mr. Danton?" John asked softly.

"We were at Luchnow waiting for news of the relief column. After our usual morning walk and inspection, we returned to the cottage. As we sat on the veranda awaiting our breakfast, a howitzer shell burst onto the veranda. A red glare blinded me for a second then all went black. When I became conscious, I was buried

147

under a substantial amount of rubble. With the exception of severe bruises, I was unharmed. I immediately looked for Brigadier MacBride. I found him fifteen feet from me. Suffice to say, he was a frightful sight." Patrick lowered his head, his hands covering a part of his brow and eyes.

"Please give us the details, Patrick," said Diana, coming out of her stupor.

"They are much too ghastly to be related with ladies present."

"I insist," Diana declared firmly. "He was my father and I want to know exactly what happened to him. If anyone present has a weak stomach, they are free to leave the room."

Patrick took a deep breath. "His left arm and leg were taken off at the joint. A gaping wound at his waist lay bare his entrails. I took him in my arms. He only had time to tell me of his wish to be buried at Bridee Castle before he expired."

Aunt Clarissa paled, but she did not faint. Though Patrick's tale of horror sorely affected me, I was glad Father's death was swift. He always wished to die in battle. Silence ensued for what seemed like an eternity. I was the one to break it.

"Have you left the regiment, Patrick?"

"I was granted a six-month leave of absence to bring the brigadier's body home and attend the funeral. I shall be returning to India at the end of the six months." He stood then and bowed slightly. "I will leave you now. Can anyone recommend a good inn in Inverness?"

"There is plenty of room here, Patrick," I said. "After all you have done, it wouldn't be civil to make you stay at a strange inn some distance from here. I am sure Aunt Clarissa wouldn't mind, would you, Aunt

Clarissa?"

"What? Oh, Mr. Danton? No, no, not at all. You must stay with us. I am sure my dear brother would want it that way." Aunt Clarissa resumed twisting her handkerchief.

"Thank you."

I finished the brandy. The heat of it trickling down my throat made me shiver.

"Are you all right, Heather?" Adrian asked.

Only then did I realize his arm still held me secure. "I think so. I will retire now. I am not fit company for anyone at present." I handed Adrian my empty glass and stood, causing all the gentlemen to stand.

"I will go up with you, Heather. The news has been most shocking. I must lay down. Jane, do see me up the stairs. I don't trust my legs. They feel wobbly," Aunt Clarissa said, extending her hand toward Jane for assistance in standing.

Good-nights were said and the three of us slowly ascended the main staircase. At the landing we went our separate ways. Jean was in my bedchamber turning down the bed. I told her the tragic news.

"I am sorry for your loss, Miss Heather," was her only comment as she helped me undress. When alone in the dark bedchamber, I softly cried into my pillow.

With the exception of Aunt Clarissa and Diana, everyone was present at an early hour for breakfast. I knew my eyes were red from crying half the night, but I didn't care. A daughter had a right to cry for the loss of a parent. No one mentioned it as I took my place at the table with a sparsely laden plate.

Bruce was interrogating Patrick regarding regimental life in India. John listened with interest. Jane appeared

149

preoccupied.

Adrian, who was seated next to me, asked, "Did you get any sleep last night, Heather?"

"On and off." I ventured a weak smile. "I stopped at Diana's bedchamber just now. I wanted to talk to her. I was surprised when the maid told me she was still asleep and didn't want to be disturbed."

"We were up late last night. In fact, Diana was still in the drawing room when I retired."

"She could have shown a little more sorrow and respect for the loss of our father." I inadvertently voiced my thoughts aloud.

"We all bear our grief in different ways. Diana probably needed to talk and be with people," he said soothingly.

"Perhaps you are right. I guess deep down I knew something was wrong in India. Father never answered any of my letters."

Adrian patted my hand. "Eat your breakfast. You are going to need your strength."

"I had better ride to the village today and make arrangements with Reverend Campbell."

"Shouldn't you discuss it with your sister and Clarissa first?"

I nodded. "I am so used to making my own decisions, I wasn't thinking straight. I have a feeling that Aunt Clarissa and Diana won't be of much help. But I will wait and talk to them first."

"If you find yourself going alone to the village, call me. I will accompany you if you wish."

"That is very kind of you, Adrian."

"I will be in the library for the rest of the morning if you need me."

* * *

Noontime was approaching when Aunt Clarissa and Diana made an appearance in the drawing room. Bruce, John, and Patrick had gone into Inverness. Jane and I were discussing the prospect of securing ready-made mourning clothes. Aunt Clarissa plunked into a well-padded chair and emitted sporadic moans. Diana went to stare out the window. Her shoulders lifted then sagged.

"Does this gloomy weather ever cease? Nothing but rain, mist, and fog. Life here is dreary enough without the weather adding to the misery," Diana declared. Suddenly she spun around. "Mrs. Burns tells me you want to see me, Heather."

"Yes. I thought we could discuss the arrangements for Father's funeral."

"What is there to discuss? I am sure you can handle it, Heather. I am not of a mood to deal with clergy and all the tedious details of a funeral," Diana said.

Diana behaved as I expected. "Aunt Clarissa, do you have any suggestions for the funeral?" I asked.

"Oh, dear me. I wouldn't know what to do. When my first husband, Mr. Pickering, died, his father tended to all the details. I will leave it in your capable hands, Heather. One thing I do insist on, I want my brother waked."

"But the casket will be closed due to the circumstances of his death," I countered.

"Nonetheless, I want him waked. I am sure James would want it that way. The tenant farmers should have the opportunity to pay homage to their laird."

I never saw Aunt Clarissa so adamant and, though I was against it, I consented to the wake.

"I would like his casket draped in the clan tartan. Perhaps Mr. Danton could obtain a regimental flag. James would like that," Aunt Clarissa said.

"Where are the men?" Diana asked.

"They went to Inverness," Jane informed her. Either she omitted the fact that Adrian was secluded in the library or she didn't know.

"Whatever for? There is much to attend to here," Diana said.

"Something about mourning bands," Jane said.

"Oh, goodness. I forgot all about a mourning frock. We shall have to go to Inverness ourselves and hope they have suitable attire already made," Diana declared. "Not only will we need a frock, but hat, cape, and gloves. I hadn't realized there is so much to do. We will leave right after lunch."

"I already have mourning clothes," Aunt Clarissa said wearily.

"What about you, Heather?" Diana asked.

"I won't have time. You know my size, Diana. I would appreciate it if you would pick out and purchase a suitable ensemble for me."

"Well, I never. Really, Heather, you get lazier every day." Diana took a deep breath, then let it out slowly. "I guess that sticks me with Jane. Jane, I do hope you have something suitable to wear to town other than your drab frocks. It is positively appalling the way you dress. And do have a maid do something with your hair. I don't want you embarrassing me."

Jane flushed.

"Right now," Diana continued, "I am going to see Mrs. Burns about having an early lunch so we can leave for Inverness immediately after."

When Diana left, I turned to Jane. "Let Jean do your hair, Jane. She has a flair for the latest in coiffures."

"I am getting tired of your sister berating me, Heather," Jane said glumly.

"Then tell her to keep her thoughts to herself," I

suggested.

"I might just do that if I don't throttle her first."

"Oh, dear me. I don't like that kind of talk in this house. Haven't we had enough tragedy?" Aunt Clarissa moaned. "An early lunch is a good idea. My nerves are so frayed, I will be in need of my afternoon nap sooner than I expected."

With Jane and Diana on their way to Inverness and Aunt Clarissa ensconced in her bedchamber, I went down the hall and tapped gently on the library door.

"Come in," came Adrian's baritone voice.

Entering, I noticed the remnants of a sandwich and tea on the desk. Adrian, sitting in the desk chair, rubbed his eyes, then stretched his sinewy arms upward. "Ah, Heather! What can I do for you?"

"You said you would accompany me to the village." I hoped he hadn't forgotten his offer.

"So I did." He closed the ledger he was working on and stood. "Let me get a few things and I will be right with you. I think it best we take a closed carriage. The weather doesn't look promising."

"If there is a closed carriage left. The men took one this morning. Jane and Diana have taken another just now," I informed him.

"They probably took the broughams. I am sure a trap will be available."

Smiling, he came toward me, cupped my elbow, and steered me into the foyer. While I went to fetch my hooded cape, Adrian dashed up the staircase taking two steps at a time.

On the drive to the kirk and manse, I told Adrian the stories about my grandfather and the portrait I had found in the ancient hall. I quickly absolved my father of any of those traits. "Have you ever heard any tales about my grandfather, Adrian?"

153

"No. I never inquired about him."

"Do you think evil can be passed down through generations?"

"Why would you ask a question like that?" Amusement sparkled in his eyes.

I shrugged. "From the first day I entered Bridee Castle I felt an evil presence there."

"What kind of evil?"

"I can't describe it. It was more of a sensation."

"The castle was alien to you, as were the Highlands. The sheer strangeness of your new surroundings could have caused this so-called sense of evil," Adrian suggested.

"I hope so," I sighed.

"Do you still have those feelings?"

"Yes. I can't seem to rid myself of them. A sense of doom seems to follow me about."

"Perhaps the death of your Indian servant lingers in your mind. And now the death of your father might have compounded that sense."

"I had these feelings before the death of Samrú and my father."

"Youth is impressionable. With the death of your father, what do you and Diana plan to do? I assume your cottage in India will go to your father's successor in the regiment."

"I suppose it will. There is no reason for us to go back to India now. I don't know what Diana's plans are, but I intend to stay at Bridee Castle for the time being."

"Did your father leave a will, Heather?"

"I don't know. I would suppose he did," I said as we pulled up to Reverend Campbell's manse.

Tea and sympathy, scones and jam, were served in abundance. Under the circumstances, we decided a three-day wake would be sufficient. A brief church

154

service and a cortege to Bridee Castle's cemetery where my father would be laid to rest was agreed upon. Once the funeral arrangements had been concluded, Adrian and Reverend Campbell had a comfortable chat about livestock.

On our way back to the castle, Adrian veered the trap to a side road. Hedgerows stood darkly sentinel on either side of the narrow lane. With a charcoal sky above us, the impression was one of moving through an eerie, unending tunnel.

"Is this a short cut to the castle?" I asked. I really didn't care. No matter where he led me, I felt safe and secure with Adrian.

"No, this lane leads to my house."

"I never noticed a road to your house. I thought the only way to get there was through the overgrown path."

"That is the short cut from Bridee Castle. The hedges practically hide this road."

"It looks well traveled," I remarked.

"By me, for the most part. I do have a couple who come to tend to the place. The man the grounds, the woman the cleaning. They also bring what food I may need if I don't bring it myself."

"Why are we going there?"

"I thought you might like a change of scenery. I trust you found nothing evil about my humble abode."

"It is a pleasant and charming home. I would enjoy a respite from Bridee Castle. Thank you for being so thoughtful."

The lane curved and twisted until we reached Adrian's large, Elizabethan-style home. As he pulled the trap up to the front door, I recognized the slim lane I had crossed after leaving the tangle of brush and trees on my first visit. He told me to enter while he un-hitched the trap and put the horse in the stable for shelter and food.

Inside, I flung my cloak off and placed it on a hook in the foyer. I wandered into the spacious front parlor. Curiosity gave way to exploration.

I walked back to the foyer and crossed it to discover a dining room large enough to accommodate thirty people for dinner. At the rear of the dining room, two doors hugged the corner at an angle. One led to the pantry and kitchen. The other opened onto a library where books dominated two walls, interrupted by a manteled fireplace on one wall. A cushioned seat stretched in front of an orieled window from which the rear gardens could be viewed.

The upstairs consisted of bedchambers, sitting parlors, a game room, and rooms with no apparent purpose. Most of the furniture in the house was of Hepplewhite's design, classic in style, but graceful in execution. Refinement and lightness masked the inherent strength of the furniture. Having satisfied my curiosity, I went back downstairs to the piano and lightly picked out a tune.

"Don't be afraid to bang down on the keys," Adrian said as he came into the parlor.

I turned and smiled. "I hope you don't mind, but I took a tour of the house. Both upstairs and downstairs."

"And what did you think?"

"Beautiful."

"No impression of evil?"

I laughed. "No evil fairies or satanic little gnomes jumped out at me."

"What about ghosts?"

"They only come out at night." I left the piano bench. "Please play for me, Adrian. It would do much to take my mind off my sorrows."

"If you wish."

He sat down at the piano and began to play with robust vigor. I settled on the well-cushioned sofa and lost myself in his passionate playing.

Dusk was falling when we returned to the castle. I went directly to my bedchamber to change for dinner. Boxes were on my bed. I opened them to find an extremely plain mourning frock and a black veiled hat that was rather dated. Gloves and a black cloth muff completed the ensemble. I was willing to wager Diana's mourning clothes would be far more elaborate and fashionable. I had no one to blame but myself. Letting Diana do my shopping was inviting mediocrity.

All were present at dinner. Evidently Jane did have my maid do her hair for it was most becoming.

"Did you see Reverend Campbell, Heather?" Aunt Clarissa asked as the soup was served.

"Yes." I related the arrangements.

"Only a three-day wake? Oh, dear me. I was hoping for at least a week," Aunt Clarissa declared.

"I don't think too many people around here knew Father. I doubt if he ever had any contact with the tenants," I said in defence of the decision. "Reverend Campbell will post notice of the wake."

"I shall have to have Mrs. Burns stock the larder with more than the usual provisions," Aunt Clarissa said.

"I have already placed an order with the wine merchant in Inverness. The order should be here tomorrow," John said.

"I took the liberty of engaging a piper to play at the funeral," Patrick said. "I know the brigadier would have liked that."

"Can you get a regimental flag for the services, Mr. Danton?" Aunt Clarissa asked.

"I have one packed in my trunk. I also took the liberty of contacting the brigadier's solicitor while we were in Inverness. He will be at the funeral. He will come back the following morning to read the will."

A hush fell around the table at the mention of a will. I decided to put a halt to any incipient tension at the table. "Thank you, Patrick. I hadn't thought of those details. Wasn't it thoughtful of Patrick to bring the regimental flag, Diana?"

"What?" A look of distress flickered on her face.

I repeated my statement.

"Oh, yes. Thank you, Patrick." Her knuckles turned white as she increased her grip on the fork in her hand.

"Is something wrong, Diana?" John asked.

"Some passing cramps. That is all."

I realized Diana wasn't feigning her distress. I knew her monthlies troubled her far more than they did me. I recalled several occasions where she had to take to her bed because of the intensity of the cramps. She managed to get through dinner, but went directly to her bedchamber after dessert.

"Diana is as lovely as ever," Patrick commented as we had our drinks in the drawing room.

"Indeed she is." John's enthusiastic reply was greeted with a sneer from Bruce.

"How did you like Inverness, Mr. Danton?" Adrian asked.

"A quaint and quiet town. And do call me Patrick. Mr. Danton is too formal for one who will be under your roof for a few months."

First names were politely exchanged. Jane showed a restrained interest in the young lieutenant. Her eyes sparkled when she looked at him, but her general demeanor was one of caution. To my relief, the evening passed amicably.

Before I padded to my bedchamber, I went to see how Diana was faring. Not wanting to wake her if she was asleep, I quietly opened the door and tiptoed in.

"Will you stop sneaking about, Heather. You know how I hate it," Diana cried.

"I didn't want to disturb you."

"Well, you have. What do you want?"

"I wanted to see if you were all right."

"I'll bet you did. You would love to see me get sick so you can have all the men to yourself. Well, I have no intention of accommodating you, Heather. By tomorrow morning I will be fine so don't get your hopes up. Now get out of here and leave me alone," Diana demanded.

I did.

Chapter Nine

The casket arrived midmorning. The sight of it being carried into the castle caused Aunt Clarissa to moan and flutter about directing the servants in arranging the drawing room to accommodate the elaborate casket.

After lunch we filed into the drawing room to pay our respects. With the exception of Bruce, who left almost immediately, we took seats and silently said what prayers were in our hearts.

An hour or more passed when I concluded my prayers and meditations. I forced myself to look at the casket that contained the body of my father and stemmed my tears.

The finely carved wooden casket had a domed lid where the carving was more elaborate. Flowers with stamens and pistils, carved to perfection, tumbled over the curved lid. One could see the veins of the leaves and the life-giving woody stems. Inlaid arabesques were of a more brilliant wood. Gilt highlighted certain sections of the casket. I was surprised, as I didn't think it would be the sort of casket my father would have chosen.

Most people from the village paid their respects while only a few tenants made the trip. I think they came more out of curiosity than any feeling for my father.

Late at night on the second day of the wake, I was restless and unable to sleep. I think I was dreading the actual funeral. Control of my emotions was difficult at best during Samrú's funeral. I hoped I could manage a brave front during my father's, but I had my doubts. To keep my mind from dwelling on the impending funeral, I thought a book of fiction would banish unwanted thoughts. I quietly opened the door. The corridor was dim and gloomy. I tightened the belt of my robe and padded toward the staircase.

Reaching the bottom step, I started to turn toward the library. Emanating from the drawing room was a faint rustling noise. Light from the room cast dancing shadows across the foyer. I didn't think too much about the glimmerings, for candles remained lighted throughout the night for a wake. I was about to relegate the noise to an overactive imagination when the sound became more distinct. I headed for the drawing room to see who was there at this hour of the night. Though I tried to be quiet, the slap of my slippers against the marble floor echoed in the still night. As I approached the room, I heard a few grunts then muffled sobs. I wondered if remorse had finally overcome Diana. I tiptoed in. To my astonishment, Aunt Clarissa was draped over the coffin and sobbing. I went up to her and put my hands on her shoulders. She jerked up and spun around, fear in her eyes.

"Oh, dear me," she exclaimed, placing a splayed hand over her bosom. "It is you, Heather. Good gracious, child, you frightened me to death."

"I am sorry, Aunt Clarissa. I heard someone in here and wondered who it was."

Aunt Clarissa pulled a handkerchief from her sleeve and dabbed at her eyes. "James was my only brother and I had no sisters. Though we didn't see much of each other, I will miss him."

"I know. His death was a shock to all of us." I led her to

the settee and sat her down. "Why don't I get you a snifter of brandy. It might help you sleep."

"Yes. Yes, Heather. Make it a large one." She leaned back and fanned herself with her handkerchief.

I poured a good amount of brandy into the snifter and poured a small sherry for myself. Perhaps the sherry would do more good than a book. I handed her the snifter and sat in a chair opposite the settee. Aunt Clarissa took a hefty swallow.

"I didn't expect anyone to be roaming around this time of night," she said.

"I couldn't sleep and came down for a book. I never realized how deeply Father's death affected you. I thought you were taking it rather well."

"Well, we must put on a brave front for all the people coming in and out. John would want me to be strong. He doesn't like it when I get sentimental."

"I am sure he wouldn't begrudge you a display of grief over the loss of your only brother."

"It is better he doesn't know I was here. You won't tell anyone about tonight, will you, Heather?"

"No. I won't tell anyone, Aunt Clarissa."

We drained our glasses, then went upstairs to our separate bedchambers.

The day of the funeral had arrived. Diana and I were in the carriage behind the hearse. Aunt Clarissa, John, Adrian, and Jane were behind us, Patrick and Bruce behind them. The cortege was large considering my father spent little of his time and life in the area.

Diana was restless and fidgety. I thought some conversation might relieve her anxiety. I knew it would mine.

"Did you know about Grandfather, Diana?" I asked.

"Father told me about him some time ago. He was not

162

fond of the old man." She looked out the carriage window.

My ego was crushed. Father had told Diana, but not me. That knowledge murdered my desire for further conversation.

We followed the casket to the open grave, then gathered around while Reverend Campbell gave his brief eulogy. Funereal masses of dark clouds scudded across the slatey sky. Diana had positioned herself between Adrian and Patrick, leaving me to stand alone. Bruce was gallant and came to my side while Jane, her father, and Aunt Clarissa had their own group. I was grateful to Bruce, for as they started lowering the coffin into the grave, tears and wracking sobs gripped me and Bruce's arm gave me support.

After the obligatory ritual of tossing dirt onto the lowered coffin, we went back to the waiting carriages. Withered leaves whirled crazily before our feet. My sister and I rode back to the castle in silence. I had nothing to say. If I did, I knew Diana didn't want to hear it.

After breakfast the next morning, various groups of us straggled into the drawing room to await the solicitor. Diana was the last to make her appearance, and when she did, eyebrows raised.

She had exchanged her mourning dress for a pale lavender taffeta day frock. Tiers of blue roses rambled around the hem. A green velvet sash cinched her waist, the ends trailing almost to the ground. White lace exposed her neck and a bit of shoulder, and ruffled around her wrists at the end of long puffed sleeves. She looked divine and prepared for anything—except mourning. Smiling at everyone, she took her seat next to me.

Divested of his cloak and tall hat, the solicitor came waddling into the drawing room. All I could think of were the penguins I had seen in the London Zoo. He was short

163

and lean with a face like a sick crow. He sat down at the table expressly positioned for him. He glanced at the people seated before him as though we were weeds in a flower bed. He coughed, cleared his throat, then perched reading glasses on his beakish nose. After reading minor bequests to the staff, he came to the bulk of the estate.

"To my sister, Clarissa Ross, I leave all the family portraits, an annuity of three hundred pounds, and my best wishes for a happy life. To my daughters, Diana and Heather MacBride, I leave equal shares in the demesne, Bridee Castle. They are to share equally in my tenanted lands, stocks, bonds, and all liquid assets contained in the vaults of the Bank of Scotland in Edinburgh. They may sell or divide the aforementioned as they wish, but equally. I also wish my daughter, Heather, to complete my memoirs from the notes I have given her. She is to be compensated from the estate upon completion of said work, the amount to be established by a reputable publisher." The solicitor removed his glasses and looked up. "Any questions?"

"Does that mean we can sell Bridee Castle and its lands?" Diana asked.

"Yes, if both of you decide to sell, that is. The monies received from such a sale would have to be divided equally," the solicitor answered. "Any more questions?"

"Do you have a list of the stocks and bonds? Also the assets in the Bank of Scotland?" Diana asked, her interest obvious and keen.

"I have prepared lists for you and your sister, Miss MacBride. They show the intrinsic value of the stocks and bonds, along with the annual revenue they generate. I have included an accounting of the assets in the Bank of Scotland, which is a sizable sum, I may add. There is also a list of the tenants and the amount of rent each produces. I am sure you will find them accurate and concise." He pulled two folders from his briefcase, stood, walked around the table toward us, and handed one folder to Diana and one to me. "I believe that concludes the last will and testament of James Angus MacBride. It goes without saying that if either of you predeceases the other, the entire estate goes to the survivor."

"What happens, God forbid, if both Misses MacBrides expire?" John Ross asked.

"The estate will go to his closest living relative, which, in this case, would be Clarissa Ross. Any more questions?" His beady eyes roamed around the room. "Then if you will excuse me, I have to return to Inverness. I shall leave a copy of the will here. Naturally the original will be put in my office safe." He nodded to everyone and left.

"I am so glad that is over," Aunt Clarissa said with a sigh in her voice.

John Ross stood and drew himself to his full height, then came to Diana and me. "You are heiresses now. How does it feel?"

"Quite good," Diana declared with a broad smile that showed her white teeth. "I think I shall sell this dreary old castle, travel the Continent for a year or so, then settle in London where the divertissements are more numerous. Don't you think that is the sensible thing to do, Heather?"

"I haven't really thought about it," I answered.

"Don't tell me you are going to be obstinate, Heather," Diana said, her smile vanishing.

"Obstinate about what, Heather?" Bruce asked as he joined the group.

I related Diana's proposal regarding Bridee Castle.

"What a shame to leave us when we've hardly had time to know one another."

"I would rather *not* know anymore about you, Bruce," Diana declared.

Bruce glared at her with hatred, then headed for the

165

sideboard.

"Touring the Continent would be an educational experience of the two of you," Aunt Clarissa said with a vague smile. "Perhaps you could take Jane with you as a chaperone."

"God forbid!" exclaimed Diana. "It was bad enough I had to be seen with her in Inverness. The Continent would be totally out of the question." Diana's laughter tinkled through the spacious drawing room. "Can you imagine plain old Jane in the capitals of Europe, Heather?"

"Yes, I can." I smiled at Jane who was flushing an angry red.

"Really, Heather. You do have a vivid imagination," Diana said.

Jane looked as though she might burst into a vituperative rage. She stalked from the room. I made a wager with myself that Patrick would be Diana's next victim.

To my astonishment, she purred sweetly to the three men gathered in a semicircle around her. My heart plummeted to see Adrian in that group cosseting her and using his substantial charm on her. I was an heiress too! Why didn't he fawn over me? I suppose the answer to that was obvious even to me. If I had my choice between a handsome rich prince and a plain rich prince, which would I choose? I guess it was in man's nature to go after the beautiful one first.

With folder in hand, I left the drawing room and headed for the library where I could peruse the contents of the folder in private. I sat down in the large leather chair behind the desk. The chair dwarfed me as I spun it around, causing the high leather back to face the desk.

The papers in the folder were explicit and concise. I never knew Father had been that wealthy. When I mentally totaled the sums, I found the extent of my share of the wealth hard to believe. I could never spend that amount of money in one lifetime. As I pondered my new status in life, the door to the library opened and closed. I was about to spin around and announce my presence, when the anxious and whispering voices caught my attention.

"What are we going to do now, Jane?" came Bruce's apprehensive voice.

"I don't know." Jane's voice cracked as though she were going to cry.

"That bitch! If we don't toady to her every whim, she is the type of she-devil who would put us out on the street without a sou. She is not too fond of us as it is," Bruce grumbled slowly. "I have half a mind to choke the life out of her."

"Don't talk like that, Bruce. What if someone heard you?" Jane warned.

"I don't care. She has been nothing but a misery since she came here."

"I don't see what we can do about it."

"We had better start making contingency plans."

"What kind of plans?" Jane asked.

"I'm not sure yet, but I am not letting that bitch put me out of here like yesterday's trash."

"What about Adrian?"

"I don't think we have to worry about Adrian." I could almost hear the sneer in Bruce's voice. "Adrian," he continued, "can take care of himself. You know very well when Adrian decides to turn on the full strength of his charm, no woman can resist him. He has the ability to manipulate women to dance to whatever tune he chooses. Besides, he always has his breeding animals to fall back on."

"What about this Patrick Danton? He was her beau in India. He might have an influence on her," Jane suggested.

"Pay no attention to him. He won't be with us long enough to matter. I am going to ride into the village. I have some friends there who seem to have solutions for every problem."

"Don't, Bruce."

"And why not?"

"I am afraid you will get in your cups and talk about things you shouldn't."

"Never fear, my dear sister. When it comes to matters as crucial as this, I know how to conduct myself."

"What should I do?"

"Keep an eye on our potty Clarissa. I don't want her pestering or riling her niece. Ta, ta love."

The door opened and closed. I was about to turn the chair around when I heard Jane let out a pitiable sigh. I remained rigid in the chair. For them to know I overheard their conversation might have deleterious consequences. Hours seemed to pass before Jane left. Actually it was only ten or fifteen minutes. I waited for what I thought was a reasonable amount of time before I left the library.

Dinner was not as somber as it should have been under the circumstances. I could see that Diana's sporadic laughter befuddled and angered Aunt Clarissa.

"Really, Diana. Only a day has passed since we interred your father. I should think this is not the time for merriment. You should act according to the solemnity of the occasion," Aunt Clarissa said.

"Father would be put out if I continually mourned for him. He liked to hear me laugh. He said it was the sound that cheered him most. Besides, Patrick has been through enough. He is entitled to a little gaiety," Diana countered.

"Clarissa, Diana's youth and beauty do not put her under the same restrictions as those of us who are more mature. One is only young once," Jane soothed.

Diana looked at Jane and raised a querulous eyebrow.

"At least Heather shows some decorum," Aunt Clarissa said. "Where is Bruce?"

"He went to the village. I imagine he is still there," Jane

answered.

"Was the monsoon heavy this year, Patrick?" I asked. Once Aunt Clarissa embraced a topic, it was hard to pull her away. I was afraid if she continued in the same vein she would disrupt the comparative calm at the dinner table.

Patrick became expansive on the subject of the monsoon which led him to the topic of the repercussions of rain during battle, much to Diana's annoyance. She preferred the conversation to revolve around her.

With Adrian and Patrick flanking her and a disgruntled John trailing behind, Diana twittered as compliments flowed her way. We were halfway across the foyer on our way to the drawing room, when Diana doubled over. She would have slipped to the floor if Adrian hadn't caught her.

"Are you all right, Diana?" Adrian asked as the rest of us formed a circle around them.

"My bedchamber," she managed to gasp between twitchings of spasmodic pain.

Adrian swooped her into his brawny arms and headed for the main staircase.

"I will go with her," I said to the gaping group, "and let you know if a doctor is needed." I lifted my skirts and raced after Adrian who was almost to the top of the stairs. Aunt Clarissa's "Oh, dear me" rang in my ears.

Once in her bedchamber, Adrian laid her on the bed, Diana's hands clutching her stomach.

"Is there anything more I can do?" Adrian asked.

I shook my head. "I will ring for a maid if I need assistance."

"Let us know of her condition as soon as you can, Heather," he said before he quietly left.

I began to remove Diana's gown, then went to work loosening the tight stays of her corset. "Is that better?"

She took several deep breaths and nodded. "Much. I

wish Samrú was here. She knew an herbal infusion that eased these miserable cramps."

"Perhaps if you didn't wear your stays so tight, you wouldn't get these severe attacks," I said.

"I must keep my figure."

"Are you willing to suffer this every month to keep your figure?"

"Don't talk nonsense, Heather. My stays were no tighter than usual." Her face contorted as another wave of constricting seizures gripped her.

I looked at her with compassion. "Are you sure there isn't something else wrong with you, Diana? I don't remember seeing you suffering this much before."

"Perhaps you are right, Heather. I might have had the maid pull the stays too tight this time. The silly twit should have known better."

"Now don't go blaming the maid. I am sure she only did as you instructed."

"That's right. Take her side. You never did stand by me in anything. You are a poor excuse for a sister. I wish you had been born a boy instead of a girl."

"I think Father had the same wish."

"Of course he did. You will never know how he lamented your birth."

I could tell Diana was feeling better. Her tongue was becoming sharper. "Should I have the doctor sent for?"

"No! I don't need some old lecher poking me about."

"Dr. Drummond seems like a very nice man."

"I don't want a doctor. Don't you dare mention it again, Heather."

I sat down on the edge of the bed. "Have you had a chance to look through the folder the solicitor gave us?"

"Not yet. I take it we are well off."

"Very. I don't think we could spend it all."

"Perhaps you couldn't, Heather, but I could and will.

170

What do you think about selling this old mausoleum?"

"I haven't thought about it. I am still trying to get used to the idea of being rich."

"Well, think about it. The sooner I get away from here the better. Spending the winter here when we could be in the south of France or Spain is like carrying coals to New-castle."

"We don't have to sell the castle to go to the south of France. There is more than enough money to tour the world if we want."

"Is there really?" She seemed surprised.

"What about Adrian and Patrick? You seem fond of both of them." It was hard for me to ask the question. I feared the answer even more. If Diana wanted Adrian, she would have him, especially if she knew I was in love with him.

"Adrian is a virile, handsome man, and so muscular! Still . . ." She paused reflectively. "I think he is after my money. He never showed much attention to me until he learned of the legacy. I cannot tolerate any man who is more interested in my money than he is in me. Patrick always did amuse me, but I wouldn't dream of marrying a lowly soldier any more than I would an animal breeder. Now that we are heiresses we will move in the circle of the peerage—dukes, earls. Perhaps in Europe we can acquaint ourselves with princes." Her eyes glittered with expectation.

"Perhaps our legacy will prove more of a curse than a blessing," I mused.

"Never. Money can give me more than any man could. At the end of the month I am going to see about making reservations for a trip to the south of France. Whether you go with me or not is up to you, Heather. I hate these Highlands. The sooner I get away the better."

"Are you feeling better now?"

"Yes."

171

"Are you sure you don't want a doctor?"

"I told you not to mention it again. I know when I need a doctor and when I don't."

"Will you be coming downstairs for some sherry?"

"I am undressed now. I really don't have the strength to get dressed again. I will rest tonight. In the morning I shall be busy making plans for an extended holiday."

"I had better go downstairs and tell them you are all right. Everyone was worried."

"Don't you dare tell them what caused the spasms."

"I wouldn't dream of it, Diana. Shall I ring for your maid?"

"Yes. Pull the cord several times. She is a lazy twit."

I pulled the cord twice and left.

Puzzled eyes stared at me as I entered the drawing room. The handkerchief in Aunt Clarissa's busy hands twisted.

"How is Diana?" Patrick asked, coming to cup my elbow. He steered me to a Queen Anne chair and I promptly sat.

"She is fine now. A bit of indigestion, I suspect."

"Should we send for the doctor?" Aunt Clarissa asked.

"I don't think that will be necessary. Besides, she absolutely refuses to see one."

"Are you sure she is all right, Heather?" Jane asked. "Her face was so pale and ashen."

"She must be feeling better. She is planning a holiday in the south of France."

"Will she be traveling soon?" Patrick asked.

"She said by the end of the month."

"I see." A glint flickered in Patrick's eyes and I knew he was considering following her there.

"Will you be going with her, Heather?" Adrian asked.

"I don't know. There is so much to be done here."

"What are you planning for Bridee Castle?" John asked,

his eyebrows clashing over the bridge of his nose.

"I was thinking of restoring the unused part of the castle and turning it into a museum in memory of my father."

"Oh, dear me. Isn't that a vast undertaking?" Aunt Clarissa asked.

I smiled. "Just a passing thought, Aunt Clarissa."

Diana improved over the days. Fortifying herself with pamphlets and books on France John brought from Inverness, her time was well occupied. Though her monthlies were over, she continued to have mild spells of indigestion along accompanied by shortness of breath. I laid the maladies down to a lack of exercise followed by sudden, energetic spurts of activity.

I rode or took brisk walks whenever the weather permitted. With Adrian paying so little attention to me, I half-decided to go to France with Diana. On those rare occasions when Adrian condescended to notice me, I was treated like a mischievous child.

John and Patrick danced attendance on Diana, helping her with her plans for the impending holiday. As Jane was Aunt Clarissa's constant companion, more and more I found myself in Bruce's company. After overhearing his conversation with Jane, I had become wary of him. He seemed placid and harmless, but an unsettling glint glimmered in his brown eyes.

As the end of the month approached, Diana hounded me for an answer about going to France with her. She berated me for hours about my indecision. But Diana had never been truly in love. I couldn't bear the thought of leaving Adrian for a better climate. Even if he never paid any attention to me, to see him and be near him brought me a delightful measure of happiness.

As Diana's breathing became more labored, she took to

173

her bed for the afternoons. I feared consumption might be the cause of her lung difficulties and urged her to leave immediately for France, or see a doctor. I also suggested a clinic in Switzerland might be the better choice. At the mere suggestion of a clinic, Diana would fly into a rage. She was furious that I thought she might have consumption and be contagious. I dropped the subject.

In the coming days, I wished I had the stronger will and insisted she leave or see a doctor.

One morning, I had completed my toilette and was on my way to breakfast. I reached the landing to the staircase and never got any farther. The sound I heard froze the very marrow of my bones.

Chapter Ten

The chilling scream reverberated through the castle, even to the uninhabited section where the sound would only startle rats and spiders. The screeching came from my sister's bedchamber. Lifting my skirts, I ran like a fury to her door.

I dashed inside to see her face a mask of terror. I started to go to her when Jane and her father appeared at the door.

"Keep them out, Heather. I don't want anyone in here," Diana demanded.

"I am sorry," I said softly as I closed the door on Jane and John. I went back to Diana. "What happened?"

"Look!" Diana thrust her hands out for me to inspect.

I scanned her hands with an impatient eye. "I don't see anything."

"You must be blind, Heather. Look here . . . and here." She pointed a finger to places on the back of one hand. "Can you see them now?"

I took her hand and peered at the small horny projections. "You mean to tell me all this was screaming about a few tiny warts?" I didn't know whether to laugh or be angry. I smiled.

"It is not funny, Heather. Look!" She pulled the collar of her robe aside to reveal a wart on her neck. "And here." She pushed up the sleeve of her silken robe. A larger wart was on her arm poking above the fine golden hairs. She sat down on the bed and removed her slipper then lifted her foot for my inspection. "Just below the ankle bone."

I dropped to my knees and examined her foot. Below the ankle bone was a good-sized, ugly wart. I stood up as Diana started to cry. I sat next to her on the bed and put a compassionate arm around her shoulder which she promptly shrugged off.

"I don't need your sympathy, especially when you are probably glad this is happening to me."

"Don't be ridiculous, Diana. I wouldn't wish warts on anyone, especially you."

"You don't fool me, Heather. You are jealous of my beauty and always have been."

I knew it was useless to argue with her when she was in this state of mind. I changed the subject. "I think it is time for us to send for the doctor."

"What? Have you lost your senses, Heather? I don't want it gossiped about that I have warts. No one must know about it. I trust you will be able to keep your mouth shut."

"Doctors don't go about telling people what is ailing their patients. I think you had better see one before the condition worsens."

"I neither know nor trust the doctors around here. I refuse to let these warts become worse."

"Wishing isn't going to make them go away."

"I am not stupid, Heather. I want you to find that gypsy you saw. Give her whatever money she wants for something that will make these go away."

"She might have left the moors to head south."

"I said find her. I don't care what you have to do, but find her. If anyone knows how to get rid of warts, the gypsies do. I wouldn't be surprised if she cursed me with them," Diana declared.

"Don't be silly, Diana. She doesn't even know you."

"Oh, my God! What will I do if I get them on my face?"

"If I were you I wouldn't be putting my hands to my face."

Her hands dropped suddenly to her lap and terror invaded her eyes. "I shall have to wear gloves and high-collared gowns and frocks until they are cured."

"Suppose I can't find these gypsies in the next day or so? You are leaving the day after tomorrow, aren't you?" I asked.

"Gracious no! How can I go to France looking like this? I wanted to have a whole new wardrobe made in Paris. I certainly can't have dressmakers viewing me. I won't leave Bridee Castle until I am rid of them. Now help me dress, Heather. The maids here are gossips. You will have to attend me until this cursed ailment disappears."

"I get up early, Diana. Are you willing to get up early in the morning?"

"If necessary. Now go look for that gypsy."

"What shall I tell everyone regarding your screams?"

"Tell them I thought I saw a mouse. Tell them anything but the truth."

"Is there anything I can do for you right now?"

"Finish dressing me then ring for the maid. She will bring my breakfast up."

When I finally entered the dining room to eat my breakfast, everyone was already seated and half-finished with their food. Aunt Clarissa was still in her bedchamber.

"Well?" John queried.

"Well what?" I placed my full plate on the table and sat down.

"What terrified Diana into screaming like that?" John asked with impatience.

"She thought she saw a mouse."

"A mouse? Good Lord! I thought the ghost of Lady Anne was assaulting her," Bruce said.

"A live mouse can be just as frightening as your Lady Anne, Bruce," Jane said.

"At least it wasn't an event to delay Diana's departure for France," Patrick said.

"Diana has changed her plans, Patrick. She has decided to defer the trip for a few weeks," I informed him while my brain scrambled for a feasible excuse for the delay.

177

"Oh? Why?" he asked.

"Something to do with clearing up some paperwork regarding the will." I wished Diana had come down to breakfast and given her own excuses. I didn't like fibbing for her.

I was mounting my horse when Adrian came into the stableyard. He told a groom to saddle his horse then he headed for me.

"Off so early?" he asked, his smile making my heart palpitate.

"Helps the digestion, I am told." I returned his smile.

"Stay off the moors. Fog is in the hollows already. The moors can be treacherous in fine weather, but with fog, they are lethal. The gypsies might still be out there. We wouldn't want them carrying you off, now would we?"

"Do you really think there are gypsies on the moor, Adrian?"

"There have been rumors. If I didn't have business in Aberdeen I would ride with you."

"Isn't Aberdeen some distance from here?"

"About eighty miles or so."

"Then you won't be back tonight."

"Perhaps. I will have to see how things go." He mounted his large steed. "We can start off together. I will be taking the southeast road just before the village."

We left the stableyard and rode in companionable silence until we reached his road.

"Good-bye, Adrian."

"Are you going to France with your sister?"

"I don't think so. Why do you ask?"

"I was curious. It might be best if you did."

"Why do you say that?"

He hesitated and the muscles around his mouth hardened. "The weather and general dreariness of the castle. Think about it seriously, Heather. Good-bye." He dug his heels into the flanks of his steed and galloped off.

I waited until he was well out of sight then veered my horse toward Culloden Moor. If I had truly seen a gypsy woman in the topiary, I felt their camp had to be close by. Culloden Moor was nearest to Bridee Castle.

I let the horse lope along and pick her way through the gorse, furze, and heather. I didn't want her stumbling, or catching her hoof in some unsuspecting rabbit hole, or, worse, breaking a leg.

After a few hours of aimless wandering, I spied a thin film of smoke spiraling in the air. I urged the mare to pick up the pace. In a place where everything was a uniform gray, the wagon, painted bright red and enhanced with designs in bright blues, greens, and yellows, became a sparkling citadel of color. As I drew closer, I slowed my horse and assumed an air of dignity.

The woman's long black hair hung loose. When she saw me, she tossed her hair back with a flick of her head to reveal large hooped earrings. Her skirt was bright red. A white, low-cut blouse was covered with a black woolen shawl. Chains of gold ringed her neck while both wrists boasted numerous gold bracelets. She was hunched down before the fire.

A man stood at the rear of the wagon, one foot on the bottom step which led into the vehicle, an elbow braced on the wagon itself. He was small in stature with swarthy dark brown skin. Black boots and black breeches were topped by a dark worn woolen frock coat. He was hatless. His tightly curled raven hair clung to his scalp and he shouted in another language, causing another man, similar to himself, to open the wooden dutch door at the rear of the wagon. Both men peered at me through narrow, suspicious eyes. The man in the wagon said something to the woman which prompted her to reply in the same alien tongue. I began to wonder if I could make myself understood.

I slid down from the horse, grasped the reins in my hand,

and held them tight. The man outside the wagon was eyeing my horse with envy.

"Do you speak English?" I asked the woman.

"What do you want here?" She maintained her position before the fire.

"I am looking for a salve to cure warts."

"No salve."

"Do you have something that will cure them?"

"You have money?" the gypsy woman asked.

"I have money."

"Gold?"

"Gold guineas."

"Three?"

"Two." Actually I had ten, but, fearing robbery, I kept the amount low.

She shook her head. "Three and I will also tell your fortune."

I fumbled in my skirt pocket, frowned, then pretended I had found an extra coin. "Yes, I do have three. But that is all."

She went into the wagon. The man inside came out. Both men sauntered over to inspect my horse at close hand. They stroked his neck then his flanks. I prayed for the woman to return. I felt safer with her present. The way the men were examining my horse was beginning to unsettle me.

A sigh of relief escaped my lips when she emerged with a jar in her hand. The men quickly moved away. She held out the jar for me to see then stretched out her other hand, palm up. I placed the money in her open hand. She thrust the jar toward me and I took it. Inside the jar were yellow-green leaves, thin in texture, slightly hairy, a foot long and two inches wide. I studied them for a moment then looked up at the gypsy woman.

"How do I use it?" I asked.

"Break leaves and stems. Put the juice on the warts."

"Thank you." I put the jar in my skirt's deep pocket.

180

When I pulled my hand out, the gypsy woman grabbed it, and pulled off my glove. She examined my palm with narrowed eyes for several seconds, then looked up at me and shook her head.

"What is the matter?" I asked.

"Go away. Leave Bridee Castle. Death lurks everywhere for foreign intruders. Only death is there for young beautiful women. Your sister is already doomed. I see only death for you at Bridee Castle."

I snatched my hand away, retrieved my glove, then mounted my horse. I kept my back rigid as I rode off. I was still wary of the gypsies and expected to be accosted for the remaining guineas in my pocket. I didn't pick up the horse's pace until we were well out of their sight.

I dismissed the gypsy's prophecy by telling myself that it was the nineteenth century and one's fate couldn't be found in one's palm. Besides, gypsies delighted in telling gloomy fortunes. It was their stock in trade. Her predictions could have been gleaned from the village. The funeral of Samrú was no secret as was the circumstance of her death. The entire village came to my father's funeral and I wouldn't have been surprised if the servants had gossiped about Diana's illness. I considered fortunetelling so much rubbish.

Though the gypsies were no longer a problem, the creeping fog was. I wasn't that familiar with Culloden Moor. I kept telling myself I wasn't lost, but I knew I was. The dense fog had obliterated the sun. I couldn't tell which was east or west without the sun's guidance. I prayed that I wasn't riding in circles. I didn't want to come upon the gypsy wagon again.

A light mist permeated the air to mingle with my tears of frustration as I rode aimlessly for what seemed to be hours. The mist swirled and meandered like unformed ghosts. Dark clouds scudded darker shadows over the moor causing inky forms to dance a mad reel. My mind began to imagine a dramatic rescue by Adrian. He would take me in his arms and place kisses all over my face until his lips found their true desire—my lips. I let the fantasy run on in my brain until reason put a cruel stop to it. Adrian was well on his way to Aberdeen, if not already there.

Despair was about to give way to panic when a solid gray form appeared in the distance. At that moment I didn't care if it were the Loch Ness monster. It was a point to move toward, not the vague fog of nothingness.

After heaving a great sigh, I smiled. Looming before me was the rear of the village church. I wasn't going to languish on the moor overnight after all.

"Whatever are you doing here in this weather, my child?" Reverend Campbell asked as he ushered me into his sitting parlor after hanging my damp cloak in the hall.

"Quite frankly, I got lost in the fog, Reverend."

"I suspect you could use a good hot cup of tea."

"Oh, that would be lovely."

"Go sit by the fire and warm yourself, Heather, while I put the kettle on. Can't have you coming down with a cold, now can we?"

He left before I could reply. I cozied up to the peat fire, enjoying not only its warmth, but the homey smell. The chill slowly oozed out of my bones.

He put the tea tray on the low table between the flanking chairs which faced the fireplace.

I poured.

"Now . . . tell me what brings you out on a day like this. I hope nothing is awry at the castle." He settled back in his chair, cup and saucer in hand.

"No, no. Everything is fine at the castle. When I left, the weather wasn't this foul," I told him.

"Didn't you see the fog in the hollows this morning?"

"Yes."

"Well, lass, you will have to learn when you see fog in the hollows in the Highlands, a dense fog is sure to follow and spread."

"I am learning." The hot tea removed the last vestige of a

chill.

"How is Mrs. Ross holding up? She was quite distraught over your father's death."

"I believe she is getting over it. It is hard to tell with Aunt Clarissa. She has a tendency to be flighty and overemotional in general."

"All these things take time."

He chatted amiably about village matters until I heard his grandfather clock chime the hour of four. I was astonished to learn I had been gone so long. I drained my cup and stood.

"This has been most pleasant, Reverend Campbell. The tea and fire have been a lifesaver. But I really must go. I didn't realize it was so late."

"I will take you in my covered trap. I am afraid the mist has turned to rain. I wouldn't want you to get soaked."

"I don't want to put you to any trouble, Reverend. I don't want you to get lost in the fog too."

He laughed. "My horse knows these roads and lanes better than any human, I daresay. I could fall asleep and he would bring me home safely."

With my horse tethered to the rear of the trap, we made for Bridee Castle.

While the groom tended to the horse, I dashed inside after profusely thanking the reverend. As I ran up the main staircase, Bruce stopped me.

"Where the devil have you been?" he asked grumpily.

"Riding and visiting with Reverend Campbell."

"When you didn't show up for lunch, it set everyone in a turmoil. Clarissa has been on the verge of the vapors. She barely touched her lunch and that is a feat for her."

"I am sorry if I upset everyone." I started to pass him, but he grabbed my arm.

"What is your hurry?" Bruce asked.

"Please let me go. I have to get out of these damp clothes." I smiled and he released me. I continued up the stairs.

"Come down soon and we'll have a game of draughts before we change for dinner," he called after me.

"If I can." I went directly to Diana's bedchamber, knocked briefly, then entered.

"Where have you been?" she said shrilly as she turned from the window.

"Looking for the gypsy woman."

"It took you all day to find her?"

"The fog impeded me."

"Did she have anything?"

I pulled the jar from my pocket and showed it to her. Diana pulled up her nose as though malodorous air had attacked her.

"The juice from the stems and leaves is to be placed on the warts," I explained.

"Let's get on with it. She unbuttoned her high collar and rolled up her sleeve. "What did you have to pay her?"

"Three gold guineas."

"What? That is ridiculous! You should be more frugal with your money, Heather. If you continue to squander it like that, you won't have much inheritance left. You should have bargained with her."

I felt like telling her they were her warts and should be her money, but I remained silent. Her eyes were red and she kept sniffling as though she had been crying. I thought the warts were punishment enough without my adding recriminations.

"Don't stand there like a ninny, Heather. Do as the gypsy told you," Diana ordered. "The neck first."

I took the leaves and stems from the jar. I stood close to her and broke a stem just over the wart on her neck. An orange-red juice flowed out and dripped onto the wart. The same colored juice ran out of the leaves as I snapped small pieces off to cover the other unsightly horny projections.

When I finished, Diana lay on the bed as though willing the warts to vanish.

"Have you been crying, Diana?" I asked.

"No. This blasted weather and castle are giving me a cold.

184

My nose and throat are hot and sore. My scalp tingles all the time."

"I think it is time you became sensible and let me send for the doctor," I advised her.

"I will when the warts go away. Now leave me. I want to rest before dinner."

I gladly left.

It was several days before Adrian returned to Bridee Castle. Sparse snow blanketed the ground. The gray mountains sparkled white in the sun and the days were shorter. The castle stones held the cold and dampness. Fires were stoked to roaring, but did little to chase the chill from the far reaches of the rooms. Diana was no better, no worse. I seldom heard her complain of warts and she resumed the use of a maid, freeing me from that chore. I concluded the gypsy's leaves had done their work. I tried not to think about the gypsy's predictions, but every once in a while they came back to haunt me.

The adoration of Diana by John, Patrick, and Adrian resumed in a heated fashion. Each, in his own way, tried to curry her favor by flattery, bon mots, and general amiability. Neither John nor Patrick's adoration bothered me, but Adrian's attentions were another matter.

Adrian was seated at the piano and alone in the drawing room when I entered. Not wanting to disturb him and — frankly miffed by his gallantries toward Diana — I turned to leave.

"Where are you going, Heather?" he asked without turning around.

"How did you know it was me?"

"The scent of lemon verbena always precedes you when you enter a room. Come. Sit beside me."

He had a way of shattering my resolve and defenses that was incomprehensible to me. I went to sit next to him.

"Is there something wrong with Diana?" he asked, his hands softly playing a Mozart opus.

"I should think you would know better than I." My tone was clipped.

"You are her sister."

"You see more of her than I do."

"Ah! Do I detect a note of jealousy in your voice?"

"Why should I be jealous of Diana?"

"My father? He still cuts a handsome figure."

"Don't be ridiculous, Adrian," I said shortly.

"Then Patrick?"

"I gave up on Patrick a long time ago."

"Me?"

I hesitated, which was a mistake. My silence revealed too much.

"I see. Do you fancy me, Heather?"

"You seem to be in a conceited mood."

"You didn't answer my question."

"I don't think it requires an answer. As you once told me, the difference in our ages is insurmountable."

"Do you really think so?" A smile hovered about his lips as he continued to play.

"You are teasing me, aren't you? Playing with me like an overfed cat would a mouse. Frankly, I prefer Bruce's company to yours. He is younger and closer to my age. We are far more compatible than you and I could ever be."

"I think you are fibbing, Heather MacBride."

"I will not sit here and be insulted by you, Adrian Ross." I started to rise, but his hand pushed my shoulder down.

"Sit," he ordered, his voice gentle. "Your sister is clever at masking her true feelings. I have a suspicion she is not well and is trying to hide the fact. Am I correct?"

"She has a cold."

"Shouldn't she see a doctor?"

"I have tried to make her, but, as you must know, she does as she pleases," I answered.

186

"I have noticed she has altered since coming here."

"I haven't noticed anything." I wondered if he had seen one of her warts.

"Her eyes look feverish and she has a tendency to clutch at her throat."

"The cold has made her eyes red and her throat sore."

"A cold would have nothing to do with her hair."

"Her hair? What about her hair?"

"It is no longer silky. It is getting coarse. Haven't you noticed?"

"Not really." I made a mental note to study Diana more closely.

"I think you should use all your persuasive powers to get her to see a doctor."

"I think you might have more influence with her than me. She seems to favor your opinions. She never did listen to me."

"Well, what is this tête-à-tête all about?" asked Diana as she swept into the room, Patrick in tow.

"We were discussing the finer points of Mozart," Adrian replied.

"How dull," Diana said, flouncing herself on the settee. "Patrick, do be a dear and fetch me a small sherry."

He did as he was told.

"How is your cold, Diana?" Adrian asked.

"Being a nuisance. I am sure when I get to the south of France it will vanish. I don't see how anyone survives in these sunless Highlands."

"You came to the Highlands at a poor time. In the spring and early summer, the Highlands are quite bonnie," Adrian said.

"Shouldn't you be dressing for dinner, Heather?" Diana asked.

"I am dressed."

"Don't tell me you are going to wear that mourning rag again to dinner. It is positively depressing."

"You bought it for me," I countered.

187

"You should have told me you were going to live in it," Diana said.

"I was under the impression one was expected to mourn the loss of a loved one for more than a day."

"Are you insinuating I didn't love Father?"

"Think what you will, Diana."

"Why, you little brat. You still live in a world of children. You will never mature and enter the world of adults. You have no conception of love or what it is about. Love is felt in the heart, not by what one wears. No wonder Father found you odd. You are a superficial, shallow little brat," Diana spewed. "Father would have despised having one of his daughters dragging herself around in black clothes. I guess you never really knew him, Heather. He wanted his daughters to be lively and pretty."

Instinct wanted me to snap back at her defensively. I thought of many insults, the first one being "wart face." But if I retaliated, I would only be proving I was still a child. I was livid with bottled-up rage until Adrian put his hand on my shoulder. His sympathetic strength flowed into me. I smiled. When I saw the frustration on Diana's face, I knew I had won without saying a word.

As I lay in bed that night, I tried to concentrate on Adrian's comforting gesture at the piano, but my mind was filled with the dire omens of the gypsy's fortunetelling. I left my bed, went to the window, and stared vacantly into the night. My vision wandered to the keep and I became riveted, staring in awe.

Chapter Eleven

The light moved up the stairwell inside until it reached the top of the keep. The glow hovered there for some time before it began its descent. Was I the only one seeing this phantom light? Why hadn't anyone else mentioned it? Surely there were other rooms in the castle that had a clear view of the keep. I watched for a while longer. When the keep remained dark for some time, I went back to bed. I fell asleep trying to remember what it was I had found odd about the top floor when I first entered that chamber of the keep.

"Have you ever seen a light in the keep at night, Jean?" I asked the next morning as she hooked the back of my mourning frock.

"Aye, miss. Several of us have seen it."

"Do you know who is going up to the keep in the middle of the night?"

"Aye, miss."

"Who is it then?"

"It is Lady Anne's ghost looking for the body of the young lass she had slain."

"Oh, really, Jean. Surely you don't believe that. Hasn't someone gone to investigate the light?"

She blanched. "No, miss. No one dare lest the ghost, see-

189

ing a living being, kill again thinking the young lass has come to life."

"Ghosts, if they do exist, don't kill people, Jean."

"Lady Anne does. The woman you brought with you from India felt the murderous knife of Lady Anne. No one has come and said it outright, but all the servants know the Indian lady invaded Lady Anne's private domain and paid for it with her life."

"I was there along with Miss Ross and nothing has happened to either of us."

Jean shrugged. "She was probably in another part of the castle when you were there and doesn't know about your visit."

I saw it was futile to pursue questioning Jean. Her mind was set. Nothing would dissuade her.

After a solitary breakfast—Adrian had eaten and left while the others hadn't come down yet—I went back upstairs to see how Diana was faring. Bitter arguments and spiteful words could not dispel the fact she was my sister. I did have a certain amount of feeling for her.

Diana was still abed, pillows fluffed up behind her, a breakfast tray on top of the covers over her lap, and a lacy shawl draped over her shoulders. I sat down in one of the comfortable chairs near the fireplace.

"Is your cold any better?" I asked.

"No, it is getting worse," she answered in a raspy voice.

"I will ride and fetch the doctor myself."

"No, you won't."

"Haven't the warts disappeared?"

"They are becoming more numerous."

"Didn't the leaves I got from the gypsy help?"

"For a while. You will have to get more."

"If the gypsies are still there." I didn't relish the notion of another encounter with the gypsies. "Perhaps you could come with me, Diana. She might have a more suitable remedy if she actually saw the warts. They may be of a special type."

Diana looked at me horrified. "Show a stranger the warts? You must be out of your mind, Heather."

"I think it would be to your advantage." I noticed she winced as she shifted her position in the bed. "What is the matter?"

"My legs are cramped. Take this tray away so I can move around."

I rose, took the tray, then put it on the table beside the bed. I noticed she hadn't touched any of the food. Only her teacup was empty. "You didn't eat anything, Diana."

"I am not hungry." She pulled her legs up and, with her hands under the covers, massaged them.

"If you still have the warts, why didn't you call me to help you dress?"

"I couldn't tolerate getting up so early. Besides, you are slow. Under the threat of being dismissed and a poor notice, I have compelled my maid to secrecy. If she mentions the warts to anyone, she will find herself in the road without a hope of finding another position."

"I will take your tray downstairs."

"Be quick about it. I want you to search out the gypsy woman immediately. Tomorrow go into Inverness. See if the chemist has a powder for colds."

"Why should I go all the way into Inverness when there is a chemist in the village?" I asked.

"The villagers gossip too much. In Inverness they won't take any notice. And do change your attire. You look like the harbinger of death. Every time I look at you I get chills."

I picked up the tray and left. I met Mrs. Burns in the corridor. She took the tray and shook her head.

"Your sister doesn't eat enough at breakfast to keep a bird alive," she said. "Such a waste."

"Hasn't she been eating her breakfast, Mrs. Burns?"

"She usually drinks the tea and leaves everything else. Once in a while I will find a piece of toast that has been nibbled at. I think she makes up for it at lunch and dinner, though."

191

"I am going for a ride, Mrs. Burns, if anyone is looking for me. I will be back before lunch."

She nodded then headed for the staircase. I went to my bedchamber where I changed into warm, dark riding clothes. Though the weather was clear, the air was bitterly cold.

I followed what I thought was the same route I had taken to the gypsy camp. Visibility had been so poor that day, I couldn't be sure I was on the right course, especially when there was nothing but the empty moor in all directions. When I came upon the remains of a long dead campfire, I knew the gypsies had gone. I searched the area for little more than an hour to no avail. Even though I knew Diana would be disappointed, I was relieved. The way those gypsy men had eyed my horse, I wouldn't have been surprised if they would try to steal it from me. I was back at the castle well before lunch. Adrian was dismounting as I entered the stableyard. He waited for me.

"Out riding in this weather?" He smiled and pulled my arm through his as we headed for the house.

"I needed the exercise. I thought the horse could use some too," I said.

"Didn't you find it a bit chilly for riding?"

"I am dressed warmly. I see the cold weather hasn't stopped you."

"I am used to it. You have never spent a winter here. I don't imagine it gets this cold in India."

"I find this air refreshing." When we reached the foyer, he released my arm.

"I will see you at lunch," Adrian said.

I nodded and went upstairs, dreading to give Diana the bad news. When I entered Diana's room, she was studying herself in the mirror atop her dressing table. She spied my reflection.

"Did you get it?" she asked without turning around.

"The gypsies were gone."

"Did you make an effort to find them?"

192

"Of course I did. I found their old cook fire. It had been cold for some time."

"They probably moved to another spot. Did you search for them, Heather?"

"I covered the larger part of the moor and they were nowhere to be seen."

"I don't think you searched hard enough," Diana declared.

"I couldn't cover the entire Scottish Highlands. They have gone. Probably went south before winter truly sets in."

"Don't forget to go to Inverness tomorrow." Diana's tone was one of dismissal.

As I padded toward my bedchamber, I couldn't help but think Diana didn't believe one word I said about the gypsies. Anger rose in me. The only fibs I ever told were *for* her, not *to* her.

A mood of defiance consumed me. I thumbed through my wardrobe to find a frock other than the black mourning dress. I selected an earthy green woolen frock with a lace collar and cuffs. Sedate, but with more color than the plain black one.

Everyone was at lunch, including Diana. Her pale face emphasized the overuse of rouge on her cheeks and lips. As we ate I watched her closely, but not close enough to be obvious. Her hair had indeed become coarse and without its normal luster. I also noticed deep ridges on her fingernails, like those of an elderly woman. She had always been proud of her tapered fingers and smooth, carefully manicured nails. Besides being ridged, her nails were chipped and broken, leaving serrated edges. Diana appeared to be indifferent to the sad state of her hands as she frequently gestured with them as she talked.

She was always garrulous and could be amusing at times. Today her incessant talking seemed to be spurred on by a nervousness.

She picked at her food, pushing it around her plate as though she wasn't quite sure where it should go. All in all, less than a forkful of food ever reached her stomach. Finally she let her fork drop on the plate and she pushed the plate away from her.

"Is that all you are going to eat, Diana?" Aunt Clarissa asked.

"I am not hungry."

Aunt Clarissa reached over and took her plate. "We can't have good food going to waste." She consumed every morsel on the plate.

Now I knew why Mrs. Burns assumed Diana ate well at lunch and dinner. Aunt Clarissa was eating Diana's food and sending an empty plate back to the kitchen.

"I have to go into Inverness tomorrow. Does anyone want anything?" I asked.

"I need some needlepoint yarn," said Jane.

"I would like a box of chocolates," Aunt Clarissa said.

"Why don't you come with me, Jane? You could pick out the colors you need," I suggested.

"I will give you some samples of the colors I need, Heather. I am not up to traveling in this weather."

"I will take you into Inverness, Heather," Adrian said. "It isn't proper for a young lady to be traveling alone to Inverness."

Diana tossed me a glance of disapproval.

"I am perfectly capable of taking care of myself, Adrian. Thank you just the same."

"It is all settled. I am taking you," Adrian said firmly.

"Heather always traveled about India alone, didn't she, Patrick?" Diana asked. He nodded absently. "There is no need for you to chaperon her, Adrian," my sister concluded imperiously.

"I need a few things in Inverness myself." Though he had a smile on his handsome face, his jaw was set. The more anyone tried to oppose him, the more determined he would become.

At supper that night, I observed Diana repeat her display at lunch, leaving her food for Aunt Clarissa to eat.

* * *

Adrian had the carriage waiting for me shortly before midmorning. I was looking forward to being alone with him.

"Diana doesn't look well," he said as we left the driveway and turned onto the road.

"I know. She doesn't seem to be eating."

"She has lost a considerable amount of weight. Have you talked to her about it, Heather?"

"When I do she becomes evasive. If she doesn't improve in the next two weeks, I am going to have the doctor look at her whether she likes it or not," I declared.

"I think that is a good idea." A comfortable silence fell before he spoke again. "I thought we could have lunch after our shopping is completed. A small acting troupe is going to do Shakespeare's *Romeo and Juliet* this afternoon. I think both of us could use some amusement. Would you like that?"

"Very much."

"Aside from my sister's yarn and Clarissa's chocolates, what do you need in Inverness?" Adrian asked.

"Some powder or elixir for a cold."

"I told you not to ride when the weather is chilling. You don't sound as if you have a cold. Preventative medicine?"

"I am fine. The medicine is for Diana."

"Perhaps the cold has affected her appetite."

"That is why I want to wait a couple of weeks before getting the doctor. Who would you suggest I get to see her?"

"Dr. Robert Drummond is a good man. You must remember him. He was the physician who examined your Indian lady."

My eyes misted as I thought of the recent funerals at Bridee Castle, especially my father's.

"I am sorry if I brought up sad memories," Adrian said, casting a sidelong glance at me.

I blinked back the barely formed tears. "I have tried to

bury the sadness I feel. Unfortunately, it comes to the surface every now and then when I least expect it."

"Time will heal the wounds, Heather. I suspect your concern over your sister tends to make you defensive."

"Perhaps."

"Have you or your sister come to any decisions regarding the demesne?"

"Diana hasn't been up to discussing it."

"I thought she was determined to go to the south of France. Has that been cancelled?"

"I believe it is postponed for a while."

"She should go immediately. The winter will only exacerbate her condition."

"I think we should decide about Bridee Castle first."

"Sell it and leave for warmer climes."

"The land too?" I asked.

"Everything. I would be interested in purchasing the land if the price isn't too steep."

"The castle too?"

"The castle is too old and in need of repairs. Can you imagine yourself rambling around that vast place? The unused rooms will rot without proper attention. A sizable amount of your fortune would go to pay for repairs and a staff large enough to maintain it. I should think you could find better things to do with your money. The sooner you and Diana decide, the better."

"You sound anxious to be rid of us."

He turned to me and smiled. "I was thinking of your welfare, not getting rid of you."

"I will speak to Diana."

Reaching Inverness we stabled the horse and carriage then went our separate ways to shop, promising to meet at the tea garden at noon.

I purchased cold powders, horehound drops, patented liquid cold remedies, and whatever else the chemist recommended. After the apothecary's, I bought a large box of chocolates and the crewel yarn Jane wanted. As noontime approached, I went to the tea garden. Adrian was already there.

"Did you get everything you came for?" he asked, rising to come and hold my chair.

"Yes. And you?"

"I left my parcels at the hotel. We will leave yours there also while we go to the theater."

Lunch consisted of hot barley soup, cold beef sandwiches, and tea. The jam tarts were topped with clotted cream and were delicious.

I was embarrassed when the play was over and the darkened theater was suddenly flooded with the light of many oil lamps. My cheeks were tear stained.

Once outside, Adrian put his arm around my shoulders and said, "I had hoped to cheer you up. Instead the play has brought tears to your eyes."

"The tears are of a different nature. The play distracted my own sorrows. I enjoyed it, truly. I thank you. It was a pleasant change."

On the way home we talked about the play and other Shakespearean efforts in the theater. Aside from the day I spent in Adrian's house, it was one of my happiest days in the Highlands.

The lowering sun was throwing a pink glow over the hilly land as we returned to Bridee Castle. Aunt Clarissa and Jane were in the drawing room. Aunt Clarissa was delighted with the chocolates and began to sample a few immediately. Jane was thrilled and surprised by the amount of crewel yarn I had purchased for her. She said she would reimburse me after dinner. Aunt Clarissa made no mention of money, not that I cared.

I rushed up the stairs to Diana's room with the parcel of various remedies. I was surprised to find her in bed, especially when the dinner hour was so near. One by one I placed the medicines on the table by her bed. She looked at them languidly.

"Is that all of them?" she asked.

197

"I purchased everything the chemist recommended."

"It took you long enough. I am beginning to think you don't really care about my health."

"Nonsense."

"Where have you been all day?"

"We shopped in the morning, had lunch, then went to see a play," I informed her.

"You mean to tell me you went gadding about having a merry old time while I lay here ill beyond words?"

"I didn't think a few hours would make a difference."

"Whenever you think, Heather, it is always to someone else's detriment. Fetch me a glass of water. I will try the powders first."

After getting the water and dissolving the powders in it, I studied Diana while she drank it. Her sallow skin was stretched over her face like fragile parchment. Hollows under her cheekbones were prominent, giving her an almost cadaverous appearance. She was not playing the histrionic heroine this time. She was ill and it worried me.

She grimaced as she handed me the empty glass. "That is vile."

"We should talk, Diana."

"About what?"

"Your leaving here and going to the south of France immediately."

"France can wait. I am unfit for traveling long distances."

"Then let us sell Bridee Castle and go to Torbay. I hear the winters are softer there and there wouldn't be that much traveling involved," I suggested.

"I will think about it. At least here Patrick and John come to visit me. Although I could do without Patrick's constant babbling about Father."

"Oh? What does he say about our father?"

"He doesn't *say* much. Mostly questions."

"Questions about what?"

"I don't remember. Don't badger me, Heather."

"I should have thought Patrick would know as much

about Father as we do."

"I could do without Aunt Clarissa's visits. She babbles on until I have to plead a headache to get rid of her. Do tell her not to disturb me, Heather. Do you think you can manage that chore within a reasonable amount of time?"

"I will try. I don't want to hurt her feelings."

"Which is more important? Her feelings or my health?"

"I will do my best. In the meantime, I do wish you would think about leaving here or letting me get a doctor for you."

"I told you to forget about a doctor. Why the sudden urgency about leaving here? You were never enthusiastic about leaving Bridee Castle."

"I am only thinking about your welfare, Diana."

She stared at me through narrowed eyes. "What are you plotting, Heather?"

"Nothing."

"I don't like the way you have changed your mind about leaving. Are you afraid Adrian will turn all his attentions to me when I am better? I don't believe you want to get away from here because of my health."

"Don't be ridiculous, Diana."

"I will leave Bridee Castle when I am ready. You are not going to push me out of here, Heather."

"Adrian also believes we should leave for our own welfare."

"Liar!"

I gave a short sigh of exasperation. Diana could be trying on one's mental faculties and emotions. I excused her on the basis of her illness. "Will you be coming down for dinner?"

"No. I told Mrs. Burns to have a tray sent to me."

"I will help you dress if you want."

"My legs are cramped. They seem to get worse if I walk or sit for any length of time. I will stay here for tonight so I can be up and about tomorrow."

"Is there anything I can do for you, Diana?"

"If there is anything else, I will let you know. Leave now. I find you tiresome and tedious."

Her eyes closed and I tiptoed out. The corridor was uncommonly eerie during the twilight hours before lamps and candles were lighted. An indefinite, but overpowering sensation of doom invaded me. Was it due to the gypsy's prediction? Or was it because Samrú and Father were gone and now Diana looked deathly ill? Were those of us from India caught in a fatal web? I pushed the silly notion from my mind. Nothing was wrong with either Patrick or me.

As my hand rested on the doorknob of my bedchamber, I paused. Sobs and moans of desperation were coming from within. I quickly turned the knob and pushed the door open. Jean was sitting on the edge of my bed, her hands over her face while she cried her heart out. I went to her and grabbed her wrists, pulling her hands from her face.

"Jean, what is it? Why are you crying?"

When she looked at me with sad eyes, I released her wrists. She waved an arm about the room. My gaze followed that gesture to behold a bedchamber that had been torn apart by a zealous searcher. I dashed to my adjoining sitting parlor to find that it, too, had been searched as though in desperation. No furniture had been overturned, but all the drawers had been pulled out and their contents scattered about. Books, ledgers, folders, notebooks, and sundry articles had been removed from my father's trunk and carelessly tossed to the floor.

Who had invaded my privacy? More importantly, why? What was he or she looking for?

Chapter Twelve

Stunned, several minutes passed before I regained my composure. I went back to the bedchamber and consoled Jean.

"Did you see anyone in here?" I asked when her weeping was reduced to a sob or two.

"Nay, miss. The rooms were like this when I came in to get your toilette ready." She sniffed. "I'll have it all set to right no matter how long it takes."

"Don't worry about it, Jean. You tend to the bedchamber. Let me know if anything is missing. I will start putting the sitting parlor to rights tomorrow."

"I'll do it, miss."

"I am in a better position to know what might be missing in there, especially the articles in my father's trunk. I would appreciate your tending to the bedchamber only."

"Aye, miss."

I washed and got ready for dinner.

"My rooms have been searched and the culprit was quite slovenly about it. The rooms are in total disarray," I announced to everyone as I took a seat in the drawing room. Shock registered on everyone's face except Adrian's. He frowned.

"Who did it?" Patrick asked.

"I have no idea," I answered.

"Was anything missing?" Bruce asked.

"I don't know. My maid is doing my bedchamber now. I

will restore order to the sitting parlor tomorrow."

"Oh, dear me." Aunt Clarissa fanned herself with her handkerchief. "We have a thief in the house. You must do something, John."

"We had better wait and see what is missing before calling the authorities," John said.

"Do you have anything someone would want, Heather?" Adrian asked.

"Not to my knowledge. I never did possess any fabulous jewels." I took comfort in the fact the intruder couldn't have been Adrian. He had been with me all day.

We continued to discuss the villainy, discussing various members of the staff and the possibility of a stranger rummaging through the house. Before we went into the dining room, John spoke to Jeffrey and Mrs. Burns, apprising them of the dastardly deed. He instructed them to have the entire castle searched for any sign of forcible entry.

"Isn't Diana coming down to dinner?" Patrick asked as we started across the foyer.

"No," I told him. "She wants to rest in order to give the cold medicine I bought for her a chance to work."

"I see," he said despondently.

After breakfast, I went back upstairs to tackle the mess in my parlor. Aunt Clarissa was bustling down the corridor toward Diana's bedchamber. I thought this would be a good time to speak to her regarding Diana's wishes. I didn't look forward to the task and hoped I could do it without hurting her feelings.

"Aunt Clarissa, may I speak with you a moment?"

"Is it important, my dear? I am on my way to see Diana. Poor dear. She is suffering so. I have new issues of *The Ladies' Companion* and *The Lady's Pictorial*. I thought they might take her mind off her ailments."

"That is very thoughtful of you, Aunt Clarissa. I will take them to her."

"But I wanted to see her." She pouted like a thwarted child.

"When she gets better, Aunt Clarissa. I spoke with her earlier and she prefers not to see anyone until she is better."

"She sees Patrick Danton and John," she said with a trace of indignation.

"Patrick is an old friend and soothes her with talk of India. As for John, I think he should curtail his visits. You will speak to him, won't you, Aunt Clarissa?" Finding an excuse for Patrick was easy, not so for my aunt's errant husband. If Diana didn't want to be bothered with Aunt Clarissa, she would have to sacrifice the visits of John Ross.

"Well . . . if you insist. Tell Diana I was asking for her." She handed me the magazines.

"I will."

Diana's breakfast tray was on the table next to her bed, the food still on the plate, the tea half-drunk. She appeared to be sleeping, but her head turned and her eyes fluttered open as I approached the bed.

"What do you want, Heather?" Her voice was raspy. She looked terrible. Dark circles under her eyes made her countenance moribund. With her facial features becoming more skeletal and her hair coarser and unkempt, she was barely recognizable.

"Aunt Clarissa sent some magazines for you," I said.

"Put them on the bureau or wherever you can find room, then leave. I need some rest."

She rolled on her side, presenting her back to me. I shrugged, put the magazines down, and left. I had too much to do without wasting time trying to make pleasant conversation with Diana.

After Jean assured me nothing was missing from the bedchamber, I went into my sitting parlor. My hands went to my hips as I stood there trying to decide what to tackle first. I started with the area around the escritoire. I picked up everything from the floor and piled it on the small writing desk. I went through each piece before neatly putting the papers and articles back in their proper place.

I followed the same routine with the bookcase. I purposely left my father's trunk until last. I wanted to peruse each piece thoroughly. With the exception of the trunk, the room was back to normal. I washed and went down to lunch.

Aunt Clarissa, John, and Adrian were absent. Jane informed me that my aunt and John went to Inverness. She had no idea where Adrian was.

"Do you know why Diana refuses to see me, Heather?" Patrick asked.

"I wasn't aware she had," I said.

"Her maid refuses to let me in, always saying her mistress is asleep and doesn't want to be disturbed. I usually visit with Diana from midmorning until noon. Has she taken a turn for the worse?"

"I hope so," Bruce grumbled.

"Really, Bruce," Jane chastised, then turned to me. "He didn't mean that, Heather."

"I certainly did," Bruce insisted. "I don't appreciate your apologizing for me, Jane. I don't like your sister, Heather. This cold of hers is probably retribution for the shabby way she has treated me. I am a very vindictive human being." He smiled boyishly at me.

"I suppose we all have our moments when we desire some sort of vengeance," I said.

"Have you found anything missing, Heather?" Jane asked.

"Not yet. I still have to sort out my father's trunk. It will be difficult to know if anything is missing from it though. I haven't looked through it since the day we arrived at Bridee Castle."

"What is in it?" Bruce asked.

"From what is strewn about the floor, mostly books, papers, and maps. I will know better when I go through all of it."

"Maps?" Patrick asked.

"Yes, I think they are maps where various battles have taken place. I am not sure. My glance was cursory at best."

"Perhaps I could see them when you have it all in order. If they are battle maps, I may learn something from them. Your father was an expert strategist," Patrick said.

"When are you going back to India?" Bruce asked.

"Soon," was Patrick's laconic reply.

The two men glared at each other, their animosity obvious. Jane looked distraught and poked at her smoked ham. I was beginning to wonder myself about Patrick's prolonged visit. At first I thought it was because he pined for Diana and hoped to persuade her to return to India with him. Now I wasn't so sure. What could he possibly be after at Bridee Castle? He hardly left the place.

After lunch I went back to the chore of cleaning up. I quickly scanned the maps and put them aside in a pile for Patrick. I found nothing of importance in them. Stacks of paper, tied with twine, made several piles. Each frontpiece was numbered. I picked up the stack marked "One." After reading several paragraphs, I realized these were the papers containing the rough drafts of my father's memoirs. I put all but number one back in the trunk in numerical order. I would read the first bundle later.

His books were mostly military history and went back into the trunk. I put Shakespearean dramas side, intending to read *Romeo and Juliet*. I was surprised to find our old Jumble book containing the fairy tales, legends, and poems Diana and I had read as children. I really considered it my book as Diana seldom read it even though it was bought for both of us. I put it on top of the Shakespeare.

The days sped by as I became engrossed in my father's memoirs. Certain passages were difficult to decipher due to his cramped handwriting.

With my mind occupied, I forgot about Diana for a couple of days. When a dreadful dream caused me to think about her, I was consumed with guilt. Forgetting breakfast, I dressed in a hurry, then practically ran down the corridor to my sister's bedchamber. A maid was sitting in a chair outside her door. She rose when I put my hand on the knob. Her hand swung out to clutch the doorjamb across from her, barring my way.

"Remove your arm immediately," I ordered, fire in my eyes.

"Sorry, Miss MacBride. Your sister said to admit no one,

205

not even you," the maid said, her arm remaining stationary.

"Remove your arm or I shall see to it you no longer work here. I am going in there and no one is going to stop me." I reached out, pulled her arm out of the way, and entered my sister's bedchamber.

I rushed over to the bed with the intention of offering profuse apologies. Instead I gasped.

Diana was lying in a semicomatose state, her breathing labored and her skin a bluish white. Her cheeks were completely sunken, emphasizing the now black circles under her watery blue eyes. I thought that she looked terrible the last time I saw her, but now she seemed as though she were embalmed. When she looked at me, her eyes were vacant, hollow as though all thought had fled her brain. She lifted her skeletal hand indicating for me to come closer. I lowered my head to her lips. Her voice was barely audible.

"Help me," she managed to murmur.

I nodded. I couldn't speak, for my throat seemed to be paralyzed. I ran out of the room, down the stairs, and caught Mrs. Burns as she was heading for the kitchen.

"Mrs. Burns," I called. "Have one of the lads ride posthaste to Inverness and fetch Dr. Drummond immediately. Have him tell the doctor it is an emergency. Hurry." The tenor of my voice caused those eating breakfast to come out of the dining room.

"What is the matter, Heather? You are shaking," said Adrian, coming up to me.

"It is Diana. I think she is dying." The realization of my words caused tears to flow from my eyes. Jane came and put her arm around me.

"Is there anything I can do?" she asked.

"Could you fix me a breakfast tray with lots of hot tea? I am going to sit with Diana until the doctor comes. Perhaps I can get her to eat something," I said, wiping my eyes with the back of my hands.

"Of course." Jane went to fill my request.

"I will go upstairs and tell Clarissa," said John, then headed for the staircase.

Bruce put his hand on my arm. "I am sorry for what I said at the table the other day, Heather. I thought she had a cold, nothing serious."

"What state is she in?" Adrian asked.

"She hardly has any flesh on her. She is cold to the touch and her skin has an inhuman pallor. Her breathing is like a death rattle. I must go to her now. You will make sure the doctor comes up the minute he arrives," I said.

"I will see to it personally." Adrian patted my shoulder. "Go ahead. I will wait here for the doctor."

Back in Diana's room, I pulled a chair up to the side of her bed, held her hand, and tried to keep the guilt from gnawing at my bones. I should have taken her illness more seriously. I should have visited her morning and night. I should have made sure she ate some food. I should have sent for the doctor sooner. I should have . . . I should have . . .

Jane came in with a tray of porridge, rashers, eggs, and toast. She had brought extra cups along with a large pot of tea. When she saw Diana her hands began to shake. I took the tray from her lest she drop it.

"Would you like some toast, Diana? Some tea? It is freshly brewed," I said, pouring a cup and starting to bring it to her lips.

She shook her head wearily.

"You must have something, Diana. Please."

Her head turned away.

I started to eat even though my heart wasn't in it. Every now and then I tried to get Diana to have a bite of food. My attempts were futile.

"How did she get in this state?" Jane asked, her hazel eyes registering shock and horror.

"I don't know. She constantly refused to see a doctor, no matter how I insisted. From what I can gather, that maid kept everyone out. She should have told one of us about Diana's deplorable state. The girl is a ninny. I am on the verge of dismissing her."

"Don't be too hard on the lass. Gossip from the staff portrays her as more afraid of Diana than anyone else and she did exactly as she was bid. You have to admit, Heather, Diana could be quite intimidating." Suddenly Jane covered her mouth with her hand and looked at Diana. "I shouldn't have said that with poor Diana lying there. Whatever will she think?"

"At this point, I don't think she cares. She seems to be in some sort of stupor. I wish the doctor would come," I said, voicing my thoughts aloud.

"Does she have a fever? I could get some cold cloths for her head," Jane offered.

I reached out and put my hand on Diana's forehead. "She is quite cool. Almost abnormally cool."

Jane sat with me as I finished my breakfast. "Shall I take the tray away?" she asked.

"Let the maid do it. Sit with me a while."

Hours passed before the tread of footsteps echoed down the corridor. When the knock sounded at the door, I jumped to my feet and bade the visitor to come in. The door opened and Dr. Drummond marched in. I could see Adrian in the doorway. He didn't enter, but quietly closed the door behind the doctor.

"What seems to be the problem?" Dr. Drummond asked, coming to the bed.

"My sister Diana," I told him, stepping away from the bed so he could take my place.

He looked down at her and frowned. He took his stethoscope from his black bag, put it to his ears, then opened the top of Diana's nightdress. The cold metal on her skin seemed to have no effect on her. He listened for a while, then felt her pulse. Finished, he stepped back and stroked his chin. He picked up her hand again and examined her fingernails. He studied her for a moment longer then turned to me.

"We must get her to a hospital immediately," he declared.

"What is wrong with her?" I asked.

He took me aside and said, "Without certain tests I can't be sure, you understand, but she has the classic symptoms of arsenic poisoning."

"Arsenic!" I gasped aloud, causing Jane to cast inquiring

eyes my way.

"I can't be sure," Dr. Drummond said. "Tell me when she first started feeling poorly and what her symptoms were."

I told him everything I could remember, in great detail.

He looked over at Diana and nodded. "You had best prepare her for traveling. Frankly, I think she is too far gone, but we should make every effort."

"She won't die, will she?" I asked, my voice flooded with anxiety.

"Miracles have been known to happen. I will wait downstairs while you ready her. Be quick. Every minute counts."

When he opened the door, Aunt Clarissa came bustling in. "Oh, dear me. How sick is our poor Diana?" she asked, going to the bed. She started to waver when she saw Diana. Jane put a staying arm around her and led her to a chair. "How did she get so ill so quickly? What did the doctor say, Heather?"

"He isn't sure. He wants her in the hospital right away." I went to the bed and pulled down the covers. The fetid odor of an unwashed body curled into my nostrils. I couldn't let my sister go anywhere like that. She would never forgive me. "Jane, will you please have hot water sent up and lots of towels."

"Of course." She left.

I went into the large wardrobe room Diana had renovated to hold all her frocks and gowns. I plucked clean underthings from the bureau drawers, then thumbed through her numerous day frocks for the warmest and prettiest garment. If she had to appear in public, I knew she would want to look her best. A bonnet would hide her straggled hair and, with cosmetics, I could cover most of her deteriorated complexion. When I returned to the bedchamber, Jane had returned with the hot water and towels.

"Jane would you mind helping me wash her. Two of us can do it much faster. I want to get her to the hospital quickly."

"I will do anything to help, Heather."

"I can't bear to look at the poor child. I am going downstairs," Aunt Clarissa declared, then left the room, her shoulders sagging.

Jane and I removed Diana's nightdress. If my task hadn't been so urgent, I would have sat down and cried. Her body was wasted, bearing little resemblance to that of a twenty-one-year-old woman. I could see Jane was repulsed, but she took a deep breath and helped me wash the fragile body of my sister.

"Something is wrong, Heather," Jane said as we dried the inert body.

I looked at Diana closely. "She is still breathing. Finish drying her while I get her clothes." I went into the wardrobe and gathered all the things I had laid out and brought them into the bedchamber.

We started to dress her, her skin cold and clammy to the touch. Diana made no effort to help us. One of us had to hold her in a sitting position while the other pulled her clothes over her head.

"We will have to get a man to carry her downstairs," said Jane after we finished dressing her. "Shall I go down and fetch someone?"

"In a minute. I want you to hold her while I fix her hair and put her bonnet on," I said.

As I tied the ribbon under her chin, Diana went totally limp. Jane and I looked at each other in astonishment and fear. While Jane eased her down on the bed, I dashed for the hand mirror on Diana's dressing table. I brought it back to the bed and held it to Diana's nose and mouth. Nothing. No mist of breath on the mirror.

"I think you should have the doctor come back up, Jane," I said, my voice pregnant with weary sorrow.

Jane nodded and departed.

I knew Diana was dead before Dr. Drummond made his pronouncement.

"I would like to take her to Inverness where I have the means to confirm arsenic poisoning. I assume I have your permission," Dr. Drummond said.

"Of course you have it."

"Was your sister in the habit of taking small doses of

arsenic?"

"No, I am sure she didn't. Besides, why would she do that?" I asked.

"Small doses of arsenic are said to be an agent for clearing the skin of annoying blemishes or rashes," he informed me.

"Her complexion has been clear since childhood. She would have no reason to use it."

"If my suspicions are confirmed, I will have to turn the matter over to Inspector Andrews. I am sure you can see why, Miss MacBride. One unsolved murder has already taken place at Bridee Castle. If it turns out your sister was methodically being fed arsenic without her knowledge, then serious mischief is afoot here."

I must have paled, for Dr. Drummond came to my side, put his arm about my shoulders, and began to lead me from the room. I halted.

"I will stay here until they come for her." I was resolute.

"It won't help your sister. I really don't think you should be left alone. I certainly don't want another patient on my hands."

"I am all right. I insist on staying here."

He shrugged. "As you wish."

I sat next to her bed, alone in the room except for Diana's dead and wasted body. I took her cold lifeless hand and held it. So many thoughts vied for attention in my head. I wished we had been closer as sisters. Given Diana's nature, though, I doubt if it would have been possible. Perhaps the most dominant words in my mind were the gypsy's warnings: . . . *Only death for you at Bridee Castle*. My grasp on reality began to waver. Fear, guilt, and sorrow were building so furiously within, that when the door opened I dropped Diana's hand and jumped up from the chair.

"I didn't mean to frighten you, Heather," Adrian said. He carried a silver salver with two glasses and the brandy bottle. "Dr. Drummond has informed us of Diana's passing. When he said you were alone up here, I thought a bit of brandy and some company would be good for you." He placed the tray on the small round table in front of the window and motioned for me to take a seat opposite him at the table. He poured brandy into the glasses and handed me one. When I shook my head, he said, "Take it. You will be surprised how it will help make things more bearable for you."

I relented, my will having deserted me. After a few sips, I told Adrian about the gypsy's warnings.

"You don't believe that, do you?" he asked.

"I don't know what to believe, especially now. Did Dr. Drummond tell you he thinks arsenic, given over a period of time, is the cause of Diana's death?"

He looked toward the bed, his eyes scanning the inert form of my sister. "He didn't mention it. He did mention taking the body to Inverness for tests."

I drained the brandy from my glass and found it soothing. When Adrian saw my empty glass, he refilled it.

"You shouldn't be sitting here, Heather," he said. "It is too morbid. You will only succeed in distressing yourself further."

"I can't leave her all alone."

"Heather, she is gone. She doesn't know you are here."

"I feel so guilty . . . so guilty." I sipped the brandy. I wanted to cry, but it seemed so many deaths had drained me of tears. "I should have had the doctor see her sooner in spite of her objections."

"Do not blame yourself for Diana's death. She knew she was ill and her vanity prevented her from seeing a doctor until it was too late. If there is any blame to be laid, lay it at her doorstep, not your own."

"I should have been stronger and challenged her pride."

"Clarissa, as her aunt and responsible for her welfare, should have summoned the doctor. She knew Diana's condition. Sometimes I think Clarissa isn't quite with this world."

I remained silent. I was beginning to feel strange. My vision blurred and the room was fuzzy. I blinked and shook my head in an effort to restore clarity. My senses were becoming numb and an overwhelming fatigue crept over me.

"Are you all right, Heather?" Adrian asked.

"I am fine." I stood. Either the room was swaying, or I was.

"I think I had better go to my room and lie down."

I made it to the door before Adrian gathered me up in his arms. I put my arm around his neck and curled up against his hard body. The sensation delighted me. I felt warm and safe as I seemed to float down the corridor. As though from a distant chamber, I heard voices. I vaguely recognized Dr. Drummond's voice. Adrian's deep tones trembled against my rib cage when he spoke.

"What has happened to Miss MacBride? I hope she hasn't become ill," Dr. Drummond said.

"All these deaths have unsettled her. I am afraid I have committed the ungentlemanly act of getting her drunk. She should sleep soundly for several hours."

"Poor child. She has been through so much in a short space of time."

"She has indeed."

"The wagon from the village is here. I came up to supervise the removal of the body."

I resumed floating down the corridor. The bed felt good when he placed me on it. I think Adrian kissed me on the forehead, but it might have been a dream for I instantly went to sleep.

The apparition came toward me dressed in a medieval costume of dark green velvet, a golden cord knotted around her waist, the ends falling in front of her. A high conical headdress was circled with a heavy black veil. As she came closer to my bed, her hand raised to reveal a long, twisted dagger. When she stood alongside the bed, I tried to see her face, but it was hidden under the veiling. I started to roll away, but she grabbed my arm and started pulling me toward her. I looked up to see the flash of the knife as it quickly descended. I started kicking and moaning to no avail. Her grasp on my arm was firm. My strength ebbed and I waited for the inevitable.

Chapter Thirteen

In my state of terror, I refuse to acknowledge the voice that was trying to penetrate my brain.

"Heather! Heather! Do wake up," came Aunt Clarissa's voice. "Oh, dear me. You don't think she has the same illness as our poor Diana, do you, Jane?"

"I don't think so. At least she has stopped fighting you. Let go of her arm, Clarissa. I will get a cool cloth for her head," Jane said.

I slowly opened my eyes and said, "Never mind, Jane. I am all right now. I was having an awful nightmare."

I related the dream to them, as my aunt stood next to my bed, her eyes wide. "I shouldn't wonder what with all that has been happening in this place," she said. "I knew when you opened the door to the keep nothing would go right or be the same. Sooner or later Lady Anne will seek to destroy all of us," Aunt Clarissa quavered.

I sat up. Glancing toward the window, I realized night had fallen. "Did I sleep through lunch?"

"Yes," Jane answered. "We were going to wake you, but Adrian and the doctor said to let you sleep."

"When we realized you weren't coming down to dinner, we thought it best to wake you," Aunt Clarissa added.

"What did the ghost of your dream look like, Heather?" Jane asked.

"I suppose like Lady Anne."

"See, I told you," Aunt Clarissa said with vindication.

"I feel awful." There was a horrible taste in my mouth and I felt shabby in general.

"What you need is a decent meal," Aunt Clarissa said.

"Perhaps you are right. What time is dinner?" I asked.

"In fifteen minutes."

"I will be down in time. I need a few minutes to tidy myself."

"We will wait downstairs for you, Heather. Come along, Jane."

"You won't go back to sleep, will you, Heather?" Jane asked.

"I won't. I am wide awake now."

When they left, I washed my face and brushed my hair. I didn't have time to ring for Jean to do my hair properly. I simply tied it back at the nape of my neck with a ribbon. Neither did I have time to change my frock. I smoothed it out as best I could and went downstairs.

In the drawing room, Adrian came up to me and asked, "How do you feel, Heather?"

"A bit groggy. I think I drank too much brandy."

He smiled engagingly. "I trust you had a good sleep." He pulled my arm through his and we went into the dining room with everyone else.

Later, when everyone had drifted off to bed, I stayed in the drawing room talking to Patrick.

"Did you find the maps of any use?" I asked.

"A little. I took some notes. I really would like to read your father's memoirs. Do you think it would be possible?"

"I don't see why not. I have finished reading some of it. I could let you have that portion tomorrow."

"I would appreciate it, Heather." He paused. "Damn shame about Diana. So beautiful and so young."

"Please, Patrick. I am not up to talking about Diana. I need time to absorb all these horrible events."

"I am sorry."

"How much leave do you have?"

He smiled. "Are you anxious to be rid of me?"

"Of course not. Curiosity prompted the question."

"Naturally I will remain for the funeral. Besides, I wouldn't think of leaving you under the circumstances. Perhaps I can be of some use in sorting out your affairs."

215

"That is kind of you, Patrick, but I wouldn't want you to incur the wrath of your superiors."

"When they learn of the difficulties that have transpired here, I am sure they will excuse a delay in my return. I feel you need me more than the regiment does right now. After all, we were close at one time, weren't we, Heather?"

He took my hand and held it. For some reason, I wasn't pleased. I pulled my hand away, causing Patrick to frown. "I was very young then," I replied stiffly.

"You are not that much older now," he said.

"I feel the months at Bridee Castle have thrust maturity on me sooner than expected."

"I suspect so. Perhaps that is why I find myself attracted to you. Forgive my boldness, Heather. I want you to be aware of my sentiments toward you."

"Really, Patrick, this is not the time to speak of such things," I quickly interjected. I didn't like the course the conversation was taking. "It is late. I must retire." I stood.

"I didn't mean to offend you, Heather. I know now is not the time to express my feelings for you. I want you to be aware that I can offer you more than friendship if you so desire. I won't mention it again. If you need me for anything, I shall be at your service."

"Thank you. Good night, Patrick."

The hall clock was chiming the midnight hour when I ascended the staircase. A sleepy Jean was waiting for me. Once she unhooked my frock, I told her to go to bed. I could manage the rest myself.

Once in my nightdress, I climbed into bed, but couldn't sleep. Patrick's declaration disturbed me. Diana wasn't even buried and he was switching his affections. And women were called fickle! How could he bring up the topic of his so-called affection for me on the same day Diana died? I was caught between anger and sorrow which made sleep impossible. I got up and went to the window.

As I stared out, the shadowy keep merged with the inky night. I could hardly make out its tall, rotund shape. Then it happened. The light again. The glow of the lamp slowly moved up the staircase to the top of the keep. The light hovered there for several minutes before beginning its descent. Was Aunt Clarissa right? Did the ghost of Lady Anne meander through the castle at will?

Tears were a permanent fixture throughout Diana's wake and funeral. Patrick became my shadow and protector while Adrian distanced himself from me. Bruce only appeared when Patrick wasn't around. I was relieved when the lieutenant went to Inverness to obtain warmer clothing.

I was in the library writing a letter to the solicitor when the door opened and Bruce's head appeared.

"Hiding?" he asked.

"No."

"I had a devil of a time finding you." He walked in, shut the door, then sauntered to a chair in front of the desk and lazily sprawled in it.

"I made no secret of where I was. Both Mrs. Burns and Jeffrey knew I was in here."

"When I heard that that Danton fellow went into Inverness, I was too elated to ask them. Is he going to be a permanent addition around here?"

"I don't think so."

"Do you want him to be?"

"Whatever made you think that?"

He shrugged then threw one leg over the padded arm of the chair. "He has been walking in your footsteps ever since the funeral. Is he wooing *you* now?"

"If he is, I am not interested, I assure you."

"Good. I don't like the fellow."

My smile was faint. "I don't think he is particularly fond of you, Bruce. I hope it doesn't come to pistols at dawn."

"I would rather use my fists on his smug face."

"Please try to curb your animosity toward him, Bruce. I don't think I could bear any more catastrophes at Bridee Castle."

"I shall do my best to refrain from fisticuffs. I will content

217

myself with leering at him behind his back."

"Why were you looking for me?"

"I never get to talk to you in private. That arrogant Danton is always around. If I do talk to you in his presence, he looks at me as though I were a bug to be stepped on."

"Why don't you forget about Patrick?"

"How can I? The chap haunts me."

"Speaking of haunting, have you seen the light that appears in the keep at night?"

"Don't tell me Clarissa has finally convinced you of her ghost."

"Of course not. I have seen this light going up the keep's staircase, then down. Have you seen it?" I repeated.

"No."

"I am not making it up, Bruce."

"I didn't say you were. My room isn't situated with a view to the keep."

"Perhaps you see it when you come back from the village late at night."

He laughed. "I am seldom in a condition to see much of anything on those nights. Do you see this every night?"

"No, last night was the second time."

"I wouldn't pay any attention to it, Heather. Probably some maid trysting with her young man."

"The light isn't there long enough," I argued.

"Perhaps they like the dark or decided to go elsewhere. I don't think it is anything to be concerned about."

Bruce was doing his best to dissuade me about the possibility of ghosts, and he was succeeding. I changed the subject. "I haven't seen much of Adrian lately. He leaves before I come down to breakfast then never shows up for lunch. His appearances at dinner are becoming fewer and fewer. I have the feeling he is avoiding me."

"Adrian is a moody, enigmatic fellow. Even I, his brother, don't understand him at times. One never knows what he is thinking. I imagine you will see him this afternoon though."

"Why? What is so special about this afternoon?"

"Didn't Clarissa tell you?"

218

"Tell me what?" I asked.

"Inspector Andrews wants all of us for questioning. It seems Diana was methodically poisoned with arsenic. Dr. Drummond's tests proved positive."

After a lunch of steamed hare, potatoes, onions and butter in a casserole, we gathered in the drawing room to await the arrival of Inspector Andrews. Patrick promptly sat next to me on the settee. Adrian gave us a cursory, indifferent glance. I felt horrid. I had thought Adrian had come to like me. I spitefully acted as indifferently as he.

"Aunt Clarissa, why didn't you tell me about the inspector's visit?" I asked.

"I did, my dear. Don't you remember? I told you shortly after breakfast. You were headed for the library at the time," she answered.

"I don't recall speaking to you."

"Well, I did, Heather." Annoyance tinged her tone.

"You have been under a great strain, Heather. No one can fault you for not remembering little things," said John in a placating manner.

I said no more on the subject. If Aunt Clarissa had told me, I would have remembered, strain or no strain.

"I hope this isn't going to take all afternoon," Bruce said. "I am scheduled for a dart game at the pub later."

"This is more important than your blasted dart game, Bruce," John said.

"I don't know why the inspector wants to question us. Surely he can't think any of us are capable of these heinous crimes," Jane said.

"He has to do something to earn his wage," Bruce said, thoroughly bored.

"I really don't see why Heather has to be here. To be questioned on top of what she has been through is not sporting," Patrick said, taking my hand.

I pulled my hand away unobtrusively. I was about to reply to his remark when Jeffrey announced the presence of Inspec-

219

tor Andrews who promptly entered the room. He took a seat then scanned each face before speaking.

"I will try to make this as brief as possible," the inspector began.

"Would you care for a whisky, Inspector?" John interrupted as he rose and went to the sideboard.

"No, thank you."

"I hope you don't mind if I have one," John said as he poured the pale amber liquid into a glass.

"I will have one, Father," Bruce said.

"Get it yourself, young man." John left the sideboard with glass in hand while Bruce rose to help himself.

"Miss MacBride, I understand that under the terms of your father's will, you will inherit your sister's share of the estate," the inspector said.

I nodded.

"Your sister's death makes you one of the richest women in Scotland."

"What is the point you are trying to make, Inspector?" I asked.

"I am not trying to make any particular point. I am searching for possible motives for your sister's death."

"Are you insinuating I might have poisoned my own sister?" I was horrified. I might have gotten upset with Diana at times, but kill her? Never.

"I am not insinuating anything, Miss MacBride. I am trying to ferret out a murderer. If anything happens to you, who inherits the estate?"

I glanced across the room at Aunt Clarissa. "My aunt receives everything."

The inspector coolly gazed at Aunt Clarissa who had the look of a startled bird.

"Oh, dear me. I certainly hope you don't think I had anything to do with my niece's death. That would be dreadful," Aunt Clarissa exclaimed.

Jane patted Aunt Clarissa's hand. "Of course he doesn't, Clarissa."

"When such vast amounts of money are involved, I find it

expedient to follow the trail of the money. For example, Mrs. Ross, if you should inherit the MacBride money, not only would you benefit, but your husband and his children would become substantially wealthier, especially if you met with an untimely accident," Inspector Andrews said.

"I resent the implication, sir!" John Ross boomed.

"Take it easy, Father," Bruce said, an impish smile on his face. "Don't you see what the inspector is saying? Each and everyone of us had a motive to dispose of Diana."

"Really, Bruce. Dispose? Couldn't you use a kinder word?" Aunt Clarissa asked as she began to twist her handkerchief.

"And you, sir, what was your relationship to the deceased?" the inspector asked of Patrick Danton.

"Diana MacBride and I were close friends going back to the days when we were in India. I was in her late father's regiment. I was very fond of Diana. You will not be able to find any murderous intent on my part," Patrick answered.

"Were you wooing the late Miss MacBride?" the inspector asked.

"One did not woo Diana. She had a flirtatious nature and never took any one person seriously," Patrick said.

"Perhaps you felt thwarted in your intentions," the inspector suggested.

"If I was, it is hardly a motive for murder."

"Murder has been committed for a lot less," said Inspector Andrews, eyeing Patrick critically.

"Inspector, the family is above reproach. Surely you must know that," Bruce said.

"I only know the villain had to be someone in this house to be able to administer the arsenic over a period of time."

"Have you questioned the staff, Inspector?" Jane asked.

"I will. Do you have information regarding the servants I should know?" the inspector asked of Jane.

She hesitated, took a deep breath, then said, "I don't want to get anyone into trouble, but Miss Diana MacBride was extremely harsh with her maid. The maid made no secret of her hatred for her mistress. It was common gossip among the staff."

"Are you accusing her, Miss Ross?"

"Gracious, no! I thought you might want to know there were others outside the family that weren't fond of Diana," Jane said.

"Are you suggesting that certain members of the family weren't fond of Miss MacBride?" the inspector asked.

"No." Jane looked around the room, her countenance grimacing in confusion. "You have me all in a muddle, Inspector. I was only trying to help."

"That will teach you to volunteer information, Sister dear," Bruce said.

"Have you any theories, Inspector?" asked the heretofore silent Adrian.

"I believe the murder of Diana MacBride and Samrú Singh are connected."

"How?" I asked.

"I think your nanny found out about the arsenic and who was administering the lethal poison. She either threatened to tell or was blackmailing the culprit and was murdered for her knowledge," the inspector explained.

"Then that absolves me. Samrú Singh was murdered before I reached Scotland," Patrick said, a smug, arrogant smile on his face.

"It is only a theory, Mr. Danton." Inspector Andrews smiled. "I have learned things are sometimes not as they appear." He braced his hands on the arms of the chair and stood. "I should like to question the staff now. Miss MacBride, will you kindly show me the way to the servant's quarters?"

"Oh, John, do ring for Jeffrey to assist the inspector," Aunt Clarissa said.

"I would prefer the company of Miss MacBride, if you don't mind." The inspector walked over to the settee and offered me his arm. "By the way, Mr. Danton, I trust you will be at Bridee Castle until we clear this matter up."

"For a while. I will have to return to my regiment in the near future."

"Let us hope it is not before we solve this matter," the inspector said.

We went through the foyer to the corridor leading to the servant's quarters. He stopped me and looked around as though to make sure we were alone.

"Miss MacBride, only you know if you killed your sister." I opened my mouth to protest the accusation, but he raised a staying hand and pressed on. "Please. I am not saying you did. I only want to caution you. If you didn't kill her, there is a vicious, calculating murderer living here. You could very well be the next victim. I am positive money is at the root of this mayhem. Do be careful. Eat and drink only what the others consume. If you feel anything unusual happening to you, do not hesitate to call on me. If I am not available, I am sure Dr. Drummond would be happy to assist you in anyway he can. My assistant, Detective Gordon, is available to you at all times. You will take care, won't you?"

"Yes. Thank you, Inspector." I watched him walk down the corridor. Once a chilling thought has been planted in one's mind, it verges on the impossible to ignore or get rid of it. Was I really going to be the next victim? The idea swirled in my head as I reentered the drawing room.

"Why did the inspector want to see you alone, Heather?" Bruce asked.

"Some personal questions about Diana." I didn't like having to fib. On the other hand, if I were in a room with a murderer, I didn't want the person to know of the inspector's warning. If anyone needed an edge in knowledge, I did.

"Well, that inquisition wasn't so bad. I will make it to the pub in plenty of time," Bruce said as he got up from the chair. "Anyone care to join me?"

"I will ride as far as the village with you," Adrian said, striding across the room.

"All this has been fatiguing, especially when I had to forego my afternoon nap. I must go upstairs and lie down," Aunt Clarissa said.

The next few days passed swiftly. My twentieth birthday fell on Christmas Day. With the exception of a few holiday decorations lodged by the staff, no celebrations were held. No presents were bought or exchanged. On Boxing Day the servants received money packets, which they seemed to prefer.

Patrick's attentions to me were deflected by his intense interest in reading my father's memoirs. He kept pressing me to read the papers faster, but my interest in the estate and other holdings was expanding. I spent a good deal of time in the library going over ledgers and land maps. I questioned John hoping to glean further knowledge, but he knew nothing about the demesne. He told me everything was left in the hands of an estate agent in Inverness.

When the day promised to be clear and the howling wind dissolved into soft gusts, I decided to see the estate agent in Inverness. I mentioned it at the breakfast table hoping Adrian would offer to accompany me. He did not offer, nor did anyone else.

The agent's office was on the second floor of a whitewashed stone building. Though my visit was a surprise, he was courteous and obliging. He gave me a list of the tenants and amount paid along with Bridee Castle's household expenses, taxes, his commission, and the amount paid to Aunt Clarissa for her maintenance. All the monies of the demesne were deposited to the MacBride account at the Bank of Scotland. He advised me to get an accounting from them. He put the papers in a large envelope and handed it to me.

The bank manager was cooperative, but maintained an attitude of superiority. As he seemed to be in a hurry to get rid of me, I placed the papers he gave me in an envelope without looking at them. I would sort it all out later. I treated myself to lunch at the tea garden, bought Aunt Clarissa a box of chocolates, then headed back to Bridee Castle.

Dark clouds began to swirl and scud across the sky. I urged the mare to increase her pace. I didn't relish the thought of getting caught in a storm. A biting wind began to fan my face. I was almost at Bridee Castle when snow dropped from the sky in cottony flakes. The melancholy howling of hounds caused my pulse to quicken. I had never heard them before. I wanted to set the horse to a gallop, but the weather was becoming dismal, limiting visibility. The eerie baying seemed to be inching closer. My heart pounded. Were they wild dogs or someone's hunters? I prayed they were domesticated animals.

The road and the moor started to merge as one vast white sea before me. I was beginning to despair of reaching Bridee Castle when I saw it. Shining like a beacon, a light sparkled intermittently from the castle's keep. I was too grateful to question the presence of a light in the keep this time of day. The mare turned up the driveway of her own accord. I was home.

"We were worried about you, Heather. One can easily get lost in a snowstorm like this," Jane said, coming into the foyer.

"I will confess I thought I might become lost. Fortunately, the horse had more confidence than me," I said with a smile as Jeffrey took my cloak and shook the snow from it. I pushed a box of chocolates at Jane. "Here. I bought these for you and Aunt Clarissa."

"Thank you, Heather." She took the box. "Why don't you come into the drawing room and sample them with me?"

"Later. I have a few things to do first." I marched down the corridor to the library.

I tossed the folders onto the top of the desk then headed for the long gallery, hoping to catch whoever was in the keep. The thought of Lady Anne's ghost never entered my mind.

My pace was swift as I walked through the gloomy dark rooms of the forsaken wing of the castle. I ran across the open courtyard and pulled the door to the hall open. The glow of a lamp revealed the intruder. My eyebrows knitted as my mouth fell agape in bewilderment.

Chapter Fourteen

"What are you doing here?" I demanded.

"I thought you were in Inverness," he answered, looking startled.

"I was. Now, what are you doing here?"

"I thought I might find some memento of your father's here. I would like a token to remember him," Patrick said, getting to his feet and moving away from the open trunk I caught him rummaging through.

"You should know by now, Patrick, that this part of the castle is never used. Only antiquated relics are stored here. There is nothing of my father's. And what did you expect to find at the top of the keep?"

"How did you know I was up there?" He frowned.

"I saw the light as I was coming home."

"Oh, this nasty weather confined me to the house and I was bored. I thought I would do some exploring." His confidence and smugness were returning. "You seem to be angry, Heather. I wasn't aware I was doing anything wrong. I assumed I had the freedom of the castle."

"Perhaps you had better start thinking of returning to India." I was annoyed. I felt he was invading my privacy.

"Ah! You are angry with me," he said in his most soothing tone. He came to stand before me and put his hands on my shoulders. "My dear little Heather. Anger is so akin to love."

Before I could shake free of his grip on my shoulders, his cold, tight lips were pressing on mine — a sharp contrast to the warm, searching kiss of Adrian.

"Excuse me," came Adrian's deep voice. His words had a

sharp edge to them.

I pushed a surprised Patrick away from me and wiped my lips with the back of my gloved hand.

"I didn't mean to interrupt this idyllic scene, but Clarissa insists on seeing you, Heather." Adrian's smile was sardonic.

"What does she want to see me about?" I asked, going to the door where Adrian stood.

"Something about Diana's maid, I believe. She is in a dither about it." He looked past me to Patrick who remained where he stood.

I headed out the door with Adrian. "Are you coming, Patrick?" I called over my shoulder.

"Must I?"

"I would prefer it." I could see he was opposed to leaving the hall, but he doggedly followed us as we proceeded to the main part of the castle.

"How did you find me?" I asked Adrian.

"Jeffrey saw you head that way. What possessed you to go to the hall after what must have been a distressful ride from Inverness?"

"I saw a light in the keep. I wanted to know who was up there."

"Well, your problem of mysterious lights in the keep is solved," Adrian said.

"Who told you I occasionally saw lights in the keep?"

"Bruce. He thinks the shock of so many deaths has disturbed your mind. He believes you see them as evidence of Lady Anne's ghost or that you are seeing things that don't exist."

"I did see lights and I don't think they were caused by the ghost of Lady Anne. I certainly hope Bruce isn't spreading that fantastic tale around."

"I am afraid he is. Not only has he told the family, I believe he is using the tale to enhance his image as a raconteur in the village pub."

"Good Lord! Tell Bruce the light in the keep had a human hand." I stopped and turned around. "Patrick, you were at the top of the keep with a lamp, weren't you?"

"Yes, I told you I was exploring."

"Have you been up there exploring before?" I asked.

"No," he answered with true conviction. "Drat! I left the lamp in the hall. I will go back and fetch it."

I watched him retrace his steps, then turned back to Adrian who said, "Do you think he will steal the silver?"

"How did you know there was silver in the hall?"

"I went through everything when we first came here."

"Is that how you got the money to buy land and livestock?" The minute the words were out of my mouth, I regretted it. He had ignored me of late and it hurt. I suppose I wanted to get back at him. I felt petty. "I am sorry. It was a stupid thing to say. Finding Patrick going through the trunks upset me. I shouldn't take my anger out on you, Adrian."

"So upset you threw yourself into his arms and kissed him?"

"I didn't throw myself into his arms. And I didn't kiss him. He kissed me. There is a difference. Besides, what do you care?"

"I don't. You are free to do as you wish, no matter how foolish."

His stride lengthened. I had to take quicker steps to keep up with him. God knows why I wanted to keep up with him when his manner toward me was so abrasive.

"Do you think it foolish for a man to want to kiss me?"

"You were foolish to let him."

"I told you. I didn't let him. He just did it. Why don't you like Patrick?"

"He is a militaristic popinjay who is after your money. If you can't see that then you are a foolish little lass who has a lot of growing up to do."

We had reached the foyer. Adrian cupped my elbow and steered me into the drawing room. He immediately went to the sideboard and poured himself a drink.

"Thank goodness Adrian found you, Heather," Aunt Clarissa said.

I looked around the room to see everyone except Patrick present. I turned back to Aunt Clarissa. "What did you want to see me about?"

228

"Diana's maid has disappeared. I thought we should consult you before notifying the inspector."

"Why?"

"You are the mistress of Bridee Castle now. I have convinced Clarissa that we should not presume to act on anything without conferring with you first," John said.

"I appreciate your deference, but it really isn't necessary. Of course the inspector should be notified, but it will have to wait until the weather improves. When was she noticed missing?"

"Shortly after lunch," Jane said.

"Was every part of the castle searched?" I asked.

"With the exception of Cook, the entire staff searched this part and the old part of the castle," Bruce said.

"She is nowhere in the castle," John added.

"Surely she wouldn't have decided to run away in this weather." I couldn't imagine anyone in their right mind exposing themselves to the biting winds and snow.

"Oh, dear me. This is so distressing." Aunt Clarissa shook her head slowly.

"Does anyone know why she would leave without notice?" I asked, ignoring Aunt Clarissa's soft groans.

"I questioned Mrs. Burns," John began. "It seems the lass was upset by the inspector's intensely questioning her. Mrs. Burns said the lass was fearful that the inspector thought she might have poisoned Diana."

"Does she have family nearby?" I asked.

"No one she could contact in a day. Mrs. Burns seems to think her family lives on the Isle of Mull. That is some distance from here and would be difficult to reach in this weather," John explained.

"I don't see why her disappearance should concern us," Bruce said.

"Just the same, the inspector would want to know," Jane said.

"Why should we tell him? Let him find out for himself." Bruce went to the sideboard for a drink. "Where is that fellow Danton? I haven't seen him around all day. Perhaps he ran off with the lass. She was fetching, if you like them plump."

"Why do you say 'was,' Bruce?" Adrian asked. "Do you know something we don't?"

Bruce shrugged. "Just a language quirk of mine, Brother dear. When someone who lives here isn't here anymore, I have a tendency to use the past tense. Don't put your sinister thoughts into my words."

John pulled his pocket watch from his brocaded vest. "I see the dinner hour is almost upon us. I suggest we change. We must not let trivial matters disrupt our routine."

I needed no encouragement to go to my bedchamber. The day had been a long one. I was ready for a wash and a change of clothes.

I went to the library first to put the folders in a more secure place. Reaching the desk, I was stunned to find them gone. I was about to ring for Jeffrey to learn who had been in the library when I decided to look around first.

I sat down at the desk and began opening drawers. When I pulled the middle drawer open, I was surprised to find the papers in that drawer. I didn't remember putting them there. I shook my head. Perhaps I did and forgot about it. The physical encounter with Patrick and the verbal sparring with Adrian could have affected my memory. I went upstairs.

As Patrick was about to take his place at the dinner table, Bruce remarked, "Tired of the lass already, Danton?"

"What the devil do you mean?" Patrick asked.

"Do sit down, Mr. Danton. My brother didn't mean anything. His humor is warped most of the time," Jane said.

"What is this about a lass?" Patrick asked as he took his seat. John Ross explained.

"I see," Patrick said.

"Was anyone in the library after I came home?" My question caused everyone to look at me with odd expressions.

"Is something wrong, my dear?" Aunt Clarissa asked.

"No," I said a little too quickly. Their stares were disconcerting me. If Bruce had spread the story of my so-called belief in ghosts, my question might seem strange to them. I changed the topic. "This venison is delicious."

"Cook salted it too much," Aunt Clarissa complained.

"It is perfect," Bruce countered.

When I entered my bedchamber later, my hand flew to my mouth to stop an incipient scream and to hold down the bile rising in my stomach. My eyes widened in shock and horror. There, in the middle of my bed, lying on a white linen cloth, was the body of a decapitated crow. When my initial daze wore off, I remembered Bruce's prank in the armory room. This looked like his type of mischief.

I compressed my lips in anger and stalked out of the room in search of Bruce. I wouldn't be surprised if he were the one who moved the folders I had left on top of the desk. He was coming out of the drawing room with John as I reached the foyer. I placed my hands on my hips and glared at him.

"Something wrong, Heather?" Bruce asked.

"You know very well what is wrong, Bruce. You have been playing tricks again," I declared angrily.

"I have no idea what you are talking about, Heather." Bruce threw his father a quizzical glance.

"I am talking about the dead crow on my bed."

"I will leave the two of you to sort things out. I dislike being involved in arguments before retiring. Good night," John said, then quickly ascended the stairs and disappeared.

"Now what is this about a dead crow?" Bruce asked.

"The dead crow you put on my bed."

"What? I don't know anything about a dead crow." He seemed genuinely surprised.

"Don't try to deny it, Bruce. Only you would think of such a grisly prank."

"Why me? Did you ever think it might be that Danton chap? He might be miffed with you for ignoring his ardent attentions. A spurned lover isn't above stupid pranks."

"He is not my lover. Never was nor has been. Besides, Patrick is much too proper and solemn to play tricks on anyone."

"You mean he lacks imagination. Let us see this dead crow of yours." Bruce took my arm and we climbed the stairs together.

I opened the door to my bedchamber and, without looking,

pointed to the bed. "There. Look at that."

Bruce entered the room and went toward the bed. "Look at what?"

I followed him. The headless crow was gone! Not even a pinhead of blood was on the pristine coverlet.

"But there was one before I went downstairs," I protested.

"Are you sure you didn't have too much sherry tonight?"

"Don't be silly, Bruce. Do I appear inebriated to you?" I scanned the room for some sign of the crow without success.

"Well, if the crow was on your bed, it isn't there now. Have you been sleeping poorly?"

"Now you are being ridiculous. How I sleep has nothing to do with what I saw on my bed."

"I don't know what to say. I swear to you, Heather, I never put anything on your bed, much less a dead crow. It would still be there if I had, wouldn't it? Being with Father and then with you, I wouldn't have had the opportunity to remove it," Bruce claimed, then added, "if it were there in the first place."

I saw the look of doubt in his light brown eyes. He was gazing at me with a most peculiar expression. I decided to drop the matter lest he think I was prone to delusions. "You are right, Bruce. I never should have accused you. It wasn't warranted. I am sorry."

"Are you now saying the crow was never there?" A taunting tone edged his voice.

"It was there. I suspect my maid must have removed it."

He gave me a sidelong glance which was slightly leering. "I had better get to my room. It isn't seemly for me to be entertained by a young woman in her bedchamber. The servants have enough to gossip about." He smiled and left.

When Jean came in to turn down my bed and help me undress, I didn't mention the crow. She was a garrulous person who never could have kept quiet about the fact she had taken a dead crow from my bed. As she didn't mention it, I could only assume she knew nothing about it. Questioning her would start unsavory rumors among the staff. I hoped Bruce would be discreet, but I had my doubts.

In that ethereal state between drowsiness and deep sleep,

some faculty in the mind can make one aware of a strangeness in one's environs. That mental sensation claimed me. Though I fought it, uneasiness forced my eyes open.

Coming toward the foot of my bed was the same luminous specter I had encountered in the ancient hall. I sat up and pulled the covers to my chin.

"Who are you?" I asked in a half-whisper.

Everything was still.

"Who are you and what do you want of me?"

The specter stopped moving. Its arms raised horizontally, lifting incandescent wings in the dark. The sight was terrifying. I opened my mouth to speak only to find my vocal cords paralyzed. Though it was fast dwindling, I still had a tiny reserve of courage. Keeping my eyes on the grisly phantom, I fumbled for the matches on my night table. Feeling one in my fingers, I turned to light the oil lamp next to the matches. I lifted the glass dome and lighted the wick. The lamp spread its soft amber light that never quite reached the dark corners of the room. I held it aloft, then turned my eyes to where the specter had stood. The luminous phantom was gone.

I slipped out of bed and carried the lamp to all the dark corners. Nothing. I padded through the open door to the sitting parlor. Again, nothing. I went back to my bedchamber, closing and locking the door behind me. I inched opened my bedchamber door and peered up and down the dim corridor. Empty. I went back to bed, leaving the oil lamp lighted, but lowering the wick.

I sat there for some time as though expecting the return of my eerie visitor. Several times I felt myself starting to doze off. When sleep could no longer be kept at bay, I snuggled down under the covers.

The same nightmares about Lady Anne trying to kill me returned. As the knife she held began its downward thrust toward my heart, I bolted up in bed. The faltering rays of the sun threw shafts of hazy light into my bedchamber. The bedclothes were rumpled and askew as though I had been struggling with an invisible beast. I put my hand to my forehead to find tiny beads of perspiration dampening my brow.

The eldritch events of the preceding evening came back to me. I knew the threatening Lady Anne was a dream. Were the luminous specter and dead crow also dreams? My uncertainty caused my spine to shudder. Fortunately, I had regained my composure by the time Jean came in to help me with the morning toiletries.

I was late to breakfast. As I entered the dining room, all heads turned toward me, their eyes full of pity mingled with suspicion. I scowled at Bruce for I was certain he had told everyone about my irritation over a supposed dead crow. Adrian wasn't present. I hoped he hadn't been there when Bruce told his wretched tale of my folly. I wanted to shout "There was a crow!" at them. Instead, I calmly filled my plate and took my place at the table, grateful no one knew about the specter or my dream about Lady Anne. They would either make merry of it or call a physician who dealt with those of diminished mental capacities. I smiled at Jane as she led a mundane conversation.

The next several days passed uneventfully. I learned Adrian had once again gone to Aberdeen. Patrick's attentions became more amorous no matter how I tried to discourage him. I avoided him assiduously.

Whenever I encountered Bruce, a mischievous twinkle would invade his eyes as if he knew something I didn't.

Aunt Clarissa and John made a few trips into Inverness. Each time they returned, Aunt Clarissa would have a new gown or frock or bonnet; John would sport a new and expensive article of clothing — all of which I found difficult to understand after reading the papers from the bank. Aunt Clarissa's meager stipend would not support that lavish a mode of living for herself, never mind John. I could only assume Adrian was contributing to the family's finances.

I was so pleased to see Adrian at the dinner table, I felt radiant. Happiness exuded from my every pore. I made no attempt to hide that joy.

"You look pleased with yourself, Heather," Bruce said. "No lights in the keep? No crows on your bed?"

I stabbed at my potato. I had a feeling he was about to spoil my euphoric state. "I have dismissed them from my mind."

"What is all this about the keep and crows?" Aunt Clarissa asked innocently.

To my consternation, Bruce obliged with an explanation.

"Oh, dear me. How ghastly for you, Heather. Why didn't you tell me? I would have rooted out the culprit and put a stop to it," Aunt Clarissa said.

I couldn't imagine Aunt Clarissa putting a stop to anything. I managed a smile. "I suppose they are someone's idea of a prank. Don't be concerned. I am not worried about it." I furtively glanced at Adrian. He was frowning at me. I diverted my eyes back to my plate as I felt my cheeks burn.

Bruce wasn't finished embarrassing me. He said, "And our Heather has had a ghost haunting her."

I looked up sharply. Had he somehow learned of the specter?

"A very corporeal ghost," Bruce added as his eyes fixed on Patrick.

"Are you implying your statement has something to do with me, sir?," said Patrick, one finger flicking over his trim mustache.

"Well, you have been zealously trailing behind Heather, old sport. You haven't made a secret of your fervid interest in her." Bruce looked triumphant.

"Hasn't your regiment questioned your prolonged absence, Danton?" Adrian asked, his eyes searching my face.

"I have written to them explaining the dire circumstances here. I don't think Inspector Andrews would appreciate my sudden departure, for one thing. Also, I am keen to read all of Brigadier MacBride's memoirs. They are of great interest to me. My regiment is composed of very understanding chaps," Patrick said defensively.

"They must be," Adrian commented.

As everyone trickled into the drawing room when dinner was finished, I stopped Bruce in the foyer.

"Why are you persecuting me by repeating those foolish tales over and over?" I asked when everyone was in the

235

drawing room.

"You are imagining things, Heather. I am not persecuting you. I think they are jolly good stories. I really don't mean any harm."

"Any harm? You have made me out to be a lunatic with whimsical delusions. I thought you were my friend."

"I am."

"If that is what you call being a friend, God forbid if you ever become my enemy. I will never tell you anything again." I turned on my heel and marched into the drawing room.

Two nights later the decapitated crow was on my bed. I folded it up in its linen cloth and hid it under the bed with the intention of burying it on the moor the next day. When the luminous apparition mingled with nightmares of Lady Anne, sleep became fitful. I was wide awake when the sun peeked its rim over the horizon. I washed and dressed myself, then waited until I knew breakfast was being put on the buffet.

Adrian was the only person helping himself to breakfast. His eyes narrowed as he studied me.

"Are you feeling poorly, Heather?" he asked.

"No."

"You don't look well."

"I feel all right. Perhaps a little tired."

"You should take a nap in the afternoon instead of working in that dank ancient hall. The place is drafty with chilling breezes. You are liable to catch cold and make yourself sick. Exactly what are you doing there?"

"I dress warmly." We took our plates to the table and sat down. "I am taking inventory of the articles there."

"Why?"

"I have written to the Edinburgh museum to see if they would be interested in some of the period costumes and artifacts. I sent them a partial list. I want to complete it before they reply," I answered.

"What about the silver?"

"I am having it brought to this side of the castle. Once

236

it is cleaned, I shall donate it to Reverend Campbell's kirk. I hope you approve."

"You don't need my approval to dispose of your possessions. Have you mentioned it to Clarissa or anyone else?"

"No."

Finished with breakfast, he leaned back in his chair, then gazed thoughtfully at me. Finally he asked, "How would you like to get away from this gloomy place for the day and come to my house?"

My spirits soared. Spending a day alone with Adrian was beyond my wildest dream. I tried not to appear too anxious. "That would be very nice."

"If you have finished your breakfast, we can go now. I would like to be out of here before the others start coming down."

In my state of joy, I had almost forgotten about the bulge deep in my skirt pocket. "There is something I have to do first. It will only take me a minute."

"I will go and see to the horses." He pushed his chair back and departed.

I dashed into the foyer, grabbed my hooded cloak, then ran out the back door to the terrace and raced across the topiaried lawn to the woods only to find the ground was much too hard to bury the crow.

With great effort, I lifted a large stone to one side, placed the linen-shrouded crow on the ground, then rolled the stone back in place. I ran to the stableyard.

Adrian quickly started a fire in the hearth once we entered his house. It rapidly burst into warming flames which seemed all the more delightful after the cold ride across the moor.

"Make yourself at home, Heather, while I brew some tea."

I removed my cloak and stood before the fire until the warmth chased the chill from my bones. In a few minutes I sauntered over to the piano and lifted the cover of the bench. Adrian returned with a tea tray as I was browsing through the piles of sheet music.

"Have you found anything you would like to play?" he asked as he put the tea tray on the low table before the sofa.

"Many pieces. Unfortunately, I don't believe I have the skill

237

for many of them."

"Come have tea, then we will see which pieces suit you."

The morning passed pleasantly as we sat at the piano and tried various compositions. Our torsos were close. The heat of his body passed into mine sending raw sensations of desire through me. But the only amorous gesture Adrian made was an occasional pat on the head as though I was an obedient student. With regret and deep melancholia, I sensed he would never think of me as anything but a child.

He surprised me by serving a delicious cold lunch of spiced venison slices, pickled beets, bread, and chunks of cheese.

"I have to check with one of my herdsman. I won't be gone for more than an hour." He took the lunch tray away. Moments later I heard the front door close.

I scanned the magazines and found one that interested me. I curled up on the sofa and began to thumb through it.

"Heather." The soft voice inched its way into my brain. I smiled when I recognized it as Adrian's. Still in a semiconscious state, I stretched out my arms. I knew it was all a dream when he slipped into them, his lips touching my forehead, my eyes, then settling on my mouth in a glorious kiss. Then he vanished from that dream. I didn't mind. The dream had been sweet.

My dream shifted to the land, where Adrian and I raced our horses over a springtime moor to the strains of melodic music. Suddenly the dulcet and lyric music gave way to harsh chords of anguish. My eyes opened to see Adrian passionately playing the piano. The light from the fire illuminated the room brightly. I sat up, surprised to find a blanket had been placed over me. The music stopped.

"You had quite a sleep for yourself, Heather. I tried to wake you earlier, but you wouldn't budge. I guess you really needed the rest," he said.

"What time is it?" I asked, pulling the blanket off and folding it.

"Time for us to get to Bridee Castle. The moor is no place

for us to be riding at night."

"You shouldn't have let me sleep the afternoon away. You asked me to spend the day with you and here I go and fall asleep on you. I was a poor companion and I feel terrible about it."

"Don't. We both needed a restful day."

"I promise to be more lively next time."

As we rode back to the castle I began to wonder if Adrian really did kiss me or if it were a dream. The thought that he might have done it pleased me greatly.

Throughout dinner Patrick acted disdainfully toward me as though I had betrayed him. I was beginning to wish he would go back to India. I couldn't understand what was keeping him here, especially when he could be enjoying the warmth of India instead of the bitter cold of the Highlands.

"You look rested, Heather," Bruce commented. "Doesn't she, Jane?"

Jane smiled. "Indeed she does. How are you feeling, Heather?"

"Fine." I returned her smile. "I am ready to get back to work in the ancient hall."

Aunt Clarissa shook her head. "I can't understand why you bother yourself with that, Heather. You should have the servants do it."

"I don't intend to work alone anymore, Aunt Clarissa. Jean, my maid, is willing to help me."

The conversation continued in a desultory fashion, even after we retired to the drawing room. Adrian had his whisky and left. Patrick was unusually sullen. When John and Aunt Clarissa retired, Patrick went upstairs with them. Jane and I discussed the Brontë sisters causing Bruce to yawn and excuse himself.

Later we climbed the stairs together. At the landing Jane turned down the corridor one way, I the other. I was feeling frivolous and gay when I entered my bedchamber. Those feelings flowed out of me to be replaced by despair and confusion.

Another decapitated crow was on my bed.

Chapter Fifteen

I wrapped it up as before and shoved it under the bed. I would dispose of it in the morning as before. Was it an omen of things to come? But more importantly, who was doing this to me?

It was late. I never disturbed Jean at this time of night. I had always done for myself in India. Our servants there were too busy attending to Diana. Diana! She seemed to creep into my mind at the oddest moments.

Sleep refused to envelop me. I probably shouldn't have slept so long at Adrian's. Tossing and turning for what seemed like hours, I finally fell into a doze.

A low moan brought my senses to instant awareness. I opened my eyes to see the outline of a form glimmering and glowing in the dark.

A flash of yellow incandescence formed the scintillating outline of a large knife. The form floated toward the foot of my bed.

I rolled over to the edge of the bed and lighted the oil lamp. As I suspected, the phantom vanished when I held the lamp aloft. I knew it would be futile to get up and inspect the bedchamber and sitting parlor. Whoever or whatever would be gone by the time it took me to light the lamp. I put the lamp back on the table and blew it out.

I lay awake for sometime, fearful that sleep would bring on the nightmares. My fears were accurate.

Father and Diana were walking around the topiary in the

rear grounds of the castle with Samrú trailing behind them. They were dressed as gypsies. I gaily ran out to greet them. As I reached them, I threw my arms around Diana and Father only to have them turn into sculptured black thorn bushes. Their spiny branches dug into my flesh as I tried to escape. They grew quickly, encasing me in painful thorns. The harder I struggled to free myself, the more the thorns tore into my flesh. I cried for Samrú to help me for I could hear her distinctive laughter. Occasionally I would get a glimpse of her in those garish gypsy clothes. I felt relief as she came closer to my thorny tomb.

When she was within grasping distance, I stretched my bleeding hand out for assistance. The instant my fingers touched her arm, Samrú turned into an enormous headless crow with a vile, nauseating liquid oozing from the stub of her neck. The wings spread ominously and the crow took to the air. The thorny branches tightened their grip as the crow landed on my head and began to tear at my head and hair with its sharp talons. I could see my red hair flying in all directions. The loathsome fluid from its neck began to drip over my face, forming a sickening mask which began to harden, choking off my air. Screams issued from my throat.

"Miss MacBride . . . Miss MacBride."

Jean's voice finally penetrated my brain. Her shaking my shoulder helped to bring me to full consciousness. My eyes opened and I sat up.

"Are you all right, miss?" Jean asked. "You were screaming something awful."

"I am all right now, Jean. I had a nightmare." I sat for a moment, clearing my groggy head. "Are you free to help me in the ancient hall today, Jean?"

"Aye, miss."

"I shall see you shortly after breakfast then."

It was midmorning before Jean and I actually got started in the hall.

"We will start on the silver first, Jean. I think Reverend Campbell could use the extra income from the sale of it. He said something about the church needing an organ," I said, voicing my thoughts aloud.

"What should I do, miss?" Jean asked, her eyes flickering around the ancient hall with a trace of fear in them.

"First we will empty all the silver out of the boxes and crates, then dust the crates and silver before we put them back in. When the silver is done, I will have a couple of the footmen bring the crates to the kitchen where the silver can be polished. Some of it is badly tarnished. I am sure Jeffrey will know what to use on them. As you pack them back in, call off each piece and I will make a list."

Jean nodded and we set to work. By lunchtime I was much too dusty to eat in the dining room. I told Jean to bring me a sandwich and tea after she had eaten her lunch.

While I waited for Jean to return, I went over the pieces that hadn't been packed. A large silver tureen with hammered and molded silver swans took my fancy. I decided to keep that one piece and put it aside.

As I study the beauty of it, an icy draft blew over the nape of my neck. I turned to face the door of the keep with trepidation. The angle of the dim gray light spilling into the hall cast the figure, standing in the door frame, in shadows. The fine hairs on my hairs began to quiver.

"What do you want?" I asked when I found my voice.

The shadow moved forward into the muted light. "I thought I might help," Patrick Danton said as he moved toward me.

My anxiety diminished. Still, I was uneasy by Patrick's sudden appearance. "What are you doing here?"

"I heard you say you were going to work here today. I thought I might be of some help."

"What were you doing in the keep? I said nothing about working in the keep."

"You weren't here when I came. I thought I would take another look at the notorious keep. What can I do to help?"

"It is filthy work, Patrick. I am sure you don't want your nice clothes covered with grime."

"They will clean. Where shall I start?"

"I am waiting for Jean to return with a bit of lunch for me. Why don't you go have your lunch? If you are still of the same

242

mind after lunch, we should be ready to go to work again."

"Excellent suggestion. I will hurry back to assist you," Patrick said.

I was glad when he left. His presence was beginning to irk me more and more. I instinctively knew he was after something, something besides me. The only thing he wanted of me was my great wealth.

Patrick did not come back.

Over the next several days, I continued to work with Jean in the hall. At night my bed was without crows, my bedchamber without phantoms, but my mind was plagued with ghoulish nightmares. To wake up in the middle of the night with cold beads of perspiration made me afraid to fall asleep again.

After six semisleepless nights, I was tense and disoriented, not to mention physically ravaged. My state of exhaustion did not go unnoticed.

"You don't look well, Heather," Jane said as the dinner soup dishes were being cleared away.

"Jane is right. Really, Heather, you should see a doctor," Aunt Clarissa added. "I certainly don't want you coming down ill like Diana." A sudden silence fell in the room. "Oh, dear me, have I said something wrong?"

Her obvious fluster made me feel sorry for her. "Don't worry, Aunt Clarissa. I am not sick. All I need is a good night's sleep."

"Why aren't you sleeping at night, Heather?" John asked. "I thought youth had no problem when it came to sleep."

I smiled. "I suppose I am overendowed with nervous energy." I caught Adrian looking at me with a frown. He seemed to be trying to read my thoughts as if he knew there were a deeper, more sinister reason for my sleepless nights, but it was Bruce who inadvertently struck the right chord.

"Mucking about in that ancient hall is enough to give anyone nightmares. All those old artifacts and the antiquity of the very walls breed nothing but evil. Didn't Shakespeare say 'the evil that men do lives after them'? So it is with that old keep

243

and hall. Evil has settled there."

"Don't be philosophically dreary, Bruce," John said.

"You do have a tendency to be overdramatic, Bruce," Jane added.

"What does the keep and hall have to do with Heather's not sleeping?" Aunt Clarissa asked.

"Quite simple, Clarissa," Bruce began. "All the time Heather is spending in that hall is causing the accumulated evil in the keep to seep into her bones and brain. Are you having nightmares, Heather?"

"Occasionally." He had caught me off guard, but there was no reason to lie.

"Perhaps you should put your chores there in abeyance for a while," Jane suggested. "We could go into Inverness and buy new bonnets. It might buoy your spirits up."

"I would like that. Let us plan on it two days from now. I shall have finished in the hall by then." I went on to describe the lovely silver tureen I had found there, hoping it would take everyone's mind off my health.

While Jane browsed through the yarn shop in Inverness, I went to see Dr. Drummond. The intensity of the nightmares had increased to the point where I purposely tried to keep myself awake.

"Why, Miss MacBride, whatever has happened to you?" Dr. Drummond asked as he came around his desk and held a chair for me. "You look gaunt. Those dark circles under your eyes does not bode well for your health. Have you been experiencing any of your late sister's symptoms?"

"No." I managed a weak smile then went on to explain the reason for my lack of healthful coloring, omitting the crows and specters. I didn't want him to think I was mentally unstable. I concluded by saying, "I don't think anyone can force me to have nightmares."

Having resumed his seat behind the desk, he pensively stroked his chin. "Do you still feel unsettled about the recent deaths you have had to endure?"

"I don't think so."

"What about your sister? At the time you seemed to be in a state of shock."

"I have learned to accept it."

He steepled his forefingers and tapped the tips of them on his lips. "What exactly did you feel just prior to her passing away? Please be honest and frank. I need honesty if I am to help you. I assure you that your candid thoughts will not go beyond this office."

"I felt terrible. I never should have listened to Diana about not wanting a doctor. I should have summoned you when she first started on the downward path. She might be alive now if I had made her see you sooner."

"Then I assume you blame yourself, in a way, for her death."

"Yes. Very much."

"You feel guilty?" Dr. Drummond asked.

"I try not to. I try to rationalize the guilt away."

"Tell me about your nightmares."

I did with as much accuracy as I could manage.

"Hmm." He stroked his chin again. "Guilt can do strange things to the mind, Miss MacBride. Perhaps if you found absolution for your feelings, the nightmares would stop. The only thing I can do is make sure you get back to sleeping soundly. The state you are in now only leaves you easy prey to more nightmares. Sleeplessness leaves your mind tired and more vulnerable to nightmares of this sort. What you need is several nights of sound and unfettered sleep."

"How do I accomplish that?" I asked.

"I am going to give you a phial of laudanum. Two drops in a glass of warm milk before you retire should induce a sound sleep."

"Then what should I do?"

"Once you are completely rested, I suggest you talk about the subject with Reverend Campbell. My mission is with the body, his with the spirit and soul. Talking with him might relieve you," Dr. Drummond said with a smile. "I will be right back."

He left his chair and lumbered to his dispensary. A wave of

245

relief swept over me. At least I was now aware of the root of my nightmares. I was certain I could now overcome those debilitating dreams.

Dr. Drummond came back and handed me the phial of laudanum. "No more than two drops. After several nights of sleep, go see the good reverend and stop taking the laudanum. It is highly addictive. I don't want you becoming dependent on it."

"I will follow your instructions to the letter, Doctor." I put the phial in my reticule and stood. "Thank you for everything, especially the advice."

"You are welcome." He grinned. "The bill will be sent to Bridee Castle."

"I would rather pay you now. It will save you the trouble of sending a bill."

"All right." He pulled a sheet from a pad on the top of his desk, did some scribbling, then handed the sheet to me.

"What about the bill for my sister?"

"Adrian Ross took care of it."

"I see." That was a puzzle. Why would Adrian pay the doctor bill? I started to go, but suddenly turned. "Do you ever see Inspector Andrews, Dr. Drummond?"

"We dine together on occasion."

"Has he mentioned any progress on the deaths of Samrú and my sister?"

"I don't believe he has. He questioned the chemist about arsenic sales only to learn the chemist hadn't sold arsenic to private parties in over two years. He feels like he has come to a dead end."

"He will keep trying, won't he, Dr. Drummond?"

"Of course, my dear. Inspector Andrews is a stubborn man who detests having to acknowledge defeat. I am sure he will sort it all out in time."

"Good-bye, and thank you again."

"Don't hesitate to call in if you need further assistance."

"I won't."

As I walked to the tea garden where I was to meet Jane for lunch, the thought that Adrian paid Diana's bill nagged at me.

246

Why didn't he mention it? After all, it was my or Aunt Clarissa's responsibility.

Jane was already seated in the tea garden when I joined her.

"You look a little more spirited," Jane said. "Did the doctor give you some sleeping powders?"

"In a way. Laudanum. Two drops in a warm glass of milk before I retire. He assures me I will sleep soundly! I hope it works," I said. We ordered our lunch.

"I am sure it will if Dr. Drummond recommended it."

"Did you know Adrian paid the doctor bill for Diana?"

"Yes."

"Why? The bill should have been given to me or Aunt Clarissa."

"Adrian said you were under too much of a strain to be bothered with bills. Clarissa made it clear that she had no intention of paying any of your bills since both you and Diana were heiresses to a fortune."

"I shall have to reimburse Adrian."

"I wouldn't mention it. Adrian is peculiar when it comes to money. Besides, I don't think he would appreciate my telling you. Please don't mention it to him, Heather," Jane pleaded.

"If you don't want me to, I won't."

Spending the afternoon shopping was refreshing even though neither of us purchased a new bonnet.

That night I had Jean bring me a warm glass of milk. When she left I put two drops of the laudanum in it. I climbed into bed with my newly purchased magazines. I drank the milk slowly while perusing the periodicals. The warm milk tasted good.

I could hear the soft tread of feet, drawers being opened, and the almost imperceptible clink of china. I was afraid to open my eyes. If the laudanum hadn't brought sleep and the specter appeared, I might really be in danger of losing my sanity. Stubborn curiosity, though, forced me to open one eye warily.

The room was flooded with light. I opened both eyes wide to see Jean bustling about the room getting my clothes ready for the day. I sat up, stretched, and smiled.

247

"Good morning, Jean."

"Good morning to you, miss. You slept sound this morning."

"What time is it?"

"Almost eight o'clock, miss."

"Gracious! I *have* slept a long time. I had better hurry or I will be too late for breakfast."

I felt alive and ravenous as I bounced down the stairs. To my surprise, Adrian was still at the breakfast table along with Patrick, John, and Jane. I filled my porridge dish, then my plate before taking a seat at the table.

"You look chipper this morning, Heather," John said. "The day in Inverness must have done you good."

"It was a delightful change. We will have to do it more often, won't we, Jane?"

"We could make it a weekly trip," Jane suggested.

I nodded. The food tasted good. I had been so tired before I never tasted the food nor had an appetite for it.

"Where is Bruce?" I asked.

"Sleeping in. I suspect he had a late night at the pub," John informed me.

"Isn't it rather late for you to be coming down for breakfast, Heather?" Adrian asked.

"I overslept."

"You look the better for it," Adrian said.

"Thank you."

"Are you going to work in the old hall today, Heather?" Patrick asked, one finger flickering over his trim mustache.

"No. We have finished the silver. The rest of the articles I shall leave there for the museum people."

"Have you heard from them yet?" Jane asked.

"No. Perhaps they are waiting until spring when the weather is more conducive to traveling," I said.

"The day seems to be sunny. Would you care to go riding, Heather?" Adrian asked.

"I would love it."

"Better bundle up. The sun may be shining, but it is still bitter cold," John advised.

248

Riding with Adrian was so thrilling to me, I didn't care if there was a blizzard outside. I noticed Patrick raise his eyebrow imperiously as he glanced from me to Adrian. To my deepest pleasure, he didn't suggest joining us.

Astride my horse I rode alongside Adrian as we left the stableyard. "Where are we going?" I asked.

"I thought we would ride down to the loch which is close enough to permit us to get back to the castle quickly if a sudden storm sweeps down on us."

We rode in companionable silence until we reached Loch Ness. We sat on our horses as the ground was snow covered and chilled. Across the loch the snow-capped mountains shimmered golden in the sun, occasionally reflecting gold in the russet-colored loch. The beauty of the scene helped to assuage the dreariness and gloom of Bridee Castle.

"You seem happy and content, Heather. Are you?" Adrian asked.

"It is good to be out and around. I think Bruce was right. I was spending too much time in that ancient hall. It must have affected my sleep."

"Jane told me you went to see Dr. Drummond while you were in Inverness. Evidently he found a cure for your sleepless nights."

"A few drops of laudanum in warm milk. I tried it last night and it worked wonders."

"So I see. Do take care with that medicine. I hear it is a highly addictive drug."

"Dr. Drummond has already warned me. He said to use it for several days only." I studied the loch.

"Looking for the monster?" Adrian asked.

I laughed. "Hardly. I was looking at that castle which juts out into the loch. What is it?"

"The ruins of Urquhart Castle, the ancestral home of the Urquhart family. In the seventeenth century Sir Thomas Urquhart was a writer whose works are probably forgotten now. A few miles beyond the castle is the celebrated Falls of

249

Foyers. The upper fall has a bridge spanning the chasm and the water cascades down about thirty feet. The lower falls are more spectacular. They leap down ninety feet in a wild waterfall shut in by gigantic rocks. If you are still here in the spring, I will take you to see them."

"What do you mean, 'if I am still here'?" I asked.

"My personal opinion is you should leave Bridee Castle immediately."

"Why? Don't you care for my company?"

"I am thinking of your safety."

"Do you think I am in danger at the castle?"

"Bridee Castle is no place for a young woman. Aside from being dank and drear, it has a history of evil and violence that centuries have not erased," Adrian said.

"What do you suggest?" My tone was cool. The fact that the man I loved wanted me to go away wasn't easy to accept.

"Tour the Continent. Go to Spain, Egypt, Italy — anywhere but here."

"Bridee Castle is my responsibility. If there is danger here, I don't intend to run away from it. I intend to find out what is causing the danger and who killed Samrú and my sister and why." I lifted my chin defiantly and stared into his ebony eyes.

"Why must you be so obstinate, Heather? Leave the detecting to Inspector Andrews."

"He hasn't done much in the way of detecting," I countered.

"These things take time. What makes you think you can do better?"

"The three of us arrived here together. Now two of us are dead. I suspect I might be next. Whoever is doing these foul deeds is against those of us from India."

"Patrick Danton appears to be in perfect health. He hasn't expressed any fear for his life. Did you ever stop to think it might be your money someone wants?"

"Or Bridee Castle? I don't think so. Money and land do not account for Samrú's death. She owned nothing."

"Then what do you suggest? Lady Anne's revenge?" Adrian was clearly out of patience.

"Of course not. Ghosts don't exist." I said the words firmly, but I was beginning to have my doubts.

"Is there any way I can talk you into leaving Bridee Castle?"

"No. Is that why you wanted me to go riding with you? To talk me into leaving Scotland?"

"One of the reasons," he admitted.

"Oh. And what are the other reasons?"

"I wanted to get you away from the castle."

"Why?"

"As I said before, I think it is affecting you for the worse. The mind is a fragile thing. When one is under a strain, as you have been, the mind can be easily warped. Be influenced in uncanny ways."

"Are you suggesting I might be losing my sanity?" Was Adrian deliberately trying to provoke me? He was being too blunt.

"I am saying so far Bridee Castle holds nothing but unhappy memories for you and it might begin to dominate your thoughts, twisting your mind in a way you have no control over. I am only trying to help you, Heather. I am sure if your father was here he would suggest the same thing."

I stared at the loch. Would Adrian always have a paternal attitude toward me? Would he never see me as a grown woman? I sighed. Perhaps he does see me as a grown woman, but has no romantic inclinations toward me. I blinked back any tears that might be forming and concentrated on the loch.

"I sense I am only irritating you, Heather. Perhaps we should go back."

"Why isn't the loch frozen?" I asked, trying to postpone the inevitable.

"Loch Ness never freezes."

"Why?"

He ventured a small laugh. "I don't know. Perhaps it is because it is so deep. Would you like to ride along the loch for a while? The sun seems to be keeping its place in the sky."

I nodded in agreement and we urged our horses forward.

Despite Adrian's obsession with me leaving Scotland, the day was exhilarating. He dropped the topic and entertained me with the legends and folk tales of Scotland.

The fresh cold air had invigorated my mind, but left me physically tired. Once I caught up on my sleep, I knew I would have my full stamina back. I looked forward to my warm milk and laudanum as I crawled into bed.

The drink had an immediate effect on me. I don't remember finishing the milk. Rather than slowly falling asleep, I seemed to have blacked out, magazines still strewn on the bed. Then the dream started.

Rough hands were wrapping me in a shroud, covering my face which caused breathing difficulties. I wanted to push the shroud from my face, but my arms seemed incapable of obeying orders from my brain. I seemed to swing from a vague awareness into an inky void. Faceless specters hovered about me as though planning evil tortures. I wanted to struggle, but my will had fled. Every time I tried to wake myself, the black emptiness smothered me, causing my head to spin into oblivion.

Suddenly I was cold—so very cold. The cold was making me sick. I could feel my stomach constricting. There was a hazy red dot in my dream. I thought if I could reach it I would be safe.

The shroud became sheer gossamer which I could tear with my hands. I clawed my way out only to find I had to crawl on all fours like an animal. I couldn't stand. My stomach contractions intensified. I had the sensation that bile was pouring from my mouth. I started to shiver. I looked up hoping to see the red speck. Instead I saw the Devil himself.

He was dressed entirely in black, his cloak lined with bright red silk. When his hand reached out for me, I fell back into that black void.

Chapter Sixteen

My body was deliciously warm and my head was cool. If the Devil had taken me to Hell, I was enjoying it. I sighed aloud and startled myself. I opened my eyes to see Jean pouring another kettle of warm water into the tub in which I was immersed. I raised my hand to find a cool cloth over my forehead.

"Jean, why am I in a tub? What happened?" I asked.

"Mr. Adrian found you out in the cemetery. He said he found you lying in the snow."

"Did he bring me up here?"

"Aye, miss. Told me to get a hot tub ready for you."

"Did he . . ."

"Miss Ross and me undressed you and got you into the tub," Jean said as though she had anticipated my question.

"What time is it, Jean?"

"Seven in the morning, miss."

"I must get dressed and have breakfast downstairs."

"Oh, nay, miss. Mr. Adrian said to keep you in bed and bring your breakfast up to you."

"I will not stay in bed and laze the day away," I exclaimed.

"But Mr. Adrian said—"

"I don't care what Mr. Adrian said. He is not my keeper. My dark green merino day frock, Jean. I want you to do my hair up."

"If you don't mind my saying so, miss, you look so much younger with it down."

"That is the point, Jean. I don't want to look like a child."

Adrian and Patrick were at the breakfast table. They had been discussing something rather heatedly, for both were flushed with anger, their eyes registering loathing. All conversation between them came to an abrupt halt when I entered the room.

"I told the maid to keep you in bed, Heather. You shouldn't be up and around. You might have taken a chill," Adrian said, looking stern.

"I will take to my bed if and when I have a chill." I turned to the buffet and filled my plate.

"Mr. Danton, if you have finished eating, I would like to talk to Heather alone," Adrian said.

"As you wish, Mr. Ross." Patrick came to my side at the buffet and in a half-whisper said, "Heather, I wish to speak with you on a matter of importance. When can I see you alone?"

"I will be in the library later this morning. I would appreciate your bringing my father's memoirs I lent you."

"I haven't finished with them."

"I would like to get started transcribing them and I can't without the sections I lent you. They compose the first part."

"If you really need them, I shall be happy to comply. I will see you in the library," Patrick replied in a conspiratorial tone, then departed.

"What was that little tête-à-tête about?" Adrian asked as I took my place at the table.

"I don't think that is any of your concern," I answered.

"I neither like nor trust that fellow. He does not have your welfare at heart. Be wary of him, Heather. I suspect he is after something."

"Are you jealous of him, Adrian?"

"Why should I be jealous of the fellow? He has nothing I want. I am puzzled by the fact he is able to stay away from his regiment for so long. Something is drastically wrong there."

"Are you suggesting Patrick might be a deserter?"

"I deem it a strong possibility." He paused reflectively, then sat back. "What were you doing in the cemetery just before

254

dawn?"

"I don't know. I thought I was dreaming."

"Are you in the habit of sleepwalking?"

"I never have before. Really, Adrian, I have no idea how I got there."

"Do you know you were crawling about on all fours and were violently ill?"

"I vaguely remember it. I was having snatches of a dream interrupted by long spells of blackness."

"How do you feel now?"

"A slight headache, a little sluggish and groggy. Why?"

"How many drops of that laudanum did you put in your milk?"

"I put the usual two drops in." I hesitated. The milk was already on my night table and did taste a little different. At the time I didn't pay it much attention. "Do you think I was drugged?"

"I am inclined to think so. Two drops would act like a sedative. I doubt if it would have put you out completely. Who brought you the milk?"

"I suppose Jean. The milk was already on my night table."

"Have you checked the amount Dr. Drummond gave you to see if an unusual amount was gone?"

"No."

"I suggest you do so."

"What reason would anyone have to drug me and leave me out in the snow?" I asked.

"I imagine someone hoped you would catch a chill and come down with a fever."

"Or undermine my sanity," I added.

Adrian stood and tossed his napkin on the table. "Be careful, Heather. You have an enemy at Bridee Castle who is ruthless and murderous."

When he left, I poured myself another cup of tea and contemplated my position. Perhaps Adrian was right. If I did have an unknown and deadly enemy at Bridee Castle, I should leave. But that was the coward's way out. Father despised cowardice. He always said problems were never solved by running away from them. I came to the conclusion I would stay at Bridee Castle even at the risk of my life.

Upstairs I opened my bureau drawer, pushed aside some cotton stockings, and took out the phial of laudanum. I had only used four drops. The phial was half empty. Only Jean knew where I kept the laudanum. Did someone pay her to drug me? What else have they paid her to do? Put decapitated crows on my bed? If only I had some proof, I would confront her. As it was, suspicion was not enough to act on. But suspicions would make me cautious. I would watch the young maid more closely now.

In the library I placed a stack of foolscap on the top of the desk, made sure the inkwell was full, checked the nib of my pen, then waited for Patrick. I didn't have to wait long.

The lieutenant blustered into the library, firmly shutting the door behind him. He strode behind the desk, grabbed my shoulders and pulled me from the chair. His arms wrapped around me and his lips came down hard on mine. I wasn't thrilled and pushed him away despite his persistence.

"Marry me, Heather. Let me take you away from here. These people don't want you here. They have no regard for you at all," Patrick said, his hands still clutching my shoulders.

"I own Bridee Castle and it is my home now. Aunt Clarissa is my father's sister, my only living relative. If the Rosses don't want me around, they are free to leave. As for marrying you, Patrick, I don't love you."

"At one time you did."

"That was ages ago. I have done quite a bit of growing up since then."

"I know you still have feelings for me. One doesn't fall out of love that quickly."

"Then you must still love Diana."

"I was never in love with Diana, only infatuated by her beauty. You must believe me, Heather."

I sighed. "Your feelings toward Diana don't matter anymore, Patrick. I still won't marry you."

"You must marry me, Heather. I refuse to have you in the grip of these people, especially Adrian Ross. His black eyes reflect nothing but evil. I don't like the way he looks at you. Can't you see that they are only after your money? I wouldn't be surprised if they tried to kill you for it. Marry me and let me save you from them." His fingers dug into my shoulders.

"You are hurting me, Patrick. Let me go."

"Not until you promise to marry me."

"Let me go, Patrick," I cried. "Let me go."

"A little more persuasion will bring you to your senses."

His mouth came down on mine again, his lips harsh and cold. When I tried to move my head, his hands left my shoulders to grip my head. I pushed against his chest to no avail.

"What is going on here?" Adrian's voice boomed.

A startled Patrick released me and stepped back. "What is the meaning of this intrusion, sir?" Patrick asked.

"I was passing by the library door when I heard Heather's voice sounding distraught. I thought I would investigate. Are you all right, Heather?"

"Though it is none of your business, Heather and I were sealing our agreement to marry," Patrick said, putting his arms about my shoulders.

Adrian's countenance darkened. "Is this true, Heather? Danton, let her answer this time."

"Of course it isn't true," I answered, pulling away from Patrick. "I have no intentions of marrying anyone."

"Was he forcing his attentions on you, Heather?" Adrian cast an icy glare at Patrick.

"Let us forget about the incident. I am sure it won't happen again," I said.

"I think it is time you left Bridee Castle, Mr. Danton," Adrian said.

"You are not the owner of this place, sir. You have no authority here. I will stay as long as Heather is gracious enough to have me. Now, if you will excuse me." Patrick headed for the door.

"Patrick, have you forgotten my father's papers?" I asked.

"I shall send them to you directly." He stalked out of the room without glancing at Adrian.

257

"What was that all about?" Adrian queried.

"Patrick asked me to marry him and I refused."

"Why? I thought you were enamored of him."

"Any feelings, other than friendship, vanished a long time ago. Now I am not sure how strong that friendship is. He has never been forceful or demanding in the past."

"For your own sake, tell him to leave, Heather."

"That is easy for you to say. Not so easy for me to do."

"Do you want him here?"

"Not really. I see no reason for his presence at Bridee Castle any longer."

"As you saw, he pays no heed to me. And he is right. You are mistress here. I have no authority over who stays or leaves. It will have to be your decision, Heather."

"I will tell him to leave but I must have some time. I want the words to be just right."

"Do it soon, Heather."

"I will."

Jeffrey knocked on the open door. "I have some papers for you, Miss MacBride. Mr. Danton sent them." He walked to the desk and set them down.

"Thank you, Jeffrey."

"I will leave you to your father's memoirs, Heather," Adrian said, then preceded Jeffrey out of the room.

Time sped by as I read and took notes. Late in the afternoon I finished the papers Patrick had sent. I went upstairs to my bedchamber to sort out which papers I would work on the following day.

Again the trunk was emptied out, its contents strewn about. This time the lining had been slashed and ripped open. I rang for Jean.

"Walie!" she exclaimed, genuinely surprised at the disorder. "What happened, miss?"

"You tell me." I shouldn't have said that. Jean had no acting skills. She was truly ignorant of what had happened.

"I don't know, miss. Really I don't."

"Did you see anyone come in or leave?"

She shook her head while staring at the scattered papers,

258

books, and objects. After several seconds, she asked, "Shall I clean this up, miss?"

"I will take care of it, Jean. Was anyone lurking about the corridor when you came up?"

"Mr. Bruce Ross was in the corridor, but he wasn't lurking about."

"Thank you, Jean. That will be all for now." I watched her leave, then set about cleaning up the mess.

I found it difficult to believe Bruce would have disemboweled the trunk. He had no reason of which I could think. What could my father have left that someone wanted so desperately? Memoirs, a few war mementos, relics of his children's childhood were not items a thief would be able to sell.

I ran my hand fondly over my old Jumble book and put it aside. I might be of a mood to skim through it later.

When all had gathered in the drawing room after dinner and were comfortably seated, I spoke up.

"Again someone has entered my sitting room, tossed the contents of my father's trunk around, and slashed the lining. I want you all to be aware that I will not tolerate this sort of vandalism. If anything of this nature occurs again, I shall be forced to call in the constabulary."

"Are you accusing one of us?" John asked indignantly.

"I think you have gone a bit daft, Heather," Bruce said with a lift of one eyebrow.

"My maid saw you in the hall near my sitting room door, Bruce," I said.

"Really, Heather. Are you going to accuse everyone who walks the corridor of being a thief? Besides, what would I want with the contents of your father's old trunk?" Bruce asked.

"I don't know. That is what I am trying to find out." My voice was becoming strident. I had to get myself under control. Jane was looking at me with a startled expression which held a hint of pity.

"Oh, dear me," Aunt Clarissa groaned. "You haven't been yourself lately, Heather. Roaming about the cemetery like some lost soul, seeing lights in the keep. You have been under too much of a strain. All the deaths. Why don't you see Dr. Drummond again. Perhaps he can recommend a different type of doctor who can truly help you."

I glared angrily at Adrian. He had told them where he had found me. I felt betrayed. My attention went back to Aunt Clarissa. "Are you suggesting I might have mental problems, Aunt Clarissa?"

"Well, my dear, you must admit you have been acting strangely of late. All that time you spent in the old hall when servants could have done the task. I don't know what to think. I do worry so about you. Your father would want me to look out for you." Aunt Clarissa twisted her handkerchief with distraught violence. "Jane, do fetch me that box of chocolates."

Jane was obedient.

"Because I like to do things for myself doesn't make me mentally unstable, Aunt Clarissa. Sometimes I am not too sure of *your* mental capacities."

"Now, now. There is no reason for you to become vituperative toward your aunt, Heather. She is only trying to help you. I know of several doctors in Edinburgh that specialize in mental aberrations. Perhaps I should send for one," John suggested.

"Mental aberrations!" I practically screamed as I jumped up from my seat. I knew my outburst was a mistake by the way everyone stared at me with charitable tolerance.

Adrian came to my side. "Sit down, Heather. As Father said, all we want to do is help you."

I glared at him with growing anger. "*Et tu, Brute?*" I grumbled at him, then promptly left the room.

I was shaking with anger as Jean helped me prepare for bed.

"Are you cold, miss? I could get more peat for the fire if you wish," Jean said.

"That won't be necessary, Jean. The fire is fine as it is."

"Then I will fetch your warm milk, miss."

While she was gone, I checked the phial of laudanum. Nothing had been taken from the half-filled phial. Still, I took it with me to put in the drawer of my night table where I could keep an eye on it.

Jean came back and placed the milk on the table. "Is there anything else, miss?"

"No, Jean. Go to bed and get some sleep."

When Jean left, I went into the sitting room and retrieved my childhood Jumble book. I clutched it as I got into bed. I opened the book and absently turned the pages, but couldn't concentrate on the words. Was Patrick right? Was I in the grip of the Rosses? Were they after my money? Was there evil in Adrian's ebony eyes?

My thoughts and emotions were reaching a breaking point. Aberrations indeed! Still, there was the luminous specter, the dead crows, and the lighted keep. I was thankful I hadn't mentioned the specter to anyone. Citing that experience would surely have them putting me in a mental asylum. I would have to keep a wary eye on my behavior. I must be rational and lucid at all times.

The warm milk tasted fine. I couldn't discern any extra laudanum in it. I only put a scant drop of the laudanum in the milk. My lids were soon heavy. I put the book aside and snuggled down into the covers.

I was laid out on a marble slab in the top part of the keep. My hands were folded over my chest, my eyes were open and I could hear, but couldn't move. Like sizzling coals, Adrian's eyes stared down at me with a diabolical glint. Soon the rest of the Rosses were standing about me, yet their faces were distorted with lascivious leers that reflected depravity. I was pierced by a distinct chill, but my body never shivered.

Revulsion filled me as their eyes took on a reddish golden glow. Their skin became scaly and their breath foul. Talons spurted from the ends of their fingers. Mold was developing between the scales on John and Aunt Clarissa. Jane and Bruce waved their claws over me.

Only Adrian kept his human appearance. Unable to speak, I tried to beg him with my eyes to save me. His smile was ghoulish as he pulled back his black cape with the red silk lining. The top of his ears elongated to a point. He gave a slow nod of his head causing the others to screech with delight. Their claws raised. Their sharp talons glistened like highly polished knives as they lowered toward my body. Hovering over all of them like a black malignant cloud was Lady Anne. As the icy talons touch my flesh, I bolted upright in bed.

Dim shafts of light heralded the dawn. I put the back of my hand to my forehead to find cold beads of perspiration had gathered there. Though the horrid nightmare had taken its toll on my nerves, at least I had slept through the night.

I was getting used to the biting cold of the Highlands. I no longer found it a deterrent to riding abroad. I did dress warmer, though. I sensed the mare appreciated my proclivity for frequent riding. The animal pranced and galloped with rare spirit and enthusiasm.

Reverend Campbell was surprised to see me. He ushered me into his modest sitting parlor, then bustled off to make tea.

"I don't know how I can express the deep gratitude I feel for your generous contribution of silver artifacts for our kirk, Heather," Reverend Campbell said as he poured.

"The silverware has been stored at Bridee Castle for centuries. I felt it was time for the pieces to be put to good use. Have you any plans for the disposal of the silver?" I asked as I gratefully sipped the hot tea.

"I hope you don't mind, Heather, but I intend to keep several of the silver candlesticks and trays for the church if that is all right with you."

"I gave them to you. Do as you wish with them."

"The rest I hope to sell to private individuals or museums."

"I thought you might have a church bazaar and auction them off," I said.

"The pieces wouldn't bring a fraction of what they are worth. The people of this parish do not have that kind of money. The church needs many repairs and I had hoped to purchase an organ. It would be so nice to have music with our hymns. I would also like to set up a fund for the needy. The people here are much too proud to accept anything that might hint of charity. They would be more inclined to accept something from the church." Reverend Campbell gave a wistful sigh.

"If you don't have enough money to realize all your aims, I will make up the difference."

"Oh, Heather, you don't have to do that."

"I want to. Please say no more about it."

"You are a generous woman, Heather. I only wish there was something I could do for you."

"Perhaps there is." I related the incidents that had occurred since I first came to Bridee Castle, including the nightmares. I held nothing back, no matter how embarrassing it was. The reverend was a patient man and listened to my outpourings with intensity. He sat for several minutes as though deep in thought before he spoke.

"I think Dr. Drummond is right. Your nightmares are stemming from a sense of guilt. What happened to your sister was in no way your fault. You must rid yourself of that thought by consciously and constantly abrogating this so-called guilt. As for the specter and the lights in the keep—" He threw his hands up in a gesture of helplessness.

"Do you think I am going insane? Couldn't guilt make one mentally unstable too?" I asked.

"No, I don't think you are going insane. Yes, I do think guilt could drive one into insanity, but I do not think your sense of guilt is that deeply rooted. I would say you have what might be called a surface guilt. The kind of guilt that leads to insanity inculcates itself over many years, going deeper and deeper. Your sister's strong will prevented you from acting when you thought you should have. Your sister wasn't a stupid woman. She knew she should have seen a doctor, but her vanity prevented her. You are not to blame."

"Do you think seeing specters stems from my feelings?"

"Could be. I certainly wouldn't rule it out," Reverend Campbell said.

"They are so real and I am sure I am awake when I see them. I even lighted the oil lamp, but the phantom vanished while I was doing it."

"If you are really seeing dead crows and specters, I would be inclined to think some human hand is behind it."

"Do you think someone might want me to appear insane?"

"That is a strong possibility. You are a wealthy young woman. If I am not being too bold, who stands to inherit your lands and fortune if you become . . . well . . . shall we say incapacitated?" Reverend Campbell asked.

"I imagine my aunt and, inadvertently, the Rosses." I never wanted to entertain that particular thought. I knew from the beginning Adrian wanted the lands of Bridee Castle. Bruce wanted, perhaps needed, the money as did John Ross. I used to wonder what Jane would do without the security of Bridee Castle. Aunt Clarissa appeared to have adequate funds and was confident I would never oust her from the castle.

"That people would resort to murder and other infamous deeds in the name of money is abhorrent to me, but I guess it happens more often than one supposes in this material world," Reverend Campbell mused, sighing.

"What do you think I should do?" I asked.

"I think your friend, Mr. Danton, had the right idea. Leave Bridee Castle. If you want to stay in the Highlands, I am sure there are nice cottages around Inverness. Or travel for a spell. You are young enough to trot around the world."

"Isn't that being a coward? Running away, I mean."

"Better to be a live coward than a dead heroine, my dear."

"Father always told us to stand firm and face our troubles head on and they would soon crumble."

"That is a noble thought, Heather. Do you think you are strong enough to face a villain who is intent on seeking your demise one way or another?"

"I will have to be."

"Then you have decided to stay, I take it."

"I would never have any peace if I didn't."

"Seeing you are adamant about this, may I make a suggestion?"

"Of course. I would welcome it."

"Go to a solicitor and have a will made out leaving the bulk of your fortune and lands to anyone but your aunt and the Rosses. Make your actions known. If the cause is terminated, so is the effect."

264

I smiled. The idea appealed to me. "Who should I make my beneficiary? I don't know anyone around here."

"An orphanage, a museum, the Royal Burgh of Inverness. I am sure a solicitor could make better suggestions than I can."

"I shall do as you suggest, Reverend. As you said, 'Cause and effect.' " I stood, and the reverend did also.

"A warning, Heather. Don't announce your intentions before you see a solicitor. Let it be known only after you have made the will. Make it a *fait accompli*, if you know what I mean."

"Yes, I do. But if I just say I am going to do it, wouldn't that make my enemy, or enemies, come out in the open all the sooner? Wouldn't they try to stop me before I saw the solicitor, perhaps becoming careless and get caught?"

"Perhaps. But it would be like putting your hand in the fire daring it to be burned. Much too dangerous if, indeed, someone is trying to do away with you. If you go to the solicitor first, any risk is eliminated."

"Well, if anything does happen to me, at least you know my story. I truly appreciate your interest and helpful comments, Reverend Campbell. I must go now. I have imposed upon your time long enough."

"No imposition at all, my dear. I enjoy having your company and happy I could be of some help. Not many people seek my advice these days," he said as he walked me to the door.

So many thoughts whirled in my head as I rode back to the castle. That Adrian might be one of the conspirators weighed heavily on my heart. But I had to know one way or the other or I would go insane. Though I knew the reverend's suggestion about seeing a solicitor first was the sensible course to follow, I decided to take the riskier path and announce my intentions. I would rather die than spend the rest of my life with doubts and suspicions.

I didn't realize the danger was more than I had anticipated.

Chapter Seventeen

I entered the castle through one of the rear doors closest to the
stableyard. I had to pass the library to reach the main staircase.
As I approached the library I could hear voices — Jane and her
father. I halted and unashamedly listened. I would need all the
advantages I could obtain if I were going to put my plan into
effect.

"What are we going to do about her?" Jane asked. "She is so
nice, an asylum seems too cruel. I have heard what those places
are like."

"I don't like it any better than you, but you know Adrian.
Once he has his mind set, there is no changing it," John Ross
said.

"I would rather see her dead."

"Bruce thinks that is the best way, but Adrian says we must
make sure of the money first."

"I don't know how long I can keep up the charade," Jane replied.

"Adrian said we must keep up the pressure on her," John
chuckled. "That is if Bruce doesn't kill her first. He has been hot-
tempered of late."

"I am tired of it all. First that Indian woman, then Diana. I
can't stand it much longer."

"Hold on, Jane. There is a lot at stake here. Do you want to be
on the road begging for a crust of bread?"

"No, but I don't want any more killing either."

"Then pacify Bruce. Adrian's plan is the best. Intensify the
pressure, she will fall apart, and we will have her committed. We
had better get ready for dinner. All outward appearances must

be kept up. We don't want anyone becoming suspicious. I will be glad when that Danton fellow is gone. He snoops around too much."

"He wanders about the old part of the castle a lot. He unsettles me with his prying into everything. I wish I knew what he wanted here," Jane said.

"It is obvious. He wants to marry Heather for her money. I am sure Adrian will put a stop to that." John chuckled again.

"How can you be so jolly under the circumstances?"

"The situation is most peculiar. We are damned if we do and damned if we don't. Come along, Jane."

I flattened myself against the shadowy wall by the staircase and watched them leave the library. I leaned my head against the wall and closed my eyes. So the Rosses were conspiring to get rid of me and Adrian was the instigator. My heart felt as though it was being pounded by the largest rock in the world. I was in love with a man who was doing everything in his power to remove me from the world of the sane. I wanted to cry. Instead, I trotted upstairs.

"Jean," I called.

"Aye, miss." She came scurrying out of my sitting parlor.

Though I wondered what she was doing in there, I didn't ask. I had other things on my mind. "I would like a hot tub. I will wear my green silk chiffon this evening."

Her eyebrows raised in surprise. "Not one of your dark gowns, miss?"

"No. I have decided to come out of mourning."

When she left, I went into the sitting room. Nothing seemed amiss. My nostrils were greeted with the smell of lemon furniture polish. The grate was scrupulously clean and a new fire was laid. The room was spotless. It was evident Jean had worked hard to make the room sparkle. I was ashamed of myself for being suspicious.

The pale green gown suited me. It emphasized the green of my eyes and enhanced the golden highlights in my red hair. Jean did an exceptionally fine job of doing up my hair. I was pleased with my reflection in the mirror.

I was late. I swept into the dining room in much the same

manner as Diana would have. The gentlemen rose and admiration shone in their eyes.

"Heather, you look ravishing this evening," Patrick said.

"Is there a special occasion we don't know about?" Bruce asked.

"No, I thought a little color would brighten up this gloomy old castle," I said.

"You sound disillusioned with Bridee Castle," Jane said as everyone resumed their seats.

"I was never disillusioned, Jane. Father had described the castle many times, but I am beginning to find it oppressive."

"Don't tell me the ghost of Lady Anne is getting to you, Heather," Bruce remarked, a sneer on his face.

"Hardly. I don't believe in ghosts."

"Well, I do," Aunt Clarissa claimed. "There has been nothing but tragedy since the day you opened the door to the keep, Heather. She wanders through the castle quite freely now. It was very naughty of you, my dear, especially when you knew how I felt about it."

"I am sorry if the deed disturbed you, Aunt Clarissa. I doubt if Lady Anne instigated tragedies here," I said. The beef and barley soup was then served, followed by freshly caught trout. Little was said as everyone savored the fish. Once the venison, boiled potatoes, carrots, and brussels sprouts had been served, I decided to make my announcement. "I thought all of you should know I intend to see a solicitor in day or so."

"Whatever for?" John asked.

"To have my will made out."

"Aren't you a bit young to be thinking about a will?" Adrian asked.

"I have such vast holdings, I thought it best. I wouldn't want the demesne and capital being sucked away by the courts and solicitors."

"I hope you will remember me kindly, Heather, and leave some small pittance to me," Bruce said.

"Really, Bruce," John admonished.

"I see nothing wrong in putting in a good word for myself, Father," Bruce said.

"I shall leave a token of my esteem to all of you. Bridee Castle and its lands shall go to the Royal Burgh of Inverness which they can turn into a museum with the tenancy supporting the up-keep. My personal fortune shall go to Reverend Campbell and the kirk," I announced with a certain amount of glee.

I was disappointed by their reactions. No emotion registered on the faces of the Rosses. Aunt Clarissa looked as though she hadn't heard a word I said. Patrick was the one who surprised me. He looked distraught to say the least.

"Do play the piano for us, Heather," Aunt Clarissa said as we gathered in the drawing room after dinner. "Something soft and soothing."

I complied. From the corner of my eye, I watched Adrian. He appeared to be deep in thought as he stared down at the whisky in his glass. He was so handsome. I found it hard to believe he had a murderous soul. I continued to play for my own pleasure long after everyone had retired.

I was neither shocked nor frightened when I saw the dead crow on my bed. I simply wrapped it up and placed it on the hearth. I suspected I would be visited that night by Lady Anne's so-called ghost. I got into bed and pretended to be asleep. I kept the oil lamp as low as possible so all I had to do was turn it up when the specter appeared. I dismissed the thought that it might really be a ghost.

The barely perceptible light emitting from the lamp cast eerie shadows about the room which began to taunt me with visions. I shut my eyes. A deep moan curled through the room causing me to open my eyes. There was my specter glowing its malignancy before me. As its guttural moans increased and the form began to waft toward the bed, I reached out to raise the wick in the lamp.

In my haste to flood the room with light, I knocked the lamp off the table. The small flame quickly ignited the finger of oil that had spread across the carpet. Creeping toward the bed's dust ruffle, the flame caught and began to lick up toward the bed. I was now more concerned with burning to death than being beset by a ghost.

I scrambled out of the bed and circled around until I reached the door. After flinging it open, I started to scream for help. The flames were spreading rapidly. I dashed for the ewer and tossed the water into the flames. I grabbed the pillow off the chaise and tried to beat down the fire with it.

Adrian and Bruce were the first to arrive. Bruce went to have water donkeyed up by means of the dumbwaiter. Adrian took off his robe and began to beat the flames along with me. The disturbance brought John, Patrick, and Jane.

The water began to arrive. We formed a line to pass the pails along to Adrian who splashed them over the dying flames. Aunt Clarissa stood in the corridor watching the scene with horror in her eyes. When the fire was extinguished, we trooped downstairs to the drawing room. By now everyone was wide awake. John poured sherries for the ladies while the men helped themselves to large whiskys.

"What happened, Heather?" Adrian asked.

"I stupidly knocked over the oil lamp." I felt foolish, but wasn't about to mention any ghost. I was determined not to let their plan succeed.

"Well, you certainly can't sleep there tonight," Aunt Clarissa said.

"You can sleep with me," Bruce impishly suggested.

"One of the guest rooms will be adequate." My eyes strayed to Adrian. He was naked to the waist. My breath caught in my throat. Thick black curly hair covered his broad chest. Hard work had sinewed his arms. I lowered my eyes lest I be caught gaping at him.

"Are you sure it was an accident?" Adrian asked, breaking the silence in the room.

"Of course," I answered.

"Were you awake when it happened, Heather?" John asked.

"Of course I was awake. What are you suggesting, John?"

He shrugged.

"I have seen you thrash about when you were sleeping," said Jane as though explaining her father's question. "Perhaps you should keep your lamp elsewhere."

Before I could respond, Aunt Clarissa spoke. "Oh, dear me. I wouldn't be surprised if Lady Anne caused you to knock the lamp over. She will set all of us on fire. I must have another sherry, John, even though I doubt if it will make me sleep now. I shall be too busy fearing for all our lives."

"Now, Clarissa, you mustn't think like that," Jane soothed. "It was an accident. We are perfectly safe and no one is going to set fire to the castle."

"Oh, I hope you are right, Jane."

"Of course she is right, Clarissa," John added. "Come along. I think we have had enough excitement for one night. We should get what sleep we can."

Everyone filed toward the staircase. As I reached the first riser, a hand grasped my upper arm. I turned to face Adrian.

"Which room will you be sleeping in?" he asked casually.

"The one on the other side of my sitting parlor," I said before thinking. I shouldn't have told him. Now everyone would know where to find me. But then everyone would know by tomorrow anyway. "Why do you ask?"

"No particular reason. Have a good night's sleep, Heather. Or what is left of the night." He released my arm.

I plodded up the stairs. A weariness began to consume me. I fell into a dreamless sleep the minute my head touched the pillow.

A leaden sky refused to let the sun greet the morning. On days like this Bridee Castle took on an aura of a dreary and decaying mausoleum. The sparse light shafting into the rooms was gray, making one's soul feel without color.

I ate breakfast alone then went to the library to resume work on my father's memoirs. His notes contained little personal information. They dealt mainly with battles, skirmishes, and the people of the regiment. I found it a boring chore, but I had given my word and felt it was the last thing I could do for him.

Several days passed without incident. The only thing of note to happen was my moving back into my regular bedchamber. The staff had done wonders with it in the short period. A new carpet replaced the old one. No traces of fire or smoke remained. Though that particular bedchamber held no fond memories for

271

me, I felt at home there.

The night I moved back into my old bedchamber, I stood at the window and gazed at the dark shadow of the keep. As I did, I came to the conclusion that once I solved the mysteries of Samrú and my sister's death, I would leave Bridee Castle. I adored the mountainous Highlands, but could never endure the dark and empty feeling the castle engendered in me. Knowing Adrian would never be my knight in shining armor removed all incentive to stay.

I stared at the inky tower while my mind concentrated on the various places where I could make my home. Perhaps I would go on a tour of the Continent. Paris, Venice—cities that lured young and old alike. As my musings skipped around my head, they were brought to a sudden halt when my eyes focused on the light moving up the keep. Again it remained there for a while before descending. When the light disappeared, I desperately tried to think what it was I found odd about the top floor of the keep. Remembrance eluded me. I resolved to go back up there tomorrow and see if the journey would jar my memory.

Adrian and Bruce were at the sideboard filling their breakfast plates when I entered the dining room.

"Aren't you up a mite early, Bruce?" I asked.

"I am meeting One-eyed Angus in Inverness. He knows where there are some good card games," Bruce explained.

"I thought you owed him money," I said, filling my plate.

"All paid up. And look." He pulled a roll of pound notes from his pocket while balancing his plate in one hand.

"Win another dart game?" I was surprised by his sudden wealth.

"Something like that." His smile was mysterious.

"Bruce has a lot of hidden talents," Adrian remarked drily as we took our seats at the table. "What are your plans for today, Heather? More work on your father's memoirs?"

"I haven't quite decided." I didn't want anyone to know I was going to the keep, especially Adrian. "And you?"

"I have things to attend to."

"Mucking about in that house of yours in the woods, no doubt," Bruce said.

Adrian raised a querulous eyebrow.

"Don't look so startled, Brother dear. We have known about your minor mansion in the woods for some time now."

"How did you find out?" Adrian asked with a complacent expression.

"I was out riding one day and came across the secluded house. I told Father and he went to Inverness to check the land records. He thought it might be a good investment if the property were for sale. He was stunned to learn you were the owner."

"Why hasn't anyone mentioned it?" Adrian asked.

Bruce shrugged. "Father said to wait until you mentioned it. As time went by, I guess we forgot about it. I am surprised you stay here when you have your own, more modern, place."

Adrian tossed his brother a sardonic smile and said nothing.

I dawdled with my breakfast, hoping they would leave before I began my trek to the keep. Bruce gulped his breakfast down and departed. Adrian seemed to hesitate.

"Has your bedchamber been cleaned to your satisfaction, Heather?" he asked.

"Yes." I reached for another piece of toast and smeared it with marmalade.

"You are exceptionally hungry this morning."

"I am."

He studied me for a moment. "I have the feeling you would like to dispense with my company."

I made no attempt to reply.

His dark eyes narrowed. "Are you angry with me, Heather?"

"I try to make it a practice never to get angry."

"Displeased then."

"Shouldn't you be getting on with all those things you have to do today?"

He eyed me suspiciously. "I can see you are in an obstinate mood today. I had best leave you to your own devices." His tone was icy, his expression forbidding as he stood. "Perhaps I will see you at dinner."

Again I said nothing. I kept my eyes on my toast. I couldn't bring myself to look at him lest he see the torment in my eyes. When his footsteps faded and the front door slammed shut, I took a deep breath. I had done it. I had denied his potent attraction. I was sure, in time, my love for this man who was trying to have me institutionalized would fade.

I could hear the footsteps of Jane and her father coming down the stairs. I quickly drained the last drops of tea and stood. I was in no mood for company. I made the usual morning greetings to them in the foyer then went to the library. I needed some time to compose myself before I went to the keep.

I sat behind the desk, my head in my hands. I couldn't stop Adrian's handsome face from taunting me.

"Are you all right, Miss MacBride?" asked Mrs. Burns poking her head through the half-open door.

I looked up and smiled faintly. "I am fine, Mrs. Burns."

"You really shouldn't keep yourself cooped up in the library all day."

"Perhaps you are right, Mrs. Burns. I think I shall take a walk to the ancient hall to make sure all the silverware has been sent to Reverend Campbell." I thought it best someone should know my whereabouts. I knew Mrs. Burns wouldn't say anything to anyone unless I was gone longer than I should have been.

"Will you be back for lunch or should I have Jean bring a tray to you?" she asked.

"I will be back long before lunch."

She nodded and left.

I pushed myself up from the desk. I stood there a minute drawing myself together. Knowing it would be cold in the keep, I went to fetch my heavy cloak.

I took my time walking down the long, dim corridor. A chill tingled my spine as I entered the weaponry room. What little daylight filtered in gave the standing suits of armor an eerie aura of time past. In a way it frightened me. I felt there was a living, breathing presence in that room. Shadows proliferated in reaction to the darkening sky outside. I wanted to flee, but the sense of being watched ceased. Perhaps this was my chance to catch the evildoer of Bridee Castle.

Bruce and Adrian had left the castle, though. At least that was the impression they gave me. They could have reentered through a rear door. But how would they know I was here? I only told Mrs. Burns.

I narrowed my eyes and peered into every dark corner of the chamber. My imagination began to play foul tricks on me. The suits of armor appeared to move. The more they seemed to be alive, the more paralyzed I became. The room started to close in on me, giving me the sensation I was being crowded from all sides. I turned around and around as if trying to protect my back at all times. With my immobility broken, I groped for sanity. When common sense finally overtook my capricious fear, I started to race out of the room.

As I reached the door frame, hands shot out. The one that swooped around my waist caught me short in my flight and knocked the air from my lungs. As I gulped in air in preparation for a good loud scream, a hand clamped over my mouth. I was dragged back into the shadows.

Chapter Eighteen

"Don't scream, Heather. I have no intention of hurting you. I will take my hand off your mouth if you promise not to scream."

I nodded my head, raw anger swelling up in me. He removed his hand. "What is the meaning of this, Patrick? Have you lost your mind? You half scared me to death. Let go of me."

"I didn't mean to scare you, Heather. I only wanted to talk to you alone."

"You could have done that in the living quarters of the castle. You didn't have to come here to accost me in the gloom."

"Every time I get you alone in the inhabited part of the castle, someone comes along to interrupt us," Patrick declared.

"Why did you wait so long before making your presence known?"

"I wanted to make sure you were alone and no one was following you."

"You are imagining things, Patrick. No one is following me. What did you want to talk to me about that requires all this secrecy?"

"Didn't Diana or your father tell you?"

"Tell me what?"

"You really don't know?"

"Stop playing games, Patrick," I demanded.

"Before I say anything, let me ask you again to marry me. We will leave this desolate place and go anywhere in the world you want."

"What about your regiment?"

"I will be honest with you, Heather. I have left the regiment for good."

"You deserted?"

"I suppose you could put it that way."

"Do they know where you are?"

"I doubt it. I used a false name when booking passage." He came closer and put his hands on my shoulders.

"If you try to kiss me, Patrick, I *shall* scream. Long and loud."

"Have I no hope of making you my wife?"

"None whatsoever. I don't love you and would never consider marrying a deserter from the army. My father trusted you. He would shudder in his grave if he knew you deserted. How could you have done such a thing. Patrick?"

"I hated India. I hated those filthy wogs. I couldn't stand being around them. Even more frustrating was the fact I was constantly being passed over for promotion. They kept bringing in outsiders to command over me. I was sick of the whole thing. When Diana left and your father died, I saw no reason to stay."

"My leaving didn't disturb you?" My pride was bruised.

"Of course, Heather, of course. I missed you most of all."

"Liar."

"Think what you will, Heather. Remember I was attracted to you first."

"All that is beside the point now. What about my father?"

"Brigadier MacBride was well liked by the native population. He did many favors for the Hindu rajahs, ranis, maharajahs and maharanees, and for the Muslim muftis and the Mahdi. They made him a wealthy man by showering him with precious gems and gold—the finest of emeralds, rubies, and star sapphires, not to mention a horde of uncut diamonds, luminous pearls whose size would dazzle any eye. Your father showed me one. Incredible! He told me he had been given a large box of white pearls along with a box of black pearls. Aside from all his investments, he said the jewels alone would keep him and his daughters in luxury for the rest of their lives and their children's lives. He told Diana about them. I presumed he told you also."

I shook my head. "I never saw any jewels. Neither Father nor Diana ever mentioned them."

"Oh, Diana knew about them all right. She knew they were here in Bridee Castle, but she didn't know where. She made half-hearted attempts to find them before she became too sick to care. Samrú would have known where they were hidden, but I got here too late to question her. I am surprised Samrú didn't tell you about them."

"Samrú said nothing of gems. How do you know they are here? Perhaps they are back in India," I suggested, still stunned by this information.

"I looked everywhere before leaving India. Besides, your father told me they were here and to make sure his daughters found them. He died before he could tell me where he had hidden them." He grabbed my shoulders and shook me violently. "You have got to know where they are, Heather."

"Stop it, Patrick. I have no idea where they could be. What interest is it of yours anyway?"

"I helped your father carry out many of the favors for the Indian bigwigs. Some of them wouldn't have been accomplished if I hadn't helped. For years your father promised me a share of the gems and gold. I am here to see that that promise is kept, no matter what I have to do to get them. I will tear this castle apart if I have to." His eyes became brittle. High emotion raced greed across his face.

"Were you the one who rifled through my father's trunk?" I asked.

"Yes."

"Both times?"

"I had forgotten about the lining. I went back to see if he had left a map or a note in the lining. I found nothing."

"Is that why you are so interested in reading my father's memoirs?"

"I thought he might have mentioned them in the notes," Patrick confessed.

"Why didn't you tell me all this sooner? Why were you so secretive about it?" He stared at me, his eyes glazed. I suddenly realized the meaning of the subterfuge and said, "You wanted it all for yourself, didn't you, Patrick?"

"Why not? I earned it. You didn't. You have all the money you will ever need. Those jewels are mine. Don't try to stop me, Heather, or you will be sorry."

"Would you kill for them, Patrick?"

"If I have to."

"Even me?"

"Even you." He turned and began to pace. "I don't want to hurt anyone, Heather. I only want what is rightfully mine. You have no idea how long I have waited for those jewels. I must have them."

His story didn't sound right to me. Father was always a fair and honest man when it came to business matters. He liked Patrick. It wasn't like him to cheat his lieutenant.

"Why didn't my father give you your share when he first received the gems?"

He stopped pacing and came to stand in front of me, a cold fury glittering in his eyes. "Are you questioning my veracity?"

"Yes, I am. I don't think you have any right to those gems — if they exist. Aunt Clarissa has more right to them than you do."

"I suppose you are going to run to your aunt and the Rosses and babble all about the jewels."

"Is there any reason why I shouldn't?"

"Yes, I am going to stop you."

His quick, strong hands were about my throat squeezing. My lungs screamed for air. I knew I had to do something before I passed out. The vision of a young Indian girl defending herself against a lustful Sepoy flashed in my brain. My physical reaction followed in a second. I brought my knee up hard and swift between Patrick's legs. His hands fell to clutch his wounded anatomy as he groaned and sank to the floor. I ran back to the safety of the drawing room occupied by John, Jane, and Aunt Clarissa. I made sure I was not alone for the rest of the day.

I wore a navy blue taffeta gown as I went downstairs to await dinner. I stopped short in the doorway of the drawing, room. Patrick Danton stood by the fireplace. No one else was in the room. As he came toward me, I had to fight the urge to run. Jeffrey was across the foyer in the dining room. One cry from me would bring him running to my assistance.

"Please don't go, Heather. I wish to apologize," Patrick said as he approached me.

"It is a little late for apologies, Patrick." My hand went to my bruised throat involuntarily.

His eyes skipped to my neck. "I am truly sorry. I don't know what came over me. It was like someone else took possession of my body and soul. I never meant to hurt you."

"Well, you did. I will never forget the incident, Patrick." Oddly enough, I was quite calm.

"I swear it will never happen again. Never," Patrick claimed.

"I know it won't. You are leaving Bridee Castle, Patrick. I never want to see you again."

"You can't mean that, Heather. We have been friends for years. Your father and I were as close as father and son. We are almost like relatives."

"Perhaps you see it that way. I don't. You are no longer welcome here." I started to walk past him toward a chair. He grabbed my arm and spun me about.

"Listen, Heather, you are not going to toss me out of here until I have found what I came here for."

"Let me go, Patrick." I tried to pull my arm free, but his grip tightened. I should have known he had great strength in his hands from the way he squeezed my throat.

"Not until you forget all about my leaving Bridee Castle."

"Blackmail only adds to my growing dislike of you. Now let me go!"

"Why don't you do as the lady wishes," Adrian said as he entered the drawing room.

Patrick released me and turned around. "Do you always sneak up on people, Ross?"

"What has been going on here?" Adrian asked, ignoring Patrick.

"A difference of opinion," Patrick answered.

"A strong difference of opinion," I added. I think Adrian would have pursued his questioning if the others hadn't entered at that moment.

Between the soup and the main course, I made the announcement. "Patrick will be leaving us the day after tomorrow." I thought that would be enough time for him to get his things together and make traveling arrangements.

"Called back to the regiment, Danton?" John asked.

"Something like that," Patrick said, giving me a surly look.

"Rumor has it that the East India Company will have to relinquish its hold on India," Bruce said.

"Rumors?" John queried. "Why, Lord Palmerston introduced a bill into the House of Commons this month to have a president and council head a new government for India."

"I doubt if Queen Victoria will approve," Adrian said.

"Why?" I asked.

"I have heard she wants India vested in her name and all the powers exercised in her name. I think she had a desire to be more than Queen. Perhaps Empress of India is more to her liking," Adrian said with a wry smile.

We spent the rest of the evening discussing politics, then retired to bed.

I only saw Patrick at meals the next day. He was quiet and avoided speaking to me. The day I had elected for him to depart, he appeared at the breakfast table early.

"I presume you will be leaving this morning, Patrick," I said when he sat down.

"Late this afternoon, if you don't mind. I make better connections that way. I shall send you my address when I have reached my final destination. Perhaps you will be generous and write to me, Heather. And if you find anything that I might have left behind, anything that rightfully belongs to me, I hope you will send it along," Patrick said, narrowing his eyes, then wiping his mustache with one finger.

"If I find anything that *rightfully* belongs to you, naturally I shall post it to you immediately." I knew he had gems in mind. But I was still of the opinion the jewels — if there were any — never reached the Highlands.

"I would greatly appreciate it, Heather," Patrick said. He rose from his chair. "If you will excuse me, I have to tend to the last-minute details."

"What was that all about?" Adrian asked, sitting back in his chair.

"You heard what was said," I answered.

"Come now, Heather. Your repartee with Danton had a deeper meaning than what was on the surface."

"You have a fertile and inventive mind, Adrian. People do forget things, especially when their visit has been an extensive one."

"At least he is leaving. He was becoming a nuisance."

"Who is a nuisance?" asked Bruce as he made his way to the sideboard.

"Danton," Adrian said.

"Nuisance is an understatement, Brother dear. The man was a positive affliction. Everywhere I turned he was there. And his questions about the castle! Are there any hidden passageways? Are there secret doors? Where are the cellars?" Bruce mimicked Patrick quite accurately. "He drove me crazy with his questions. One would think he was going to purchase the place. I am thoroughly delighted he is leaving. Now we can have Heather all to ourselves." Lust sparkled in Bruce's eyes when he looked at me. Or was it a desire to get on with the plans they had for me?

"You are hardly here, Bruce," I said.

"Perhaps I shall stay around more often now. Between your late sister and that Danton chap, I found the atmosphere here quite disagreeable."

"No matter what the atmosphere is like here, Bruce, you will always find the racetrack or pub more agreeable than anywhere else," Adrian said good-naturedly.

Bruce smiled, making him appear impish as he sat down at the table.

"What have you planned for the day, Heather?" Adrian asked.

"Work on Father's memoirs."

"Why don't you come riding with me? The day promises to be sunny."

"Watch him, Heather. I think my brother wants to get you alone in his hideaway," Bruce said.

I flushed red as Bruce uncovered my most fervent desire.

"Heather has nothing to fear from me. I think she knows that. Will you come riding with me, Heather?"

"Yes, I will go up and change." I left the dining room, my heart beating wildly. My feelings toward Adrian were so ambivalent. I could neither hate nor fear him when he was near me. Love pounded that fear from my heart.

After a brisk ride over the moor, we did indeed go to Adrian's lovely house. But we were not alone. A beautiful young woman in her mid-twenties opened the door to greet us. She graciously took my cloak, then Adrian's cape. Fortunately, I had enough self-control not to gape at the woman.

"Kitty, this is Miss MacBride. I believe we would enjoy a good hot cup of tea," Adrian smiled at her.

"Aye, Mr. Ross." She returned his smile with adoration shining in her eyes.

Adrian cupped my elbow and steered me into his parlor. A fire was already crackling its warmth in the hearth. I sat down on the sofa while Adrian went to poke at the fire. I tried not to be jealous, but I was. I couldn't ignore the thought that this Kitty was the reason Adrian spent so much time here.

"Why so quiet, Heather?" Adrian asked as he came to the sofa and sat beside me.

I managed to make my lips form a smile. "I have nothing to say at the moment."

"I didn't think you would take Danton's departure so hard. He was your first beau, wasn't he?"

"I suppose so." I didn't want to talk or think about Patrick. I really wanted to talk about this Kitty. But to do so would reveal my jealousy and, perhaps, my true feelings for Adrian. I had too much pride for that, especially when Adrian was the head conspirator in a plot to rid me of my inheritance. How could I love so sinister a man?

"For what it is worth, I think you are well rid of him."

Kitty came in and placed the tray on the low table in front of the sofa, her eyes never leaving Adrian.

When she left, I smothered my pride and asked, "Who is she? I don't believe I have ever seen her in the village."

"Kitty isn't from the village. She is the daughter of one of your tenant farmers."

"Has she been here long?"

"A few months. She does odd jobs around here," he said, pouring one cup of tea. "This will warm you up." He handed me the

283

cup.

"Aren't you having any?" I asked.

"Not right now. I have the urge to play the piano."

The tea tasted a bit strong, but it succeeded in chasing the last chill from my bones. Adrian softly played one of my favorite pieces. I kept trying to keep my eyes open, but my eyelids were becoming leaden. My entire body felt fuzzy and numb. I knew I couldn't sit upright or stay awake much longer. A frightening thought struck me: had Adrian decided to kill me and poisoned my tea? Then came oblivion.

The room was dusky. Only the waning light of day remained. I could hear voices in the far distance as my eyes began to open wide. I was stretched out on the sofa, a knitted blanket over me. I sat up, pulled the cover off, and put my feet on the floor. I wasn't dead after all, but there was no doubt in my mind I had been drugged. Why had Adrian done it?

"Ah! You are awake," Adrian said, striding into the parlor. "I never knew my music put people to sleep. It usually has the opposite effect. I trust you had a good sleep."

"Yes. What time is it?"

"Time for us to get back to the castle. Are you awake enough to ride?"

"Of course." I stood up.

In the small foyer, Kitty brought my cloak and Adrian's cape. I wondered what they did while I was asleep. I refused to let my mind dwell on it, but it did put me in a foul mood. Riding back to the castle, I remained silent.

At dinner Patrick's absence was evident, especially to Aunt Clarissa.

"Where is Mr. Danton?" she asked, her eyes searching every face at the table.

"Don't you remember Heather telling us he had to go back to India, Clarissa?" Jane asked.

"Oh, dear me. How foolish of me. Yes, I remember now. I do hope he has a good trip. What a long journey that must be. Going to Edinburgh is long and tedious enough. I doubt if I could endure a trek halfway around the world."

"It is not as bad as it sounds, Aunt Clarissa. The days pass more quickly than you think. There is much to do aboard ship," I told her.

"What did you do during your sea voyage?" Bruce asked.

I gave a detailed account and tried to make my commentary interesting. I suspected it wasn't interesting enough for Adrian, since he left immediately after the main course. I hated myself for envisioning Kitty in his strong arms. It was causing me to work up an anger.

I wasn't surprised by my inability to sleep that night. After all, I had slept for most of the day at Adrian's. After tossing and turning for what seemed like hours, I finally left the bed. I wandered to the window hoping to see the mysterious light make its way up the keep. It would have provided a distraction of sorts. Though I stood there for some time, no light appeared. I gave up, lighted the lamp, and sat on the edge of the bed. I toyed with the idea of going down to the library and working on Father's memoirs, but the notion didn't appeal to me. I padded into my sitting parlor and retrieved the novel I had been sporadically reading then went back to bed.

I didn't know exactly when I fell asleep, but dawn was streaking light into my bedchamber when my eyes opened.

"You are up early, Jane," I commented at the breakfast table.

"I couldn't sleep," she said.

"Where is your father?"

"I imagine he is still abed. I suppose you will miss Mr. Danton now that he is gone," Jane said.

"I doubt it."

"Why?" she asked with astonishment.

"When his attentions turned to Diana back in India, my attitude toward him altered. Nothing unfriendly, mind you. I no longer thought of him in a romantic light. I was glad to see him when he first came to Bridee Castle, even though the circumstances were tragic. To be honest, harsh words were beginning to pass between us of late. His departure has relieved some of the tension."

"I suppose my brothers didn't help. They made their dislike of

Mr. Danton quite obvious."

"You liked him, didn't you, Jane?"

A smile dashed over her lips. "I must admit he was good-looking and charming. He was always polite toward me no matter how my brothers treated him."

"Patrick was always a gentleman when it suited him."

"I hope he has a good trip back to India. At least the Sepoy trouble is over," Jane said.

I decided not to spoil Jane's memory of Patrick. Let her think he was going back to his regiment in India. I didn't know where Patrick was going to settle, but it certainly wasn't India.

"I am surprised Adrian isn't here. He is usually up by now," I said.

"I don't believe Adrian came back to the castle after he left last night. In fact, I am sure of it," Jane informed me, then sighed. "His life is so erratic. I do wish he would settle down before he drops from exhaustion."

Falls from exhaustion into Kitty's arms, I thought maliciously. "And Bruce? Do you think he should settle down?"

"I doubt if a woman could cure him of his predilection to gamble."

"Perhaps he will fall in love one day and forget all about gambling," I said.

"I don't think One-eyed Angus would approve of that. He makes a fair living off my brother."

"Where does Bruce get the money to gamble so frequently?"

"I guess he wins on occasion. And then there is Father."

"I didn't know your father was that well off."

"He isn't really. Clarissa dotes on him. He knows he can cajole an extra pound or two from her," Jane said.

"Good morning, ladies," Bruce greeted cheerfully as he entered the dining room. He filled his plate and sat down.

"Isn't it a bit early for you, Bruce?" Jane asked.

"I could hardly wait to get out of bed and face this glorious day — a day without that Danton fellow dogging my heels. Besides, I am meeting One-eyed Angus. He has some sure things going."

Jane glanced at me as if to say "I told you so."

Bruce was of a mood to talk. As he waxed expansive, Adrian came in. He looked tired and flushed, yet he seemed pleased with himself. I couldn't bear it. Having finished my breakfast, I left while he was still at the sideboard. Jeffrey was waiting for me in the foyer.

"Miss MacBride, I wonder if you have a minute," he said.

"Of course, Jeffrey. What can I do for you?"

"I am afraid something is amiss. One of the maids was cleaning the guest room which Mr. Danton inhabited. She found the room most peculiar," Jeffrey said.

"Have you spoken to Mrs. Burns about it?"

"Yes, miss. She looked the room over and thought there was nothing out of the ordinary. I looked about the room and didn't think it peculiar. I thought that seeing you know Mr. Danton best, you should look the room over yourself. Perhaps you can offer an explanation for what we found there."

"What did you find?"

"I would rather you see for yourself, Miss MacBride."

"Very well."

I followed Jeffrey up the stairs and down the corridor to the guest room. When I entered, Mrs. Burns was standing in the middle of the room. I looked around until a frown crinkled my brow. Something was indeed amiss.

Chapter Nineteen

I went to the bureau. Patrick's silver brushes rested on top. Mrs. Burns didn't say anything, but pointed to the large wardrobe cabinet. I looked in to see a pair of leather walking shoes. Otherwise the wardrobe was empty. She motioned me to follow her into the water closet. Resting on the wash basin was Patrick's shaving mug and brush.

"Why would Mr. Danton leave these personal things behind?" Mrs. Burns asked.

"I don't know. Perhaps he forgot them." The excuse I offered was feeble at best. I knew Patrick was proud of his silver brushes and never would have left them behind unless he was using them as a ruse to have me keep in contact with him. Or as an excuse to return to Bridee Castle. Of course! That was it, damn him. "Is everything else of his gone?" I asked.

"Yes, miss. Clothes and valises—all gone. Funny thing though. No one remembers seeing him leave or taking his baggage down."

"Knowing Patrick, he was used to doing things for himself. He probably hired a carriage from the village to take him to Inverness and left by a rear door so he wouldn't have to say goodbye. Patrick hated good-byes. I wouldn't worry about it, Mrs. Burns. Have those things he left behind packed in a box. I will post them to him later." I left the room and never gave the incident another thought.

As I plodded toward the library, sharp stomach pains caused me to double over and sink to the marble floor. Waves of nausea convulsed me. My head was in a whirl and the dizziness blurred my vision. I couldn't get enough air into my lungs and began to gasp for air. My stomach heaved and I retched on the shiny marble floor. I heard shoes clicking closer, then heard no more.

I was in my bed when consciousness returned. Dr. Drummond was sitting alongside the bed watching me.

"How do you feel, young lady?" Dr. Drummond asked.

"Shaky. What happened to me, Doctor?"

"You were sick then passed out from what they tell me. You were in bed when I arrived. Do you recall what happened?" he asked.

"Sharp stomach pains brought me to my knees. I became dizzy, vomited, then passed out."

"Did you eat anything you wouldn't normally eat for breakfast?"

"No, I ate my usual breakfast."

"Was it brought to you?"

"No, I helped myself from the buffet like everyone else."

"Hmm. Are you sure you didn't take food not eaten by the others?"

"I am positive. Are you suggesting I might have been poisoned?"

"I was thinking along those lines, especially in light of your sister's demise."

I was stunned. I knew I would be subject to danger after announcing my intentions of making out a will. However, I thought I would see my nemesis, rather than be subjected to a covert attempt on my life. I had been foolish.

"Do you think it was arsenic?" I asked.

Dr. Drummond shrugged. "Hard to say, considering I have nothing on which to base any tests. The marble floor has been scrubbed clean and the residue of your retching disposed of."

"What about the rags used to clean the floor?"

"Unfortunately, by the time I got here, all the rags used to clean the floor had been tossed into the kitchen stove. So you see I can't say it was poison with any certainty."

"Was anyone else sick?"

He shook his head slowly. "I cannot understand it. Did you drink something the others didn't?"

"Jane and I had tea from the same pot. Bruce had coffee."

289

"I don't know what to tell you. When you are feeling better perhaps you should come into my office and have a complete physical. The two murders here might have made me jump to the wrong conclusion. Your illness this morning might not have been an attempt on your life. You might have some physical ailment."

"Such as?"

"The onset of a cold, severe indigestion. I will come by tomorrow to see how you feel." Dr. Drummond stood. "Stay in bed for the day."

"Should I restrict my eating habits?" I asked.

"No, eat as you normally do, but only what the others eat."

"How can I do that if I am to stay abed?"

"If you can manage it, go downstairs for your meals. If not, and a tray is brought to your room, do not eat anything that smells or tastes peculiar. If you have another attack, have someone bring you to my surgery immediately. I will see you are placed in the hospital for a few days. Get some rest and, as I said, I will see you tomorrow." He felt my forehead, nodded, then left.

Jean fussed about the room and informed me I had missed lunch.

"I'd be happy to have Cook fix a tray for you and bring it up," she offered.

"No, thank you, Jean. I am not hungry." My stomach was still queasy and a foul taste in my mouth had destroyed my palate.

When she left, I searched my mind for a food I had eaten and the others had not. I even visualized the breakfast buffet and what I spooned or forked onto my plate. Between these mental exercises, I dozed.

Shortly before dinner, I rang for Jean to help me dress. Though I felt a little unsteady, I was sure going down to dinner would not present a problem. Fortunately, it didn't.

Adrian bounded to his feet and came to greet me when I entered the drawing room.

"Should you be up?" Adrian asked, his dark eyes searching mine.

"I don't see why not. Besides, I am famished."

"You look pale to me, Heather," Aunt Clarissa said.

Adrian put his arm about me and led me to a chair.

"What did Dr. Drummond say was wrong with you?" Bruce asked.

"He wasn't sure. He will be by tomorrow. I might have to go into Inverness for a complete examination." I thought for a moment, then added. "I will probably see the solicitor at the same time." I wanted to get this ugly situation out in the open as soon as possible. I would go insane if I had to endure this uncertainty any longer. With my suspicions growing, I didn't know who to trust. My heart wanted to trust Adrian, but my reason wouldn't let me.

"Would you like me to go into Inverness with you, Heather?" Jane asked.

"Yes, I would like that." Could I trust Jane? Or was there a sinister nature lurking behind her pallid, innocent face?

I ate sparingly at dinner. A little of the quail, boiled potatoes, carrots, and turnips. I declined dessert as my hunger was quickly assuaged.

Tea was brought into the drawing room. Aunt Clarissa rejected it in favor of a sherry. Jane poured two cups and handed one to me as she settled in the chair with her cup.

I reached for the sugar bowl but dropped my hand as though the sugar bowl had become molten hot. All of a sudden it came to me, the one thing I had taken this morning that no one else had. White sugar! No one in the house used it except Diana.

I had grown to like the brown sugar or honey in my tea and on my porridge. The bowl with the white sugar had been on the breakfast table and I had inadvertently spooned it on the porridge and into my tea. I could feel the blood draining from me. I stiffened and stared at the lethal white sugar.

"What is it, Heather?" Adrian asked.

"Are you going to be sick again, my dear?" Aunt Clarissa queried. "If you are, I will have John get a bowl. I would hate to have this beautiful Persian carpet ruined."

Adrian's hand came down on my shoulder and broke my self-imposed trance. "I am not going to be sick, Aunt Clarissa." I settled back in my chair and sipped the unsweetened tea.

The realization that the white sugar could contain arsenic

didn't solve a thing. Anyone could have put the poison in the sugar bowl from Adrian to the lowliest of scullery maids.

"It might be best if you made an early night of it, Heather," Adrian suggested.

"I would prefer to listen to you play the piano, Adrian," I said.

"That would be nice," Jane agreed.

"Only if he plays soft music. That harsh music of yours gives me a roaring headache, Adrian," Aunt Clarissa declared.

"As you wish, Clarissa."

The music was soothing and it gave me a chance to study the people in the drawing room. Bruce was fidgety and drank his whisky in gulps. He seemed startled when his glass was empty and quickly went to refill it.

John Ross appeared to be in another world. I doubt if he even heard the music. Every once in a while his eyebrows would bounce together in a frown as though his thoughts were disturbing. If ever there was a picture of an unhappy man, John Ross was that picture.

Jane's hazel eyes darted about the room as though searching for something she knew wasn't there. She kept smoothing her hair back nervously. Her breast rose and fell with rapid breathing. Though she was normally pale, there seemed to be a more intense pallor to her countenance.

Aunt Clarissa had a beatified expression as she was obviously enjoying Adrian's piano renditions. Her head swayed in time to the music's cadence.

Adrian's face was dark and inscrutable. I sensed he wanted to lash out his with emotions on the keyboard, but struggled to keep his true feelings out of the music. After an hour I supposed the strain became too much for him and he ceased playing.

"Thank you, Adrian. That was lovely," I said.

"It was rather nice for a change," Aunt Clarissa agreed. "One more sherry and I am off to bed."

"I think I shall go now," I said.

"Are you going to Inverness tomorrow, Heather?" Jane asked.

"No. The doctor will be coming here. If everything is all right, I might only go to see the solicitor."

"I think there will be snow tomorrow. I could smell it in the air.

The doctor might not be able to get here," Bruce said.

"Then we will go to Inverness on the first nice day. Good night," I said, leaving the chair.

"Would you like me to walk upstairs with you, Heather?" Adrian asked.

"That won't be necessary. I feel fine and can make it on my own."

Before climbing into bed, I retrieved my old Jumble book I had left in the sitting parlor. I wanted to revert to the happy times of childhood. The gloom of Bridee Castle with its tragic events was beginning to take its toll on me. The urge to stay on and discover the fiend behind the deaths was beginning to pale. I was starting to believe the compulsion was a foolish one, especially when my own life was at stake. Tomorrow I would give serious consideration to leaving the castle. For now I would concentrate on the silly old childhood book.

Stories and poems about animals comprised the Jumble book along with one-dimensional animals drawings. As I slowly thumbed through the pages, remembrances of my childhood came to the fore. I even smiled several times. As a child, my favorite poems were about the elephants, since they played such an integral part in life then. When I reached them, I was surprised to see each line was underlined in red ink. I was positive I hadn't done it. I hadn't looked at the book since I was eight or nine. At that age Father forbid us the use of ink, especially red ink. I had to assume Father had done it as he packed the trunk. And he must have done it purposely. Why? I proceeded to read the poems slowly and carefully.

The elephant sucked and blew through his nose,
An act that was natural, I suppose.
Hollow inside,
He used it with pride
Till an arrow struck outside.
The trunk which was his life
Now caused him strife.
The outside hole dripped
Whatever he sipped.

He mourned the hide that was ripped.

The second poem read as follows:

The elephant's trunk was long and hollow.
He sucked up water to swallow
Then used it like a hand
With a flourish that was grand.
Tough hide was in Nature's plan.

Several of the words were underlined twice: *Outside, Trunk, Hide, Hollow, Hand.* I was keenly aware Father was trying to tell me something. I fell asleep before I could ponder the puzzle thoroughly.

When I woke in the morning, I recalled my dream. As I relived the dream, I started to giggle.

Aunt Clarissa was riding an elephant and chasing the specter of Lady Anne through the jungle. I was still giggling when Jean entered. She didn't say anything, but she did give me a peculiar glance. I stopped chuckling.

The humor of my dream stayed with me as I went down to breakfast. The sugar bowl on the table snapped me back to dangerous reality.

"The doctor won't be coming today, Heather," Bruce said, placing a laden plate before him as he sat down.

"Why?"

"Haven't you looked out the window?"

"No."

"Snow is coming down as though it wants to bury us alive," Bruce said gleefully. "Disappointed?"

"Not really. I have enough tasks here to keep me busy."

"Oh? What?"

"Odds and ends."

"Sounds like something final. Are you leaving Bridee Castle?"

"Who is leaving Bridee Castle?" Adrian asked, striding into the dining room.

"Heather," Bruce answered.

Adrian looked stunned as his eyes darted to lock with mine.

"Is this true, Heather?"

"Not at all. As long as it is snowing today, I said I thought I would take care of some odds and ends. Bruce misinterpreted my meaning."

"I assume you won't be going into Inverness today," Adrian said.

I shook my head. "I hope Jane won't be too disappointed."

"Don't let it bother you. Jane is tougher than she appears," Bruce said.

"Are you going to work on your father's memoirs?" Adrian asked.

"I don't think so. Why?"

"I was going to do some work in the library if you weren't going to use it."

"Go right ahead. I shall be busy upstairs. What do you do on a day like this, Bruce?" I asked.

"Play chess with my father. Annoy the maids. Whatever I can think of to pass the time. I might come upstairs and pester you."

"Don't listen to him, Heather. He will flit away the morning, eat heavily at lunch, then sleep all afternoon," Adrian said.

"That sounds promising, Brother dear."

The repartee at the breakfast table was light, almost cheery. Still, I sensed an undertone that bordered on grimness. The more capricious their banter became, the more tension filled me. I went upstairs.

In my sitting parlor, I mulled over my Jumble book and the elephant poems. Obviously my father was referring to his trunk. Hide. He had hidden something in it. Patrick must have thought the same thing. He had gone so far as to rip the lining out. Whatever my father had hidden there, it was on the outside of the trunk. I had solved all the words save two. Hand and hollow. If hand was for handle, they certainly weren't hollow. The only handles on the trunk were made of leather and couldn't possibly be hollow.

I sat down at my escritoire, took some paper from the drawer, then dipped the pen into the inkwell. I wrote the words *hand* and *hollow* over and over, trying to think of every possible variation. I must have pondered the conundrum for an hour or more, but couldn't come up with anything that made sense.

My mind began to wander into the realm of daydreams. I saw myself riding to Adrian's manor house where we sat close and played four-handed piano pieces. He would ride back to the castle with me. The picture of him on his black steed was vivid. The animal was as handsome as its rider. Then it came to me. The horse.

Father knew of my proclivity for horses and riding. *Hand.* Of course. A horse was measured in hands. A hand was equivalent to four inches. Whatever my father was referring to was on the outside of the trunk, hollow, and measured four inches.

I left the escritoire and went to study the trunk. To my dismay, everything appeared to be four inches from the hasp to the brass strappings to the heavy corner fittings.

The brass straps were flat and obviously not hollow. That left the hasp and the ornate brass corner fittings. With a pair of strong, stout scissors, I pried the hasp apart and found nothing. The corner fittings were next. The first one revealed nothing. On the second one I was rewarded with the discovery of a tightly folded parchment paper three inches square. I took it to the escritoire and carefully unfolded it, revealing a letter from Father.

Heather, it began. No "dear Heather." That preface was saved for Diana. I began to read the contents.

> *I am sure you will find this letter given enough time. I knew you would read your old Jumble book. By this time I shall be long buried and you and Diana safely in the Highlands. I am writing to you knowing you are far more curious than Diana. I fear she may leave the trunk unopened for eternity.*
>
> *I have accumulated a large store of jewels and gold given to me by those grateful for my services in India. I leave them to you and Diana as an extra legacy. I sincerely hope you are both married by the time you have found the jewels.*
>
> *You mother's coffin is identical to mine. Perhaps you wondered why the lids on our coffins were domed. Ghoulish, no doubt, but it was the only way I could think of to get the gems out of India and to the Highlands without being scrutinized by custom officials.*
>
> *You will not have to open the coffins themselves. There is a spring*

on the right-hand lip of the dome. I am sure I can trust you to divide the gems equally. I especially want Diana to have the diamond necklace and tiara. I would also like her to have the black pearls. I believe those are in the dome of your mother's coffin.

Patrick Danton knows about the jewels. In one of my weaker moments I promised him a few of the gems, but you need not tell him you know where they are. Let them think they are buried somewhere in India.

Father

So Patrick was right. He *was* entitled to a portion of the riches. As soon as he forwarded his address, I would either take him his fair share or post them to him. First I would have to dig up my parents' coffins. More time would have to pass before I could bring myself to undertake the gruesome task. Diana would have had the stable boys digging in the snow. Jewelry was a weakness of hers. She would have been ecstatic at the sight of the gems. A tear or two trickled from my eyes. She was so young and had so much to look forward to in life, especially as an heiress. I left my sitting parlor, threw myself on the bed, and had a good cry for myself.

I cried long and hard. It was the final release. When I was done, I felt purged. I went to my dressing table and stared in the mirror. My eyes were red and puffy, my lips scarlet from chewing on them. I unpinned and brushed out my tangled hair. A knock on the door startled me. Was Bruce carrying through with his threat to annoy me? I was not in the mood for his company. I hesitated, causing the knock to intensify.

"Heather . . . are you in there?"

It was Adrian's voice. I went to unlock the door, then opened it, unmindful of my appearance.

"What is wrong, Heather?" He stepped into my bedchamber.

"Nothing."

"Don't tell me 'nothing.' Obviously you have been crying. From the looks of it, you have been doing a great bit of it. Don't you feel well?"

"I feel fine. Nothing is wrong. I was going through my father's trunk and started thinking about everything that has happened since I came to Bridee Castle. I suppose the sorrow of losing those I loved overwhelmed me. I am over it now. What did you want to see me about?"

"Lunch is being served. When you didn't come down, I thought I would see if you were all right," he explained.

I turned my head and glanced at the ormolu clock on the mantel. Ten minutes past noon.

"I forgot about the time. Let me tie my hair back and I will be right down."

His hand raised, his fingers twining in my hair. "Shiny copper," he murmured. He dropped his hand as though it had been burned. His expression hardened. "I will go and tell them you will be down in a few minutes." He turned and quickly left.

I had the impression he was garnering some affection for me, but was crushing it out of existence so he could get on with the task of erasing my sanity.

At lunch Aunt Clarissa was unusually animate and loquacious.

"Oh, dear me. This weather is beginning to scratch on my nerves. Next winter we should go to the south of France or Egypt. Cairo would be nice. Yes. So warm and sunny. What do you think, John?"

"We shall see, Clarissa," he said languidly.

"Jane, what do you think?"

"Whatever you wish, Clarissa."

"The next fine day we shall have to go into Inverness and get some books on Egypt. I can hardly wait to see the great temples, the pyramids, and the desert. What a novelty it would be to ride a camel. Have you ever ridden a camel, John?"

"No, my dear," was the bored response.

"Am I invited, Clarissa?" Bruce asked with a twinkle in his light brown eyes.

"Of course. All of us shall go. Except Adrian. He will have much to do here. Besides his herds to tend to, he will have to get someone in to make sure Lady Anne is back in the keep and locked up. I shall never be at peace until she is imprisoned in her proper place. Don't you think Egypt would be a pleasant respite from a Highland winter, Heather?"

"Yes." I smiled. I wasn't going to smother Aunt Clarissa's sudden enthusiasm for Egypt. Besides, it wasn't a decision one had to make immediately. Who knew what next winter would bring? If the Rosses had their way, I probably wouldn't be at Bridee Castle.

As I climbed into bed, my mind dwelled on Aunt Clarissa's proposal to go to Egypt. If it ever came to fruition, I could just visualize the mounds of luggage it would entail. Trunk after trunk. Perhaps huge chests of bonnets and skirts.

As the image of a huge chest floated into my mind, I suddenly remembered what it was I found so peculiar on the top floor of the keep. The chest. Though everything else in the keep was swathed in dust and cobwebs, the chest was clean, almost polished. Yet when I lifted the lid, it was empty. I couldn't solve the puzzle. I would have to have another look at that chest. Why wasn't it dusty like everything else there?

Though the snow had stopped, the morning sky remained sooty. I brought my woolen hooded cloak down with me and left it in the foyer. Adrian, who was on the verge of finishing breakfast, made casual and cool conversation as though he were either preoccupied or tired of my company. I hoped it was the former. He soon left and I finished my meal alone.

In the foyer I swung my cloak on. As I headed for the corridor that would take me to the frigid part of the castle, a voice stopped me.

"Where are you off to, Heather?" Bruce called from the top of the stairs.

"Nowhere in particular. Just wandering about," I said as I turned to watch him bounce down the stairs. "You seem energetic this morning."

"Had a good rest yesterday. Seriously, where are you going all bundled up like that?"

"I thought I would take a closer look at the other part of the castle."

"How dreary!" He narrowed his eyes and stared at me for a second. "Don't tell me you are going to that bloody keep again."

"Do you want to take another jaunt up there with me?"

"I am not *that* energetic. I don't intend to waste my strength climbing up those wretched steps. I can put my muscles to better use."

"Lifting a pint and playing darts?"

"That's right. And if I were you, I would stay away from that dreadful place. It is too spooky up there, especially since that Indian woman of yours was butchered up there."

"You aren't going to bring up that Lady Anne story again, are you?"

He shrugged. "One never knows about ghosts. I believe one shouldn't tempt fate. If you do go, don't say I didn't warn you." He turned and headed for the dining room.

Having hurried through the neglected section of the castle, I came to the courtyard. The wind curled in and around the area with such rapidity it wailed as though in warning. The great hall was as desolate as before. I went directly to the door of the keep. I fumbled for the key in the pocket of my skirt. I inserted it into the lock, but, to my surprise, the door was open.

I started up the spiral stone steps, my mind on the chest. By the time I reached the top tier, I was breathing heavily — but not so heavily that I couldn't let out an ear-shattering scream.

Chapter Twenty

Patrick Danton hadn't left Bridee Castle after all. He was sprawled on the floor, a large knife protruding from his back. My screams had scattered the rats gnawing on his body.

I stood there gaping and screaming until the air in my lungs could no longer push the screams from my throat. When the initial shock wore off, I ran back to the castle and sought out Jeffrey. I came across Mrs. Burns first.

"Mrs. Burns," I began. "Please send one of the lads to Inverness for Inspector Andrews. Quickly!"

"What has happened?" Her eyes widened and fear spread across her face.

"I don't have time to explain now. Please hurry."

She scampered away after casting a worried glance my way. I went into the drawing room and poured myself a small brandy. My hands were shaking to the point where I needed both of them to raise the glass to my lips.

"So early in the morning, Heather? I am surprised at you," Bruce said as he came into the drawing room. He started to laugh. When his mirth subsided, he put his hand on my shoulder. "Why, you are really trembling. You went to the keep, didn't you? And the ghost of Lady Anne besieged you. I told you not to go up there."

I shrugged his hand off my shoulder, went to a well-padded chair, and sat down.

Bruce plopped down on the settee across from me, his elbows on his knees, his hands dangling between them. "You don't look so good, Heather. Are you ill? Would you like me to send for the doctor?"

"No, I will be all right."

"I was only teasing you about Lady Anne. I hope you didn't take me seriously."

"I thought you were going to the village."

"I am eventually."

As I sipped the brandy, Bruce told humorous tales of certain habitués of the pub. I listened with half an ear, trying to make sense of all that had happened.

Inspector Andrews and his assistant, Thomas Gordon, arrived shortly after lunch. Dr. Drummond accompanied them.

"To what do we owe the honor of your visit, Inspector?" John Ross asked as we all filed into the foyer from the dining room.

"I sent for him," I said.

John looked at me quizzically, as did everyone else. "Whatever for, Heather?"

"I have something to show them," I said to John, then turned to the inspector. "This way, gentlemen."

I grabbed my cloak from the marble table where I had left it and started down the corridor. Inspector Andrews, Thomas Gordon, and Dr. Drummond dutifully followed me, John and Adrian lagging behind. Adrian caught up with me and cupped my elbow.

"What is this all about, Heather?" Adrian asked, bending his head so his lips were near my ear.

"You will see for yourself."

I stiffened my back and continued to march with a purpose. Adrian still clung to my arm.

"Is it much farther, Miss MacBride?" the inspector called.

"The top of the keep," I answered over my shoulder. I heard Dr. Drummond exhale a low moan.

302

On the landing just before the top floor of the keep, I halted. "I can't go up there. You will have to go without me." I stood aside and let the men pass.

In a flash a pale John Ross came thumping down the stairs. He dashed by me to continue his flight from the keep. Several minutes later, Adrian came down with Detective Gordon. Gordon gave me a nod and hurried on his way. Adrian stopped.

"I am sorry, Heather. I suspect he meant a lot to you. Why didn't you say something at lunch?"

"I didn't want everyone rushing to the keep, perhaps destroying vital evidence. It also occurred to me that someone might remove the body to make me look foolish."

His expression darkened. "I take it you don't have a very high opinion of the Rosses. What have we done to make you distrust us?"

I was tempted to tell him of the conversation I overheard between John and Jane, to tell him of his duplicity by drugging me at his manor house. Instead, I said nothing.

He glared at me with his inky, inscrutable eyes. "Your silence speaks for itself." He turned on his heels and rushed down the spiral staircase.

I was tempted to run after him, but the thought of Patrick lying dead on the floor above me, murdered like Samrú, prevented me. A maniac was loose in Bridee Castle and it had to be one of the Rosses. Until I knew which one, I couldn't allow myself to trust any of them, not even Adrian.

I waited until I was sure Adrian was in the living quarters of the castle. I began the trek back to the drawing room. I had no idea how long the inspector and doctor would be.

"Oh, dear me. That poor, poor man," Aunt Clarissa moaned as I entered. "You must be beside yourself with grief, Heather. Jane, do get Heather a sherry."

"Please don't bother, Jane. I had a brandy earlier. I could not tolerate another drink." I sat down in a Queen Anne chair. "Where are John and Adrian? They came down long

303

before me."

"After Father informed us of the tragedy, he went outside for some fresh air. I don't know where Adrian is. Bruce is at the pub, I believe," Jane said.

"Does Bruce know of Patrick Danton's demise?" I asked.

"I don't think so. He left directly after lunch," Jane informed me.

"Are you all right, Heather dear?" Aunt Clarissa asked.

"That depends on what you mean. Physically I am fine. After the first shock, I think my nerves are calming down. I just can't understand why anyone would want to kill Patrick. He would have been leaving Bridee Castle today. There was no reason for anyone to kill him."

"Lady Anne works in mysterious ways. The keep is her domain. Anyone who violates it must pay the price," Aunt Clarissa said, her eyes glazed.

"And how would that account for the murder of Miss Diana MacBride, Mrs. Ross?" Inspector Andrews asked as he strode into the drawing room, Dr. Drummond trailing behind.

"Would you gentlemen care for a whisky?" Aunt Clarissa asked.

"A welcome thought, Mrs. Ross, especially after the scene we have just witnessed."

"Dr. Drummond, would you do the honors?" Aunt Clarissa waved a directional hand toward the sideboard. Dr. Drummond poured two large whiskeys, handed one to Inspector Andrews, then took a seat.

"You haven't answered my question about Diana MacBride, Mrs. Ross. Has she ever been in the keep?"

"I think I can answer that, Inspector," I said. "My sister was never in the keep nor in that part of the castle."

"Perhaps she went on her own and told no one about it," the inspector suggested.

I shook my head. "She never would have gone there alone. If she had, she would have told me or someone about it. She was not the type to keep things to herself. Did you discover any clues up there?"

"Nothing concrete. I can only assume the victim, Mr. Danton, was caught unaware or the murderer was someone he trusted implicitly. He was an able-bodied man in first-rate physical condition, capable of fighting off an opponent, even a formidable one. But there was no sign of a struggle. I am afraid I am as much in the dark on this murder as I am on the other two. With the exception of the victims being from India, there is nothing to link the murders together. Miss MacBride, do you recall anything from the past in India that might have a bearing?"

"No, nothing." Andrews looked at me as though he were wondering why I was still alive.

"I wish you would give it some thought, Miss MacBride. I wouldn't want to think you were holding anything back." His eyes narrowed as he looked at me. He tossed the remainder of his drink down and stood. "Detective Gordon went for a wagon. He should be back shortly. Where will the funeral be held?"

"At the parish church. I will speak to Reverend Campbell about it. In deference to my father, we will bury him in Bridee Castle's cemetery. Patrick had no living relatives," I said.

"We shall take our leave now. If anything comes up, I shall notify you immediately." Inspector Andrews nodded at Dr. Drummond and they left.

"Another funeral. Oh, dear me. Where will it all end? What will become of us? Are we all going to be murdered?" Aunt Clarissa twisted her handkerchief violently. "I must go and rest though I know I shan't sleep." She pushed herself from the chair. "Jane, do help me up the stairs. This nasty business has me shaking."

"Of course, Clarissa."

As I sat alone in the drawing room, I tried to think of an event in India that might connect the three murders. I had never thought seriously about it. Inspector Andrews seemed to think it was a strong possibility. Then I remembered the

305

way he looked at me. A shudder convulsed me. Did he think I was behind the murders?

I swallowed hard when I realized he had good reason to think so. I received my sister's fortune. Why Samrú? Because she favored my sister with more attention? Patrick because he showered affection on Diana and not me? In a stranger's mind these could be strong and palpable motives. I sat for some time in a stupor. I wasn't sure if I were stunned or outraged.

The church service was brief. The eulogy at the cemetery was even briefer. At least the day was sunny and only a moderate chill pervaded the air. I could feel Inspector Andrews's eyes boring into me. How could he think me capable of murder? My insides were so roiled I couldn't bring myself to shed a single tear for Patrick.

After a small repast at the castle for the few attending the funeral, I went upstairs and changed into my riding clothes. When I came downstairs, the guests had departed. I went directly to the stable.

I rode hard across the moor, then let the mare pick her way down to the banks of Loch Ness. I dismounted, tethered the horse, then walked to the edge where the water gently lapped at the shore. I stared out over the loch, my breath coming in tremulous sighs.

What could I do to prove my innocence? Flush out the real culprit? Was I clever enough for that? Or would I be the next victim?

I stood there for more than an hour contemplating my options. I came to the conclusion that the only thing to do was tempt fate and spend as much time in the keep as I could.

As though that poor solution had solved my predicament, I rode back to the castle with less turmoil churning my stomach.

Two days after Patrick's funeral, I decided to put my

shoddy plan into action. I dressed warmly and tucked a book into my skirt pocket. If nothing else, I didn't want to be bored during my vigil.

As I approached the top floor, I thought of the rats and my resolve began to weaken. Visions of Samrú and Patrick's gnawed bodies undermined my determination. I tiptoed up high enough to peer at the top floor. No sign of a rat. I screwed up my courage and boldly marched onto the top tier of the keep. I sat down on the chest prepared to read, but jumped up almost immediately. My desire to examine the chest was the reason I had found Patrick's body in the first place.

I lifted the lid. Empty. I scrutinized the chest from every angle. Something was wrong, but my mind didn't quite comprehend what it was. Several minutes passed before the discrepancy became obvious. The chest was much deeper on the outside than it was on the inside.

Putting my hand inside the chest, I fingered the entire perimeter of the bottom. On each side was an indentation imperceptible to the eye. With both hands in the chest, I placed my forefingers in the notches. To my surprise, the floor of the chest lifted out easily.

To someone watching me, it might appear that I gasped, but no sound issued from my throat. Before me, in the concealed bottom of the chest, rested a king's ransom in jewels. I was about to reach in when I heard the slight swish of material behind me. I turned around. This time I did gasp aloud.

I beheld the creature of my nightmares—the ghost of Lady Anne. At least the creature was dressed as such—long draping sleeves; a tight bodice coming to a vee in a full skirt; a tall conical black hat with thick veil circling it. Underneath the veil a pierrot mask hid the face. Long black gloves covered the hands and arms. All this I beheld in a fleeting glance before my eyes quickly focused on the long butcher knife glinting in the creature's upraised hand.

I dashed behind the sacrificial dais and looked around for

a weapon. To my dismay, none was at hand. As the creature began stalking me, I kept circling around the dais attempting to draw my enemy to the far side of the circular room so I would be nearer the stairs. The creature surmised my plan and dashed back to cover any exit I might attempt. I commenced screaming. It was the only weapon I had at the moment.

We circled around the dais eyeing each other warily. When we came to the narrowest part of the dais, the creature's hand shot out and grabbed my wrist. The strength in that hand was phenomenal. No matter how hard I tried to free my wrist from that grip, it remained firm. The masked person maneuvered his body so that he was now on my side of the dais.

The hand with the knife started to angle down toward me. I raised my free hand and curled my fingers around the creature's wrist. My hand met flesh and blood, not the stuff of a ghost.

I knew I couldn't hold the knife-wielding hand off much longer as it steadily inched downward. My hoydenish childhood stood me in good stead. I gave my attacker a good hard kick in the shins.

The grip on my wrist slackened, enabling me to pull my hand free. Using all my strength, I managed to slam the knife-wielding hand down hard on the marble dais. The knife skittered across the dais to fall to the floor on the other side. Infuriated, the creature slapped me so hard I crumpled to the floor. Before I knew it, the so-called ghost of Lady Anne hovered over me, the knife once more in its grasp ready to plunge into my heart.

"Stop!" boomed Adrian's voice.

The creature glanced at him momentarily, then set about the original task. A swift downward plunge streaked toward my bosom. Enough of my wits remained and I rolled out of the knife's path. As the creature moved toward me, Adrian was upon him. The creature wildly fought to be free. John Ross came to his son's aid. Between the two of them, the mythical ghost was subdued.

"Are you all right, Heather?" Adrian asked.

"A little shaken, that's all," I said, getting to my feet.

"I shouldn't wonder," John said.

"Would you care to do the honors?" Adrian asked as he nodded to the mask.

"I would be delighted." I pushed the veil aside, then pulled the mask off. I gaped then murmured in disbelief, "Aunt Clarissa."

"Hello, my dear." She smiled at me.

"Let us get her downstairs," Adrian said to his father.

"We had better send for the inspector," I suggested as I followed them on shaky legs.

"The minute I heard you scream, I sent for the inspector and Dr. Drummond," Adrian said as we progressed toward the drawing room.

Jane was sitting there wringing her hands when we entered. She got up, came toward us, and put her arms around me. "I prayed to God that you would be safe. I imagine you could use a sherry. Let me get you one."

I sat down in the first chair I came upon, my mind in a muddle. I accepted the glass Jane handed me and absently sipped it. Over the rim of my glass I gazed at Aunt Clarissa placidly sitting on the settee as though she was waiting for Jeffrey to announce dinner.

We all sat thinking our own private thoughts until Inspector Andrews, Detective Gordon, and Dr. Drummond arrived. Adrian went to the doorway and spoke to them briefly. John sat down beside Aunt Clarissa and took her hand in his.

"Clarissa, these gentlemen would like to talk to you. You will answer their questions as best you can, won't you?" John asked.

"Oh, dear me. I hope the questions won't be too hard." She was smiling, but her eyes had glazed over eerily.

If Inspector Andrews was curious about Aunt Clarissa's costume, he never mentioned it. "Tell me, Mrs. Ross, why

309

did you try to kill your niece Heather MacBride?"

"Me? I wouldn't harm a hair on her head. It was that awful Lady Anne. I told Heather not to let her out of the keep. But she wouldn't listen to me. Now Lady Anne roams the castle taking her revenge."

"Did this Lady Anne kill the Indian woman?" the inspector asked.

"She had to, didn't she?"

"Why?"

"That Indian woman was sneaking about the castle and she started to interfere with Lady Anne's plans for getting rid of that conniving Diana."

"Ah! Did this Lady Anne poison Diana MacBride?"

"Naturally, she had no choice. Diana was plotting to take John Ross away from her. Lady Anne doesn't like people who try to take loved ones from her."

"How did Lady Anne feed the arsenic to Diana Mac-Bride?"

"In the white sugar, of course. Diana was the only one in the castle who insisted on using white sugar. Lady Anne is a very clever woman, don't you think?"

"Quite," the inspector said. "I don't understand why she killed Mr. Patrick Danton. He was no threat to her. Do you know why, Mrs. Ross?"

"He was a thief. She caught him trying to steal her jewels. Those jewels provided the means for her to give John everything he wanted." Aunt Clarissa giggled. "Danton was so busy fingering the jewels, he never heard her come up behind him."

"How do you know all this, Mrs. Ross?" Inspector Andrews asked.

"Lady Anne told me everything."

"I thought you were afraid of her."

"I am. She told me she would kill me one day, but not for a long time."

"Let us return to the original question. Why did Lady Anne want to kill Miss Heather MacBride?"

310

"She didn't at first. She liked Heather. Oh, she had many chances, but she just wanted to frighten her away. She knew Heather was the clever one and Lady Anne wanted her away from Bridee Castle before she discovered the jewels. She had a feeling Danton told her where the jewels were. She followed her to the keep and watched. When she found the secret compartment to the chest, Lady Anne knew she had to kill her."

"May I ask a few questions, Inspector?" I asked.

"If you wish."

"Aunt Clarissa," I began.

"Yes, my dear," she responded.

"Where did Lady Anne get the dead crows?"

"The gypsies. They would do anything for a few baubles. She had them carry you to the cemetery that day. They obeyed her implicitly. Strange people. When you became too interested in the keep and wanted to give Lady Anne's clothes to a museum, she wanted the gypsies to put her in a sack with stones and drop Heather into Loch Ness. They refused no matter how many jewels she offered them."

"How did she make herself glow in the dark?" I asked.

"That was really clever of her, wasn't it? She had read about an Italian cobbler who, a long time ago, discovered that calcined barite would glow in the dark after exposure to light. She had the gypsies purchase this barium sulfide from a chemist in Glasgow, the same place where the gypsies bought the arsenic for her. Lady Anne is a shrewd woman. She knew how to make efficient, well-thought-out plans."

"Very clever," I said. "How did she get the jewels?"

"I let her come down from the keep to see your mother's beautiful casket. As she traced her fingers over the delicate carvings, she accidentally released a spring that caused the dome to open and there lay the jewels. She put them in a pouch, then took them to the keep. When your father's casket proved to be a duplicate, she looked for and found the same spring. More beautiful jewels to add to her collection." The room fell silent. Aunt Clarissa looked around and smiled at everyone. "They were easy questions. Are they all over?"

"I have a question or two for you, Mrs. Ross," Dr. Drummond said.

"Yes?" Aunt Clarissa's smile widened and her face brightened.

"Before you came to live at Bridee Castle, you were Mrs. Pickering, were you not?"

Aunt Clarissa's smile vanished, her eyes narrowing with suspicion. "Why do you ask?"

"Mr. Pickering was very ill and you were very poor. Am I correct, Mrs. Ross?"

"I don't like these questions."

"Just one more, Mrs. Ross. Didn't you ask your father for money in order to pay for doctors and hospitals for your husband?"

Aunt Clarissa jumped up, her eyes blazing as she paced back and forth. "That bastard! I told Lady Anne about him. He denied me my rightful inheritance because I married a man of whom he didn't approve. Gave my brother everything, he did. He always hated me for not being a boy. I never had pretty clothes nor jewelry. He treated me like a servant, making me wait on him like a scullery maid. Oh, how I hated him! When I came to Bridee Castle to beg him to loan me some money to pay the medical bills, he laughed at me and told me to get out. He didn't want to see me ever again. I decided to make sure he never would see me again."

Aunt Clarissa raced over to Dr. Drummond, grabbed his hair, and pulled his head back. She ran her finger over his throat as though it was a knife. She let him go as Inspector Andrews got to his feet and started for her. Her strident, maniacal laughter filled the room.

"Gordon, let us get this woman to Inverness before she does anymore harm," said the inspector. The two of them took the laughing Aunt Clarissa away.

"What will become of her, Doctor?" I asked as John handed the man a large glass of whisky.

"She will be interred in an insane asylum for the rest of her life, I'm afraid. She is completely mad, you know." He took a large swallow of the amber liquid.

"I can well afford the best for her. Please keep that in mind when you place her, Doctor," I said.

"I will."

"Shall I pack her things and bring them to her, Doctor?" Jane asked.

"Wait until I get her settled."

"She can't go around dressed in that ridiculous costume," Jane protested.

"Pick out suitable clothes for her and I will take them with me."

Jane left the room and I could hear her feet dashing up the stairs.

"What made you question my aunt about Mr. Pickering, Doctor?" I asked.

"When she started blaming a mythical Lady Anne for the murders, I had a suspicion her dementia had deeper roots in the past. Once before I had a case like Clarissa Ross. I was still studying medicine at the time, but it made a lasting impression on me. As I sat listening to her rantings, I remembered the unsolved mystery of your grandfather's murder. I suspected she had harbored a good deal of guilt for years. When she moved back into Bridee Castle, where the deed was committed, that guilt intensified and her mind began to deteriorate under the strain. The old tale of Lady Anne's ghost suited her purpose admirably. She could absolve herself of any wrongdoing and thrust it onto Lady Anne. In short, she became two people living inside one body, if such a state of being is possible."

"Do you think she will get better?" John asked.

"No, I believe she is too far gone. Even if she did return to normal, she would have to stand trial for three murders. Under the circumstances, I would suggest a swift divorce, Mr. Ross."

Jane came into the room with a valise. "I think these will

do nicely."

Dr. Drummond stood. "I will be on my way. I'll keep you informed regarding Mrs. Ross." He picked up the valise as John rose and walked the doctor to the door.

"I am going into the village to fetch Bruce. He should be here," Adrian said.

Jane and I talked about the chilling events at Bridee Castle for almost an hour, then Jane went upstairs to begin packing Aunt Clarissa's clothes. I was alone in the drawing room.

Suddenly I felt as though the room was closing in on me. My breathing became labored and my lungs screamed for fresh air. I opened the French doors and stepped out onto the rear terrace. I strolled amid the sculptured yews and box hedges. I felt very much alone which caused me to think about leaving Bridee Castle. There was no reason for me to stay in the Highlands any longer. I had accomplished what I set out to do—find Diana's murderer. I bemoaned the fact it was Aunt Clarissa. I would have been happier if the murderer had proved to be a total stranger.

A slight breeze stirred. My nostrils flared to greet the scent of approaching spring. I looked up at the blue sky with its puffy white clouds and sighed. Hands came down on my shoulders to place a shawl about them. I spun around to face Adrian. His expression contained a mixture of pity and uneasiness.

"You knew about Aunt Clarissa all along, didn't you?" My eyes searched his.

"I was never really sure. I certainly didn't think she had gone completely mad. I sensed a change in her when we moved here. She became increasingly restless, not to mention a tendency toward eccentricity that seemed to swell with each passing day. When you and Diana arrived, she became unaccountably calmer. I felt something was wrong, but I could never put my finger on it or prove anything."

"I overheard your father and Jane talking about putting her in an asylum. Bruce wanted to kill her. At the time I

314

thought they were talking about me."

Adrian smiled broadly. "One should never eavesdrop, especially on private conversations. They were talking about Clarissa's state of mind. I suggested we take her to a doctor specializing in mental disorders. Bruce said, 'Let's kill her.' One of his less than humorous jokes. What makes you think I would want to harm you?"

"If I were dead or tucked away in an insane asylum, Aunt Clarissa would inherit everything which would benefit all of you. They said something about you wanting to make sure of the money first. What did they mean?" I asked.

"I wanted to learn where she was getting the money from. I suspected she was embezzling from your father's estate. I kept going over the ledgers, but couldn't find anything. I didn't know about the jewels. She must have been selling or pawning them for cash."

"The light in the keep must have been her going for more jewels to sell. I wonder what she did with Patrick's things."

"Probably gave them to the gypsies. Did you really think I was after your money?"

I nodded and lowered my eyes.

"Oh, Heather." He took me in his arms and held my head to his chest. "I have been so afraid for you since your sister died. Why do you think I drugged you and kept you at my house? Jane said Clarissa was acting extremely strange that day. I thought it best to keep you out of harm's way."

I put my arms around him and held tight. I wanted to burn this moment into my memory. The spell broke when he took my shoulders and held me at arm's length.

"What are you going to do now, Heather?" he asked.

"Get rid of Bridee Castle. I could never be comfortable there now."

"Where will you go?"

"I don't know yet. Perhaps Jane would like to accompany me on a tour of the Continent. I have enough money to live quite royally no matter where I go. More pointedly, what are Bruce and your father going to do?"

315

"Father will probably go to Edinburgh. He likes city life and has always managed to fend for himself. I imagine he will get Clarissa's small yearly stipend that your father left her. He can live quite comfortably on that. As for Bruce, it is about time he learned to make his own living in this world."

"You could hire him to run your farms," I suggested.

Adrian laughed. "Never! He would bleed me dry for gambling money and not do a lick of work. Never hire relatives is a law with me. I will make sure Jane gets a monthly stipend from me to live comfortably."

"You could have her live with you."

"I like my privacy."

To be with Kitty, I thought. I had nothing more to say. "I am going back to the house. The chill out here is getting stronger." I headed back to the rear terrace. Before I reached it, I turned to see Adrian standing where I had left him, head bent, hands behind his back in an attitude of despair.

A tear came into my eyes. I couldn't walk away from him without revealing my true feelings for him. Pride be damned! I lifted my skirts and ran to face him.

"Adrian Ross, I am in love with you and have been from the first moment I laid eyes on you." I was breathless with audacity. "I shall always love you. You can think me a hoyden for being so bold. I don't care. I have spoken my heart and mind. Make of it what you will." With a toss of my head, I started to walk away, but Adrian grabbed my arm, then pulled me into an embrace. His lips on mine, his kiss was deep and urgent in its exploration. I was breathless when he finally released me.

"I have wanted to hear those words from your lips more than anything in the world. The first time I saw that picture of you as a ten year old, you claimed a piece of my heart. When you walked into the drawing room that day, those green eyes of yours took the rest of it. I wanted to tell you then how much I loved you, but common sense told me to

316

wait until you came to know me."

"You said you were interested in Diana," I reminded him.

"I also said 'not the way you think.' I was curious about Diana's reasons for her obvious attentions to my father. I could see it was bothering Clarissa, though she did her best to hide it. I thought I might be able to draw her away from Father. I had no real interest in her."

"Why didn't you tell me?"

"I had decided to tell you of my love, but then Patrick Danton came with your father's casket. You became an heiress and I realized you would think I was after your money and estate. Patrick Danton was another reason. I thought you were in love with him. I was the happiest man on earth when you spurned his advances and told him to leave."

"What about Kitty?"

"What about her?" He was genuinely surprised.

"Well, she is in your house a lot."

He laughed. "Poor Kitty is a little simple. Her mind isn't fully developed. I give her odd jobs to make her feel important and to give her a little money to spend on herself while she is still in the Highlands. She will be leaving soon. The family is going to America. Were you jealous?"

"Yes."

"Are you still of a mind not to marry anyone?"

"That depends." My pulse raced.

"On what?"

"Who is asking."

"And if I ask?"

"Ask what?"

"Heather, you are an exasperating woman."

"At last I have you thinking of me as a woman. Now what is your question?"

"Heather MacBride, will you marry me?"

"I thought you would never ask." This time I threw my arms around his neck and kissed him with all the passion in me.

317

"I presume I have your answer. And I shall never doubt your womanhood." Still embracing me, Adrian smiled at me warmly.

"Yes, yes, yes!" I clung to him in joy.

"We had better get back to the house and tell everyone the good news," Adrian said as he took my arm and pulled it through his. "By the way, what do you intend to do with the jewels?"

"As you will be my husband, I feel it prudent to keep them in the family. I shall divide them between your father, Bruce, and Jane. They can do whatever they wish with them. Why do you ask?"

"I would like the largest emerald among them and have a jeweler fashion a betrothal ring for you."

"You can have all of them, Adrian."

"Only the emerald, love. I already have the brightest jewel in all of India. I need no other."

FIERY ROMANCE

CALIFORNIA CARESS   (2771, $3.75)
by Rebecca Sinclair

Hope Bennett was determined to save her brother's life. And if that meant paying notorious gunslinger Drake Frazier to take his place in a fight, she'd barter her last gold nugget. But Hope soon discovered she'd have to give the handsome rattlesnake more than riches if she wanted his help. His improper demands infuriated her; even as she luxuriated in the tantalizing heat of his embrace, she refused to yield to her desires.

ARIZONA CAPTIVE   (2718, $3.75)
by Laree Bryant

Logan Powers had always taken his role as a lady-killer very seriously and no woman was going to change that. Not even the breathtakingly beautiful Callie Nolan with her luxuriant black hair and startling blue eyes. Logan might have considered a lusty romp with her but it was apparent she was a lady, through and through. Hard as he tried, Logan couldn't resist wanting to take her warm slender body in his arms and hold her close to his heart forever.

DECEPTION'S EMBRACE   (2720, $3.75)
by Jeanne Hansen

Terrified heiress Katrina Montgomery fled Memphis with what little she could carry and headed west, hiding in a freight car. By the time she reached Kansas City, she was feeling almost safe . . . until the handsomest man she'd ever seen entered the car and swept her into his embrace. She didn't know who he was or why he refused to let her go, but when she gazed into his eyes, she somehow knew she could trust him with her life . . . and her heart.